A Killer in the Wind

A KILLER
IN THE WIND

ANDREW KLAVAN

The Mysterious Press

an imprint of Grove/Atlantic, Inc.

New York

Published simultaneously in Canada
Printed in the United States of America

ISBN: 978-0-8021-2225-4
eISBN: 978-0-8021-9370-4

The Mysterious Press
an imprint of Grove/Atlantic, Inc.
154 West 14th Street
New York, NY 10011

Distributed by Publishers Group West

www.groveatlantic.com

14 15 16 17   10 9 8 7 6 5 4 3 2 1

This book is for Bill Korchinski and Cynthia Withers.

Acknowledgments

My sincere thanks to Chris Saffran for helping me better understand police procedures and the organization and methodology of the NYPD. And to Toby Bateson for patiently explaining various avenues of criminal investigation. Thanks as well to Cynthia Withers, MD, for her medical expertise.

My thanks as always to my agent Robert Gottlieb of Trident Media and my editor Otto Penzler.

And thanks beyond words to my wife Ellen Treacy, whose worth is far above rubies.

I

A Killer in the Wind

MAYBE IT WAS the dark house on the edge of town, the murderer waiting for me inside, but I thought about the ghosts that night, that last April night before they all came back to haunt me.

We had gotten a warrant a week before. Out of Tennessee. A killer in the wind. Frank Bagot, his name was. He had beaten a girl to death in Nashville—God knows why. Had outrun the police when they moved in on him, shooting one officer in the leg, shattering his shinbone. He was armed and dangerous, without much to lose. And I had a feeling from the start he'd be heading my way.

He had a sister in my little corner of downstate New York, that's why—that's why I was expecting him. Bess MacIntyre. In her thirties. Mother of two. Managed the home department at Wal-Mart. She'd crossed my path a couple of times: a harried bottle-blonde with an edge of tenderness I kind of admired. Losing her looks early—which was probably just as well, since her looks hadn't helped her much but only drew in a string of men with the sort of personalities that would've been much improved by a shovel to the back of the head. The last one—the last man, I mean, two or three in after the MacIntyre who'd left her with his name and the second kid—was a local lowlife, Harvey Salem. Took to cooking up meth in the little toolshed in her backyard. Finally, one day Harvey fireballed the shed and blew himself home to Jesus, assuming Jesus was in one of his forgiving moods. I caught the investigation. Took me about seventeen seconds to find the cash he'd hung up in the septic riser. I glanced down at it, glanced up—and saw Bess watching me from the house window. That was about a year's pay to her in that plastic bag down there. No way she'd be able to keep the house without it. I just closed that riser right up again. Investigation over.

So I'm not saying she owed me, but she did owe me and she knew it. That's why I figured when brother Frank came to her looking for a place to hide, I might be the best one to go see her and smoke him out.

And so it came to pass. Because that's the thing about being a fugitive: You can't run away from your own life. Oh, it's easy enough to disappear in this country. You slip your local cops, leave the state, get a fake ID, you're gone. On television shows, a hunted man has to always be looking over his shoulder wherever he goes. Police are watching for him on every corner, newscasters are putting his picture on TV, helicopters are flying around searching the area, and so on. Maybe it would be like that in real life too, if police had the same budgets as television shows. But, of course, in real life, we haven't got the manpower or the time. I've got enough trouble patrolling my own territory without looking for trouble that escaped from someone else's. And the newscasters—well, they have too many drunken starlets to talk about for them to waste time helping us catch Frank Bagot. Hell, the girl Frank punched to death never even made a music video. Why should the media waste time covering her?

No, a man like Bagot can easily slip into oblivion. All he has to do is cut the strings that tie him to his existence.

But he can't do it. Nine times out of ten, those strings bind him. Wait around long enough, keep your eyes open, and one of these days, he's going to send his mom a birthday card, or drop in on an old girlfriend or borrow money from his brother or hide out with Sis—not because he's sentimental or horny or broke or has nowhere else to go, but just because his life has a hold on him, his past has a hold on him, the past shaped his desires and so his desires draw him back into the past.

So that's where I'd be waiting for him.

All I had to do after I saw the warrant was keep tabs on Bess's bank activity and credit cards. Sure enough, exactly seven days after Bagot went invisible in the South, Bess's food bill at the A&P skyrocketed and I knew he'd come to see her.

It was late evening when I got the word. I was alone in the Sheriff's Department's BCI—the Bureau of Criminal Investigation. I went out into Processing and found Deputy Hank Dunn typing up his dailies.

"Deputy Dunn. You want to go catch a mad-dog killer?" I asked him.

Deputy Dunn is about twelve years old, or maybe twenty. He looks like a crew cut and an Adam's apple pasted to the top of a stalk of corn. But there's an eager mind and the makings of a noble heart in there somewhere, so he practically leapt to his feet, as I expected he would.

"Sure!"

Only later, sitting in the passenger seat of the Beamer 5 heading out to Bess's house, did it occur to him to have second thoughts. Probably thinking about Sally, the schoolteacher he was engaged to, who was well worth thinking about.

We were on a stretch of Route 52 outside of Tyler. Forest close to the road on either side of us. No houses in sight. No light but the headlights and a three-quarters moon disappearing and re-appearing from behind the treetops.

"So who're we really after?" Deputy Dunn asked me with a nervous laugh. "You find your gas thieves finally?"

"I wouldn't lie to you, Hank. It's a lady killer," I told him. "Fugitive out of Tennessee. This woman we're going to see, Bess MacIntyre—she's his sister."

3

"Well, that doesn't mean he's out there, does it?"

"He's out there. She's been buying him groceries."

Deputy Dunn went quiet. I glanced over at him from behind the wheel. Saw the Adam's apple bobbing up and down in the cornstalk. Smiled to myself in the dark as I faced forward and guided the blue Beamer round another turn. I was almost twenty years older than he was, nearly forty, but I remembered what it was like to go into action for the first time—real action, violent action. Hard to tell the difference between excitement and fear. Maybe there is no difference.

"Shouldn't we have some backup?" Deputy Dunn said after a while. "I mean, if you're not just putting me on. If it really is a killer. We could have the staties send tactical."

"Seems a lot of taxpayer money to waste on one scumbag."

"Right," he said—trying to laugh like he meant it. Then, after another pause: "Guess you got used to this sort of thing down in the city."

"I won't let you get killed, Dunn," I said. "And if you do, I'll take good care of Sally for you."

"Ha ha."

"She'll never even miss you."

"Thanks. I feel a *whole* lot better now."

"That's what I'm here for, my friend. I'm glad we could have this little talk."

I turned the Beamer 5 off the highway onto Lawrence Post Road and off the Post Road onto the long dirt drive that bounced down between forest and swampland toward Bess's place. Middle of nowhere. Had to ease off on the gas to make it over the corrugation without dropping a strut. Over the *thumpety-thump* of the tires—even with the car windows up and the air on—I could hear the racket of frogs and crickets in the nearby swamp water. I could see the house lights through the trees, then the house itself, the gibbous moon bright in the April sky just above it.

"Vest in the back," I said to Dunn.

I didn't have to tell him twice. He popped his seat belt and practically climbed back there to get at the Kevlar.

As he worked the body armor on, the Beamer 5 bounced over a last stretch of road. We came into the open dirt space Bess used for a driveway. Both her cars were there: her rusty, trusty '94 Accord —and it was somehow just like Bess to own the most stolen car in America—and the old Mazda pickup Harvey the meth man left her when he metamorphosed into a cloud of cold medicine and dust.

I turned the Beamer sideways at the end of the road and shut her down. I unlocked the LTR, the black tactical rifle, from the rack between the two front seats.

"Take that," I told Dunn. "Stay behind the cars. If anybody kills me, you kill him right back and teach him a lesson, you hear me?"

"Yeah," he managed to say, taking out the rifle.

"Move as close to the house as you can under cover, but make sure our boy's not sleeping in the back of the Honda or the truck bed so he doesn't pop up and blow your brains out. Or, even worse, mine."

"Right."

"And hey, there are kids in there, by the way. A six-year-old boy and an eight-year-old girl who say their prayers and believe in Santa Claus. So if you decide to shoot someone by accident, try to make it yourself."

"You sure we shouldn't call the staties?"

"You're gonna be fine, Dunn," I said, pushing the door open. "Tonight, Sally's gonna be having sex with a hero."

"Can't wait."

"I wasn't talking about you."

Dunn and the LTR rolled out on the far side of the car, all saucer-sized eyes and adrenaline.

I shut the driver's door and started across the dirt.

The house was a run-down two-story shingle with a porch out front. Lights on upstairs and in the back of the first floor, but I couldn't see anyone moving. Dunn was ducking from car to car, checking the truck bed and the back of the Accord like I told him. He settled behind the Accord with the rifle braced on top and pointed at the house's front door. I headed for the porch.

As I came close, the moon went behind the roof, casting the porch's recesses into deep shadow. I could make out the shape of a swing just to one side of the front door and a rocker just to the other, but farther in than that everything was blackness.

I went up the stairs. I didn't draw my 19. I still had an undercover's instincts and figured I could talk my way out of pretty much anything. I stepped onto the porch. Deep darkness on either side of me. No noise but the frogs and crickets riddling and peeping in the swamp nearby. I reached out to pull open the screen.

The next second, the night was all roaring and snarling as a dog, a huge German shepherd, launched itself at me out of the blackness to my right. Lance, Harvey's drug dog. I'd forgotten all about him. I saw his dripping fangs flash and his angry eyes burning even as I stumbled backward, arms wheeling, off the porch onto the top step. Lucky I hadn't drawn my gun. If I had, I'd have shot the creature dead. Then I'd have had that on my conscience along with everything else because old Lance was chained up and couldn't reach me. He snapped the chain tight and hung off the end of it, his front legs suspended in air as he snarled and yammered at me in a helpless rage.

Bess opened the front door, turning on the hall light inside as she did.

"Who's there?"

"Dan Champion from the Sheriff's Office."

"Dan?"

"I'd like to talk to you, Bess, and I don't want to have to shoot your dog to do it."

"Quiet, Lance! Quiet! Go lie down!"

Lance gave a last disdainful woof and figured to hell with it. Receded into the porch shadows and lay down in the darkness. My heart was knocking at my ribs like a cop's fist on a whorehouse door. Had to breathe my pulse back to normal as I stepped up onto the porch again.

"Sorry about that," said Bess. "Harvey trained him. It's all show. He doesn't hurt anyone."

She tried to smile but she was too worried to pull it off. That tenderness I sometimes noticed in her eyes was a hunted tenderness now. Plus she'd been crying and had black mascara rings highlighting her eye pouches. Reminded me of a cornered raccoon—just like a cornered raccoon, in fact: defiant and terrified.

I stepped up close to her, towered over her. The dog growled from the shadows. I spoke low.

"I'm here to take your brother, Bess. I don't want the kids to get hurt."

She looked up at me, right at me. Her lips trembled. "He's not here," she said, starting to cry.

"I don't want the kids to get hurt," I said again. "Where are they?"

She barely managed to get the words out: "Upstairs in their bedrooms."

"And Frank?"

The mascara streaked her right cheek as the tears rolled down it. "Hiding on the cellar stairs," she whispered. "Behind the door in the kitchen."

I squeezed her shoulder. "Go up to your babies. It'll be all right," I said.

She nodded quickly. I held on to her arm, guiding her back into the house. I went in with her and let the door close hard so Frank could hear it, maybe think everything was back to normal. I nodded at the stairs and gave Bess a little shove that way. She glanced back at me once but then went, scurrying up to the second floor.

I moved on, past the staircase, toward the bright light of the kitchen in back. Down a narrow hall. I could see the cellar door just at the end of it, just where the kitchen began, on the wall to my right. The door was hinged to open toward me.

I knew Frank would come out of there gun first and he did. Meaning to curl around the door, take a shot at me, and run for it. I was there too fast. As the door swung open, I kicked it back on him. It smacked him in the shoulder. The pistol fired, a deafening blast. A china serving tray on a kitchen shelf exploded into fragments and white powder. A black hole opened in the flowery wallpaper. Then I was on him. I grabbed his wrist. I snatched the gun out of his hand and dragged him into the kitchen by his shirtfront and smashed the gun butt into his face, breaking his nose. I hate a scumbag with a gun, hate it. I twisted his shirtfront in my free hand and slammed his back full force into the wall. Held him there with a forearm and stuck the barrel of his own weapon into his eye socket.

"You pull a gun on me?" I said. I slapped him in the face with the barrel. "You hit women. That's what you're good for. You don't pull a gun on me. Not on me."

I slapped him again just to see his eyes spin around. Then I hustled him and his bloody face back down the wall, past the stairs, to the front door. I heard the German shepherd going nuts on his chain again and when I pulled the door open I saw Deputy Dunn and his rifle trying to edge around the creature's teeth to reach the door.

I pushed Frank out onto the porch.

"Shut up, Lance!" I shouted, but the dog kept barking.

I went past him—and past Dunn—and threw Frank down the stairs. He landed face-first in the dirt below and lay there, dazed and groaning.

"Kill him," I told Dunn.

"What?"

"Oh, all right, cuff him then, and get him in the car. Shut up, Lance!"

The dog howled and squealed and barked some more.

While Deputy Dunn kneeled on Frank Bagot's back and wrestled his arms behind him for the cuffs, I stepped into the house again. Went to the bottom of the stairs. Looked up to where Bess now stood on the landing, a frightened child huddled one under each of her arms.

"It's all right," I told her. "Someone'll come by tomorrow, pick up his things and take a statement from you. Tell them how he held you hostage, threatened your kids."

"He did, you know," she said, sniffling.

"Well, you tell them. And you ought to get rid of that dog too, before he hurts one of you," I said.

"I will," she said.

But she wouldn't. Or if she did, she'd get herself a man just as bad and he'd do the damage instead of the dog. That's how it was with her, with everyone more or less. By my reckoning, maybe 15 percent of the suffering of life is unbidden sickness and disaster, the rest we bring on ourselves.

I hesitated a moment at the base of the stairs. Beautiful kids too. A porcelain girl with silk blonde hair. A dark solemn boy with farseeing eyes. It was a shame what was going to happen to them in this house. But there was nothing I could do about it. Nothing anyone could do.

I gave them a nod. "You have a good night," I said.

The dog was still straining and barking as I stepped out onto the porch again, but I think it was beginning to get tired of the sound of its own voice. When I glared at it now, it whimpered and shut up and circled the floorboards, its chain scraping. Finally, it lay down again. I went down the stairs to the dirt drive.

Dunn was just working Frank Bagot into the backseat of the Beamer. I stood where I was a while and composed myself, considering the night sky: the gibbous moon rising and the Big Dipper bright and the bright stars and planets flickering out from behind the trees, making the woods seem mysterious and deep. With the dog quiet, I could hear the swamp creatures again. Whistling, chattering, humming, groaning like bulls. There was a peacefulness about it after the sudden violence, an atmosphere of rightness and content as if things were working in the dark of the forest the way they were intended to.

That's when the ghosts returned to me—the memory of the ghosts, I mean. The memory of the city with all a city's suddenness and jarring noise. I was thinking about Frank Bagot and the way he came back to his past and the way the past comes back. I had lived three years in exurban Tyler County, but New York was always with me. I was always half-afraid that I would turn this way or that and see the little boy who wasn't there, see him staring at me with his phantom eyes. Or the woman. Samantha . . . The past shapes your desires and your desires lead you back into the past.

I took a deep breath of the cool spring air, rich and moist and somehow green, full of the swamp and the forest. *You're fine,* I told myself. *Fine.* But I guess the thing is: Once you've been crazy, once you've seen ghosts and lived with delusions, you can never be quite sure of yourself anymore. Reality seems fragile to you. You're always worried it'll crack and you'll step through it into the bad time again.

I heard Deputy Dunn shut the Beamer's rear door. I walked over to the driver's side.

"Nice work," I said.

He nodded, big-eyed, big Adam's apple going up and down. He was still all fired up and confused. But I could see by the look of him that he was beginning to realize he had come through it, and he'd have a good story to tell his Sal tonight.

We both got into the car, me behind the wheel.

"You bastard, you hit me," said Frank Bagot out of the back.

"You're lucky I didn't shove that gun up your ass and blow your brains out," I told him. I started the car.

I paused for a moment there, my hand on the gearshift. Looking out the windshield at the lighted house with the moon above it. Finally, with some small trepidation, I scanned the edges of the surrounding forest. Fearing I would see those old ghosts standing there, watching me, from just within the trees.

But there was nothing. Of course not. I felt fine. Good. I had for years. Not likely ever to see what I once saw, what I saw back then, down in the city. The boy. The woman. Not likely.

But once you've been crazy, you can never be quite sure.

2

Flashback: The Emory Case

THIS WAS A little over three years ago. I was NYPD back then. An undercover vice detective in Manhattan North—what in cop-speak we called an *uncle*. I had the whole uncle routine going too: the longish hair, the motorcycle, the cigarettes—and the ganja, when off-duty—not to mention the complete disdain for rules and procedures that goes along with the undercover trade.

I had been a while finding my calling. Raised in orphanages and foster homes, I'd bummed around for a few years after high school. Did construction work here and there. Drank hard. Broke hearts. Punched people. Then, on the advice of a deputy sheriff who'd just finished kicking me in the stomach, I joined the Army. Traveled to the Hindu Kush, met exotic, *Pakol*-wearing evildoers, and killed them. Came back, got my degree in law enforcement at Syracuse, then applied to the NYPD.

I became a white shield uncle in PMD—the Public Morals Division—right out of the academy. You can do that in Vice. It's not like Narcotics. You don't have to serve three years on patrol. So I scored my gold shield after eighteen months. And now I was a detective—thirty-three because of my late start, but still plenty young enough to be on fire with ambition.

And I was more than on fire. I had nothing else in my life to distract me. No wife, no family. Nothing but the job. I worked it hard. I developed a hunger inside me. I hammered through my two-week eighty-hour pay periods and then past the twenty-five overtime cap whether the department approved the money or not. Then I worked on into secret, sleepless, unknown nights, and screw the union rules. I combed through hot cases and cold cases. I pawed through buried files in basement boxes that had never even been scanned into the system. I busted my way up from prosses to pimps to mobster traffickers in women and children—all manner of modern slave-traders who preyed on foreigners and the poor. I even did my part to bring down a state senator once, a man of the people trading his vote for high-priced call girls on the side.

Over the course of a couple of years, I developed . . . I'm not sure what to call it—a preoccupation, say, with a perp known to me only as the Fat Woman. She was a specialty broker. A seller of human beings without flaw or blemish, supplying the finest in flesh and souls—in women, girls, and boys—to the very highest class of clients. That's what my sources told me at least. There was no record of her anywhere—no pictures, no prints. She was just a word on the street, a passed remark, a knowing mutter over the body of a dead child. An elite and legendary monster, like the devil himself. In fact, it's a good comparison because, as with the devil himself, you only saw the effects of her while she remained invisible. As with the devil himself, some people, even some police, didn't believe she existed.

But I did. I believed. And I wanted her. I had an eye out, always, for any sign she had passed by.

Then came the day—it was deep winter—I got a call from a friend in the one-seven. Their module was working a luxury pross ring run out of a building on Sutton Place. My friend, one of the investigators, a detective named Monahan, had been camped on the street outside for a week. He'd snapped a stakeout photo of a john who frequented the place.

If uncles like me were the rebels and artistes of the force—
the "dope smokers and faggots," as Monahan poetically put it—
investigators like him were usually big, meaty, Irish, or spiritually
Irish, guys who didn't need uniforms to look like cops. Monahan, in
particular, was one of these thick-necked musclemen who stretched
his shirts to the breaking point. Face of an overfed schoolboy. Red
hair worn belligerently short, except on his knuckles, where it
was long.

"Dig this," he said. He was sitting on the edge of his desk. He
pointed to the computer monitor, the picture there. I leaned in
for a better look, pressing my fists against the desktop. "The john's
name is Martin Emory. Private financial consultant. Referrals only.
Works with millionaires. *Is* a millionaire."

The building that headquartered the luxury pross ring was a
tower of red brick and concrete. In the photograph, this Emory
guy was just pushing out of its black glass front door and stepping
onto the sidewalk.

"Now watch what happens," Monahan said.

He tapped the keyboard to change the shot, then changed it again.
I saw Emory move from the building to a sleek black Mercedes
parked at the curb. In the next picture, he was inside the car, in
the passenger seat.

"Yeah?" I said. "So?"

"See the driver?" said Monahan.

I couldn't. Not much. The car's window was rolled up and dark.
But if I squinted, close to the screen, I could make out the shape
of her: a woman, immensely obese.

I wagged my head—a kind of shrug. "Maybe it's his mother," I
said. I said it as blandly as I could. But the truth was, I felt like I was
a buzzer that had just gone off. It was *a* fat woman anyway—and
who knows, maybe *the* fat woman I was looking for. "Any better
shots of her?"

"Just this one."

Monahan clicked to his last picture. The woman was turned
toward us now, toward the camera, nervously scanning the street.

But all I could see—all I seemed to see through the window's darkness and the buildings reflected on the glass—was a bizarrely piebald oval of flesh framed in short, darkish hair.

"Where the hell's her face?" I said.

Monahan's massive shoulders lifted and fell under the straining shirt. "Beats me."

"What, is she wearing a mask?"

"Maybe. Could be the light. Could be the glass."

"I guess. It's spooky. What about the car? You check the car?"

"Rental. Phony ID. Dead end."

"So that tells us something right there."

"Exactly. I'm thinking maybe he gets his expensive thrills inside the building—and his *very* expensive thrills from her."

I didn't answer, but I was still buzzing, buzzing more in fact, more every second. "It's a leap. I don't know. The phony ID is definitely something. Otherwise . . . she's in the fat half of the female half of the human race."

"I got a way in for you if you want it."

"Yeah?"

"One of Emory's clients is also a john," Monahan said. "William Russel. Runs a very exclusive private school. I don't think he'd want to do the perp walk with the *Post* snapping pictures. If I lean on him, I'm pretty sure he'd give you a referral to Emory."

I kept peering into the monitor. Spooky: that featureless, piebald oval where her face should've been. Must've been the glare on the glass.

"What do you think?" said Monahan as I hesitated. "You want to make contact with him?"

I was only pretending to think it over. I already knew what I was going to do.

"Yeah," I said. "Sure. I'll make contact."

Which I did, about a week later, posing as a wealthy video game designer. I figured I played video games and read about them and Emory probably didn't, so it was a good cover. Monahan put the squeeze on his private school perp, Russel, and got me the referral I needed.

We met on a Wednesday in Emory's apartment, which doubled as his office. It was a penthouse on East 52nd Street, right above the river. Wraparound windows and a balcony over the water. Polished wood floors and elaborate carpets. A lot of stuffed white chairs and glass furniture. A lot of black-and-white photographs on the wall: famous actresses and athletes, reclining nudes, plus one of a nude woman kissing another woman who was wearing a veil. I recognized some of these photos. I'd seen them before in magazines. But I guessed these were the originals or early prints or something—something expensive. The whole place felt aggressively expensive, an advertisement for Emory's investing skills, I guess.

But that wasn't all. There was an atmosphere about the place, a subtle atmosphere of creepy sexuality. Maybe it was the photographs that did it: the sprawled poses of the actresses and the drooping eyelids of the nudes. Even the rippling six-packs of the boxers and ballplayers might have had something to do with it. Even the furniture: sparse and spare, yet oversoft like rotten fruit. It was the whole place—I don't know; I couldn't put my finger on it. Could've just been me, my jaded point of view, my cop instincts. But I didn't think it was me. I thought it was Emory. I already suspected what the guy was under his pink polo shirt and khaki slacks. I thought he meant the place to feel the way it did. I thought it was a kind of subliminal tease built into the décor, his private joke, his private perversion—whatever it was—hidden in plain sight, mocking any visitor who wasn't in the know. Anyway, all I'm saying is: The place made me queasy.

His short, bustling Puerto Rican maid let me in. Then Emory turned from the river view at the far wall of windows and walked across the living room to greet me. I shook his hand and I thought: *He's evil.* I did, just like that, right off. He was round-faced, bland-faced—flaccid-faced somehow though he was barely forty. Pale and soft, with short, sandy hair and green eyes embedded in wrinkled folds of flesh. There was something coy and provocative in the way he looked at me. It was the same attitude I sensed in the apartment generally, the same giggly hint of a barely hidden secret, a cherished pet wickedness that only the initiated were allowed to see full-on.

We sat in his office down the hall. Wooden paneling. Leather-bound books. A vast mahogany desk with a glass top and gold trimming. We sat side by side and examined my fake portfolio displayed on his computer monitor. He gave a speech about diversification and hidden opportunities in the current market. He made it sound like he was addressing my case specifically, but I could tell it was a speech he'd made before. For my part, I played it strictly straight, nothing out of line. I was supposed to be one of these creative types who made a lot of money but didn't understand the ins and outs of high finance, so I nodded a lot, as if I were pretending to understand what he said but didn't. All the while, I was buzzing inside, wired, electric. There was something about this guy that felt like bingo. For the first time since I'd heard of her, I thought I was on the trail of the Fat Woman.

Only when we were done, only when we were shaking hands again, out in the living room, out by the door, did I drop my bait.

"This all sounds very good," I told him. "I'm going on vacation next week, but I'll call you as soon as I get back."

"Oh, where are you going?" Emory asked politely, because that's what people politely ask.

"Bangkok," I told him. "Thailand. I spend a lot of time there," I added, averting my eyes.

"Good food, I hear," said Emory. And then, as if joking: "And lots of prostitutes, right?"

I laughed and said, also as if joking, "You got to spend your money on something."

He laughed too, but his mocking eyes caressed me.

I knew I'd set the hook. I knew I had him. I wouldn't have to do anything else, not yet. He'd come back to the subject on his own. They all do. They can't help themselves, these guys. They want to tell. They want to share. They want to convince themselves that everyone is secretly like them, deep down.

I couldn't sleep all that week. I never slept much but this was different. I lay wide awake, staring at the ceiling, night after night after night. Thinking the same thing over and over, the same words: *I've got her. I've got her.* I didn't even know why I thought that. I didn't even know how I knew. But I knew. Monahan was right. The Sutton Place hookers were just a pastime for Emory, a stopgap. He was into something else—something dark, something nasty, something only the Fat Woman could supply. *I've got her. I've got her.* Night after night. I couldn't sleep a wink.

"How were the prostitutes?" That's what he asked me the next time I saw him. Sitting in his living room with the wraparound windows. With the gray winter sky and the gray winter river. Me on the sofa, him in a chair. "How were the prostitutes?" As if he were joking.

"Young and cheap," I said with a laugh. As if I were joking.

"Seems like a long way to travel just for a good time," he said. Laughing. As if he were joking.

"Depends on your definition of a good time," I said. As if.

"Well, whatever it is, I'm sure with your money, you could find it a lot closer to home." Laughing, he opened a folder on the glass table between us. Portfolios. Opportunities. "I, meanwhile, have been using *my* time more productively on your behalf . . ."

See, now he had tossed out *his* bait, *his* hook: *You could find it a lot closer to home.* And I was supposed to say: *Really? Are you serious? What do you mean?* And I would say it. But not today. That would have been too eager. It might have tipped him off, put him on his guard. I had to seem to be cautious. I had to seem afraid. Take it slow. Step by step.

That was the hard part. The waiting. The slow pace and the tension and the constant buzz. No sleep, night after night. Night after night.

★ ★ ★

I called him about a week later. Asked him if we could meet somewhere. A restaurant maybe. Have a drink.

"If you're going to be handling my money, I'd like to get to know you better," I said.

We met at his club. We sat in leather chairs at a small square table under a white marble fireplace the size of a studio apartment. I was wearing an Armani suit I'd DARed—charged to the city on my Daily Activity Report. I thought it was the kind of suit you might wear if you had money but didn't *know* money. If you only knew the famous names like Armani. I ordered Laphroaig, a single malt. Just a little water, no ice. I'd learned about that on singlemalt.com. But I pronounced the name of the scotch wrong and the waiter corrected me. That was an accident, but luckily it suited my cover.

"So let me ask you something," I said. Kind of shyly. Smiling, but not laughing now. This was beyond the point where I could pretend I was joking. This was it. I was making my play. "When you said I could probably find my pleasures closer to home, whatever they were, what did you mean? Were you serious?"

Emory smiled, an impish, boyish smile, looking down at the table, then up at me. "Are we being naughty now?" he said—and he wrinkled his nose like a dowager talking to her poodle.

It turned my stomach. This was the thing, the thing that was keeping me awake at night. Not just the scent of the Fat Woman. Not just the feeling that I was getting close. It was this: the evil. I don't know any other word to describe it. My growing sense that I was in the presence of evil.

See, I'd seen that look before. That wrinkled nose, that laughing sparkle in the eyes. In the movies, the evil guys laugh out loud. Bwa-ha-ha. Or they chuckle suavely, swirling their drinks in their glasses. But this is the real deal, the real look most of these monsters have. A sort of cute, dainty, delicate recoil from speaking the thing out loud. The forbidden joke of it.

Are we being naughty now?

Naughty to me is snapping your girlfriend's butt with a towel. *Naughty* to these guys is the unspeakable.

Emory gave me no other answer. He bluntly changed the subject. "Let's talk about other things for the time being."

For the time being.

I had another sleepless night. Lying on my back. Staring at the ceiling. *I've got her. I've got her.*

Are we being naughty now?

The next day, I caught someone watching me. White guy in a sweatshirt and jeans, baseball cap and headset. Trying to look like just-a-dude, but a sinewy bone-crusher beneath the costume. Professional talent.

A friend of the department had agreed to loan us his upper Fifth Avenue apartment while he was in California for the winter. It made a convincing address for a rich guy like I was supposed to be. I hadn't been spending my nights there—I'd been staying at my place in Jackson Heights—but I decided to stop there in the morning to drop off some clothes and equipment before heading in to the cop shop for the daily tactical meeting.

I spotted the thug as I approached the front awning. I managed to turn back before he saw me. I went around the corner and assessed the situation. I hadn't been expecting to meet with Emory today and wasn't dressed for the part. Just wearing a leather bomber jacket and jeans, carrying my DAR ed clothes in a suitcase. I'd parked my Harley in a nearby garage. I could go back and get it and blow before the thug saw me. But then I'd lose him. Better to get inside and watch him from there.

Quickly, I thought up a cover story to explain the suitcase. I'd stayed with a girlfriend last night. We were in the process of breaking up. I was bringing my clothes back from her place. Something like that. It would pass, if I needed it. I came back around the corner, nonchalant-like, and headed for the building. The doorman had been prepped and gave me the nod as I passed the front desk.

Once I was upstairs in the apartment, I took a better look at the guy from the window, curling around the frame, snapping shots of him through a Canon zoom. I was on the eighth floor, with a view of Central Park across the street. The thug was hanging out by the wall, by a bus stop, ducking his head and moving his body like he was bopping to the music on his headset. Just a dude waiting for a ride downtown. He was strapped but you couldn't read it. Not like he was some punk, with the gun bulging or throwing off the line of his clothes. This guy was smooth.

I lay the camera aside on a small end table. Sat down in a flowery upholstered chair. This was a nice place, furnished like something in a museum. The chairs and sofa had carvings on the wood. In the bedroom there were cherubs painted right onto the ceiling, cherubs flying in dawn-colored clouds.

I pinched the bridge of my nose, closed my eyes. I hadn't slept all night. I hadn't slept for weeks of nights. My head was foggy. I looked at my hands and saw they were shaking. My heart was fluttering too.

I blinked hard. I tried to clear my head, tried to work things out. I didn't think Emory had sent a thug like this. I didn't think he had the connections, not directly. I tried to imagine another scenario. What if, after our meet in his club, Emory called his supplier, say? The Fat Woman, say—or whoever was getting him whatever he got. What if *she* was the one who'd sent this punk to check me out?

The idea made sense and amped my excitement. I called Monahan.

"I got a watcher on me now."

"You're kidding. Where are you?"

"The Fifth Avenue place."

"Don't you have a life?"

"No. What would I do with one of those?"

"Where's your watcher?"

"Across the street. I'm looking at him. Caucasian male, five-eleven, one-eighty, brown hair, narrow face. Wearing jeans and a rapper sweatshirt. Yankees cap and headset."

"Professional?"

"Oh yeah. An ex-con too, definitely."

"I know what you're thinking," Monahan said.

"Then we both know."

"I'm gonna come up."

"Good. Just don't let him see you. You look like a fat Irish detective."

"It's a clever disguise. I'm really a skinny wop."

I sat in the chair, watched the watcher from the window. Twenty minutes later, I saw Monahan cruising downtown on Fifth. A sea-green Lexus at the center of a moving swarm of yellow cabs.

I phoned him.

"Nice wheels."

"Borrowed 'em from Narcotics," he said. "Thought'd be less conspicuous than a Crown Vic. How'd I look."

"Like a fat Irish detective in a Lexus."

"I'm gonna go around the corner, drop it at the museum, come back down through the park on foot. Even you won't see me."

The Lexus moved to the edge of the cab swarm, turned the corner, and was out of sight. I sat by the window. Watched the bebopping thug across the street. Watched the park too. But Monahan was right. I didn't see him. Another ninety minutes went by. Finally, the thug made a gesture. He unconsciously lifted his hand to his headset before catching himself, dropping it to his side. He was getting a call.

After a few seconds, he started bebopping away.

I called Monahan. "He's on the move."

"I'm right behind him."

I scanned the park. It was January. The trees were bare. I had a good view of the walkways leading down from the museum. I saw women walking their dogs. Nannies with their kids all bundled up and stiff in winter clothes. I could see yellow cabs on the East Drive. But no Monahan. The guy was the size of a small truck and I couldn't spot him. You had to admire that.

My cell rang. There he was. "Guess what?" Monahan said. "A yellow cab picked him up on the corner of Park."

"Picked him up? He didn't hail it?"

"Cab just stops. Door swings open. Guess who's inside?"

I licked my lips. My mouth was dry. "You saw her?" I wished I could clear my head. I wished I could get some sleep.

"Just a flash," said Monahan. "Mostly her big, fat body."

"Not her face?"

Monahan hesitated. "Just a flash, it . . . I couldn't see, it . . ."

"Where the hell's her face at? Who is this woman?"

Another pause. "It was dark in the cab. Hard to make out," Monahan said.

That night I stayed in the cover apartment, just in case the thug came back. The bed there was big, the mattress thick and soft. The painted cherubs looked down from the ceiling above me.

I turned from side to side. I lay on my back and stared back at the cherubs. *I've got her. I've got her.* Sleep was impossible. I didn't get a minute of it, not a wink. I got up, sitting on the edge of the mattress, holding my head in my hands. I was so tired. I found a decanter of brandy. Drank some. It didn't work. I had a few sleeping pills—pretty standard-issue equipment in Vice. I took them too. They made my thoughts fuzzy and vague but didn't stop them. *I've got her.* I kept seeing the featureless, piebald front of her head. *Where the hell's her face at?* I kept seeing Emory with his cute, wrinkled nose, like an old woman cooing to her poodle. *Are we being naughty now?* What were these people up to? Evil. Something evil. The big word kept coming back to me.

Finally, I threw the comforter off me, cursing. Jumped out of my bed, bare feet to the carpet. I needed something. I'd never been like this, never. I had to get some sleep or I wasn't going to make this case. Brandy and Ambien weren't going to cut it. I had to stop thinking. The thinking was driving me crazy.

I got up and got dressed. Christ, it was almost two in the morning. I had my Harley parked in the building's garage. It roared to life, the noise echoing off the concrete walls.

There was a guy I knew. Janks. A CI—a confidential informant—who'd helped me bring down a kiddie porn ring. Janks dealt in anything you could smoke or swallow. He had extensive contacts in the medical profession.

I found him in the Harlem Lounge, like any buyer would. No one blinked to see a white man walk down the bar past the line of all-night drinkers to the stool at the end that was Janks's headquarters. Even Janks didn't look up when I sat down next to him.

"I need something," I told him.

Janks was scrawny and solemn. A dark brown undertaker type with a self-important air. He fancied himself a proper pharmacist or doctor, dispensing his medicine to the sick or sick-at-heart.

"What you think you need?" he said, from on high, his chin lifted.

"I can't sleep."

"You can't sleep or you crazy?"

"I'm crazy and I can't sleep," I said.

"Take some Ambien, man."

"I did. I'm in Vice, dude. You see the stuff I see, Ambien's like an after-dinner mint."

"All right. Wait here."

I waited while he went into the men's room. I tried to flag the one-eyed bartender, to order a drink. The one-eyed bartender showed me his empty socket and wouldn't look at me. The Harlem Lounge reserves the right to refuse service to white junkies.

Janks came back. He slipped me a Baggie full of white pills.

"This be Z. You know Z?" he said.

I shook my head.

"This be powerful shit, nome saying? You take this, you won't be crazy. You'll sleep like you're waiting for Jesus."

"It's not Jesus I'm waiting for, believe me."

"Don't be drinking with it."

"All right."

"It's powerful shit. Don't say I didn't warn you."

"All right."

"You get an erection lasting more than four hours? Don't be bringing it to me."

I slipped the Baggie into my bomber jacket. Slipped Janks some money. Down-low. In case there were any cops in the place, ha ha.

I popped the first pill the moment I got back to the apartment, before I even took my coat off, before the door even shut behind me. Then I got undressed and lay down on the bed. I looked up at the cherubs on the wall.

Janks was right. It was powerful shit. It didn't make you woozy or knock you out or anything like that. It just sort of melted inside you into a fresh, white puddle of new attitude. Then the puddle of attitude spread out all through your body. Within about twenty minutes, I had developed a philosophical approach to the presence of evil in the world. *What can you do?* I thought. *That's just the way it is.* After that, I fell asleep.

It was a good, sound, peaceful sleep. I only woke up once, near dawn. I had a dream that the apartment was on fire. My eyes flashed open. I smelled smoke. I lifted my head and looked around me to make sure the place wasn't really burning. I had a sense that someone was standing in the shadows of the bedroom, looking back at me. But I peered and squinted and didn't see anyone. I was too tired to get up and check it out. I lay down again and closed my eyes. I was philosophical. *Such is life,* I thought. The next thing I knew it was late morning.

The thug was outside again, bopping by the bus stop by the wall of the park. I got dressed and went out. He followed me at a discreet distance. I led him downtown to the Sony Building, the big rosy one with the hole in the top and the vast arches and pillars on the ground floor that make it look like a science fiction cathedral. I slipped lobby security a glimpse of my shield and they let me go up to the office floors. I spent forty-five minutes wandering around the halls, then went back down. When I came out of the building, the thug was smoking a cigarette by the revolving doors of the tower across the street. He followed me to the French café where I had lunch on the city. He stuck with me all the way back to the apartment on Fifth. After another hour, he bopped off to the make-believe rhythms in his headset.

I took another Z pill that night. I grew philosophical and fell asleep around ten. I didn't remember dreaming, but when I woke up I smelled smoke again. I don't know what time it was. It felt late. I lay for a few minutes staring up at the ceiling. I could see the cherubs up there, naked except for their white feathery wings, floating in the white feathery clouds.

Suddenly something moved—something in the doorway. I threw the comforter off me and was up, my heart beating hard as I stared into the shadows. I listened for a sound, a footstep, anything. Nothing.

My 19 was in its holster on the bedside table. I drew it out: a boxy semiautomatic with a nice solid feel. The weight of it in my hand calmed me.

I got up. I was wearing shorts and a T-shirt. I padded barefoot to the doorway, the gun down by my thigh. I peeked around the jamb, looked down the hall. It was shadowy, but not pitch black because so much city light was coming in through the living room windows and the glow bled into the corridor.

That's when I saw him, the first time I saw him. He was down at the hallway's end, down by the front door. I could just make out the shape of his body, small and thin: the body of a hungry child. His big eyes glinted in the half-light as he stood staring at me.

Somehow I knew his name was Alexander. Somehow I knew he was dead. The knowledge made the center of me clutch in helpless, childlike fear. For a long moment, I was paralyzed, my gun hand quivering, the cold barrel tapping against my bare skin.

The boy just stood there. Silent. Staring. Finally, by pure force of will, I came out of the bedroom. I made myself take a step toward him. Then another step. I could see the end of the hall more clearly now. There was no one there—no dead boy, no one. Of course not. I walked to the end of the hall. I walked through the whole apartment. There was no one anywhere. Of course not.

I went back to bed. I lay looking up at the ceiling, at the painted cherubs. They seemed sinister now in their cloudy surroundings, more like demon imps than cherubs. Grinning, feral, ravenous, their eyes gleaming. Mocking me, like Emory's eyes.

It's the pills, I thought. *I should stop taking the pills.* But I knew I wouldn't stop. Because I couldn't stand the thoughts that came to me as I lay awake. The Fat Woman's missing face. Emory's delicate evil.

Soon, my breathing slowed. The chemical calm descended on me. *What the hell?* I thought. I slept.

The next morning, early, I went to Emory's apartment. I slipped past the doorman and made my way to his apartment, unannounced. I pounded on the door with my fist until I heard his footsteps inside. I saw a flicker of shadow at the peephole.

It was just past 7 A.M. Too early for business. Too early even for the maid. I figured he'd be alone.

He was. He opened the door. He was wearing a plaid bathrobe.

"What on earth are you . . . ?" he said.

I stormed in past him.

"Shut the door," I told him.

"The doorman didn't ring. How'd you . . . ?"

I went back to him and took the door out of his hand and shut it forcefully. I put my face close to his. I made myself look afraid. Maybe I really was afraid.

"That thing I said to you. At the club the other day." When he hesitated, I said harshly, "You remember."

"Yes," he said. "Yes. Of course." He was being cautious, watchful.

"Well, forget it. I didn't mean it. It was a joke."

"What's wrong? What's the matter?"

I wiped my mouth with my hand, really playing it, really looking panicked, tapping into that tension, that buzz that was all through me whenever the Z wore off. I dropped my voice low. "Someone's been watching me. Staking out my apartment. Must be the cops. Has to be. Who else could it be?"

It took a moment before Emory understood what had happened. Then his pale, flaccid face relaxed. He smiled a superior smile.

"Oh, no, no, no. Relax, relax." He said it singsong, as if he were talking to an old woman or a child. "Don't be so paranoid."

I pretended his attitude was a revelation. "You already knew! Did *you* send him?"

"No, no, not me. But the people I deal with . . . They're cautious. They have protocols. You have to expect that. It's only reasonable."

I paced, pretending to think it over. Paused. Stared at him. "These are, like, your suppliers?"

"Don't look so worried. It's all right. You check out just fine."

I stared at him another moment, then let a breath out as if I were relaxing. "You should've told me."

"Now that would have spoiled the whole idea, wouldn't it," he said—and once again, he wrinkled his nose, cute, an old woman talking to a poodle. My stomach turned over. "I'm surprised you spotted him. They tell me he's very good."

"Look, this isn't . . . ? I mean, you're not some sort of . . . ?"

"What?" he said. "Policeman? Please! Of course not. You came to *me*. Remember?"

I hesitated—then I nodded.

"All we'll require now is a money transfer," he went on. "One computer to another, easy as that."

I nodded again, looking antsy—feeling antsy.

Emory took a step toward me. He put his hand on my shoulder and gave it a reassuring squeeze. I wanted to rip his arm off and beat him to death with it. Him and his sick desires. "It's all right," he said again. "You're nearly there. You've almost arrived. You've come to the right place, found what you're looking for." The green eyes buried in the soft folds of his pale skin gleamed out at me and I remembered the imps on the ceiling of the bedroom. He went on in a soothing, hypnotic voice: "No more half-starved, half-drugged yellow trash. What we're talking about is white. Fresh.

Safe. Completely safe. No history. No future. She'll exist only in your moment of ... absolute delight."

It was an effort to keep the expression of horror off my face but I managed it. I managed somehow to manufacture an expression of rapt expectation instead.

"You'll be receiving a call," Emory said majestically.

And with a friendly pat on the arm, he sent me on my way.

The street outside Emory's building—the little branch of 52nd dead-ending at the river—was quiet. A cab was making a U-turn. A doorman was pacing. The day was cold, gray, windy, heavy with the threat of rain. I stuck my hands into the pockets of my overcoat and ducked my chin into the collar as I walked to First Avenue.

When I reached the corner of the avenue, I paused and scanned the scene. An instinct. To see if the thug was still tailing me. The avenue was where all the action was. The morning rush hour: yellow cabs packed tight curb to curb, delivery trucks double-parked and blocking traffic. On the sidewalks, pedestrians were passing in a steady flow. Men and women carrying briefcases and coffee cups. Working guys with crates in their arms. Older ladies walking little dogs.

My eyes went over all of them—then stopped. I lifted my chin. My mouth opened and I felt a catch in my throat.

The dead boy was standing by a lamppost across the street. The boy I'd seen in the apartment: Alexander. He was just standing there, gazing at me. I could see him clearly in the gray daylight. He was small—maybe eight years old, but small even for his age. And frail—underfed. He wasn't wearing a coat or anything, just a thin button-down white shirt and grimy corduroy pants, a pitiful pair of worn-out sneakers that had once been red. He had thick black hair and a narrow, emaciated face. Big eyes—giant eyes above those gaunt, sunken cheeks. And he just stood there. Watching me. Without expression. Without movement. Just watching.

He kills them, I thought.

It came to me like that, all at once. Emory said he would find me someone completely safe . . . *No history. No future. She'll exist only in your moment of . . . absolute delight.*

Right. Because when I was done with her, he would kill her. Because murder—that was *his* absolute delight. He sold his victims to his customers to earn back the Fat Woman's purchase price—and when the customer was done, he killed the victim for his own pleasure. Maybe he watched the customer at work first, maybe that was part of it too, but it was the killing he lived for. I was certain of it.

The boy—the dead boy; the ghost I called Alexander—gazed and gazed at me from across the street, from out of his limbo-world of unforgivable suffering and injustice. I had the powerful urge to cry out to him through the rush-hour traffic, to cry out words that came into my memory out of nowhere, words one of my foster mothers had read to me from the tattered Bible open on her kitchen table.

I wanted to cry out to him: *Vengeance is mine. I will repay.*

But before I could speak, a bus came between us, rumbling uptown. When it passed, I saw that the dead boy had vanished.

After that, a week went by—more than a week, ten days maybe. Nothing happened. No calls from Emory. No meetings. Not a word. A sickness of suspense and revulsion gripped me. It was my constant state of feeling. There was no relief from it. I spent every day at the cover apartment on Fifth Avenue. Every evening, I took the Z. I knew what it was doing to me, but I couldn't stop . . .

She'll be completely safe. No history. No future. She'll exist only in your moment of . . . absolute delight.

I'd seen a lot of bad stuff, a lot of bad stuff. I didn't know why this time should be different, but it was. This time, I couldn't face the evil without the drug.

One night, the final night of waiting, I woke fully dressed, sprawled in a plush chair in the living room. The lights were on. The room was full of smoke. I knew—I could tell—that the smoke was in my mind, that my mind was swirling and unclear, and yet I could also see the smoke in the room: twisting tendrils of gray mist expanding into a general fog. It was as if the smoke itself obscured the borderline between the world as it was and the world inside my brain.

There was something else too. I had heard something. Just before I woke up, there had been a noise. A strange, piercing cry of a sound. Was it in my dream? In reality? In reality, I thought. Somewhere in the apartment . . .

Yes. Someone was there. Someone else was in the apartment with me. Living or dead. Someone.

When I stood up, I stumbled, my legs weak under me. I reached for the holster in the small of my back, but it wasn't there. I had taken the gun off when I came in that evening. It was in the bedroom, on the bedside table.

I took an unsteady step toward the bedroom door. It shifted in the smoke as the smoke shifted. The dark rectangle of the doorway faded in and out of my vision. The whole room tilted and I nearly went falling across the floor toward the windows. The damned drug. I grabbed hold of the back of the sofa to steady myself. I pulled my way along it, making for the bedroom through the smoke.

I reached the tilting door. I braced my hand against the frame to keep myself upright. The bedroom was dark. I didn't want to go into the darkness. I reached inside and found the light switch. The light came on. I stepped in. The smoke was in there too. I could see the bed only hazily, coming in and out of view. I didn't want to look up but I couldn't help it. I raised my eyes to the ceiling.

The cherubs grinned down at me, their sharp teeth bared.

I made a gagging sound and put my hand up to my brow, shielding my eyes from the horrible sight of them as I tumbled through the doorway, stumbled through the smoke toward the bedside table. My gun and holster lay there, next to my cell phone. Shielding my eyes from the grinning, feral cherubs on the ceiling, I reached forward through the smoke. My fingers touched the table. Touched my holster. I grabbed my gun. That was all I wanted. I had to get out of there.

I spun back around—and the dead boy was standing right in front of me. He was holding out his arms to me as if he wanted me to lift him up. He stank of the grave.

I cried out and reeled back through the smoke toward the bed. The blood-eyed cherubs reeled through my vision, laughing. That sound that had awakened me—that high cry—pierced the room.

It was the phone. I saw it light up on the bedside table. I saw it plainly—and when I looked around the room, the smoke was gone. The air was clear. The boy had vanished.

I dared—just barely dared—to look up at the ceiling. The cherubs were cherubs again, overcute, chubby angels gamboling among the dawn-lit clouds.

The phone went on ringing. I snapped it up.

"Tomorrow night at nine." It was Emory. He told me an address in the suburbs, a landmark to look for. Then he hung up.

I sat on the edge of the bed, my head hung down, the gun dangling from my hand.

The next night, I was in a car, the green Lexus we had borrowed from Narcotics. I was driving up Interstate 95, the streetlights glaring, the city skyline at my back.

"I don't know," Monahan was saying. "I'm looking at a lot of manpower for just a hunch."

He was stationed at the address already, out in the woods with the statie tac team and the rest of the task force. His voice came into the Lexus over its speakerphone. It was a comforting presence as I maneuvered through the night. It tethered me to reality, kept me from floating away.

"It's not a hunch," I said. "I'm telling you: He kills them."

"Because he said they were 'completely safe'?"

"Yes. And had no future. And because I just know."

"That sounds suspiciously like a hunch to me."

I didn't answer. I drove on. The city fell away. I traveled into Westchester. The highway grew darker. I blinked hard, trying to clear my vision. My head was foggy from the Z. Sometimes the fog came out of my mind and drifted through the night on the far side of the windshield. The cars around me would dim and waver like they were underwater. White headlights and red taillights would turn distant and gray. The sounds of the ride would grow muted and soft. Then after a mile or two, the mist would dissipate and the scene would snap back into clarity. The rumble of the engine and the rumble of the tires on the road and the steady sough of the air passing would rise and surround me again.

And there was Monahan's voice on the speakerphone: "You know what I think?"

"I care very deeply what you think, Monahan. Never doubt that."

"Yeah, I think Vice is getting to you."

"Nah. Vice is nice," I said. It's what we always said because the work was so much cleaner and safer than in Narcotics.

"Vice is nice," said Monahan, "but it gets to you. The perps and their shenanigans. They'd get to anyone."

"Shenanigans," I muttered. The highway seemed to telescope away from me and snap back. The hallucination was so real and sudden it nearly made me gasp. I shook my head to clear it. The damned drug.

"And you, with nothing else," said Monahan. "No life to distract you. That's the problem right there."

"This again."

"You need a life, Champion."

"I have a life. This is my life."

"You need a girl."

"I have girls."

"Your girls," said Monahan. "You take 'em to dinner Saturday night. Monday, we bust them on the street."

I laughed. It made my head hurt. "Combining work and pleasure —it saves time."

"You need a real girl. A wife," said Monahan.

Monahan had a wife. Cheryl her name was. A little Italian whirl-wind. Came up to his belt buckle. Always had two of his kids under her feet and one on her hip. Always shouting at someone. She made these pasta dinners that could've sunk an aircraft carrier. You could've put a plate of her lasagna on the deck of the USS *Ronald Reagan,* the Reagan would've just upended and sunk to the bottom, *blub blub blub,* with all hands lost. Two days in a row with Cheryl and I'd've gone nuts, but Monahan loved her.

"I don't like New York women," I said. "They're too . . . busy. Noisy."

"Eh. New York. Women are women. They're all noisy. But the good ones, you treat 'em nice, they'll do anything for you."

"I'll have to try that sometime. Here's my exit."

I left the highway. A couple of turns, a couple of miles of driving and I dipped down onto a narrow lane through the woods. It was dark here, really dark. No houses in sight. No lights. No moon visible through the heavy cloud cover. The forest on either side of me seemed dense and impenetrable. A drizzle started and as I turned on the wipers, a mist trailed up off the black pavement in front of me. I couldn't tell anymore whether the mist was real or in my mind.

"Your guys ready?" I said.

"You should see this army," said Monahan. "After we arrest this guy, I think we're gonna invade New Jersey. Right now, you're the safest guy in America. Press your thing."

I felt my pocket. I had a key chain in there with a flashlight about the size of a quarter. If I pressed the flashlight button, it lit up like a regular flashlight—but it also sent a radio beacon to the task force. I pressed the button through the cloth.

"There you are," said Monahan. "Every fifteen minutes, right?"

I was going into Emory's place without a wire or a gun. Emory was careful, suspicious. I knew he'd search me. The flashlight-beacon was the only way I had to call the cavalry. One signal meant I was okay, two meant it was time to launch the invasion. If they didn't hear from me after fifteen minutes, they'd come in without any signal at all. That was just in case Emory took the flashlight away.

"Every fifteen minutes," I said.

The drizzle grew heavier. So did the mist. I leaned forward, squinting, trying to see. The headlights picked out the end of the pavement. The next second, the Lexus was juddering over a dirt road. I felt the forest pressing in on me. I saw it moving at the edge of my vision—I thought I saw it; I thought I saw it creeping up to the windows of the car. When I turned to look, the trees were still, but the spaces between the trees were so black that the darkness seemed almost a solid wall.

Once, deep in that darkness, I saw a figure—the figure of a little boy—standing amidst the trees, watching me go by.

When I looked ahead, the mist was everywhere, clinging to the pavement, to the windshield, to the air. The rain on the windshield made streaks on the glass.

Then I saw an old stone root cellar to my right—that was the landmark Emory had told me to look for. To my left, hidden in the bushes, a driveway wound down away from the road.

I turned the wheel. The Lexus came bouncing off the rutted dirt onto the smooth pavement of the driveway. Now the trees really did close in around me as the car descended into a narrow forested valley.

"I'm signing off," I said.

"Go with God," said Monahan.

I disconnected. I felt the solitude flutter down on me like a shroud.

I came around a long curve and the forest fell away. The driveway continued to descend over a great sweep of sloping lawn. The house was at the bottom of the hill. It was a vast place, a mansion. Three stories of red stone. Roofs, gables, chimneys—I counted four chimneys—and graceful balconies. White pillars holding up the porch roof. More pillars supporting a round conservatory or something off to the side. The newspapers next day said the place had been built in 1900 in the Colonial Revival style, whatever that means. To me, it just looked pompous and grand—and grandly secluded too, sitting down there at the bottom of the hill with the lights from the windows dying into the blackness of the woods on every side.

As I traveled the last few yards of the drive, I saw something that I would remember later. A light went out somewhere. A yellow glow went out on the lawn, right where the lawn met the base of the house. I hadn't even noticed the light until it snapped off, and then I couldn't see where it had come from. There was no window there. There was nothing. I would remember that.

I felt my throat go dry as I rolled up to the four-car garage on the right. My head seemed to expand painfully, then snap back into place painfully. I was nauseous and woozy and I cursed the drug.

The rain grew heavier. It pattered on the roof of the Lexus. The fog was encroaching on my vision again. I blinked it away but it kept returning. I switched off the engine and sat taking deep breaths. Finally, I popped the glove compartment and checked one last time that my Glock was there. Then I pushed open the door.

I had to concentrate hard to walk steadily over the wide slate path across the lawn to the front steps. The rain dampened my hair, rolled down my face. The rain felt thick to me; gelatinous.

I climbed heavily into the darkness of the porch—and as I did, the lights just behind the front door came on. The mist seemed to swirl away for a moment so that I knew it was only in my mind. I checked my watch. Nine exactly, right on time. I reached into my pocket. Pressed the button of the flashlight. Fifteen minutes.

Now the huge front door swung open. Emory stood there. He was dressed almost formally for him, wearing slacks and a turtleneck and a navy blazer. His bland face creased with a bland smile. He stepped back to let me enter.

"You seem surprised to see me," he said. He closed the door.

"The house was so grand, I was expecting ... you know ..."
He pretended not to understand. Stood with his head cocked in
a question. "A butler, a maid or something," I said.

He gave a strangely feminine little giggle. "On these special
nights, I prefer to be alone."

These special nights. He said the words in that way he had, wrin-
kling his nose, gleeful and wicked. *Are we being naughty now?* I
wanted to clutch him by the throat. I felt a thickness in my brain
like fever. The room swam in mist all around me.

We were standing in a vast foyer. A massive chandelier with
prisms sent rainbows over the walls. There was a sweeping turn of
stairs in the shadows beyond the chandelier's reach. Dark wood
banisters twisted out of sight into the upper stories. Mist.

"I'm afraid I have to search you," Emory said.

I rolled my eyes. That's what I thought an innocent man would
do. "You're kidding me."

"I know, I know," he said, "but the world is full of philistines
and we really have to be careful. Would you mind removing your
overcoat?"

I gave an elaborate sigh and stripped the coat off and handed it
to him. He went through the pockets, examined it back and front,
felt the linings. He was thorough and expert. He had done it before. When he was finished, he hung the coat neatly on a hanger
in the foyer closet.

"Empty your pockets please," he said over his shoulder.

I gave him my wallet, my phone, and my keys. He turned the
phone off and set it on top of a short bureau by the closet door. He
set the wallet there too. Then he looked at the key chain, pressed
the flashlight button. He was satisfied when the light went on. He
put the keys on the bureau beside the wallet.

Finally he patted me down. Again, he was thorough and expert.
I've snuck guns past the searches of some pretty hard-boiled street
characters, but Emory and his soft white hands would've been
hard to get around.

He smiled then. "Sorry about that."

I shrugged. "Whatever. Can I have my stuff back?"

"Just leave it there for now. You won't be needing it anytime soon."

I didn't want to leave the flashlight-beacon behind but I couldn't think of an answer that wouldn't arouse his suspicions.

Emory gestured toward the archway behind him. "Shall we sit and have a drink together?"

I hesitated. The clock was ticking. Emory had pressed the flashlight-beacon again so the fifteen-minute count had restarted, but it might not be enough. I didn't want the tac team to come bursting in before I'd had a chance to get some solid evidence against him.

I tried to move things along, pretending to be a nervous first-timer. "You know, I think I'd rather just . . . get on with it, if you don't mind."

Emory laughed. "No, no, no. Don't be that way. Everything's fine. Now that it's all out on the table between us, you and I are going to be good friends. Let's get to know one another. Please."

There was no getting out of it. I glanced at my watch as I followed him through the archway. It was just after 9:05. Around 9:20, tac would come through that door like the Allies crossing the Rhine.

The living room was expansive. There was one wall of high windows. They were dark except where the interior light winked off the raindrops running down the panes. The other walls had elaborate wallpaper and paintings—one green and hazy landscape after another with ruined temples on their hills.

"Single malt, if I recall," said Emory.

I sat on the flowery sofa. The thickness in my head came and went and came again. The mist drifted in and out of the room's corners. Finally, it gathered all around me, blurring the borders between my body and the room. Made me feel as if I were going to melt somehow into the fabric of the place. I shook the feeling off.

Emory handed me a drink and took one of his own to a chair on the other side of a low coffee table.

"To the good life," he said, and drank. Then he laughed. "Oh, relax, really. This is part of the pleasure of it: being accepted for who you are. Not having to make excuses anymore. Not having to live a lie."

I barely sipped the scotch—barely sipped the sting off the surface of it—and yet it hit me instantly, hit me hard. I felt my stomach roll. I saw the world go dreamy. Thick white fog pressed hard against the windows across from me, threatening to permeate the walls, the room, my mind.

"Let's face it, we live among troglodytes most of the time," Emory went on. "People are so incredibly backward, so incredibly insensitive to differences in points of view. I mean, God, this is the postmodern world already! There are cultures on the globe where we'd be perfectly accepted, cultures where we'd be priests and kings. What are they going to say now? 'Only our way is right?' By what argument? 'Oh, I *feel* it. You're evil. I feel it in my bones.' It's absurd. Socrates himself was . . . What's the matter?"

I had been staring past him at the fog gathered at the windows. It seemed to roil and push against the glass like a living animal, seeking access. Then all a once . . . a shadow on the fog . . . a small dark figure moving through it, toward me . . . reaching out for me plaintively with his desperate little hands . . .

The ghost boy. Alexander.

Emory looked over his shoulder to see what I was gaping at. But the dead boy sank back into the fog, and the fog sank away into the darkness.

I glanced at my watch. Almost ten minutes had gone by since he'd pressed that flashlight button. Another five or so and the tacs would invade and we might well be left empty-handed. Emory would slip the net.

I plunked my drink down on the coffee table. "I'm sorry," I said. "I guess I really am tense. I'd feel a lot better if we could . . . you know, convene and have a drink afterward maybe."

Emory sat and gazed at me a long moment, a bland, meditative gaze. With his legs crossed at the knee, he swung his foot back and forth as he considered. In my feverish brain I thought I could practically hear him calculating whether or not to trust me. For a moment, in a waking dream, a waking nightmare, I saw him reach under his blue blazer and draw out a .38, ready to shoot me dead. I caught my breath—but the moment passed, the hallucination passed. He was just sitting there, just gazing at me.

Then he smiled. He leaned forward in his chair. Set his drink down next to mine.

"Afterward, you won't want to, you know. That's the problem. You'll scuttle away—you'll see. But . . ." He slapped his knees resolutely and stood. "I understand your . . . anticipation." He gestured toward the archway. "Shall we?"

I followed him back out into the foyer, then up the stairs. It was a hard climb for me. My body felt distant, as if I were running it by remote control from somewhere far away within myself. When we reached the landing, there were several halls going in different directions. So it seemed to me anyway. The place seemed to me a maze, a mad maze that was a living reflection of the mad maze in the haze of my mind. Down we went now along a corridor of doors and dark wood paneling. Around a corner . . . down another corridor. Lights like candles flickered in sconces on the wall. The mist curled around the lamps. Their light faded and the shadows threatened to swarm and overcome me. The tendrils of mist threatened to wrap themselves around me like skeletal fingers.

I didn't want to look at my watch, but all the while I felt the time tick-tick-ticking away. Around another corner . . . down another hall . . . Any minute, I thought, any second, Monahan and the staties were going to break down that door and come pouring in here.

Not yet, I thought. *Not yet.*

We came at last to the end of a corridor. There was a small triangular table set in the corner there with a vase of flowers on top of it. Emory bent to move the table aside, lifting its legs carefully over the runner so as not to jar the thing and tip the vase over.

"You'll like this part," he said to me with a sly smile. "Very gothic."

Then he straightened. He pressed his palm against the wall, then pressed it harder and made a curt upward motion. A section of the wall snapped open, swung out toward us. Very gothic. Right.

Emory moved back a little and gestured for me to go in. I stepped across the threshold.

There was a tremendous blast as the door downstairs exploded inward. A dozen voices filled the house, an army of men shouting: "Police!"

The tac team had arrived.

Emory reacted fast—much faster than I did. I was too feverish, too drugged, too foggy in my mind to move quickly. But Emory—the moment he heard the sounds below, he threw his shoulder into me. Unsteady on my feet, I stumbled, reaching for the edge of the open wall. I missed it. I fell to my knee in the inner chamber. I caught a glimpse of a room draped in red velvet . . . a four-poster bed . . . expensive stuffed animals against one wall . . . Very gothic.

Emory darted down the hall out of sight, quick as black lightning. I staggered up to go after him, seizing hold of the open wall to propel myself forward.

But before I could, I sensed a presence behind me. I looked back over my shoulder and saw the girl.

She was beautiful—a beautiful child—and forlorn, so frail and forlorn. She stood trembling in a purple nightshirt with a faded picture of a cartoon princess on it. Her wrists were tied around the bedpost.

She was seven or eight years old. She had long brown hair and green eyes with a dusting of freckles on her pug nose. She wasn't crying. She was frightened beyond tears, desperate beyond tears. But her expression—lost, helpless, hopeless, terrified—would have shattered the heart of a statue.

I leapt to her, the rage flaring in my chest like a living flame.

"I'm a policeman," I told her, nearly choking on the words. "No one will hurt you. No one."

I worked at the ropes quickly, blinking back tears.

"I want to go home," she managed to say—and her voice broke and she gulped and started to sob.

The ropes came loose. I swept her up into my arms. She weighed nothing; nothing at all.

"Hold on to me," I said. "Don't be afraid."

I carried her out the door. Through the crazy maze of corridors. I don't know how I found my way. The corridors snaked and twisted endlessly. The floor was dipping and swaying beneath my feet like ocean waves. The darkness curled in mistlike tendrils off the walls, and mist like darkness swirled around me. My body seemed a dead and raglike thing. Only the flame of rage inside me propelled me forward. Only my arms had strength, clutching the child against my chest.

I came around a corner and almost ran into the barrel of a submachine gun. A tac in black armor, helmeted, masked, loomed out of the mist of my mind, monstrous.

"It's Champion!" I shouted at him.

But he'd already seen the little girl, already thrown his arms up, pointing the rifle skyward. He cried out a curse, his voice cracking.

"Where's the stairs?" I shouted—but I saw them, just a few yards away. I had made it through the maze.

The little girl was sobbing and trembling now as I carried her down the sweeping curl of steps to the foyer below. I had to hew close to the wall because men in black armor were pouring up the stairs past us, holding their machine guns at the ready. I could hear the tac team shouting all around beneath me and above me as they searched each room of the massive mansion:

"Clear!"

"Clear!"

"Clear!"

Just as I reached the ground floor, Monahan stomped immensely into the foyer. He was coming out of one of the halls. He was waving a .45 semiautomatic in the air, shouting, "Check the grounds!"

"Jimmy!" I called to him. I set the girl's feet on the floor. "Help me! Take her!"

Monahan looked down at the child. He blinked once. He holstered his weapon. He lowered his enormous body to one knee in front of her. He wrapped his gigantic arms around her and pulled her against his vest. I heard him murmur to her in a voice like a dove cooing, "You're safe now, baby."

I left him there, staggered away from him, staggered through the mind-mist to the foyer table. Grabbed the keys that Emory had left there and staggered out the front door.

A cold rain was dropping heavily from the sky now. It washed down my face as I stepped off the porch. It carried away my tears and momentarily cleared my head. All around me, in the black forest surrounding the house on every side, beams of light were slashing here and there through the dark and the rainfall as the tac team searched for Emory among the trees. Bursts of static and muttering voices joined the shouts still coming from inside the house. They could not find him.

Nauseous, feverish, weak as I was, I was still able to jog along the path back to my car. I pressed the button on the key to unlock the door, yanked the door open, and stuck my head in. Inside, I popped the glove compartment. I drew out my Glock 19.

When I stood up straight again, I swayed, dizzy and sick. I became aware of red and blue lights flashing—the first flashing lights I'd seen. An ambulance. It came quickly and quietly up the drive. I saw Monahan striding across the lawn to meet it, the child nearly lost in those massive arms.

I had to force my legs to move so I did, I forced them. I marched back up the path to the mansion's front door. I paused there, leaning in the doorway, steadying myself with my hand against the jamb. Then I swung inside again.

The tac team had spread out through the house. I could see black armor and flashlights any way I looked. I could hear them shouting everywhere.

They could not find him.

I turned to the right, away from the living room archway, toward a smaller archway into a smaller den. I went through—across a prim, green sitting room—through the sickening and smothering mist that was gathered there, toward a closed door on the far wall. The room was dark and shadowy. As I went through it, I thought I caught a presence in the corner of my eye. I thought I saw a child, enthroned in an armchair, watching me pass, expressionless. The dead boy. I didn't turn to look. I didn't dare. I stumbled across the room to the far door, through the door, and into a narrow corridor beyond.

A flashlight beam hit me in the eyes as the officer searching the hall swung his gun my way. The beam lanced painfully into the core of my head, the mist exploding away from me, then swarming back around me even thicker and more nauseating than before. The cop nodded at me as we passed in the hall.

"Clear," he said.

I was too woozy and confused to nod back or answer. I just kept stumbling forward. I charged down the narrow hall past more pictures of ruins or maybe the same picture again and again, I didn't know, couldn't tell. I came to a door at the end of the hall, yet another door in this puzzle box of a house. I pulled it open. A walk-in linen closet. I stepped inside. Turned the light on. Pulled the door shut behind me.

I was in a close little pantry. There were shelves on two of its walls. The third wall was empty. Nothing but wood paneling.

I had seen that light outside, that glow on the grass as I was driving up to the house. I had seen the glow go out as I approached. There was no place that light could have come from. There was no window there, not even a cellar door. I remembered that. It had been in the back of my mind from the moment Emory had opened the secret bedroom upstairs.

That light had come from somewhere near here.

I reached out to the wood paneling in the linen closet. I pressed my hand against it. Then I pressed my hand against it harder—much harder—and felt it give very slightly. I made the same curt upward motion I had seen Emory make—and yes, a section of the wall snapped away and swung toward me. Very gothic.

There was a stairway within, leading downward, becoming invisible in deep darkness. I went down. The open section of wall swung shut behind me. The dark closed in on me. It pressed tight. It seemed to seep into me and meld with the darkness already inside me. It was impossible to tell where the dark ended and I began. I went down and down.

I reached the bottom. I nearly collided with the wall before I saw it. Then I did see it, and I saw a thin, thin line of dim white light hanging in the air just above my head. I pressed my hand against the paneling, pressed harder, lifted—and again, the wall opened. Light—dazzling brightness—spilled out over me. Shielding my eyes with my hand, I stepped into it.

From this point on, my memories of that night are more like dreams. Glimpses and fragments that waver and fade. The light, that bright white light, and the smoke and the smell, so thick, so sharp; and the fog in my brain—it all came together and overwhelmed me.

I staggered forward. I saw the source of the light: four white circular objects packed with halogen bulbs. I could not think what they were at the time but now, looking back, I know they were lights from an operating room. Their brilliant beams reflected, gleaming, off the steel operating table beneath them. They flashed off the loathsome instruments that were laid out in readiness on a stand beside the table and hanging from hooks on the white walls.

The smell—the smell was disinfectant. A smell so harsh and raw I could almost see it in the air like heat. Emory had a red plastic gallon container of the stuff. He was splashing it wildly over the walls and the floor.

The smoke, meanwhile, was billowing out of a metal trash can just near him. Papers and photographs were burning there. Through the fog and fever and stench and smoke, I caught a glimpse of one of the pictures, one of the photographs. I saw what it was before it curled and blackened. I thought, *My God, my Jesus God.*

Emory spotted me then. He started back, throwing his hands out, flinging away the red plastic container. It slid across the tiled floor and rattled to rest. The green disinfectant came gulping out of the open neck so that the smell grew even worse, grew overpowering.

Emory's weak, round features were wild with terror. His green eyes lanced laserlike at me out of their folds of flesh, burning with terror and with rage.

"Traitor!" he shrieked.

I pointed my gun at him. "Who's the Fat Woman?" I said.

"Traitor!"

"Where is she?"

My voice sounded bizarre in my own ears, drawn out and distorted like a recording played back at slow speed. I was drowning in the feverish atmosphere down here. I was losing myself in it, falling away from myself, farther and farther away.

"You think you're Justice?" Emory screamed—at least that's what I think he screamed, that's what I remember. He started to cry. "You're a traitor to everything!"

But his voice was growing distorted too. He was slipping off into the atmosphere, slipping away from me. Both of us were lost and swirling in the swirling and unreal confusion that crossed and erased the borderlines between me and the world I saw.

The rest is all like that, all darkness and unreal confusion, all mist and smoke and bright white gleaming lights and the choking stench, all of it filling me up with darkness—filling up all reality with darkness, so that reality and I became one dark thing, darkness itself, darkness alone.

I think Emory went on screaming in that darkness. I'm not sure. I don't remember.

I don't even remember killing him.

3

War Stories

THERE WAS A restaurant called Salvatore's on Main Street in Tyler. Nothing fancy: pizza and burgers and sandwiches, that sort of thing, plus a full bar. A lot of county office workers went there at the end of the day. A lot of families and some high school kids sometimes—the good kids, the clean kids. It was the sort of place you went for dinner and a good time and no trouble. And there never was any trouble, because it was where the county's law enforcement officers hung out too—Sheriff's Department deputies and BCI inspectors and state police and prosecutors and assistants and all.

Salvatore cultivated our trade. He named drinks and sandwiches after us, especially the inspectors. Mine was a veal and onion submarine he called the Champion Hero, a name that always got a lot of laughs. Plus he put in one of those old Bally pinball machines especially for us. It was called "Police Force," and was all about these lion and tiger cops chasing down weasel and reptile bad guys. Everyone had a good time with that as well.

The day after Deputy Dunn and I tracked down Frank Bagot at his sister's house was a Thursday. Salvatore's was crowded as the workday closed. The story about Bagot had been in the local daily, the *Tyler Dispatch:* "Sheriff's Men Track Down Tenn Murder

Suspect." The story took up most of the front page. Sheriff Brady had given the official statement, but Dunn and I had both been interviewed. Dunn was interviewed on the local radio station too. There was even a brief report about the arrest on the TV news out of Danbury across the state line.

So when I laid off work and walked into Salvatore's that evening, the crowd there erupted in a big cheer. A lot of them stood up and everyone started applauding. I couldn't help grinning as I made my way through a gauntlet of handshakes to the big round table by the storefront window that Salvatore reserved for police.

Young Dunn was already there, having a beer. So was another young deputy, Rob Wilder. Grassi and Sternhagen, both BCI, were present and accounted for, with a red wine and a scotch respectively. And Anne Brady, who was the sheriff's daughter and a part-time administrative assistant in the department, was there with a beer as well. Anne was hoping to be a deputy when she finished college and she liked to be thought of as one of the boys. We tended to oblige her.

"Well, I ordered a Champion Hero and here it is," said Sternhagen.

"Well, don't hold back then, go on and bite me," I said.

"That's the plan."

I pulled out a chair and sat with them. "And you must be that Deputy Dunn I keep hearing so much about on the radio."

Dunn blushed from his crew cut to his Adam's apple. "That's me."

"Tell us again how you pumped that mad dog full of lead, cowboy," Grassi teased him.

The whole table laughed and Dunn blushed even redder, hanging his head so low he nearly went face-first into his beer.

Grassi slapped him on the back. He was a dark little man, broad at the shoulder, bright white teeth when he smiled but always kind of sinister in the eyes, if you asked me. He had a penchant for checkered sports coats no one could talk him out of. We'd had a run-in once after I answered a call for a domestic dispute at his house. He'd given his wife a black eye and I told him right in front of her I'd run him in if he did it again, member of service or not. Wouldn't have done much good, of course. Sheriff Brady was expert at losing paperwork like that when he had a mind to. But Grassi felt I'd humiliated him in front of his wife and he took it hard. We'd made it up since—we had to, working together as we did—but it was a brittle relationship at best.

"Am I too late to make Champion Hero jokes?" That was Bethany, one of Salvatore's waitresses.

I looked up over my shoulder at her. She smiled her heart-stirring smile. "No, go on. I always love those," I told her. "They make me laugh and laugh."

"Now Bethany, you know what they say about hero sex," said Grassi, pointing at me. "You might want to get in on a good thing here."

Bethany rolled her eyes. Grassi always took this sort of thing right up to the edge of too far. "What can I get you, tough guy?" she asked me.

"A Sam Adams would be great, Beth, thank you," I said.

I was still looking up at her as she wrote it down on her pad. She lifted her eyes to me. They were big, green eyes that were deep with tenderness and need. She knew they went right through me. I had told her often enough.

"I'll get that beer for you," she said, and went back to the bar.

"So you talk to him?" said Sternhagen. Sternhagen was a nice enough guy. Fifties, lean, steel-haired with a weak sort of face. A good cop once, serving out his time now. "This Frank Bagot. He say anything to you?"

"I recall he complained of his treatment at the hands of our local constabulary," I said.

"That Dunn," said Grassi. "He's a wild man, you let him loose."

"True that."

"You didn't hard-hand a visitor to our county, did you, Champion?" said Sternhagen.

"We had a free and frank exchange of views."

Bethany set my beer in front of me. I thanked her and took a good pull. It had been a long day: I was ready for it.

"You ask him why he did it?" Sternhagen asked. "Strangle the girl, I mean."

"He didn't strangle her. The Nashville boys say he punched her to death. He told us she liked the rough stuff."

Sternhagen laughed. "He didn't."

"That was his reason."

"There's criminal logic for you. 'Gee, if you like a slap on the ass now and then, well, honey, you're *really* gonna enjoy being beaten to death.'"

"It was total crap too," Dunn chimed in. "She was a local girl. People knew her."

"Yeah, and you're an expert on that stuff, right, Dunn?" said Grassi. "That teacher you go out with, I heard she's into all that."

"Shut up, Grassi," Sternhagen said. "Jesus, man. Fuck's wrong with you?"

I was glad he said it so I didn't have to. Dunn tried to look like he was taking it well, but I could see he wasn't. He didn't like jokes about Sally.

Anne Brady chimed in as peacemaker, changing the subject. "Bastard'll probably get himself a psychiatrist to declare him insane or something," she said. "Like, yeah, he's suffering from Evil Dirtbag Syndrome."

We managed to laugh and move on.

"I remember when I was in uniform," Sternhagen said. "I got a call once. Guy killed his wife. He says, 'She drove me crazy.' I said to him, 'Well, why didn't you divorce her?' He says, 'Oh, I couldn't do that. She never would've forgiven me.'"

We laughed, shook our heads.

"Had one like that last year," said young Deputy Wilder. He was a great big slab of a fellow with a strangely babyish face. "Said he couldn't get a divorce cause he was Catholic. So he killed her."

"Yeah, I think the church allows that, don't they?" Sternhagen laughed.

Grassi smiled wryly into his wineglass. "Way these scumbags think," he said, and took a swig. Which was rich coming from him, being just this side of a perp himself.

Anyway, the storytelling went on from there and I had another beer. Then after a while, I noticed Bethany trailing out of sight into the corridor in back that led to the restrooms. I pushed away from the table.

"Excuse me a moment," I said. "Police business."

"Take a whiz for me while you're at it," said Grassi.

I met Bethany in the dark of the hall. She was a good-looking woman in her thirties. She had long blonde hair, in a ponytail tonight. She had a terrific figure which did terrific things to her waitress uniform, a short black skirt and tight white top.

"I'm off at nine," she said—quickly, softly. "You coming by?" Her breath was warm on my face and her scent, even with the sweat of her working, was delicate and sweet.

"You want to test this hero sex theory, huh?"

Her bright smile flashed but she shook her head. "That Grassi. He's such garbage."

I nodded. "Don't let him get to you."

"I might let you get to me, though. You gonna come by?"

"I don't know how I could resist."

She seemed about to say something else but then she pressed her lips tight to keep it in. "Don't even think about resisting," was what she said instead.

She went back out to the main floor. I went into the restroom for a moment or two, then came out and went back to the table to join the others.

It was funny, strange, given what finally happened that night—given the way it all came back to get me like some hand in a horror movie coming up to grab you out of the grave—it was strange that I thought of the past again as I was driving my G8 over to Bethany's. Maybe it was the fact that it was April—the start of spring—and the air had that April feeling to it that makes you long for something but you don't know what. It was almost as if the past was in the atmosphere.

Or maybe it was Bethany herself. How good she looked, how sweet she was. That gentleness in her eyes and the way she almost said something to me in the corridor but didn't. I knew why she didn't. I thought I knew why. There wasn't really anything more to say between us. We had had it all out and it was what it was, no more. If she said too much, if she went too far, well, it just caused uneasiness between us.

She had asked me once why—why it was I couldn't love her. All she wanted was to do for me, she said. She had gotten emotional and asked me if maybe I might not come to love her over time. I don't recall what I answered. What could I answer? I didn't want to see her lower herself in that way. I wasn't going to let her spend her life in some hell of reaching for something in me she just couldn't touch, that no one touched.

Of course, I asked myself the same thing, privately. Why couldn't I love her? That cold and watchful incapacity of mine—what was it? But of course I already knew. I didn't like to think about it, but you always know these sorts of things, deep down.

I couldn't love Bethany because I was in love already. I was in love with a woman I could never have. You hear people talk about that sort of thing. Usually it's some guy who carries a torch for someone else's wife or maybe can't get over a girl who left him or is even pining away for someone who loved him once but died. And those are all sad stories, right enough. But this was worse than any of them. Well, it was weirder anyway.

I couldn't love Bethany because I was in love with Samantha. And it was thinking about her—driving the lonely backroads over to Gilead in the night and thinking about Samantha—that drew my mind back into the past again.

4

Flashback: Samantha

I WOKE UP IN the hospital. That was the first thing I knew after the mansion in Westchester, after my meeting with Emory in the secret cellar, with him shrieking "Traitor!" and me falling away into a fog of drugs and smoke and confusion. I opened my eyes and saw the white ceiling and thought: *I don't remember.*

I sat up slowly. Gray daylight was at the windows, coming through the slats of the venetian blinds to lie in bars across the fringe of the bedsheet. I drew a breath and turned my head—and there was Monahan. Sheepish and hunched, he looked like a pile of boulders that had tumbled from a mountainside, burying the small blue plastic chair on which he sat.

I dragged my hand over my face and cursed. With my eyes closed, I saw a murky brainscape: swirling, impenetrable red-brown smog with clipped, spastic moments of memory and motion flashing out of it briefly, then dying away like the light from a falling flare.

"The girl . . ." I said. "The little girl."

Monahan nodded glumly and spoke on a long sigh. He looked as if he hadn't slept all night. "She's okay. She'll be okay. Docs say no one touched her. They were saving her for you."

I pressed my lips together and didn't answer for a moment. You have to savor these things, these little victories. "What about me?"

I said then. I patted myself. My chest, my belly. "Was I shot or something? What am I doing here?"

"No," said Monahan. "You just went down." He targeted me with his close-set eyes so I knew there was more he wasn't saying. The doctors must have found the Z in my bloodstream. Of course they had.

I rolled my legs over the side of the bed. "Who is she? The girl."

"We don't know. She doesn't know. No one seems to have reported her missing. She has a name. Eva. That's it. She says she used to live in a place with other children, then she went to live with the Fat Woman."

"The Fat Woman." I felt a choking surge of rage as more of the night came back to me. "She remember anything about her?"

Monahan blinked rapidly. With that schoolboy face of his, he looked like a baffled ten-year-old. "She said the Fat Woman told her to call her Aunt Jane."

"Aunt Jane!"

"I asked the kid what Aunt Jane looked like. She said Aunt Jane had no face."

"Oh, for Christ . . . What the hell is this, Monahan?"

Monahan turned one hand in his lap: a helpless gesture.

"Emory's going to talk to us," I said. "Lawyered-up or not. He and I are going to have a private conversation."

"Not unless you're planning a road trip to hell."

"What—he's dead?"

"It was an understandable reaction to the fact that you put five slugs in him."

My mouth opened. I meant to say something but only a slow breath came out. I tried to see the scene through the fog: Emory screaming . . . me with the gun . . . "Did I?" I murmured finally.

"Three in his chest, two in his head," Monahan said.

"I don't remember."

Monahan lifted his chin and did his best to give me a meaningful look. "The fool drew down on you, bro," he told me. "Tried to put a .357 in you with an 850."

I held his eyes only a moment, then looked down at the gray and white tiles of the floor. I saw flashes in my mind of Emory—only flashes. He had been holding a red plastic container when I first came in. Then later, his hands were empty. I tried to remember him with a gun but I couldn't. Certainly not a CIA 850. That was a classic throwaway. That's what Monahan was telling me, see, with that meaningful look of his. He—or someone—had planted the gun on the dead man after I'd blown him away in cold blood.

"I don't remember," I said again. I felt it, though. I felt sick inside. The drugs . . . "Too bad. He could've told us more."

"Yeah, he could've."

I stood up. I was wearing one of those thin hospital gowns they give you, my ass hanging out the back. I yanked the gown off, tossed it aside. There was a blond-wood bureau against one wall. I pulled open the drawers until I found my clothes. I started to get dressed.

Monahan could see how I felt, I guess. "He deserved to die. He deserved worse."

"It's true," I said. "He did."

"No, you don't even know yet. You were right about him."

I buckled my belt. "Was I? What do you mean?"

"We found a graveyard in the woods behind the house."

I had my shirt halfway on. I stared at him.

"Eight children so far," Monahan said. "They laid off digging last night but they'll be back at it this morning. They're sure to find more."

I went to the window, buttoning my shirt. I felt strange. Heavy and strange and distant. Suddenly I remembered the photographs I saw Emory burning in the trash can. *My God, my God,* I thought, *the things people do to one another.*

I looked out through the slats of the blinds. We were on the second story. There was a courtyard below. Grass and paths and benches and a couple of small plane trees, leafless in the winter cold. No one was out there. Nothing was moving but a gray-brown squirrel. I pulled the string of the blinds and lifted them. I knew somehow the dead boy would be waiting—and there he was, small and frail and shivering beneath the naked branches of a tree. Gazing up at me, expressionless, with his large dark eyes.

"Were they girls and boys both?" I asked Monahan. "The bodies they found. Were they both girls and boys?"

"Yeah, both."

"Any IDs."

"We're working on it."

Alexander, I thought. One of the dead children would be named Alexander.

"If you get any hits let me know," I said over my shoulder—and when I looked out the window again, the courtyard below was empty. The emptiness had a feeling of finality to it.

I did not think I would see the ghost again.

After a while, Monahan left. I needed a doctor to give me release papers so I badgered the nurses until they sent one. He was a small, serious-looking Asian man named Lee. He held a clipboard in his hand. He had a round face and big glasses. He had no expression on his face, none whatsoever.

"You have any idea what it was you were taking?" he asked me.

I shook my head. "The dealer called it Z."

"Zattera," said Dr. Lee. "It was developed as an antianxiety medication but the FDA banned its ass because it makes you nutty as a brainless ape." He said this deadpan. It was kind of comical. "Hallucinations, hyperaggression. Stuff's not good for you, Detective."

"No kidding."

"Tell you what's even worse: going off it cold. It'll make you nuttier than the drug, plus you'll puke your guts out. Taper off, say over the course of two weeks or so."

"Right," I said. But I was lying. I was never taking that crap again. Whatever cold turkey was like, I would get through it and be done.

"Have any good hallucinations?" asked Dr. Lee.

"I saw a ghost. A dead kid. He followed me around."

"That's pretty cool."

"I don't recommend it."

"Wait till you try to quit. You'll see things that look so real that reality will pale by comparison."

"Can't wait."

"Like I said: Taper off it. Slow."

"Right."

"Right." He studied his clipboard, expressionless. "I'd appreciate it if you could keep your mouth shut about this."

"The drug?"

"I'll lose my license if it comes out I'm covering for you."

"Are you covering for me?"

"You killed a man in cold blood while doped out of your mind, Detective."

"Yeah. So why are you covering for me?"

"Because you couldn't have killed that son of a bitch dead enough to suit me."

"Right. Thanks."

"Also your friend Monahan asked me to and I'm afraid he'll beat me up."

"He is big, isn't he?"

Dr. Lee nodded. He signed a page on his clipboard, tore it off, and handed it to me. "Give that to the front desk and they'll set you free to do more damage to yourself and others."

Something happened then. Just a small thing. I didn't think much about it at the time, but it would come back to me. It was what I guess you'd call a sort of blackout. When I went to leave the hospital, I remembered walking past the reception desk, walking toward the doors. Then the next thing I knew, I was on the train headed back to the city. I didn't know how I got to the train station. Walked, I guess. It wasn't far. I didn't know how much time had passed. Maybe half an hour. It was gone completely.

I shrugged it off. Just the drug, I figured.

Like I said, I didn't think much about it at the time.

★ ★ ★

I made my way back to my apartment, the old place in Queens. I was on administrative leave until a grand jury could decide about the shooting. I wasn't worried about that, though. The "House of Evil" was a big news story. There were pictures all over TV and the Internet. Child-sized corpses being carried in body bags from their forest graves. Fuzzy surveillance shots of the "Mystery Woman"—the Fat Woman—Aunt Jane. Long investigative portraits of Martin Emory, a Wall Street player and a serial killer who made a profit selling his victims to johns before he tortured them to death.

There was not a grand jury anywhere on the planet that was going to charge me with wrongdoing for having blown him away.

My only concern was to get that drug out of my system. I could still feel it working in me. It came in waves of mist and distortion. Weird little fits of distance. I kept catching glimpses of movements at the corners of my eyes. I tried not to turn toward them. I didn't want to see whatever hallucination was standing there.

My place was on a residential street off the main boulevard. A gray two-story clapboard house with white trim around the windows. I lived on the second floor. The landlord lived below. Ed Morris, his name was. He was a cranky but basically decent old gramps who owned a couple of the houses on the street and spent his time complaining about the tenants.

I had a private entrance. A flight of white steps on the house's side. I remember climbing the stairs heavily with a bag of groceries under one arm. I remember my apartment door swinging in. I remember stepping out of the gray day into a bleak and irascible darkness. The blinds in the apartment hadn't been opened for days. Sandwich wrappers and beer cans were still on the low coffee table. I'd never gotten around to fully furnishing the place and it looked particularly empty and uninviting now, like a cheap motel room at the end of a long day's ride. Nothing there but a TV and a sofa and the coffee table.

What else do I remember before the withdrawal hit full force? I flushed what was left of my supply of Z down the toilet, shaking the Baggie at the water even after it was empty—just in case I got tempted, I guess. I cleaned off the coffee table. I sat on the sofa. I cracked a fresh beer. I turned on the TV with the remote. Skipped past the video of bodies being brought out of the woods. The "House of Evil" surrounded by cops. "A noted psychiatrist says Emory may have been the victim of abuse himself..." A school snapshot of a smiling little girl, one of the victims who had been identified. I stopped on the sports channel. Stared at the screen and sipped my beer. I wondered if I'd pumped all five bullets into Emory at once or stood over him after he went down and planted the last two in his head more deliberately.

Well, there was no point getting sentimental about it. Monahan was right. The bastard deserved much worse.

It took about two hours for the real withdrawal horror show to get started. Once it was under way—Dr. Lee was right: It was pretty impressive.

The sportscaster on TV had just finished speculating about some off-season trade the Yankees were planning.

"If the Yanks don't fill the holes in their roster, they could be looking at another long season," he said. Then, he turned in his seat just slightly and looked directly at me. He said, "Aunt Jane is waiting for you, Champion. She's waiting for you in hell. You're going to burn down there with her forever."

Well, that was kind of creepy—and it got worse. The sportscaster started spewing obscenities at me, a long, guttural rant of unbroken filth. He grinned and his eyes burned through the TV screen. The tirade went on and on and on a long time without commercial interruptions.

After a while, I found myself lying on the carpet at the base of the sofa. I was curled into a ball, clutching my midsection in pain. The sportscaster did a sizzling, staticky fade into the bowels of the machine. He was replaced by images of horror—images of the children Emory had tortured. I saw them tortured. I saw them killed.

"A noted psychiatrist says Satan may have been a victim of abuse himself," the announcer said.

But at this point, I had other things to divert my attention. There were, for instance, the snakes and spiders covering every inch of the walls, oozing down and spreading over the carpet toward me like a twining, chittering stain. I writhed and screamed in agony and terror as they came toward me.

And oh yeah, Dr. Lee was right about the vomiting too. That also went on and on and on.

I wasn't sure how much time had passed. I wasn't sure whether it was night or day. It didn't matter. I didn't want to know. There was only one thing I wanted now. I wanted the strength to crawl to the door . . . to tumble down the outside stairs . . . to reach my motorcycle . . . to get to Harlem . . . to get to Janks . . . to get some more Z and make this agony stop.

I was in the process of clawing my way across the carpet to that end when I heard the knocking—or no: when I realized that I had been hearing a steady knocking for some time. I rolled halfway over and peered through a blood-colored haze at the door. I fought to focus. Yes. Someone was tapping, lightly tapping with a small fist—a woman's fist, I thought.

"Hello?" A woman's voice. Dim. Muffled through the door. "Hello? Can you hear me? Can you get to the door? Should I call an ambulance?"

No idea—no clue—how I found the strength to climb to my feet. As I did, the room seemed to plunge from the sky in a nauseating spiral. I fell through the air till I smacked against the door.

I managed to pull it open, staggering back from the effort. Staggering back against the couch and dropping down onto it, hard.

I sprawled there, clinging to the sofa back to hold myself at least partly upright. I stared at the doorway. It was day, as it turns out—bright day. The doorway was a tall bright rectangle of blue and white. The woman stood in silhouette in front of it.

"Oh, my God," I heard her whisper.

★ ★ ★

She shut the door and came to me. Bent over me, put her hands on my shoulder, then quickly moved one hand to my forehead. That was my first good look at her. I don't know if she was really as beautiful as she seemed to me at that moment. It was probably just that she was the first thing I had seen in I don't know how long that wasn't all cruelty and ugliness. I gazed at her. I was too racked with cramps and nausea to feel desire. I just gazed up in wonder at the sweetness of her face. She had a tumbling pile of auburn hair falling all around her high cheeks. She had red-gold cheeks dusted with light freckles. She had thin, prim, certain lips that suggested a fine, high virtue. She had large blue eyes so warm with compassion they were mesmerizing. Even through my own stench and the stench of the room, the smell of her reached me, fresh and clean. Her hand on my forehead was firm and cool and gentle.

"It's all right," she said. "Here, take it easy. Lie down."

She helped me shift back farther onto the sofa so I could stretch out. I gave a cry as I saw the multilegged creatures crawling on the ceiling above us. I pointed at them to warn her they might drop down on top of us, fangs and all.

"No, no, no," she murmured. "It's all right. There's nothing there. Close your eyes. Lie still."

I lay still but I didn't close my eyes. I didn't want to stop looking at her. Her face was a consolation. I didn't want to lose sight of it.

"I'm sick," I murmured to her.

"I know. It's going to be all right," she said.

I think I must've fallen asleep as she sat hushing me, because at some point I jolted awake with a start, afraid she had gone, thinking she must have. But no, there she faithfully sat on the edge of the sofa. She had been wearing an overcoat before, I remembered, but it was off now, tossed over the sofa arm. She wore a skirt and a gray cotton blouse. Her hands were folded in her lap and she sat very still, looking down on me with concern.

"Who are you?" I said weakly.

"Samantha. From downstairs."

"With Ed?"

"I'm staying with Ed. I heard you through the ceiling."

"Sorry."

She smiled and laid her hand on my forehead again, a gesture of almost intolerable kindness. "You were making quite a fuss."

I ran my tongue around my thickened, rancid gums. I wanted to ask her how she knew Ed, what she was doing hanging around with old Ed. But all I could say was, "God, I'm sick. I'm so sick."

"Well, no one could blame you. Anyone would be." *What did she mean by that,* I wondered vaguely. She must've seen the confusion on my face. "Ed says you're the detective they keep talking about on TV. The one who shot that monster. Going through something like that would make anyone sick."

I closed my eyes. "I don't remember. I mean, yes, I am the detective. But I don't remember shooting him." I forced my eyes open. I regretted closing them, all those seconds I had wasted not looking at her. "I was stoned on some kind of tranquilizers. Don't tell anyone. It's a secret."

She smiled gently and pressed a finger to her lips.

"It was the only way I could stand to do it," I told her.

"To shoot him?"

"No." I laughed weakly. "I could've shot him straight. It was the only way I could stand to get in on him. To pretend . . ."

"Oh, to be one of his . . ."

". . . customers."

"Yes, that must have been awful."

"I couldn't sleep. The drug was the only way I could get any sleep."

"Of course. But you had to see it through. It had to be done."

I nodded. I was relieved she understood. It made me feel better. "There was a little girl . . ."

"I'm sorry?"

"In the house . . . There was a child. He had her tied up in there. Do you understand? He was going to . . ."

"Oh, yes, of course, yes. I understand. Of course. That's why you had to do it."

"That's it." I was so relieved she understood.

"That's why you do what you do."

"Right. Right," I said. "Not just for her but . . . all the others . . ."

"And there would've been still more too, if you hadn't stopped him."

I nodded eagerly. After so much horror, her simple sympathy and understanding moved me—powerfully, deeply. The emotions made my eyes fill.

Samantha turned her head away as if something across the room had caught her attention. She was giving me time to get control of myself, see. She knew a guy like me wouldn't want a woman to see him lose it. It was such a kind gesture. Delicate. Womanly. It moved me even more.

She gave me more time. She didn't turn back to me, but instead stood up and walked across the room. I wiped my eyes dry with my hand while she wasn't looking.

When she reached the corner of the far wall, she settled gently on her haunches. The room was dark. The curtains were still drawn though there was daylight at the edges of them. I had to squint to see her through the shadows . . . the flash of her knee, her skirt like drapery. I saw her fiddle with the wainscoting at the bottom of the wall. She pulled a small section of the wooden panel away, revealing a hole in the wall behind it.

"My secret hiding place," she said, still without looking back at me. "Even Ed doesn't know about it."

I watched her through the dark as she reached into the gap in the wall.

"What is it?" I asked her, my voice rough.

She stood. She came back to me, back to the sofa, cradling something in her hand. She sat down beside me again and laid the thing on the table. It was a candle—what was left of a candle. She had a pack of matches too. She set the candle upright on the coffee table and lit it. The flame rose, bright in the darkness. I watched her by its wavering light. I watched her set the matches down. I watched her slender, graceful fingers. I checked to see if she was wearing a wedding ring or an engagement ring. She wasn't. I was glad.

She turned back to me and I think she caught my glance, maybe even read my mind. She smiled. "Could you manage to eat something?"

"Maybe. Maybe some eggs. I think I bought a dozen before I came home."

"I'll make some for you. Meanwhile, try to get some rest."

She started to move away through the flame-lit shadows.

"Samantha," I said.

She stopped and looked back at me. I had had some idea of asking her why she was here, why she was staying downstairs, what she was doing with Ed. But now, I just gazed at her. I realized I had only wanted to say her name out loud and see her face again. She seemed to understand. She smiled and went out of sight, into the kitchen.

I lay on the sofa and listened to the jangle of silverware, the clank of pots and pans. I heard the eggshells crack and heard the eggs sizzle as they landed on the hot skillet. Then I smelled them and I smelled bread toasting. I started to feel hungry.

I lay and watched the interplay of candle-glow and shadow on the ceiling and listened to the noises from the kitchen and smelled the smells. I turned my head toward the candle and watched the flame. I watched a line of wax roll down the shaft to the tabletop. As the wax touched the surface, the heat of it made a little section of the table's cheap plastic coating whiten and curdle and crack. Later—years from now—I would tease Samantha about how she ruined my table the day we first met. The thought made me smile.

I felt calm now, wonderfully calm for the first time in weeks, for the first time I could remember. I felt a sense of deep satisfaction, a sense that a great journey had come to an end, that it had ended the moment I saw Samantha. It wasn't that I loved her already. How could I? She had just walked through the door. But I already knew I was going to love her. More than that. I knew I had been waiting to love her all my life. It was as if I had always known that she was out there somewhere and now I had found her and recognized her on sight. I didn't know stuff like that really happened. But apparently it did.

I smiled into the candle-glow again. Then I let my eyes sink shut and fell back to sleep.

I woke in the dark. After a few seconds, I became aware that something was different. Better. Then I realized what it was. I felt clean inside. The sickness had passed. I had survived the with-drawal. I had kicked the drug.

I sat up on the edge of the sofa, my elbows on my knees, my face in my hands. Something else came to me as well. I remembered that something good had happened. What was it? Oh yes. It came back to me: Samantha. I recalled that sense of calm and satisfaction. It was still there. The woman I had been waiting for my whole life had shown up. At my lowest moment. Just like that. And everything was going to be all right now. I knew it. It was a great feeling.

But the apartment was quiet.

I called out to her, "Hello?"

There was no answer. The place was empty. Samantha must've gone out. I was sorry about that. I missed her already.

I looked down at the coffee table. Even in the dark, I could make out the plate there. A knife and fork lying on it. Hardened streaks of egg yolk. Bread crumbs.

I don't remember.

I guessed I must've woken up at some point. Samantha must've brought the eggs to me and I must have eaten. But when I tried to bring the memory of it back, there was a kind of barrier in my mind, a resistance I couldn't overcome.

I let it go. I tried to stand up. The room tilted and my legs went weak under me. I sank back down. After a few deep breaths, every-thing steadied. I tried again. Made it this time. Shuffled like an old man across the room. Found the light switch. Flipped it up. The light came on. It was a deeply unpleasant experience: the visual equivalent of having some guy clash a pair of cymbals together with my head in between them. I debated whether to claw out my eyes to make it stop but decided that would be an overreaction. Instead, I went into the kitchen and started some coffee brewing.

I went into the bathroom. I pissed and showered and shaved and brushed my teeth. I went dripping naked into the bedroom. Put on new jeans and a new sweatshirt. These were all major plot points in the story of my returning humanity.

I walked from room to room. I saw that Samantha had cleaned the place. She had cleaned up the vomit on the carpet. Rubbed the stains out. She had taken away the candle and removed the melted wax from the surface of the coffee table. She had turned off the demon-possessed television and pushed it into a corner. *Take that, you TV demons.* In the kitchen, she had washed out the skillet and left it in the drainer.

Imagine, I thought. *Imagine someone doing that. Cleaning up like that for a perfect stranger. Cleaning a stranger's vomit off the carpet, cleaning the stains out.* Again, it struck me as such a generous and womanly thing to do. I was moved, really moved, deep down.

I poured myself a mug of coffee and went back to the living room. I went to the window. Opened the curtains. It was early evening. The end of a clear blue day. The people on the sidewalk were hurrying home in their winter overcoats and woolen caps. Their breath was visible in the darkening air.

I sipped my coffee and watched the scene like it was Christmas morning. I felt good, really good. The Emory case was over and the poison was out of me and now there was Samantha.

Samantha.

I went downstairs to Ed Morris's place. Ed was one of those old guys you see sometimes who seem to be deflating in slow motion. Getting smaller, softer, more slouched and shapeless, bit by bit, day by day. He was a black guy with iron hair and rheumy eyes. Grumpy was his good mood. When he was in a bad mood, he got silent or whiskied up.

"Don't tell me I gotta clean your shit up there." That's what he said when he opened his door and saw me on the front step. That was his version of hello. "I don't wanna hear it."

"Be thankful you don't have to dispose of my body, you nasty old son of a bitch."

"Sounded like I was gonna. Way you was carrying on. Smell the upchuck all the way down here." By then he had turned his back on me and gone shambling back into his apartment. "Only reason I didn't call the cops on you is you *are* the cops, I know they would've sided with you, rousted my ass." I followed him in. Followed his hunched figure down an unlit corridor toward the bright kitchen.

"They would've, too," I told the back of his flannel shirt. "They'd've dug up every evil deed you ever did."

"Oh, I know it. Don't think I don't."

"So quit bitching. You got off easy. Plus I've lived to overpay you for another month. What else do you want?"

"Overpay me!" He was in the kitchen now. He opened the refrigerator. I leaned against the doorway. "I see on TV your boys been doing good work, though," he said. "Sending that evil mother-fucker to hell. That's a good day's work right there. You tell them I said good job."

"I'll pass it on."

"Whoever done it. TV say he's undercover. You tell 'em: He's a good man. Good job."

He handed me a bottle of beer. I tipped it to him. "Will do."

"Hope he did it slow too. Put one in his goulies. Man doesn't know how to use 'em shouldn't be allowed to keep 'em."

"True that. There oughta be a law."

By now, I was already thinking this was strange. Samantha said Ed had told her I was the detective who killed Emory, but now he didn't seem to know. The department had shielded my identity, kept my cover. That was standard procedure. So how *would* he know? Maybe he had guessed. Maybe he was just being discreet or . . . or something. It was strange.

Ed made it across the room and settled into a wooden chair at the kitchen table—really, just like he was deflating. He already had a beer bottle open there and a plate of some mess he'd been eating. Had a small television set up right in front of him, playing the local news at low volume. He started eating again. Watching the TV as if I weren't there.

"Didn't mean to disturb your dinner," I told him.

"What'd you think you'd do coming down here around this time of night?"

"That crap you're eating—I did you a favor."

"Well, you got that right, at least."

"Anyway, I'm not looking for you. Who would be? I wanted to talk with Samantha."

Ed went on eating his crap and drinking his beer and watching his TV. He didn't even seem to hear me. Then he said, "Who that?"

"What do you mean, *who that?* Samantha. The girl. The redhead. Said she was staying down here with you."

He glanced at me. "You see any redhead girl down here? There's no redhead girl down here. There was a redhead girl down here, I wouldn't be talking to you, I'd be doing her."

I started to laugh as if he were kidding, but I could see he wasn't kidding so I didn't laugh. I said, "There's no one staying down here with you?"

"What am I telling you? Who'd be staying here? There's no one been here since Livi died but me and my ulcer."

I took a hit of beer, stalling for time, trying to figure out how to react, what it meant. "Well, do you know a girl named Samantha?"

The old man shrugged. "Know a lot of people." He actually turned away from the television long enough to give it some thought. "But I don't believe I *do* know a Samantha, now I think about it."

"Beautiful redhead in her thirties."

"I *know* I don't know *that* Samantha."

I still didn't know what to make of it—not in my mind at least. But my gut knew. My gut went sour. My sour gut told me: *This is not good. This is bad, in fact. This is something very bad.*

★ ★ ★

Upstairs, I stood just inside the door to my apartment. I surveyed the room. I considered the possibilities.

Why would she lie about staying with Ed? She didn't look like a girl who would lie about anything. Why that? How had she known to come up here if she hadn't heard me fussing through the ceiling, like she said? Was she running some sort of game on me? Was she some sort of agent for Internal Affairs? Or for Emory? Or maybe for the Fat Woman? Had she come to get information out of me, to find out how much I knew? I tried to think of what I'd told her. That I'd been on drugs when I killed Emory. What else? Nothing I could remember. But then . . .

I gazed at the plate on the table. The streaks of yolk. The bread crumbs.

I don't remember.

I didn't remember eating the eggs. Part of my memory was gone. Maybe I'd told her more than I knew.

I moved from the door to the table. I stared down at the plate from above. Then my eyes shifted and moved over the tabletop. Something was bothering me. Something was making that sour feeling in my gut grow worse.

It took me a second or two to figure it out, but then it came to me.

I remembered lying on the sofa, watching the candle burn. I remembered how the candle wax had dribbled down onto the tabletop and the heat of it had marred the table.

But the burn on the table was gone.

That made no sense. Samantha could have taken the candle away. She could have cleaned off the ring it left on the surface. Thrown out the matches she'd used. Washed off the melted wax. But she couldn't have made that burn disappear. The burn was permanent. I was going to joke with her about it, years from now, when we were married.

I knelt down next to the table. I went over every inch of it with my fingers and my eyes. There was no heat damage to the surface anywhere. The mark was completely gone.

Slowly, a new idea came to me.

I turned to look across the room—at the wainscoting in the corner.

My secret hiding place.

She had removed a piece of the wainscoting. I remembered now. There had been a hole hidden behind it. She had reached into the hole to get the candle.

I went to the corner. Crouched down. Put my hand on the panel at the bottom of the wall. I pushed it, pulled it, clawed at it. I used that movement Emory had used in his house, placing my palm against the surface of the panel and pushing in and lifting. The wainscoting was solid. There was no way to budge it—not with my bare hand. There was no secret panel there. No hole behind it. There was nowhere she—or anyone—could've hidden a candle.

I straightened and moved heavily back across the room. I sank down onto the sofa and sat there staring at . . . at nothing really. At the air between the ceiling and the floor. I guess it took a few more moments before I could admit the truth to myself.

No one could have fixed that burn in the table while I slept. No one could have filled in that hole in the wall or replaced that loose panel. No one outside the job could have known that I was the detective who had killed Martin Emory.

I raised a hand to my face, pinched the bridge of my nose, and shut my eyes. I remembered what Dr. Lee had said about quitting the Zattera.

You'll see things that look so real that reality will pale by comparison.

Finally, I understood. There had never been a Samantha.

The moment the thought occurred me, I knew it was true. I tried to resist it. I tried to argue myself out of it. *Who made the eggs then?* I thought. *Who cleaned up the apartment?*

I don't remember.

But that was a lie. I did remember. I was starting to remember some of it anyway. Moments were coming back to me in flashes—like those flashes of the moments before I shot Emory. I saw myself in the kitchen, moving like a zombie, frying myself some eggs as the nausea of withdrawal passed and gave way to hunger. I saw myself in the living room, on my knees, cleaning up my own vomit . . .

There was no Samantha. She wasn't real. How could she have been? She had been the very image of my heart's desire. So tender, so generous, so feminine. Hardly a woman at all, more like a principle of womanhood. How could she have been anything but the creation of my mind, the last side effect of the drug, the last mirage of my addiction?

I sat on the sofa and stared into space. I pretended I felt nothing. What was there to feel? I had had another hallucination, that's all, a final hallucination. So what? It wasn't as if I had fallen in love with her. How could I have fallen in love with her? She wasn't even real. She didn't even exist.

I went on sitting there alone in the darkness for a long, long time.

5

The Body in the River

I THOUGHT OF SAMANTHA as I lay in the dark with Bethany soft beside me. Bethany's cheek against my chest, Bethany's hair against my cheek, Bethany's skin against my hand, I thought of Samantha. More than three years had gone by since the Emory case. You would think that was time enough to get over a drug-induced hallucination. You would think so. But I never really had.

It was almost as if, in some bizarre way, I really *had* fallen in love with her, shadow that she was. I daydreamed about her. I dreamed about what our lives together would have been like. My eyes searched for her sometimes on a street or in a movie theater. I judged other women against her, against her tenderness and generosity. I remembered that feeling I'd had in the few moments she was with me—that feeling of calm and satisfaction, as if I'd finally found the woman I'd been looking for all my life. I yearned to feel that again.

Her image was with me all the time. I couldn't let her go.

Bethany stirred and breathed and kissed my cheek. I felt the consolation of her breasts against me, her legs around me, her damp center pressed against my thigh. She was a tender girl too, a generous girl who liked a man taking pleasure in her just as she liked watching him eat the food she made. I wanted to love her. I really did.

"What're you thinking?" she whispered.

"Nothing," I said.

Bethany shook her head close to me. "You are one strange son of a bitch, you know that?"

I gave a low laugh. "Just what a man likes to hear after making love to a woman."

"Oh, you know the lovemaking was fine."

"Just strange, huh?"

"I didn't say it was strange. I said you were."

"All right." I shifted so I could press my lips to her forehead and her dark blonde eyebrows. I tasted her makeup and the heat of her. "What's so strange about me?"

She spoke so close I felt her soft words vibrate against my throat. "Well, I listen sometimes when you're at the table." She meant the round table by the window in Salvatore's, the one where the lawmen sat. "And everyone's telling war stories and everything."

"Uh-huh."

"And you never do."

"Never do what?"

"Tell war stories. 'This happened to me way back when.' 'I once arrested a guy who did so-and-so.' You never say anything like that."

I laughed again. "Oh yeah?" I grabbed at her waist, making her squirm and squeal and giggle. "I'm the strong, silent type, what's wrong with that?"

"Stop!"

"I don't know, should I?"

"Dan!"

"One of these days I may show you just how strange I can be."

I let go of her. She settled back against me. I held her there, kissed her. After a while, she lay quiet, thoughtful, her fingers fiddling with the hair on my chest. A car went by on the street outside. The glow from its headlights passed in an arc over the bedroom's ceiling and the far wall. The sound of its passage rose and faded.

When it was gone, I listened to the little house settle back into quiet and darkness. Bethany's mom had left her this place. It had a comfortable, purple, musty atmosphere to it, like coming home for a visit. I thought sometimes it was the atmosphere of Bethany's girlhood. I could imagine her as a child here, playing with dolls in a corner or something, daydreaming about how one day she would have a house and family of her own. Kind of pitiful when you thought about it: the two of us lying in bed together, her with her daydreams, me with mine.

Then she said, "Sometimes with you, I used to think . . . I'd be chattering away, you know, and I used to think, *Well, isn't this nice? Here's a man who actually knows how to listen to a woman.*"

"Yeah? And now?"

"Well, now I wonder: *Maybe the only reason he's always listening is 'cause he's never talking.*"

"Man oh man. 'Listen to me, don't listen to me, talk, don't talk.' Try to please a woman. I dare you."

"I know. But you know what I'm saying."

Well, I suppose I did. And it was true enough: I had my secrets. The reason I had come to Tyler County, for instance—that was one of them.

With a little deadpanned perjury from Dr. Lee, I had managed to keep my drug use out of the grand jury hearing on Emory's death. But at One Police Plaza, the brass knew. After I was cleared of wrongdoing, I was called into the office of the chief of detectives, Harry Fine. Fine was a fat little man with mild eyes and a mild smile and nothing else really mild about him.

"You did a great job, Champion," he said, shaking my hand across his desk. He gestured for me to sit in the visitor's chair. As I lowered myself into it, he added, "And now you're through."

I had been half-expecting this. "Am I?" I said.

"Oh, yeah. Hell yeah. You kidding me? Five slugs in a suspect while under the influence? That's 'Good-bye-nice-to-know-ya,' in anyone's book. Be prison too if you ever open your mouth about it."

I nodded. I was thinking about the Fat Woman. She had been my mission—my obsession—for years. I'd never get the chance now to run her to ground. It was going to be hard to let her go.

"Only question is how you want to handle it," said the Chief of D's. "We could send you to Psych Services, put you on 'limited' for three months, retire you at half-pay plus benefits. No one could blame you for cracking up after a case like that. It's not a bad deal."

It wasn't, but I waved it off. Hard to get a job in law enforcement after they put you on psych disability.

"Would you back me if I applied to another force?" I asked him.

Chief thought about it. He looked me over, drumming his chubby fingers on the desk. "*Should* I back you? How crazy are you anyway?"

"I'll get over it. It was the drug mostly."

He drummed his fingers some more but finally he dropped a nod. "You go to some rural force. Small town. Bust some teenaged potheads, clean up a meth lab now and then. Guys killing their wives or whatever. You could handle that. I'd back you on something like that, sure. They'd be lucky to have you."

"Thanks, Chief."

"It's plausible too, a plausible story. After a dirty case like this, a guy gets tired of the big city. Wants some fresh air, wants to do some fishing. You like to fish?"

"I do."

"Well, there you go. It's a plausible story." Then he pointed one of those chubby fingers at me. "But you write your memoirs, or go online or come to Jesus where anyone but Jesus can hear you, I will personally react with shock and dismay tempered by sorrow and compassion and then prosecute you till the end of days. Understand that, Detective. If you tell anyone about this, you will go to prison. The NYPD does not perform executions in the field. And we don't cover them up. It just doesn't happen. It never happened. Hear me?"

"I hear you."

He stood up. I stood up. He shook my hand again. "And like I said: good job. I hope you let that evil bastard suffer before you double-tapped him."

I shook my head. "I don't remember."

"Shame. It's memories like that that warm the lonely evenings of our golden years. Have a good life, Champion."

So yeah, Bethany was right. There were things I wouldn't say—actually couldn't say—about my past. Maybe that made me wary of story-swapping around the table, especially after a drink or two.

"I mean it's not just swapping war stories in the bar," Bethany went on—and it was as if she had read my mind and was speaking directly into my thoughts. She could be a genuine pain in the ass that way. "I mean, I don't care what perp you had to slap around or how bedbug-crazy some evildoing so-and-so was."

"You do listen in, don't you."

"You and I have been in and out of bed together almost a year." She was talking low, looking up from my chest, her lips near my jaw. "You know how I feel about you . . ."

"Bethany . . ."

"No, I'm not gonna get off on all that. I'm just saying. I've got no complaints about the way you treat me, God knows."

"Well, after all, I am a stone funky love machine . . . Ow!"

"I'm not just talking about that, thank you," she said, removing her knuckle from my ribs. "I know you're the big bad lawman of the world and all that, but I swear I never met a man so naturally sweet-natured behind closed doors."

"Of course, now that you know that, I'm gonna have to kill you."

She reached up and touched my lips with her finger, I don't know whether to shut me up or simply to do it. She said, "It's just: I don't know the first thing about you. When I think about it. I don't know one damn thing."

"Oh, come on, that's not true."

"It is."

"I've told you things."

"Your resume. 'Then I went to Afghanistan, then I joined the police ...'"

"And growing up in foster homes and all that. I don't discuss that with just anybody."

"Mm," she said.

"How come women don't have to make a logical argument? How come women just get to say, 'Mm,' like that?"

"I don't know. That's how God made it. You don't want to mess with God, do you?"

"Well, all right, what is it you want to know?"

"I don't know. Anything. Something personal, something about yourself."

"Like what?"

"What's your favorite color?"

"*That's* what you want to know?"

"Well?"

"I never thought about it. Chartreuse."

"Oh, you don't even know what chartreuse is."

"Sure I do. It's purple."

"It's green."

"Oh. Well ... brown then. I have a brown jacket I like. Kind of orange-brown. It's nice."

"What kind of things are you afraid of?"

"Conversations like this, for one."

"Not like guns or dying or something like that. Something stupid. Something you're embarrassed by."

"Let's see. I never liked spiders much."

"Hate spiders."

"Ugly little bastards, aren't they? And they can jump at you, some of them."

"What's your earliest memory?"

"Oh, Christ ... Playing catch in the backyard with one of my foster fathers. He coached Little League, you know. Wanted me on the team. He was shocked I'd never even played catch before so he taught me."

"Was he a good guy?"

"Yeah, he was."

"Did you have to leave him?"

"Yes. He got sick or something. I don't remember."

"That must've been hard."

"Oh, man. Does this have to be some kind of sob session about my sad childhood?"

"Oh, no, we wouldn't want that," Bethany said. "Big tough fellow like you actually having emotions. Completely unacceptable."

"I have emotions. Is *being annoyed by a lot of questions* an emotion?"

"All right, we'll move on."

"Or we could stop."

"What about your first girl? And no, I don't mean for sex. I don't want to hear about some Russian hooker."

"She said she was a Kansas farm girl. She did talk kind of funny now that I think about it."

"Who was the first girl you had a crush on, the first girl you ever loved?"

"You know what?" I reached down and smacked her backside.

"Ow!"

"I'm tired of this game." I threw my legs over the side of the bed and sat up, my back to her.

She came up behind me and laid her fingertips against me. "Just tell me *something* you love, Dan. I just want to know what it's like."

I had my hands pressed into the mattress, ready to push up and stand, but I lingered a while, breathing her scent. She had a nice scent. It wasn't her perfume, either—it was her. She smelled clean and natural; innocent somehow. I always liked that about her.

"What's the point?" I said. "Look, it's no secret: You grow up how I grew up, it does something to you. You're never entirely comfortable in your own skin."

"I know that."

"Maybe nobody is. I'm not complaining. It was what it was. I got myself straight in the Army and now . . ."

She stroked my back. "Now what?"

"Oh, I don't know. I just want . . ."

"Me to leave you alone?"

"It's not that exactly. It just does no good for me—always talking about everything, thinking about everything. What good does it do? When things are over, they're over, you can't change them. I just want to go about my life, go about my business."

"Agh, Dan!" She came up on her knees and wrapped her arms around me. It was a pleasure to feel her press against me. "You're such a great guy and you're so exasperating!"

"Am I?"

"You make me so crazy! Couldn't you just . . . ?"

"What?"

"I don't know. Let me in? Just a little. You don't have to love me, sweetheart. Really. Just let me in."

I started to say something. I don't know what—some dodge or other. Luckily, I was rescued from the whole business by my phone's ringtone.

Then it's hi-hi-hey—the Army's on its way . . .

The phone was in the pocket of my slacks. My slacks were lying on the floor. I had to root around for them, and then root around in the pocket. During the whole process, the phone sang and sang.

For where e'er we go, you will always know, that the Army goes rolling along . . .

"Damn it." I couldn't get it. Finally, just as I managed to yank the phone out of the pocket, the singing stopped. The readout showed it had been Sheriff Brady calling. "Oh, hell."

"What?" said Bethany.

"It was the boss. Something must've happened."

I was about to dial him back when the phone started ringing again. *Then it's hi-hi-hey . . .* I answered before the first verse finished.

"Hey, Sheriff, here I am," I said.

"We just got a 911 call," said Brady. "Floater in the Hudson just south of the picnic grounds. Figured you might be at Bethany's, nearby . . ."

"Yeah, I'm, like, a minute away. I'll be right there."

"Send that good woman my apologies ..."

It really was barely a minute's drive from Bethany's place to the river. I got there just behind the sirens. The blue and red lights of a couple of cruisers and an ambulance were flashing as I pulled to the curb. The deputies and EMS workers were already climbing out of their vehicles in the shifting, colored glow. More sirens sounded, more lights flashed against the night as two more cruisers came racing to the scene.

Walking quickly, I passed Hannah and Mike from the EMS as they paused to snap open their rolling stretcher. I stepped onto the asphalt of the river walk. Deputy Stinson, a husky veteran, was already there. He was shepherding the small crowd of onlookers over to one side. I stood and looked down the dirt slope toward the water. The moon was almost full. It hung directly above me. A line of its silver light lay glittering on the river's surface. I scanned the water for a moment, searching for the body, but there was nothing there.

Then Deputy Holbein, walking ahead of the EMS stretcher, lifted a handheld spotlight and turned it on.

There she was. Lying not in the water but on the narrow bank. Sprawled stark naked and facedown, one foot in the water, one hand stretched out over the grass in front of her, as if she'd been trying to climb onto the land when her strength gave out. I could see in that first instant that she was beautiful—strikingly white; pearly white ... and beautiful, the shape of her as full and graceful as a statue.

Carrying an oxygen canister, Hannah raced ahead of the stretcher to get to the body. She knelt down beside it and felt around its neck and spine.

"Hold that light steady," I said to Holbein. Then I stepped down off the walk into the broad misty glow of the spot.

I was standing right above the woman when Hannah turned her over. The spotlight was shining on all three of us, catching us in its ghost-white beam. The light transformed the deathly pallor of the nude body into something resembling marble. But she wasn't marble. When Hannah turned her over, I saw her flesh ripple and flow.

I caught my breath. I felt the blood drain out of my face. I looked— I stared—I gaped down at the body. An involuntary noise—an unspoken word, choked off in my throat—escaped through my parted lips. I heard it as if it had come from someone else, as if it were the sound of someone else's wonder and amazement.

It was Samantha. The woman lying on the grass was Samantha.

There was no mistake, no possibility of a mistake. It was her, all right. I had never forgotten those features. How could I have? I had dreamed about them every day for years, preserving every detail in my memory.

Now I stood staring down at her in something like shock. It was impossible. How could it be possible? She wasn't real. She never had been real.

Dumbstruck, I stood and watched as Hannah—with what seemed to me dreamy slowness—pressed the oxygen mask over Samantha's mouth, then raised her free hand in a beckoning wave to her partner Mike. She shouted at him to bring the stretcher.

I just went on staring. Staring and wondering how it was possible, how it could be possible . . .

And then Samantha opened her eyes.

"Good God!" I said.

The words broke out of me. I sank to one knee in the grass beside her. I gazed, still gaping, at that sweet, pale, beautiful face. I watched as she struggled back to consciousness.

Her eyes moved back and forth above the oxygen mask, searching the scene around her, searching the faces that were hovering over her.

She came to my face. Her eyes stopped moving. Her gaze rested on me.

I stared and stared down at her, stunned into silence.

After another moment, Samantha's white hand lifted weakly. She pulled the mask away from her mouth. She turned her head and coughed up water.

"Samantha," I heard myself say.

She turned back to me weakly, her eyelids fluttering.

And then—so softly I could barely hear her—she whispered, "They're coming after us."

6

Death and Death

NOW I WAS in the hospital, sitting in a plastic chair against the wall. The dead glare of the lights made the hallway seem sterile and spiritless. The nurses and aides went back and forth in front of me. They looked like silent figures in a white, white dream. Sitting against the wall across from me was Deputy Holbein. He had been assigned to guard Samantha's room. He was drinking coffee, lifting the paper cup to his lips. He stared into space as he drank, saying nothing, as if he were some kind of automaton. The soft sounds of gurney wheels and opening doors, elevator tones and footsteps, even the occasional sound of voices—they all struck me as flat and mechanical, as if I were inside some gigantic machine.

I was stunned and dazed, I guess. Everything seemed far away and alien. Ever since I had seen Samantha on the riverbank, I had felt like this, like a stranger in the world. I kept thinking and thinking about it, but I couldn't get it to make sense.

"Champion."

I looked up. Grassi was standing over me. Despite the colorful sports coat, his usual sinister energy seemed dimmed. His mean-boy smile was nowhere in evidence. His eyes were dulled—with alcohol, probably. With his hands in the pockets of his slacks, he looked here and there over the hallway, as if he were bored, fitful, searching for a way to escape. Well, it was late.

I managed to lift my chin to him by way of greeting.

"How's the girl?" he said.

I shrugged. "We're waiting to hear."

"Boss says you know her?"

"Not sure. She looked familiar. I may have met her once." *In a hallucination,* I added bleakly to myself. "I don't remember where."

"You don't remember."

"No."

"You know her name?"

"I think her first name is Samantha. That's all I know."

"Amazing though. Right? She washes up in Gilead. You're in Gilead. You maybe know her. What're the odds?"

"None," I murmured. "She must have been looking for me."

"Or you tossed her in the drink in the first place. You didn't toss her in there, did you, Champ?" There were those white teeth of his now. Because he was only pretending to joke about it. He had his suspicions—or maybe his hopes.

"Yeah. When did I do that?" I asked him with a weary sigh. "I was drinking with you all night."

"Oh, what, I'm your alibi now? Hell, I never saw you before in my life."

"Then after Sal's, I went home with Bethany."

"Ooh, lucky man." He pumped his hips obscenely with a mirthless laugh. But I could see he was still turning the whole thing over in his mind—the woman in the river; the fact that I had spoken her name—he was trying to find some way to make trouble for me. Then, as if it were an afterthought, he muttered, "Oh—the boss says you should head in and make a report. I'll take lead here. Since you know her and all."

I couldn't work up the energy to protest. What was I going to say? I don't know her. I only dreamed her. Anyway, Grassi was just passing on the sheriff's orders. I'd take it up with Brady later.

"Go on, get out of here," Grassi said. "After all that wrestling with Bethany, you must need the rest." He pumped his hips again.

"I will," I said. "I just want to wait until we find out how she is."

"I'll call you, let you know."

"I'll wait."

It wasn't long. I stood up when I saw the doctor push through the swinging door into the hall. Dr. Owens. A tiny caramel-colored woman. Looked competent and either humorless or exhausted beyond any emotion at all, I wasn't sure which.

Grassi approached her and I hovered behind him.

"She's going to make it," Dr. Owens said—and I let go of a breath I didn't know I was holding. "It was close though. She almost drowned, almost froze. But yeah, she's going to pull through."

"Can we talk to her?" said Grassi.

Dr. Owens shook her head. "She's intubated and under sedation while we bring her temperature down. It's going to be hours before she's awake. You might as well come back in the morning."

"Awright."

"She say anything?" I asked.

"No. Not a thing. She's been unconscious since she got here."

"Well, I guess there's not much point in hanging around then," said Grassi. It was late, like I said. He wanted to go home.

"Any other injuries?" I asked.

"Plenty. Cuts, bruises, contusions. She was all banged up."

"From the river or did someone work her over?"

"I was focused on trying to keep her alive. I didn't do an inventory. But I didn't notice anything either—anything specifically handmade. Be hard to tell."

"No handprints or ligature marks or anything like that."

"No, I'd've noticed that," Dr. Owens said.

"All right," Grassi said, stretching his shoulders back. "I'm lead here now, Champ. You're supposed to go back and file. I'll take over."

"I want to see her," I said.

She looked like a corpse in the morgue—or no, like a corpse in some kind of horror show medical experiment. Lying on her gurney in her little cubicle off the ER. Marble-skinned. Still. A white sheet over her, ankle to throat. Tubes running into her nose and her arm and down below. Big tanks of fluids hanging above her. Like some sort of macabre experiment where they preserve the body alive in order to do who the hell knows what to it.

I remembered her as I'd seen her last—or as I'd imagined her last—back in my apartment in Jackson Heights. I remembered her sitting on the edge of the sofa, looking down at me sweetly, laying her cool hand sweetly on my feverish forehead. And as I stood over her now, my hands in my pockets, my mind in outer space, that memory, that dream, whatever it was, seemed almost more real and alive than the bloodless, motionless creature lying on the bed in front of me.

Back at BCI, I typed up my report in the same stunned daze, with the same weird distant quality of mind. I obsessively went over everything that had happened, trying to piece the puzzle together. It frustrated me at every try. Any way I arranged it, it wouldn't work, wouldn't make sense. It couldn't be an accident, her washing up here. She had to have been looking for me. But how could she have known me? How could she even be here when she wasn't real? She had to have been real then, right? Back at the first when she came to my apartment. But that didn't work either. There was no pull-away panel in the wainscoting. No hole behind it. No candle damage on the tabletop. I had cleaned the apartment. I had cooked the eggs. And what about Ed Morris downstairs? She said she was living with him but he had never seen her. She said she knew who I was, but she couldn't have. It was possible she had lied, possible she was part of some sort of bizarre plot against me—but I didn't believe it . . . None of it made sense.

They're coming after us.

And yes, there was that too. Those words she had spoken on the riverbank. If she had spoken them. It was after midnight now. At that foggy hour, in my foggy brain, I was no longer sure I had heard her right. Hannah, the EMS girl, had been shouting to her partner Mike at the time. She hadn't heard a word. Maybe I'd imagined it. I was no longer sure. I was no longer sure of anything.

They're coming after us.

What could it mean? Who was coming after us? And who the hell were *us*? Me and her? What did we have to do with each other? How would she know if someone was after me? How could she know anything about me at all?

She wasn't even real. She had never been real . . .

As I signed the report, a wave of nausea went over me. More than that. It was as if the floor beneath my feet had turned to water. As if the desks and chairs and clocks and flyers of the BCI cop shop had become watery and transparent. It felt, for just a second or two, as if I were trapped in a dream.

And I thought: *Maybe I am.*

I drove home slowly over a winding, silent two-lane. Nothing but forest on either side of me—forest and then, sometimes, open rolling fields, or sometimes a single house on a high hill, black against the moonlit sky. I lived in Hickory, a dying town. It was zoned and regulated for rich weekend people from the city. They owned those houses on the hills. They didn't want any industry or development tainting their air or blocking their views so there were lots of woodlands and open spaces, but no jobs or housing for the residents. What had once been the main street—Post Street—a series of local shops by the railroad station, was now a row of boarded storefronts. I lived on the little dead-end lane just past that, just by the train tracks.

I lived here because it was cheap and private, but it wasn't much of a neighborhood. There were only four houses on the lane. One was empty, with broken windows and dust blowing through abandoned rooms. One was trashed with the husks of cars and dead refrigerators strewn over the uncut grass. Some hungry-looking longhair lived there. I'd see him give a paranoid peek out his screen door from time to time and I knew that one of these days, I'd have to get around to busting the knucklehead for whatever it was he was up to. In the next house, there was an old lady. She kept a defiant patch of garden in one corner of her crabgrass yard. I'd see her there sometimes, kneeling in the dirt in her faded pastel dressing gown. She always said a pleasant hello whenever I went by.

My house was the last one on the block, pressed up against hedges and a concrete wall that marked the border of some rich guy's scrubland. The place was a rental and the rent was low for all the obvious reasons—plus there was the fact that freights went screaming by in the middle of the night three times a week after the passenger runs were finished. The glare of the trains' headlamps would go through every window, the wheels' thunder rattling the panes, the whistle shrieking. Still, the house had its charms. It was a tightly made two-story clapboard with a covered porch and a pitched roof. Big and rambling inside, with high windows that let in plenty of sun during the day. It had come furnished with lots of stuffed chairs and sofas so I could wander through it and sprawl with a beer in any room and watch whatever view presented itself. I felt comfortable there somehow.

I parked the G8 at the curb out front. Went wearily up the path. Wearily up the stairs onto a porch sunk in deep shadow. The outside lamp had a pull-chain so I could turn it on and see to fit my key in the front door. I reached for the chain and pulled it down.

The light came on—and there was a man who looked like Death standing next to me. He was thrusting a knife blade toward my ribs.

He really did look like Death—like a living skeleton. Tall—as tall as I am—but starvation-thin, with a bone-white, skull-shaped face, the eyes enormous, yellow and glowing. He was grinning like a skull grins too, staring at me with insane fascination as if he couldn't wait to see what I would look like when the knife went in and the life bled out of me. He was wearing black, a black windbreaker over a black T-shirt and black jeans. It set off the strange pallor of his skin, made it seem almost incandescent.

The sight of that gleaming death's head might have hypnotized me while he stabbed me, but the blade caught the porch light and it flashed and I saw it. My hand—the hand holding my key—was still on the light chain. I swept it down fast, and turned the knife thrust aside. The blade cut through my shirt and sliced my side, then went past me, into my jacket. I jabbed with my keys—fast—hit the skull-man with the key-point close enough to his eye to make him flinch and stumble back. That gave me time to grab his wrist and twist it. The bloody knife fell, clattering on the porch floor.

You wouldn't think a man that thin would have any strength in him but he did. As I twisted his hand harder, working to bend him over, he punched me, a swift, expert left in the temple. The pain and impact rocked me and I let him go, reeling backward against the porch rail. He was off-balance too and stumbled against the front wall.

We faced each other. The split second froze. Everything was pulse and action inside me, fear and racing thought.

I saw his hand go into his jacket. I went for my gun. He drew out a Glock and I drew out mine at the same instant.

I shouted, "Drop it!"

He leveled on me. I pulled the trigger.

There were four deafening blasts, rapid-fire. I put three slugs in his chest. He let off the fourth as his arm flew up and his hand spasmed. The porch post near my ear splintered as his bullet went in. Then, like a puppet with its strings cut, the skeleton-man danced and collapsed in a heap. I fell back against the railing, panting, stunned beyond fear, stunned beyond anything now but the electric pounding moment.

Slowly, the heap of the skeleton-man keeled over. He let out a long, long, rattling breath and lay still.

★ ★ ★

I kept the gun on him as I edged forward. The muzzle of his pistol—a .45-caliber Glock 30—was sticking out from under his crumpled form. I put my foot on it and tugged once, twice, until I pulled it free of his weight. I picked it up and slipped it into my jacket pocket. Then I knelt down beside the still killer. I put my hand on his neck. His flesh was uncannily cold. I felt for a pulse. There was none. He was dead.

I hesitated a moment, crouched there. Then I started running my hands over him, feeling through his clothing for a wallet. I knew I should've waited for the inspector on the case, but I figured what the hell. They were going to put me on administrative leave now, take my gun and badge away at least until a grand jury ruled on the shooting. The case would go to someone else. I'd have to finagle for information. I didn't feel like finagling. The man had tried to kill me. I wanted to know who he was—now.

I found his wallet in his pants pocket, front right. Worked it out. Opened it. Cash inside. A lot. More than a thousand dollars in hundreds and twenties. A driver's license. John Jones. Sure. Nothing else. Not a single thing.

I put the wallet back and felt around his pockets some more. Found a cell phone in the other front pants pocket. It was a burner, a throwaway. I turned it on and took note of the number. I didn't have time to do more than that. I put the phone back too.

A whistle screamed in the distance. Freight train on the way. I stood up and holstered my 19. The movement made my side flare with red pain. I looked down and saw the bloodstain spreading quickly over the side of my shirt. I parted the torn cloth with my fingers. The skull-man's knife blade had lanced a red gash in my side. The pain flared again. I flinched and released a breath.

Moving carefully, I drew my phone out of my pocket and called dispatch. The night dispatcher was named Hillary.

"I need backup and an ambulance," I told her. "Some clown just tried to kill me. I'm cut and he's dead."

I lowered the phone with a shaking hand. I was feeling the effect of adrenaline now. I was shuddering head to toe. Images were flashing in my head. The knife coming at me. The grinning man. His eyes. All the ways it might have gone down. All the ways I might have died. I looked at the corpse as I slipped the phone into my pocket.

They're coming after us.

Right, I thought. Like Grassi said: What were the odds? What were the odds this was unconnected to Samantha's warning? None. Not the way I figured it.

The freight whistle blew again. I saw the first glow of its headlamp through the hedges. The slice in my side was really beginning to burn. My damp shirt clung to the wound uncomfortably. I needed to get inside. Find a towel or something to stop the bleeding.

Where was my key chain? I'd dropped it in the fight, not sure where or when. I looked around and there it was, by the dead man's knee. Holding my side, gritting my teeth against the pain, I bent down and swept it up. My eyes came level with the dead man's eyes. He was still staring at me with fascination, still grinning. I straightened and moved around the body to the door.

I worked the lock and stepped into the house. It was dark inside but the moonlight shone in from the rear and filled the living room with shapes and shadows. As the door closed behind me, the whistle of the freight train shrieked once again. The train came nearer. I could feel the vibration of it in the floorboards. I could see the first out-glow of its headlamp. It came through the window and sent the shapes and shadows of the room into swirling motion.

And out of that light, and out of those shadows, a man who looked like Death—the same man who lay dead on the porch behind me—rushed at me, screaming.

It was the same man, so help me, only instead of that eerie grin of fascination, his skull-like face held a wide, shrieking grin of rage. He screamed and the train whistle screamed and the white of his face and the black of his outfit reeled out of the reeling white of the train lamp's glare and the reeling black shadows—and I was so startled and so confused by the impossible sight of him that he was on me before I had a chance to react at all.

He hit me hard in the face and body, then carried me down to the floor. His hand was on my throat. His knee was in my belly. I smacked down against the thin rug, the air going out of me. That screaming skull loomed over me as the train screamed again and the lamplight flared over us and the shadows swirled.

He jammed a gun barrel into my eye. I was dead. I knew it. It was a feeling like falling helplessly, endlessly—down and down, raging, grasping, terrified, helpless forever.

But then, in a harsh rasp, the killer said, "No—too quick." Grinning, eyes gleaming. He pulled the gun away from my face and jammed it into my groin for a fatal gut shot.

In that quarter second, as he shifted the gun, I drove my thumb into his throat.

He gagged. I hurled him off me. I rolled to my feet as he crashed into a low dresser. I rushed at him. He was already clawing at the dresser-top, pulling himself up, twisting to train the gun on me again. He'd never dropped the damned gun.

Furious and frightened and in a world of blood-red pain, I kicked at him, screaming. I went for his wrist. My foot hit. The gun flew out of his hand.

The train lamp glared bright white. The train whistle shrieked. The house shook and rattled as the freight rushed toward it. I grabbed the front of the skull-man's shirt with my left hand and drove my right fist at his face. Then the freight went past and the glare went out. The light went strobic, flashing by. The skull-faced killer blocked me in that pulsing flicker. He struck back, the blow silent in the deafening roar of the passing train. He launched himself at me and then we were locked together, falling, clawing, wrestling on the quaking floor of the quaking room. In the swallowing vortex of shadows, I saw his grinning death-head glow. I felt the power in his sinewy arms as he tried to pull free of me and I tried to pull free of him and strike him dead. I cried out in pain as we rolled over and the gash in my side tore wider. My cry was buried under the train noise and the train whistle answered with a stuttering blast that seemed to engulf us. I felt the killer's hand go under my arm. He was reaching for my gun. I grabbed his wrist. The weapon came free of its holster. We wrestled for it. In a final shock of strength against strength, I bent his wrist. The Glock fell spinning into the spinning shadows and flickering light—and in that same shock we broke away from each other, rolled away from each other, leapt to our feet, face-to-face in the noise and the vibration and the vortex of darkness.

I was gasping for breath. My face was twisted with pain. I was expecting him to attack again. I was crouched and ready. Losing strength. Sagging. Afraid to die, expecting it. I could see him clearly, his face so white it seemed to glow, his eyes so wide they seemed as bright as his face, and brighter. His whole deathly presence seemed to stand at the still center of the rushing noise and pulsing light.

In the next moment, with startling suddenness, the freight went past. The light went out. The noise diminished swiftly—faded swiftly and was all but gone.

In the shocking quiet afterward, I heard—we both heard—the distant wolflike howls of sirens: the cruisers and ambulance on their way.

The skeleton-man cocked his head to listen a moment. Then, instead of attacking, he stepped back quickly into deeper darkness. His voice trailed out of the shadows in a rasp.

"Next time, I'll make you beg to die," he said.

I hesitated only a second. Weak and frightened as I was, I didn't want to live with that, didn't want to spend my days waiting for him. I cursed and charged into the shadows after him.

But he was nowhere. He was gone.

Gasping for breath, clutching my side with one hand, reaching out to feel my way with the other, I staggered across the room. I banged my thigh against a chair and shouted with pain. But I pushed forward. Hit the wall. Found the light switch. Turned it on.

The place had been ransacked. Furniture overturned. Sofa and chair cushions sliced open, the stuffing on the floor. The closet was opened and jackets and junk had been yanked out of it, strewn everywhere. Drawers had been pulled from bureaus and tables, the contents dumped. I could see more chaos through the kitchen door: utensils and boxes splayed across the counters and the floor.

I was too dazed to wonder much what the killer had been looking for. I just stood staring at the mess, leaning against the wall, trembling. I could still feel the killer's hands on me, was still reliving that falling, helpless moment when he'd stuck that gun in my eye—and still trying to make sense of the fact that I had left him on the porch, that I had left him there dead, and he had still been inside, waiting for me . . .

It hurt to move but I had to find out the truth. I kicked through a pile of clothing on the floor and went to the door. I heard the sirens growing louder outside. They grew even louder as I pulled the door open.

There he was. The skull-man. The same man. Crumpled on the porch. Dead. Of course he was dead. He had to be.

I stepped out onto the porch and stood over him. Looked down at him. Shook my head. A man who was dead but wasn't dead. A woman who was alive but wasn't real. I couldn't think about it anymore right now. I couldn't think about anything. Samantha had to have the answer. Samantha had to *be* the answer somehow.

They're coming after us.

Somehow she had known.

I looked up and saw the red and blue glow of the approaching cruiser lights. The cars themselves were still out of sight around the corner. Exhausted, I stepped heavily over the body. I moved to the porch stairs. Holding on to the banister, I lowered myself carefully until I was sitting on the top step. I put my face in my hands, blocking out everything—Samantha, the killers, all the insanity of the night—everything.

I was sitting like that when the first cruiser pulled to the curb.

★ ★ ★

"You're making it sort of tough for me to get any sleep," said Grassi.

He stood on the porch behind me, looking down at the dead man. When he glanced back at me, I could see that his eyes were clearer than they had been at the hospital. The night's booze must have been wearing off. With a sigh, he reached into his back pocket, started to tug out a pair of white rubber gloves. Hannah from EMS was kneeling beside me, cutting the shirt away from my wound. Hannah was a short girl, all breasts and butt. Pretty face, the color of chocolate. Kind, wary, sardonic.

"This what he cut you with?" Grassi said.

I flinched, looking over my shoulder to see the knife. A Ka-Bar Baconmaker. A nasty killing tool. I didn't bother answering. I knew Grassi was just asking to ask.

"You don't know him," he said.

I shook my head. "No. Or the other guy."

"There was another guy?"

"Inside. After I called you. He tried to kill me too."

Grassi looked at me, the white teeth flashing. "You're messing with me, right? There were two of them?"

I let out a groan as Hannah put pressure on the wound to stop the bleeding. "We gotta take him in, get him sewn up," she said up at Grassi.

Grassi nodded. But he said, "You're serious about this. There was another guy."

"Yeah."

"Is he dead too?"

"No. He got away."

The colored lights of the cruisers at the curb played over the front lawn, over the porch steps, over me. Inside the house, deputies were moving past the windows. Deputy Stinson was on the front walk, thumbs hooked in his utility belt, guarding us all.

"You get a look at him? This other guy?" Grassi said.

"Yeah," I told him. "He looked just like this guy."

"Like this guy?"

"Exactly. Only alive."

Grassi tilted his head, looking down at the killer. "Looks like a ..."

"Skeleton," I said.

"He does, doesn't he?"

Hannah looked too, out of curiosity. "Look at that. He really does."

Grassi started to work the rubber gloves on over his hands.

"I figure they were brothers, maybe even twins," I said.

"You're joking, right?"

"That's the only sense I can make out of it. Skeleton Two was inside tossing my house while Skeleton One waited out here to kill me."

"Pretty confident of the skeleton boys, splitting up like that," said Grassi.

"They were skeleton professionals. The way they fought ... They were ex-military—something. Ah!" I let out a shout as Hannah pressed hard against my wound.

"Oh, you are such a crybaby, Champion," she said. "It's not that bad."

"I'm sure it's fine on your side of it," I told her.

Grassi crouched beside the body. Started to go through the pockets, as I had. "A skeleton military," he murmured. "I saw a movie like that once."

I said to him, "They were expecting Skeleton One to gut me with the Baconmaker—quiet, don't wake the neighbors. I figure Skeleton Two inside heard the gunshots. Knew something had gone wrong, but didn't know which of us was still standing—me or Brother Skeleton."

"Must've assumed it was Brother, seeing how confident they were," Grassi said. He had found the wallet now.

"Yeah, that's what I thought. But he's a careful skeleton. He creeps from whatever room he's in to the front parlor, gets there just as the front door is opening."

"Then you walk in, and he knows his brother is dead."

"And he becomes perturbed."

Grassi chuckled. "Perturbed."

"He had me, I'll give him that. He could've blown my head off. But he wanted to make me suffer."

"Who wouldn't?"

"No-o," said Hannah. "We *love* Champion."

"Hey," said Grassi, making me look his way. He waggled the killer's wallet at me. "How come there's blood on this?"

I shrugged. "I looked at it. I was curious to know who wanted to gut me."

"Not exactly protocol there, boy-o," Grassi said. His easygoing friendliness was all make-believe. He was looking over his shoulder at me and I could see his eyes were not friendly at all.

"Sorry."

"Yeah. 'Cause you knew you'd be put on leave, didn't you?" He went through the wallet. "John Jones! Gimme a break."

"There's a cell phone pants pocket left," I told him.

"Oh, yeah? What's in that?"

"You're the inspector. Inspect it."

"All right," said Hannah. "Playtime's over. I gotta take this young man in and get him sewn up."

Grassi had his back to me again. Vulturing over the corpse. Bringing out the cell phone now. "Before you go, I just want to make sure I have this straight. A floater washes out of the mighty Hudson River in a town no bigger than a gnat's asshole."

"Inspector Grassi, may I remind you there's a lady present," Hannah said. "Come on, baby, stand up for me." She draped my arm over her shoulder to help me off the stairs.

"And the detective who happens to be in this gnat-ass-town fuh—excuse me, sweetheart—*banging* his waitress girlfriend actually *knows* this floater on sight. He recognizes her."

I would have responded here, but the effort to haul myself to my feet, pulling on the porch banister with one hand, bracing myself on Hannah with the other, took up all my attention.

"And later the same night, this detective returns to his home in the next town over," Grassi went on. "And holy cannoli, what do you know? Two skeleton twins are waiting on his porch to kill him."

"Only one on the porch ..."

"One inside tossing the place. Which raises that whole issue: They're looking for something. What're they looking for?"

"Don't know."

"No clue."

"None."

Grassi stood up, tapping the killer's cell phone against his palm. "Let me ask you something, Champ-man," he said. "If I told you this story, would you believe me?"

If you told me this story, you'd probably be lying, you wife-beating piece of shit—that's what I wanted to say. Instead, I said, "Well, it's a mystery, Grassi. That's why we have detectives."

"Right. Right."

"Like I said at the hospital: Samantha—the floater—her showing up here ... it can't be a coincidence. Me being at Bethany's, right around the corner—maybe *that* was chance. But aside from that, she had to have been looking for me."

"And Dead Skeleton here and the Skeleton Who Got Away? Are they a coincidence?"

"Look, I just ..."

"... don't know—right—no clue."

"Come on, Champ," Hannah said. "I can't hold you up forever."

But I hesitated. The red and blue lights played over me as I stood on the porch stairs, as I clung to the banister and to Hannah.

"Look," I said to Grassi. "I think she was trying to warn me."

"Who? The girl?"

"Samantha, yeah. She said something to me."

"She said something? You didn't mention that."

"It was so soft, I wasn't sure."

He cocked his head, gave me a look.

"I think she said, 'They're coming after us,' " I told him.

"What're we, making this up as we go along? You just add stuff as it comes to you?"

"I'm just telling you. When Samantha regains consciousness, we'll go in there . . ."

"There's no 'we' in this," said Grassi, his eyes sparking with anger even as his teeth flashed in another smile. "This is my case, my friend." Then, under his breath, so low I almost didn't hear him, he muttered, "Anyway, she's plenty awake already."

"What?"

"I said, 'She's plenty awake . . .'"

"Samantha?"

"If that's her name."

"They said she was gonna be out all night."

"Yeah, well, they forgot to explain that to her. Apparently, five minutes after they told us that, she woke up."

"Did you talk to her?"

The way he looked at me just then—I couldn't decide which I regretted more: that I had made an enemy out of him by threatening to run him in in front of his wife, or that I hadn't actually run him in and booked him as he deserved.

"No," he said. "I did not talk to her. Nobody talked to her. Nobody even saw her."

"What do you mean?"

"The monitor flatlined at the nurses' station and when they went in to check on her, she was gone."

"What do you mean?"

"You keep saying that."

"What do you mean 'gone'? Damn it, Grassi."

He made a vague gesture with his hand, waggling his fingers to show she'd vanished as in a magic trick.

For a second, I just stared at him. I couldn't answer. I couldn't believe it. I didn't want to believe it.

"But Holbein . . ." I said.

"He was outside her door."

"She had tubes . . ."

"She pulled them," Grassi said. "Or someone did."

"Someone?"

"Hey, maybe another skeleton. Maybe the skeletons are triplets, who knows."

I went on staring at him, speechless.

"Come on, Champion," Hannah said, grunting under my weight as she started to draw me down the stairs.

"Didn't she leave a note? A trail? Anything?" I said back at Grassi.

"Just some blood on the floor—from the catheter, the doctor said. And fingerprints all over the place. We'll find her."

"You got a BOLO on her, right?"

"Yeah, yeah, yeah," Grassi said. He was no longer looking at me. Already turning his attention back to the dead man. Slapping the cell phone against his palm. "Girl who looks like that—in a hospital gown—someone'll spot her."

Hannah kept drawing me down the stairs, down to the front path, down into the flashing red and blue lights.

"How could she just disappear?" I called back over my shoulder. "For Christ's sake, Grassi!"

"Yeah, yeah, yeah," Grassi said bitterly.

7

Meet the Starks

I SLEPT IN THE hospital that night. I had bad dreams. Go figure.
I woke in the bright early morning. I went into the bathroom.
Looked in the mirror. What a disaster. My face was bruised and
scratched, purple and red. My body was bruised. My ribs ached.
Under the bandage on my side, the slice in my flesh felt like it was
tearing open every time I moved. I kept having flashbacks to the
night before. The grinning skeleton, his knife coming at me . . .
The grinning skeleton—the other grinning skeleton—rushing
at me out of the swirling darkness, shrieking, the train whistle
shrieking . . .

Then there were other flashes too—flashes of the nightmares I'd
had last night. Samantha standing at the end of a hallway. Flame
at the edges of my vision. Smoke curling around her, suffocating
smoke. I was trying to run toward her, to save her, but I couldn't
move, the way you sometimes can't in dreams. It was like running
underwater. I couldn't reach her. I was screaming in frustration. I
could not, could not, get down the hall . . .

I turned away from the mirror. I went back out into the hospital
room. Rays of sunlight came through the venetian blinds, throwing
bars of brightness and shadow on me. I had asked Deputy Stinson to
bring me a change of clothes the night before. They were there, on

a plastic chair, the shirt and jacket draped neatly over the back, the pants folded on the seat. I put them on and headed for the department, where the sheriff was going to take my badge and gun away.

Deputy Holbein was young, tall, muscular. Blond and cruel-faced and actually cruel. He was the sort of cop you hope the cop who pulls you over isn't. The deadpan guy who calls you "sir" but is really waiting for an excuse to slap you around. Aside from that, he was competent, responsible, and ambitious. For instance, he was still at work, off-shift, when I got there. Writing his report, ready and willing to answer for any mistakes he might have made in letting Samantha escape from the hospital.

I sat on the edge of his desk. I was angry about Samantha's disappearance, but I tried not to show it. "What the hell happened, pal?" I asked him—sympathetically like that, one professional to another.

Holbein glanced toward the hallway door—that's where Sheriff Brady's office was. "I gotta go in there and explain it all to *him* in a minute," he said unhappily.

"But you didn't leave her alone or anything?"

"No, hell no. I never did. I never even took a leak." He glanced at the hallway again. Dropped his voice. "But, you know, she was right there on the first floor."

"So she went out the window, you mean."

"Yeah! Into the . . . there was a courtyard right outside." He shook his head. Gave his computer keyboard an angry push. "They said she'd be unconscious all night."

"I heard that."

"You heard that, right? They said that."

"I'll vouch for you with the old man if anyone questions it."

"Thanks, Champ. I appreciate it."

I pushed on. "You think someone could've come in? Through the window? You think someone could've come in and taken her?"

"Champion."

I turned. Sheriff Brady was standing in the doorway. Tall, dark, sour-faced. Lean, except for his potbelly. Good sheriff, but never a happy man. Something about his digestion. It was always acting up on him. He looked even less happy than usual this morning, the dyspeptic misery twisting his lips.

I lifted my chin to him in greeting.

"In my office, please," he said. And he left the doorway and went back down the hall.

I turned back to Holbein. "Didn't anyone see her leave?"

"Now, Champion!" Sheriff Brady shouted from out of sight.

Holbein hesitated but I didn't move. I waited him out.

"No one saw her leave," Holbein said finally. "But I don't think anyone came through the window and took her or anything like that. There were just her footprints—in the grass out in the courtyard. And there was a trail of blood too."

"A lot of blood?"

"No. Just a drop or two. Doctor said it was probably because of the Foley tube, the catheter. I guess it has—I don't know—a sort of bulb on the end, makes it hard to pull out. Doctor says it probably hurt her . . . you know . . ."

"Urethra."

"Right," said Deputy Holbein. He looked even more unhappy than before. His eyes shifted back to the door where the boss had stood. He had large blue eyes and usually there was a lot of brutality in them. But they weren't brutal now, just worried. "Shouldn't you get in there?"

I nodded. Sighed. Stood off the desk. I was still angry—seething—but not at Holbein. It was just everything. The pain in my side. A couple of skeleton bastards trying to kill me. Brady about to pull my badge. Samantha . . . Mostly Samantha, suddenly gone again. Out of reach, like in the dream about the burning hallway. I think it was mostly that, mostly Samantha.

"The blood tell you anything?" I asked Holbein.

"What?"

"The trail of her blood. You get anything from that."

"It was just a few drops. It was consistent with her walking out on her own."

"Where'd it lead to."

"We think she just crossed the courtyard. Went through a door on the other side. Then right out again, through an emergency door into the parking lot." His lips pulled back, baring his teeth. He dropped his voice nearly to a whisper. "I wasn't guarding against her escaping. You know? They said she'd be unconscious all night."

"Well, maybe the experience of your own shortcomings will teach you compassion for others."

"What?"

"Just kidding." I patted him on the shoulder. "You'll be fine." I walked away.

Sheriff Brady pushed an old-fashioned wooden out-box across his desk at me. He didn't even say anything. Just tilted back in his chair and waited, the fingers of his two hands interlaced on his paunch. I pulled my 19 out of its holster, laid it in the box. Drew out my shield. Spun it in, like tossing a card in a hat.

Brady had a sharp widow's peak of black hair. It accented his dour features. With his black suit, complete with vest, he looked more like an undertaker than a lawman. He sat with his long figure framed between the American flag on the pole to his right and the state flag on the pole to his left. He flinched and shifted and massaged his gut discreetly with one thumb. "Don't hang around here, either," he said—the first words he'd spoken since I walked in. "Don't ask anyone questions, don't put your nose here and there. Don't come back at all, in fact, until the grand jury convenes."

"Did you have to put Grassi on this?"

He shrugged his narrow shoulders. His lips worked uncomfortably. "It has to be someone. It's none of your business who. It's not your case."

"Yeah, but Grassi hates my guts. He wants to make some kind of conspiracy out of it."

"Maybe it *is* some kind of conspiracy—how do I know? It's a pretty weird goddamned story, the way he tells it."

"It's a weird goddamned story, all right, but that's my point. I don't understand it either."

Brady sat forward. He grabbed the box with my gun and badge in it. Dropped it into one of his desk drawers and closed the drawer decisively. "Wish the girl hadn't bunked on us," he said.

"Me too."

"But you don't know anything about her. Right? You know her but you don't know her. That's your story."

"I recognized her. I'm pretty sure I've seen her before." How could I explain it? I couldn't. I couldn't think of a way.

The sheriff shifted his body around, like he was trying to work out a cramp. "I also wish you'd stop killing people, while we're on the subject of things I wish for," he said. He looked up at me. I was still standing in front of his desk. He hadn't invited me to sit down. "This is the second time you've ventilated a citizen in the line of duty, isn't it?"

"He drew down on me, Sheriff. Would you prefer I'd let him shoot me?"

"Would've been a hell of a lot easier to explain to the papers." He slumped in his chair now, shaking his head, forlorn. "I just want to make sure it's not your idea of fun, that's all. That's why I put Grassi on it. Way he feels about you, if you fucked up even a jot or a tittle somewhere, he's gonna find it."

"Great."

"I'll ride herd on him. Don't worry. I just want to know the worst."

I didn't answer. What was there to say?

"The important thing is that you stay out of it," he told me. "Don't muddy the waters. Don't make things worse. I hear about you questioning witnesses or doctors or deputies or pulling records on the sly, I'll put you at a school crossing with a lollipop." He made a noise of pain, stiffened as his hand went back to his belly. "That's assuming you get your badge back at all."

"I appreciate your confidence."

"Ah, you'll get your badge back. You're a great lawman, Champion. I'll make sure the grand jury convenes in the next couple of days. I'm sure they'll find everything was right and proper."

"I'll live in hope. You didn't get an ID off the girl's prints yet, did you?"

"Don't ask me that. Don't ask me anything. What've I just been saying to you? It's none of your goddamned business."

"All right, all right."

"And don't leave the county. Have I said that already? Do not leave the county without letting Grassi know."

I held up a hand in surrender.

He leaned back in his chair again, a dismal figure between the two flags. "You look like absolute shit by the way."

"Thanks."

"Enjoy your time off."

I stood alone in my ransacked house again, and the craziness of the whole business hit me full force. As I kicked through the pile of coats on the floor of the entryway, stepped over the debris in the living room and the spongy stuffing from the gutted sofa and chairs, felt the glass of a broken pitcher crunching under my shoes, my whole life seemed as much of a mess as this—the last three years of it anyway.

Three years since I'd left the city, come here to Tyler. Three years I'd spent not thinking about Martin Emory, not remembering how I'd shot him dead. Three years I'd tried to forget about the Fat Woman too and how she'd escaped me, and to forget about Alexander, the little dead boy who'd haunted me through the streets of New York.

Three years I'd spent dreaming about a girl I'd seen once in a drug-induced hallucination, *loving* a girl I'd seen, or dreamed I'd seen, just that once . . .

If someone had told me that those three years had been a lunatic's delusion, that this, this now, was a lunatic's delusion and I was really in some institution somewhere, straitjacketed and howling in a padded room—well, I would not have dismissed the idea out of hand.

I trudged up the stairs. Trudged down the landing to the bedroom. The damage there seemed worse than in the rest of the house. It was as if this had been the main focus of the killer's search. The mattress was upended, half on the floor, half on its frame. Slit in a dozen places, the foam torn out in handfuls, strewn around. My clothes had been dumped out of the dresser and the closet. The dresser drawers had been pulled out and hurled across the room— hurled so hard that one of them had broken and splintered when it smashed against the wall. There was a hole kicked into the wall too, down near the base.

Skeleton Two had found my spare piece, of course—a Glock 19, same as my service gun. I kept it in a metal lockbox, on the floor of the closet, by my shoes. I don't know how he'd managed to pry the box open—it had a strong lock—but he had. He'd tossed the gun and its holster and magazine aside, torn up the foam in the box, and left everything on the floor, where it got buried under a bunch of shirts and sports coats.

I unearthed the weapon and slid it into the holster under my jacket. I wondered if the deputies had also found the gun when they went through the place last night. I doubted it. Grassi probably would have ordered them to take it if they had.

I found my gym bag and threw some clothes into it. Threw in my toiletry kit and so on.

Then I stood a moment and surveyed the shambles. What had they been looking for? It made no sense. Just craziness. All of it.

I went downstairs, got in my car, and drove out of the county, heading for Manhattan. I needed some answers, Grassi and the sheriff and the grand jury be damned.

"This is Monahan."

I smiled at the sound of his voice coming over the G8's speakerphone. It reminded me of the old days. I hadn't spoken to Monahan in over a year.

"It's Champion," I said.

"He-ey! There's a voice from the past."

"How you been, buddy?"

"Good. Great. Cheryl's great. Got a new kid."

"Jesus! What's that—seven?"

"Four. Five—something like that. How about you? How's life in the boondocks?"

Outside the windshield stretched the pale spring day, the sky pale blue, the sun pale yellow, the trees' new leaves pale green. The highway wound south. It was lined with dense stands of willows, elms, and maples. I could catch only brief glimpses of the suburbs gathering behind them.

"I need help," I said.

"I sorry. I no speak da English so good."

"Very funny."

"What do you need?"

"I killed a man last night."

"Again?"

"Once you get started, it's hard to stop."

"Yeah, I'm like that with peanuts. So what're you calling me for? Don't they have anyone in Mayberry who knows how to plant a throwaway?"

"Believe me, I didn't need a throwaway with this guy. He put a slug in a porch post half an inch from my ear. I can still hear the wood splintering."

"Okay."

"I need an ID on him."

"He's dead, right? Check those little finger thingies at the end of his hands. They usually have prints on them."

"They're not gonna find anything off a print—and if they do, they're not gonna tell me."

"Uh-oh."

"I'm pretty sure you'll only need to make a couple of calls to get everything there is on the down-low."

"All right. Give it to me. What've you got?"

I flashed back on the moment I turned the porch light on. That grinning face. The knife coming at me . . .

"There were two of them," I said.

"Two? Good shooting. You killed them both?"

"No, one got away."

"That's not like you, Champion."

"I think they were brothers. They had to be. Maybe even twins. They looked like skeletons."

Monahan didn't answer. He didn't have to.

"They really did, buddy, I'm not kidding you," I said. "Pale, bony, bald, sunken cheeks. Probably ex-military. Definitely professionals. Crazy as cats on fire, the two of them. Totally nuts. The one who got away? Swore he'd come for me. Swore he'd kill me slow by way of revenge."

"It's nice when brothers love each other."

"Right. He meant it too. It wasn't just the usual I'm-gonna-torture-you-to-death chitchat. My friends in the Sheriff's Department are investigating whether I dotted my i's before I blasted Skeleton One, meanwhile I'm gonna wake up one night tied to my bed, Skeleton Two standing over me with a syringe and a skinning knife."

Monahan chuckled. I'm not sure why. "Anything else?"

"I got the number off his burner."

"Excellent."

I gave it to him. There was quiet while he wrote it down. I watched the clustering trees at the side of the highway. They parted like a curtain at an exit, giving me a view of gas station signs and stores and streetlamps. The city was less than an hour away.

"All right," said Monahan finally. "I'll make some calls. And don't worry. If this guy is really a professional, he's not gonna expose himself by torture-killing a cop."

I nodded. I guided the G8 over the twisting pavement.

"Consider me reassured," I said.

★ ★ ★

I stopped off in Queens to visit my old apartment. The house in Jackson Heights was just the same as when I lived there: a gray and white two-story clapboard, a flight of stairs going up the side to the second floor. There was a fresh paint job but otherwise nothing had changed. Made me feel for a moment like I could walk right back into the world I'd left behind.

But that feeling went away fast when I knocked on the door downstairs and Ed Morris opened it. The old man had withered, as if he'd aged fifty years in three. He'd always looked like he was deflating downward into the ground, but now he was collapsing inward too. Gaunt, sunken, his clothes baggy around him, most of his iron hair gone.

"Well, well, well," he said—his voice was hoarse and more gentle than I remembered it. It was almost as if he were pleased to see me. "Detective Champion. You look like someone been beating on you, boy."

"Must've been something I said."

"I'll bet it was."

"How about you, old man? How you doing?"

"How I look?" he said, and laughed and coughed.

"What, you sick?"

"Oh, yeah. I'm dying, Champion. Just a few months left, they say."

"Ah, shit, man. I'm sorry."

"Me too."

He led me into the living room. The curtains were drawn. It was dimly lit. The air smelled two weeks old. He settled himself carefully in an aging armchair. It had a brace on the arm supporting a metal tray. There was medicine on the tray and water and a bowl of half-eaten soup. The television was playing some god-awful thing—women screeching their stupid opinions at one another, I don't know what. Ed only just managed to gesture with a trembling hand toward a worn green sofa. I sat down on the edge of it.

"So? What you want?" he said. "You didn't come to see my—" he coughed roughly—"smiling face."

"You remember that time I was sick upstairs?"

His sallow eyes shifted, searching for the memory. "Yeah. Just at the end of you staying here. Yeah, I remember."

"You remember I came down here afterward and asked you about a girl."

He searched the corners again, vague, thwarted. "My memory . . ."

"A pretty redheaded girl named Samantha. You said you didn't know her."

"Nah . . . Oh, wait. Back in the kitchen there. Yeah. Yeah. I didn't know her."

"That's what you said. I gotta ask you something."

"All right. Go ahead."

"Did anyone make you say that? Threaten you? Offer you money?"

"Money? What do you mean?"

"Did someone tell you to say you didn't know the girl, that you'd never seen her? I'm sorry, Ed, I need the answer. Were you telling me the truth? You really never saw her?"

It took him a moment to grasp what I was asking him, but then he did. "Nah. Nah. No one threatened me. Or paid me. That's crazy."

"There was just no girl."

"There was never any girl. I swear it. You must've been seeing things."

"You never saw two guys, twins. White men. Scary-looking. Like twin skeletons. They never came here. You never saw them."

He shook his head. "Nothing like that."

"No one's ever threatened you . . ."

"Who could threaten me now? Or buy me either? What I got to lose or pay for? Wives don't talk to me, kids don't talk to me. I'm dying alone here, Champion. I got no reason to lie to anyone anymore."

Before I left, I went upstairs to see the old place. I'm not sure why exactly. I'm not sure what I was expecting to find. I think I just wanted to get a sense of the past, a sense that the past had really happened, that it wasn't just a figment of my drug-addled memories.

Ed told me there was a young couple living upstairs now. Only the girl-half was at home when I got there. A skinny creature in her twenties with dyed black hair and a bad complexion. Wearing sweatpants and a T-shirt. Sporting a spiderweb tattoo on her arm, a ring in her nose, and a stud on her tongue. Cocaine eyes. And, oh, yeah, a baby on her hip.

She opened the door, took one look at me, and went blank and scared. She knew a cop when she saw one.

"Albert's not home," she said instantly.

"It's all right, sweetheart," I told her. I waggled a finger at the baby's nose. The kid stared at it, cross-eyed, openmouthed. "I'm on personal business. I used to live here. I just want to look around."

"Well, I'm just . . . I'm not . . ."

"It's all right," I told her again.

She didn't know what to do, so she let me in.

I stood in the center of the room. The place was littered with baby stuff. A playpen, brightly colored plastic toys, stuffed animals. There was a round dining table in one corner. A box of crackers on it. Also, cracker crumbs and trace amounts of white powder.

The girl stood next to me as I looked around. She kept eyeing the cocaine residue on the table. Her aura of fear and panic was distracting. I just wanted to stand there and get a feel for the old days.

"We're just . . . you know . . . bringing up our baby," the girl said to me. Trying to sound wholesome. Ruining the effect with a nervous laugh.

Annoyed, I just held up my hand in answer. I wished she'd be quiet. I also wished she'd stop doing blow while she was taking care of her baby. And dump her dealer boyfriend. And go home to her mother—or any clean relative she had. But mostly I just wished she'd shut up and let me think.

I looked around the room. At the places I'd been. At the places where Samantha had appeared to me.

What the hell? I thought. How was it possible? What the hell was happening to me?

I moved to the wainscoting, crouched down, and checked the panel—just as I had back in the day. I didn't need to do it really. I knew there'd be no secret hiding place. There never was.

I straightened up. I thought of the woman who had washed impossibly out of the Hudson. The same face, the same hair, the same eyes. The same woman as had appeared to me in my hallucination. Samantha.

They're coming after us.

What the hell? I thought. *What the hell?*

I was waiting for Monahan when he got home. Nice suburban house in Little Neck. Cheryl had assigned me to their front room and plunked me on the sofa by the window there with a bottle of beer. The front room was the formal living room. Clean carpeting and stuffed furniture with embroidered upholstery. Family portraits taken by professional photographers. A painting of Jesus holding a lamp—the light of the world. Putting me in there, I think, was Cheryl's version of treating me as an honored guest. Plus the formality of the room was supposed to keep the kids away from me. That didn't work much. Tribes of the midget barbarians kept drifting in, drifting closer, gazing at me. Man, there were a lot of them.

"Why is your face all hurt?" one of them asked me.

"I punched a bad guy with it."

"You can't punch with your face!"

"Oh, now you tell me. Where were you when I needed you?"

Cheryl would keep shouting from somewhere, "Kids, leave Mr. Champion alone, you know you're not supposed to be in there!" But that would only disperse them briefly. Then the little savages would come back, drifting closer and closer, bolder with each return.

By the time Daddy got home, they were swarming over me like the bloodthirsty cannibals they were. Then Monahan stepped through the front door and I was unburied in a single sweeping rush. The kids launched a heedless charge at the thick-necked muscleman and a second later were dangling from his enormous arms and body like

Christmas ornaments. Cheryl came out of somewhere too, carrying the new baby on her hip—a mess of a thing covered in some hideous green substance. Monahan nevertheless bent his big body low and kissed it and even paused down there to plant one on his wife as well. Cheryl handed him a bottle of beer.

"Come on, kids," she said then.

Monahan shook them off him and said, "Outta my sight, you criminals. I'll be in in a little while."

Cheryl herded them away—all except the oldest boy, who hid behind a chair and aimed his finger at me like a gun, making shooting noises.

"I potted this one, like, ten times already," I complained to Monahan. "He won't stay dead."

"Yeah, they're like zombies, you gotta go for the head shot." Monahan pressed a finger to the kid's temple and said, "*Blam.* Now get outta here."

That did the trick. We were finally alone.

Monahan sat on the edge of one of the embroidered armchairs, his elbows on his knees, his beer bottle hanging out from beneath one huge paw. The chair was a big one, but it looked like doll house furniture under him. I sat on the edge of the sofa and we bent our heads together until they were almost touching. Monahan kept his voice low so his family wouldn't hear him.

"Their names are Roy and Robert Stark," he murmured. "They're professionals, like you said. Top of the line. Twins, like you said too. There's not much background on them. Some rumors they worked security for the Arab slavers in North Africa."

"Nice."

"Then out of nowhere, maybe five years back, they blew into town, cut the throats of a couple of freelancers, and consolidated the business."

"What business?"

"Murder for hire, security, debt collection—a sort of temp agency, I guess you could say: one-stop shopping for all your enforcement needs."

"Damn. This was five years ago? I never even heard of them."

"They probably didn't advertise in the *NYPD Shield*."

"That must be it."

"The thing is though—according to what I hear—the Stark twins themselves have mostly graduated from the bloody stuff. They bring in people to do the wet work for them."

"Not this time. Not with me."

"Well, right. So if they came after you themselves, maybe you stepped on their territory somehow. Have there been any big busts up in Nowhereland lately that might've gotten Roy and Rob ticked off?"

I shook my head. "A fugitive killer out of Tennessee. It was just a domestic rap, though. Killed his girlfriend. Could've been a pal of theirs, I guess."

"The other possibility, I'm thinking, is that you somehow made yourself an enemy powerful enough—rich enough—to hire these guys to do you with their own skeleton-white hands."

When he said that, I thought of the Fat Woman. Or, that is, I tried not to think of her, as I had tried not to think of her every day for the last three years.

"What?" said Monahan. He was watching me carefully. He must've seen the idea go through my mind.

I shrugged. No point telling him. Why would the Fat Woman come after me? Why now? It was just my old obsession acting up. "What else you got?" I asked him.

He leaned even closer to me, spoke even lower. "The burner. The number you gave me."

"Right, right."

"There were only three calls on it, all of them three days ago, all of them to one other burner."

"So twin-to-twin probably."

"Probably. The calls came out of a town called Greensward, Pennsylvania. From a coffee shop there—The Grind, it's called—on State Street. The caller was in the vicinity at least ninety minutes, roughly seven-thirty to nine A.M."

"Good, that's good," I said, feeling a touch of excitement. It was a place to start, anyway. Greensward, Pennsylvania. "What else?"

He shifted uncomfortably, averting his eyes. "Some of this stuff I heard . . . You know how it is with guys like this. When they first hit town, they took out some top-level talent. A lot of bloody, dramatic stuff, laying claim to the territory, inspiring fear. They went after one guy's face with a power sander . . ."

"Yeah? So?"

"So, I'm just saying, it's like . . . they're urban legends now. Everyone you talk to has a story about them."

"Spit it out, Monahan. What're you trying to tell me?"

"Well . . . remember what you told me? How Stark was gonna make you beg for death and all?"

"Yeah?"

"And I said he wouldn't expose himself by coming after a cop." I nodded.

Monahan took a swig of beer before continuing, a swig of courage. "I don't know which one of them you killed. I don't think it matters very much. These guys . . . apparently they were . . ." He held up two fingers close together. "Heart to heart. You know? Like they were still in Mommy's tummy. They thought the same thoughts. Even went at girls together, one on one end, one on the other. So the point is, when you killed one of them? It's like you ripped a single guy in half."

"So you're telling me he was serious about coming after me."

"The word is he's brought in his top talent to help look for you—that's two, three, maybe four expert killers on your trail, not counting Stark himself. And their orders are to take you alive . . ."

"Right, right, right. So Stark can really go to work on me, make me beg for death."

Monahan blew out a worried breath, ran his sausage-sized fingers up through his bristly red hair. "Look, I know the sort of stuff you did in the 'Stan. I know you can mix it up with anyone. But in this case . . . maybe I should arrange to get you some police protection, maybe even witness protection . . ."

I didn't answer. I just smiled at him. We both knew the police couldn't protect me from this. No one could.

"'Cause the thing is," he said, "they're good at this stuff, Champ. The Stark boys, I mean—that was their rep. They were always good at the torture stuff. They learned the techniques in Africa. Those Arab slavers, man. Not nice people."

"Well . . . maybe you've just been hanging around the wrong Arab slavers." I gave a pale laugh as I said it, but when our eyes met, the big cop's schoolboy face was so full of concern for me it was kind of touching.

"All right, boys," said Cheryl. She had come into the room's archway to fetch us. She stood framed there, children clinging to her legs. "Lasagna's ready."

Monahan and I traded gazes another moment. "Screw it," he finally said. "Dinner'll probably kill you anyway."

I spent the night in a hotel near the airport. I skimmed over the surface of sleep. Every few minutes, my eyes opened, checked the door. I kept my gun on the bedside table.

Cheryl had offered me the sofa at the Monahan house. "What do you mean a hotel? You're not going to a hotel. You stay with us." Monahan stood behind her nodding his big head and saying, "Yeah, you should stay." But he was looking at me the whole time, telling me with his eyes: He didn't want me there. Skeleton Stark—whichever one of them was left—was coming after me. Him and his top talent. Two or three or four expert killers. Monahan wasn't going to have me bringing death and destruction down on his wife and kids.

So I lay on the hotel bed, alone, and watched the door.

In the morning, I left New York for Pennsylvania. It was a windy spring day. The vertical stone city opened like curtains as I crossed the river into Jersey. The narrow corridors of sky grew bright and wide. Soon, green farmland stretched into blue distances. The shadows of large clouds drifted over rolling hills. Hours of highway rolled out ahead of me. I watched the traffic in the G8's rearview. I didn't spot a tail.

I tried to listen to the talkers on the radio, but they kept fading out as I traveled. It interrupted the train of their conversation. It was annoying. I tried to listen to music instead but it didn't occupy my mind. That was the trouble. My mind wouldn't leave things alone. I couldn't figure the situation out but I couldn't stop thinking about it either. I couldn't stop asking myself: Who sent the Stark twins to get me and why? Where had Samantha come from? How could she even exist?

The gash in my side throbbed. So did the sore spots on my face and my body. There were still flashbacks too. The porch light coming on to reveal the skeleton face standing next to me. The knife just slipping past. The gunshots, the bullet just missing, the porch pillar splintering by my ear. The Glock jammed in my eye . . .

I couldn't stop thinking that if one of those skeleton bastards had nailed me—the knife in the gut, the bullet in the head—I would've died without a clue to the reason for it. Not that it would've mattered much, I guess. But a fellow likes to know these things.

I forced the questions out of my mind, but they kept slipping back in, my thoughts kept returning to them.

And to the Fat Woman. I couldn't stop thinking about the Fat Woman. The old obsession back again.

I reached the town of Greensward around 11 A.M. It was a nice old town set in the hills above low farmland. Fine old white buildings on the outskirts and fine old brick buildings at the center. Views of the valley at the end of every avenue.

I parked the car in a public lot and toured the area on foot. The neighborhood was quaint and artsy. Brick brownstones with bay windows. Cafés with sidewalk tables. It was Saturday now and there was plenty of traffic. Plenty of pedestrians and people in the shops. Young, most of them, college age. There must've been a college somewhere nearby.

I found the coffee shop I wanted. The Grind. That's where the now deceased Stark twin had used his phone. The place was busy when I got there. A gusting breeze made its green and white striped awning shudder and flap, but despite the cool weather, the tables on the sidewalk beneath the awning were filled with kids nursing their coffees and pecking their laptops. The tables were filled up inside too and there was a line at the counter, people waiting to place their orders.

I leaned over the end of the counter. Flagged a girl barista as she rushed by me carrying an empty pot. I told her I wanted to speak to the manager. She was the manager. Funny. She looked to me to be about twelve years old. Five foot nothing with her brown hair in pigtails that stuck out of the side of her head like bike handles. Only her smart, suspicious eyes looked as though they had reached majority.

"I'm looking for someone who was here three days ago."

"Why? Why are you looking for him?" she asked.

"I'm a police detective. He's a bad guy."

"Oh, yeah? You have, like, a badge or something?"

I didn't have a badge anymore, but I had my business cards with the sheriff's star on them so I gave her one of those. I kept asking questions so she didn't have time to think about it too much.

"Were you here three days ago? Seven-thirty to nine A.M. You work that shift?"

"Yeah. Three days ago? Yeah. It's a busy time, though. It's, like, rush hour."

"Guy I want has a pretty distinctive look. Looks like a skeleton. Really like. White face, hollow cheeks, big—great big—spooky eyes. You might've noticed him."

"No." She handed the card back to me, shaking her head. "I don't remember a guy like that. So many people come in here at that hour, though. When you're working, you mostly have your head down."

"Mind if I ask your people?"

She glanced toward the registers. "Only Jack was here. Jack," she called to him.

The kid came over. He looked like he was twelve too. Scrawny blond guy with spotty skin. I asked him about the skeleton-man. No, he hadn't seen him either.

"Listen . . ." the girl said. She tilted her head toward the line of waiting customers. "I gotta go."

"Sure. Thanks."

She went through a door into the back of the place, taking her empty pot with her.

I went outside and stood on the sidewalk beside the shop's tables. My eyes scanned the neighborhood.

The Grind was on the corner. There was a small white office building to my left. Across the street, there was a line of shops, buildings rising above each one, two or three stories of brick. I thought of Stark sitting here at the café three mornings ago. At least ninety minutes, seven-thirty to nine. Calling his twin brother three times, checking in, bringing him up to date. He must've been waiting for something or watching for something, I thought. Waiting for someone to come in or for someone to go by . . .

My phone rang. I dug it out of my pocket, still watching the shops, still thinking it over.

"Champion," I said.

"Where the hell are you?" It was Grassi.

"I'm right here," I told him.

"Here where?"

"Here. At home."

"Yeah, well, bullshit, okay? Because I just came from your home."

"Oh. Yeah, that's right. I went out. I forgot."

"Did you leave the county?"

"No. No. I'm in the county."

"So where are you?"

"In the county. Driving around. I'm driving around the county. Hey, did you get an ID on the dead skeleton yet?"

"No. And it's none of your fucking business so shut up. You better get back here, you hear me? I'm serious. I got questions I gotta ask you."

"Like what?" I stepped off the sidewalk. Turned my head to check the traffic in both directions. Crossed the street, my phone to my ear. "Ask me whatever you want."

"No, no, no. I want you here, Champion. At the shop. I want to look you in the eye."

On the opposite sidewalk, I stood between a drugstore and a gourmet deli. There was a glass door here, an entry into the apartments on the floors above the deli. There were two rows of doorbell buttons by the door, eight in all. One button was labeled "Super."

The cool wind whipped up and came down the street again. It smelled faintly of fertilizer from the farmlands.

"I'll come in on Monday," I said into the phone.

"No. Not Monday. Now."

"Now? It's Saturday."

"Right now."

"Oh, all right. I'm on my way. Hey, what about the girl? You get a hit on the girl's prints?"

"Fuck you," he said—and he hung up.

"Hell of a coincidence," I muttered, slipping the phone back into my pocket. "That's exactly what I was going to say."

I rang the super's doorbell.

The super was a bookish little man in his sixties. The aesthetic saggy-cardigan type with a theoretically peaceful demeanor. Long white hair, small round glasses. I handed him my card.

"I'm Inspector Champion from the Tyler County Sheriff's Department," I said. "I'm looking for a woman who might live here."

He held up the card. He smirked. "This county is in New York. You're out of your jurisdiction."

I smiled at him the way you smile at an idiot. "It's not a matter of jurisdiction, sir. She's not in any trouble. I just have some information to give her." Then I kept talking to ride over whatever stupid thing he was going to say next. "She's in her thirties. Very pretty. A lot of dark red hair—auburn hair. Blue eyes. Good figure."

"You don't know her name?"

"I don't." She had only told me the name *Samantha* in my drug dream, after all.

"But you have information to give her?" the super said suspiciously.

"That's right," I said, showing him the idiot smile again and waiting him out.

"Well . . . that's Samantha Pryor," he said after what I guess he considered an appropriately suspicious hesitation. "She lives upstairs in 3B."

Made sense. The skeleton-man had sat across the street, waiting for her, watching for her. Who else could he have come here to find?

"Great," I said. Still smiling, I pressed the button for 3B.

"I'm pretty sure she's away," said the super. "I haven't seen her for a couple of days. Her mailbox is full too."

"You know where she works?"

"I don't know if she would want me to tell you that."

"Believe me, she's going to want to talk to me," I said.

"Well, I suppose there's no harm in your knowing. She works at the public library over on Cannon Street."

"Leaves for work every day around eight, eight-thirty."

"I guess."

"Okay. Thanks. I'll try her there. Give her my card if you see her, would you?"

"All right."

I lifted my hand in a fond farewell to the pompous son of a bitch and walked away. There was a security camera above the door, so I kept walking even after he went back inside. I walked around the whole block. It gave me a chance to enjoy the spring weather, visit the historic Civil War monument on Main Street, and make sure no one was following me on foot. I also took a moment to stop off at my car and get the pocket-sized leather pouch full of burglar picks I kept in the glove compartment.

Finally I came full circle back to the apartment building. I figured the super had probably stopped watching the security monitor by then.

The lock was a simple dead bolt and I was always handy with a pick. I got the door open quickly. I moved to the stairs without a pause and started up before the door swung shut behind me. I went two steps at a time to the second floor, then around the bend to the third. Apartment 3B was right off the stairs in the middle of the landing. Another dead bolt there. Half a minute later, I slipped into Samantha Pryor's apartment.

I turned on the lights. I recognized the skeleton's work right away. He'd trashed her place, same as he'd trashed mine. Sofa cushions slashed and gutted. Tables overturned. Drawers and closets emptied onto the floor.

I drew my Glock. I moved through the rooms quickly, kicking debris out of my way, turning lights on as I went. Just wanted to make sure I was alone in here. There was a kitchenette off the front room—all the drawers and cabinets opened, all the silverware and plates and pots and pans dumped on the counters and the floor. There was a bedroom—the mattress gutted, lady clothes piled up everywhere, the closets emptied. I caught sight of a picture frame on the carpet, a photo of three women behind the broken glass. The woman in the middle of the group was my Samantha, sure enough, exactly as I remembered her.

I went on into the bathroom off the bedroom. All the toiletries had been dumped into the sink and the bathtub. There was lots of broken glass sparkling under the top light. Lots of girl gunk that had dried in gelatinous streaks of color as it oozed toward the drain.

I was about to pull back into the bedroom when something stopped me. I hesitated in the doorway. Drew a series of short breaths in through my nose. I smelled something. I moved back into the bathroom again, sniffing around like a dog on the trail. Finally I found what I was looking for in a corner of the tiled floor.

A bottle of perfume. The glass was too thick to have broken during the search but the stopper had come out. There was only a small yellow puddle left inside. The rest had spilled out onto the floor.

I lifted the bottle to my nose and drew in the scent. It was her scent—Samantha's. I remembered it from when she'd sat beside me on the sofa in my apartment. In fact, the smell brought back the memory of her so powerfully it made me ache with longing.

What the hell? I thought. How do you hallucinate a thing like that?

I holstered my gun as I stepped back out into the bedroom. I kicked aside a pile of clothes. Some sort of chiffon nightgown or top or something clung to my leg. I picked it off, lifted it, smelled it: the same scent as the perfume. Samantha.

As I stood there, holding the fabric to my face, I contemplated the wreckage around me. Obviously skull-boy hadn't found what he was looking for or he wouldn't have had to toss my place too. But whatever he was after, I was pretty sure I didn't have it, so maybe Samantha did. Maybe she kept this much-desired thing at the library. Or maybe it was here somewhere and Stark had missed it. His searching methods were comprehensive but not exactly methodical. Maybe her hiding place was just too good for him.

The minute I thought that, an idea struck me—and I let go of Samantha's chiffon. It wafted slowly to the floor.

I knew where to look. It didn't make any sense that I knew. Why should I know? But nothing made any sense. I knew.

I went to the corner of the wall behind the bed. Crouched down and examined the wainscoting at the bottom. I probed and pulled at it, but it didn't move. I got up and walked around the bed to the opposite corner and tried again. Again, nothing.

I stood up and looked around. I looked at the bedroom door, the bottom of the door. The door interrupted the wainscoting on that wall so that on one side the panel was only about eight inches long. I went to the short panel. Crouched down. Worked my fingernails into the top of it. A spark of excitement went through me as the section of panel came away in my hand to reveal the hole that had been broken into the plaster behind it.

Amazing. Amazing and weird. And even more amazing was the fact that I wasn't surprised at all.

I reached my hand into the hiding hole and felt the slim paper object inside it. I worked it out. A small manila envelope. I undid the clasp and reached into it. Drew out a sheaf of folded pages. Crouched there, I unfolded them. I looked at the top page. I felt the breath come out of me in a long slow involuntary hiss.

I was looking at a photograph. Originally from a newspaper, I thought, but it was reprinted on a sheet of standard paper. I recognized the picture instantly. It was an NYPD surveillance shot of Martin Emory—the same photo that had first got me interested in his case. There he was, sitting in a sleek black Mercedes parked at the curb outside the Sutton Place brothel. And there was the driver, barely visible behind the tinted window: a fat woman with a piebald oval of flesh where her face should have been. The ghostly image had been circled with red marker.

I shuffled the top page to the bottom of the pile and looked at the page beneath. A news story. From the *Post*. "House of Evil." I pulled that aside to look at the next page—and as I did, something slipped out from amidst the pages and glided in a swift arc to the floor.

It was a square of paper. It had landed facedown but I could tell it was an old snapshot. I picked it off the carpet. Turned it over.

What a bizarre sensation. To see the face in that photograph was as bizarre as anything that had happened to me yet. It was heartbreaking too somehow: the formality of the pose, the child all dressed up in tie and jacket, the smile put on for the camera—but the eyes . . . the eyes lonesome, lost, and sorrowful, helpless in a world of adult cruelty and corruption. The color of the photo had faded to little more than a range of yellows, and the paper was crimped and wrinkled, making the image unclear. But I could see it as well as I needed to.

I recognized the living image of the ghost child: Alexander.

★ ★ ★

My hands were unsteady as I stuffed the picture and papers back into the envelope. I slipped the envelope into my jacket pocket. Then I worked the wainscoting panel back onto the wall.

I stood up. My phone rang, startling me. I made a face, figuring it must be Grassi again. I pulled the phone out of my pocket with one hand as I flicked off the bedroom lights with the other, getting ready to leave.

"Champion," I said. I went into the bathroom and reached for the light switch there as well.

"In Africa, I learned how to skin a man alive."

My hand froze on the switch. My mouth went dry in a finger-snap. A cold sweat started at my temples and at the back of my neck. I remembered that voice—that rasping whisper; how could I forget it? In a flash of memory, I remembered the death-head vanishing into the shadows, that harsh sound trailing after it: *I'll make you beg to die.*

"We'd do it to slaves who tried to escape, mostly," he went on. "We'd tie them up, still living, in a bag made of their own skin and let the others watch them struggle so they knew not to try to run away. There were always some who would try, but we always caught them. Always, Champion. Every time."

I drew a trembling breath as I forced myself to move again. I pulled the switch and shut the bathroom lights off.

"You sound like a fun guy, Stark. Or maybe like a sick, evil, twisted bastard—I always get those two confused."

He laughed. It was a sound I never wanted to hear again.

I drew my gun. Holding the phone in one hand, the gun in the other, I edged out the door, into the living room.

"Oh, you don't know the half of it," Stark said. "Something like that—skinning a man, flaying him—that's just for show really. To spread fear, you know. The Arabs like that sort of thing. Well, they're savages, aren't they? The truth is, if you want to cause pain, just pure pain over a long period of time, you don't need all that blood and guts. It gets in the way really. It works against you. With the right tools, you can go straight into the brain, neat and clean. Right to the pain centers of the brain. You can keep a man alive indefinitely that way—forever, in effect. You can cause him an agony beyond anything imaginable—forever and ever."

I swallowed. It wasn't easy. It felt like I'd eaten a rock. I moved slowly across the living room, scanning the corners.

"A more sensitive man might take that as a threat, Stark," I said. "But I know you're just making conversation."

"You killed my brother."

"He was getting on my nerves."

"I loved my brother. He was all I loved."

"That's a touching tale. I'm all misty, Stark. No, really."

I reached the light switch in the kitchenette. Turned off the light in there. Moved through the debris in the living room to reach the last light switch by the front door.

"You know what I do now?" Stark rasped. "With all that love, you know what I do? I think about you, Champion. I think about you all the time. I make plans. I plan what I'm going to do to you."

"It's nice to have a hobby. Takes your mind off your troubles."

"I'll be seeing you, Champion."

"Why? What do you want, Stark?"

"Just you."

"What're you looking for?"

"Just you."

"Someone sent you after me. Who was it?" My mouth was so dry I could barely get the words out.

"It doesn't matter," Stark said. "That's over now. Now it's all about you. You and me. It's all about what I'm going to do to you."

"Was it the Fat Woman? Is she the one who sent you? Aunt Jane—isn't that what they call her? She's the one who got your brother killed, Stark. Who is she? What did she send you to find?"

"Count the minutes till it begins, Champion. That's all there are now. Minutes. Hours maybe. Not even a full day till it begins. And once it begins, it will go on and on and on. Like hell, a hell on earth. I made a promise to my brother's soul. Hell won't be the half of it."

Fear set a red burst of rage off inside me. I nearly choked on the words as they sputtered out. "You better hope you get to me, you son of a bitch. You better hope you get to me before I get to you."

But nothing came back except that laugh again. That awful sound. Then silence. He was gone.

Still holding the phone to my ear, I leaned my head against the wall. Then I slowly lowered the phone, lowered my trembling hand to my side. My scalp was clammy with sweat. The back of my shirt stuck to me, damp. I still couldn't swallow. Mouth too dry. Throat too thick.

A team of killers after me with orders to bring me alive to that skull-headed monster. And him set on torturing me forever and ever. Not a pleasant situation. Hard to see the sunny side of it.

"All right," I murmured aloud. "Keep it together."

I straightened with a breath, stiffened my back with a breath. Slipped the phone into my pocket with one hand, still holding my Glock with the other, feeling the pebbled butt of the gun against my sweating palm.

I had to get away from this place. Somewhere safe where I could think. The crazy killer's threats were repeating themselves in my mind, as mocking and insistent as a bully's schoolyard taunts. *An agony beyond anything imaginable forever . . . hell won't be the half of it . . . count the minutes till it begins . . .* I could barely think with all that interior noise, could hardly consider what I'd found here—what the Starks or their employer had been looking for, but only I had found.

Samantha Pryor—whoever the hell she was—had been onto the Fat Woman. That had to be it. She had known it was Aunt Jane who'd been supplying Martin Emory, selling him the children he'd buried in the woods. What else had Samantha known? What else was in that sheaf of papers? Who was she, for Christ's sake? Just a librarian?

I took one last glance around the shambles of the apartment. Then I turned to the door, holding my gun low, keeping it pressed against my pants leg. I unlocked the door and began to draw it open.

Suddenly, the door was kicked in, throwing me back. A giant of a man charged into the apartment as I staggered. He was massive—towering—massive in the middle, broad in the shoulders. Muscles stuffed into his jeans and baseball jacket. He was young, in his twenties, with styled, sandy hair and a sandy goatee. Nothing in his expression but businesslike professionalism as in one swift, unbroken motion, he pushed the door shut behind him and came at me.

I tried to bring the gun to bear. He was too fast. He was on me. Grabbed my arm with his left, brought his right up into my center. I never saw the Taser. I just felt the blast. My body went rigid, a tremor of muscle-clenching pain fanning out from the gun through all of me in a flash. The thug held the weapon against me and went on holding it. Then he snapped it off, pulled it back, and let me fall.

I collapsed into myself and crumpled down, dropped to the floor like a dead weight. I heard a curse come out of me without my even thinking to curse. What I was thinking was: *Hold on to the gun.* I tried, but I couldn't. My spasming hand wouldn't respond to my brain. The Glock dropped from my slack fingers as I toppled down.

I lay on the floor now, still clenched and shuddering. Unable to move but fully conscious. I could see the big thug swooping down to snap up my Glock. I could see him stick the gun into his belt. Then, trembling, helpless, I watched him unzip his baseball jacket. He had a T-shirt on beneath, his muscles bulging through it. With another quick, calm, professional motion, he pulled a roll of canvas from an inside pocket, tossed it onto the floor next to me. I saw it start to unroll. A canvas sack. I knew he was going to stuff me in there.

Now—still swift, still calm—he unzipped another pocket. Brought a leather pouch out of it. Opened the pouch, fished inside it with his fingers.

Terror wildfired through me as I lay watching him bring out a syringe.

An agony beyond anything imaginable forever ... hell won't be the half of it ...

I had to move. I had to move but I couldn't. I fought for control of my body but it was a thing apart, a shivering, unresponsive corpse with me trapped inside.

The thug held the syringe needle up and pushed the plunger just enough to clear the air from the canister. All the while his demeanor was bland, blank, serious, professional.

I let out a strangled noise through my frozen jaws as he dropped down onto one knee beside me.

Count the minutes till it begins, Champion.

I had to move. Had to fight. Had to get away or Stark would have me.

I couldn't do it. I couldn't move.

The thug plunged the syringe's needle into my neck. I was thinking, *No, no, no!* as I lost consciousness.

8

The Road to Hell

I STARTED TO WAKE slowly and then the memory of what had happened came back to me and the terror came back to me and I jolted awake fast.

I was in total darkness. I didn't know how long I'd been under. I found I had control of my muscles again, but I still couldn't move, I could only struggle. My hands were pinioned behind me. I was in a close space and couldn't extend my legs. I thrashed for a second in blind panic, trying to tear my way free by main strength. Then I stopped. Lay sweating and breathless, my heart pounding. I fought to keep still, to take stock.

My gut burned from the Taser. My neck ached from the shot. My mind was still slow and sluggish from whatever the thug had drugged me with. The effect got worse as the adrenaline of panic seeped away. I began to feel like a great, strong hand was wrapped around me, trying to drag me back down into unconsciousness. My eyes began to flutter shut . . .

But that voice—Stark's hash rasping skeleton voice was alive in my mind again. *Hell won't be the half of it . . . count the minutes till it begins . . .* And that laugh: a sound like a snake slithering and rattling inside my head. Fear and desperation rose up in me again and overcame everything—the sluggishness, the pain . . . everything. I forced myself to think. I had to get free. I had to get free before it was too late. If it wasn't too late already.

I took two long deliberate breaths to fight down the panic, to slow my racing thoughts and clear my head. Where was I? Inside the trunk of a car. Yes, I could feel the motion, hear the noise of the engine, the noise of other cars passing outside. I was on a highway. Traveling somewhere. Traveling to Stark. Traveling to hell.

Two more deep breaths. *Don't panic. Fight the panic.*

My hands—what about my hands? Handcuffs? No. Twisting my fingers around, I could feel the extended plastic tab of a nylon zip-tie pulled tight around my wrists.

I drew another breath. It wasn't easy. There wasn't enough air in here. The air was hot and close. Not a lot of room to move, either. Like being in a coffin—which added to the frenzy of dread inside me. At least I wasn't inside that canvas sack. That was something anyway.

I shifted my body so that my fingertips could brush the bottom of the trunk, so I could get a sense of my surroundings. The trunk was carpeted. Empty too, as far as I could make out—kicking around with my feet, turning my body. Nothing in here but me.

All right, at least I was thinking now. Empty trunk. Locked. Me inside, hands tied up. What do you do? It's no simple thing to open a car trunk from the inside. That's why new cars sometimes have emergency tabs in them: phosphorescent plastic pull-tabs you can see in the dark so you can grab them and pop the trunk open if you get trapped somehow. If I could find a tab, maybe I could pull it . . .

I twisted around some more. Every motion brought back to me how restricted I was. Stuffed in that small space, my hands bound. Every time I tried to move I had to breathe down another fresh gout of panic.

Still—grunting, straining—I managed to twine my body over far enough so that I could get a broad look at the darkness surrounding me. No phosphorescent tab that I could see. No simple way to get the trunk open.

The failure brought a fresh wash of sweat down the front of my face. I had to blink the sting of it out of my eyes. But I forced myself not to go crazy over it. Just a setback, that's all. You had to keep trying, right? You had to go on thinking: There was no emergency tab, so what else could I find in the trunk of a car? What else?

Tools.

The idea lit a faint glow of hope in me. If I could find something—anything—to use as a saw or a lever, I might be able to break through the zip-tie, free my hands, give myself at least a fighting chance when Stark and his thugs came to get me. Even a sharp edge somewhere might help me cut through the plastic.

The hope glowed—and then the glow dimmed almost to nothing. In a lot of trunks, the tools for changing tires are kept with the tire beneath the trunk floor. No way for me to lift the trunk floor while I was lying on top of it as I was.

In some cars though, it's different . . .

I began to shuffle and hump my body across the small space. It was hard. Hard. Moving first one half of me, then the other, like a snake. I writhed to one side of the trunk. Got myself in a position where I could run my fingers over the trunk wall.

I felt nothing there. Just more of the same, more of the smooth carpeting. No sharp edges—not a one. Had to move up a little. Every inch a strain. The sweat pouring out of me, the breath breaking from me in little grunts and gasps. But now—yes— my fingertips brushed over a ridge in the surface. What was it? Something. My eyes filled with tears of frustration as I tried to work my restricted fingers under the edge of it, tried to test if there was a break there, something that could be pulled away from the rest.

Then something budged. Just a little. I felt a break in the carpet. One fingernail—one sliver of one fingernail—worked its way under the ridge in the trunk wall. I worked to get a better grip.

Please, God, I prayed. Squeezing my eyes shut so that the tears fell from them, mixing with the sweat.

The car hit a bump. My fingernail slipped out of the ridge.

I let out a broken cry of frustration. I could've sworn I heard Stark's skeletal laugh. *Count the minutes till it begins, Champion ...*

With a growl, I hurried to twist back into position. To find the ridge, to get my fingernail back under it. There it was. I wedged the nail in. Curled my finger. I felt the ridge shift, pulling away from the rest of the wall.

Please ...

Now I could work my fingers into the space. Now I could pull again. A piece of the wall came loose. The space widened. I struggled to shift my body. Worked my hands in deeper. Pulled again.

A small square section of the wall fell free. I felt as if my heart was about to leap out of my chest. What was it? What had I pulled out? I couldn't turn to look. I wouldn't have been able to see it in the dark anyway. But I prayed I had opened the tool compartment. It had to be. It had to.

Before I could find out, the motion around me changed. I felt the car turn. I felt it slow. I lay very still, trying to hear over the noise of my hammering heart, trying to get a sense of what was happening in the big, free world outside this smothering darkness.

The car was leaving the highway. It slowed some more. It rolled to a stop. My breathing stopped as well. Had we reached our destination? No, not so close to the exit ramp. We'd just stopped for a moment. A stop sign at the end of the ramp—that had to be it. But maybe the driver had left the highway because he heard me moving back here. Maybe he was going to come back around to check on me. Maybe he'd see that I'd worked the tool compartment open and hit me with the Taser or the syringe again, or maybe ...

No. The car started up. Moving now on a slower road. A local road.

I licked my dry lips. *We must be getting close,* I thought. *Nearing our destination. Where Stark was waiting for me ...* I felt my heart, my hopes sinking. Not much time left.

But some time. Some.

I opened my mouth wide and pulled as deep a breath as I could. Prying the cover off the wall compartment had given me some hope. Now the sense that time was running out gave me fresh urgency. I needed the energy from both. The muscles in my shoulders were strained and burning, sore from the effort of moving my fingers with my wrists bound behind me. Every movement in that coffin of a place made me draw my lips back, bare my teeth in pain. Only hope, and the fear of what was coming—what was coming fast, coming soon—pushed me on, mind against body, mind forcing the body to try again.

I had to work the separated section of the trunk out of my way. Then I pressed close to the wall. Found the opened compartment. Forced my restricted hands into it.

My fingers touched cold metal right away. I hardly dared to feel the thrill of it. I scrabbled desperately to get a grip on the metal. A cylinder of iron. The car's tire iron. Wedged into some sort of holder in the wall.

Fresh tears sprang to my eyes—tears of desperate desire now. The hope that I could get that tool brought fresh fears with it: fear that time would run out before I got the thing, fear that the nylon of the zip-tie would be too strong, fear that my movements were so restricted I wouldn't be able to use the iron at all.

I strained back, wrapped the fingers of one hand around the cool cylinder. I arched my body. Kicked with my feet, grunting. I came away from the wall—and, yes, pulled the tire iron free.

I fell slack. Panting from the effort, gulping in lungfuls of the hot air. My shirt was soaked through with sweat, clammy on me, heavy on me. And my arms hurt so much I had to lie still another moment to let the muscles rest, let the pain subside.

As I paused like that, blinking through sweat, staring into almost pitch blackness, the car's movements once more forced themselves on my attention. We were traveling slower than before but our progression was just as steady. I figured we must be on a smaller highway now, maybe a two-lane. Traveling through open country, I imagined. Sure: traveling to someplace secluded. Someplace where Stark could go to work on me in private, without interruption, for as long as he wanted . . .

Stark's voice started to whisper in my mind again: *With the right tools, you can go straight into the brain* ... But I chased him off with a fierce shake of the head, a silent curse, my teeth gritted against his hissing, skeletal presence.

All the while, I kept hold of the tire iron in one hand. Now I tightened my grip, began to try to twist it around so I could wedge it between my wrist and the plastic, get it inside the loop of the twist tie. Oh, man, it was slow work. Slow, hard, so frustrating. So many failures. So many times I lost my grip and then—then I dropped it, and dropped it again—and each time I heard the clunk of the iron on the trunk floor, I made a noise in answer like a beast whimpering in the jaws of a trap. I got hold of the iron again. I got the wedge under the plastic of the zip-tie—then it snapped away again. I had to stop to rest my shoulder, gasping for breath. But almost at once, I tried again. Got the wedge in a second time, scraping my skin, making it burn—and *bump*: The car turned, went off the road, went bounding and rumbling over a new, rough surface.

I knew where we were—or at least I thought I knew. We were on a broken road now, maybe a dirt road. The sort of road that leads into the middle of nowhere, to a place where no one would hear me screaming, where I would never be found until Stark's long vengeance was over.

My heart sped up and my breath grew shallow. Exhausted, sick, hurting, gasping, I felt a fear beyond fear, a scarlet mindful of fear that almost torched my panic again. But the wedge was in this time, in beneath the zip-tie well and truly. I worked it in deeper with one hand. Then deeper, bit by bit. Then I began to try to wrap the fingers of my other hand around the shaft.

The car juddered over the broken road, dropping into a deep hole with a jarring jolt. But I still had the tire iron gripped in both hands. I started to twist it against the zip-tie, using it as a lever to stretch the plastic, to pull the bonds away from my wrists, farther away, and farther, trying to get it to break.

It wouldn't break. I couldn't get enough leverage. I relaxed the pressure, gasping. No choice. My shoulders were burning with pain. My wrists were aching, my hands weak.

The car bounced and slowed and my heart seized in me. I thought we'd reached the end of the line. But no, we were only working our way more slowly over the broken road, edging forward, maneuvering past the potholes.

I didn't try to stretch the tie again; I knew it wouldn't break. Instead, I shifted my grip on the metal bar. I worked my hands into position. I drew breath. Held it. Then all at once, I let the air burst out of me as with a single concerted motion—a single effort of strength that tore the sinews in my arms and sent a sparkling burst of agony through the darkness behind my eyes, I twisted the tire iron in the zip-tie sharply—one hand pushing one way, one pulling in the other—and the plastic snapped.

My hands were free.

The shock of the release, the joy of fresh hope, the relief to my arms—all of it sent a new burst of strength through me. Quickly, I tore the zip-tie off me completely. I curled around in the cramped space. I ran my fingers over the metal of the trunk cover, trying to find a spot where I might wedge the tire iron in, break the lock, and pry the lid open.

But the damn thing seemed built to thwart me. The trunk lid overlapped with the body of the car in such a way I didn't think I'd be able to get the iron in between them—and even if I did, I wasn't certain I'd be able to get the leverage I needed to snap the latch.

I cursed, my heart falling as quickly as it had risen. I had to steel myself against breaking—because I was breaking, my spirit was breaking and I had to fight to keep it alive. I told myself I had a chance now—I had a weapon now, free hands, the element of surprise—I could do battle if I had to. But I remembered the calm, professional, expert demeanor of the young muscleman who'd put me in here. He had a Taser. He surely had a gun. He probably had allies—even Stark himself—waiting for him wherever we were going. If I was still stuck in this rolling coffin when we reached the end of the line, I was a dead man, and worse than dead.

"All right, all right," I whispered. My voice was barely audible above the noise of the tires banging over the rough road.

I had to think again, had to go back to the beginning. What did I have? What could I use? What could I find that would help me get out?

The jack.

I started moving at once. Twisting around. Gasping, puling with the effort. Working my body into position to get my hands in the compartment, to get the jack. I grabbed it, pulled it out of its holder. It was a good one. A heavy, solid scissor jack. I set it on the trunk floor. Feeling my way, I worked the iron into its slot. I lay curled on my side next to it. I started to pump the bar.

The jack cranked up inch by inch. I could hardly see it in the dark and had to keep putting my hands on top of it to find out how high it was. I wasn't sure it was tall enough to reach the lid, but there was no sense worrying about it. I didn't have any other ideas. I tried not to think. I just kept pumping.

And the car kept moving, bouncing slowly over the dirt road. How much farther would it go? How much time did I have?

Curled on my side, moving my arm up and down, I listened to the grinding jack rise, feeling the sweat pour off me, feeling it soak my clothes.

The jack touched the ceiling of the trunk. Again, new hope, new strength went through me. I kept pumping—harder, then even harder as the trunk lid resisted the rising jack. I felt the metal of the lid begin to buckle and dent. I heard it. Would the driver hear it? No, not over the noise of the road. I gritted my teeth. I pumped harder. Now the lid had bent as far as it would go. Now the metal held, resisting. I pressed down on the iron. It seemed to press back up against me, refusing to budge. I leaned on it, grunting, lifting my body off the trunk floor, pressing down with all my weight.

The latch snapped. The lid flew up. The trunk sprang open.

The driver must have seen it. The car stopped at once, stopped hard. At the same time, light—blue evening light—and air—cool evening air—washed in over me, and by some magic chemical reaction all the terror and hope and desperation inside me turned instantly into a killing rage.

I grabbed the tire iron. Yanked it free of the jack. Climbed out of the trunk and tumbled out onto the road.

I was in a forest of towering pines, the sky twilit above me. Everything was falling into silhouette as the daylight died.

I stumbled a few steps, then planted my feet on the rough dirt. I clutched the cold iron in my hand. I was weak and unsteady and drenched in sweat, but the fury was like lightning in me, one long blast of white-hot power, animating my failing flesh.

I saw the dark shape of the car door coming open, framed against the low glow of the car's running lights. I saw the dark shape of the thug rising out from behind the wheel. An animal cry tore out of me and I rushed him.

He was halfway out of the car, half turned away from me with his hand still on the door, when I reached him and brought the iron down on his head. The blow wasn't hard enough to knock him out but it stunned him. He threw his two hands up in self-defense and tried to stagger away.

I went after him, roaring. I hit him again. This time I only connected with his hand. I heard him make a noise. I saw something drop from his fingers. I heard the sound of plastic hitting the dirt. The Taser. He'd been planning to shock me again. To knock me out, keep me alive for the skeleton's tortures. The jagged bolt of rage inside me danced with fresh fire. I roared—I couldn't stop roaring—and swung the iron again.

He threw his arm up, blocked the blow. I could feel the strength in him: the muscle, the power. Even dazed as he was, he managed to wrap his arm around my arm and capture it, twist it, force me to drop the iron bar. At the same time, he tried to jab his free hand into my eyes. But we were close now—too close for blows. We grabbed hold of each other, spun away from the car, and tumbled down together into the dirt.

We rolled and clutched at each other in the glow of the running lights. He was too strong for me. Quickly, he had me wrapped up, held fast. He got around behind me, wrapped his arm around my throat. I had my chin tucked in to keep him from strangling me but he was forcing me down under him. Desperate, all I could do was keep my body loose, slither my arm out of his control, reach for a pressure point.

Just before he pinned me to the earth, I found it. My hand slipped between his thighs. I made a fist.

He grunted and his grip on me loosened. I pulled away but kept clutching him. In the thrashing force of his agony, he lashed an elbow into my temple. That made my head ring and knocked me away. I rolled across the dirt, a throbbing pain behind my eyes. But I was out of his clutches and I knew I only had seconds before he recovered. I had to rush. Had to get my best shot at him fast.

I rolled up onto my hands and knees. An owl *hoo-hooed* in the high pines. A wind whispered through the branches. I saw the tire iron in the dirt by the light of the car. I reached for it, wrapped my fingers around it.

The day had darkened even further now. The air was deep blue, except where the double beam of the running lights cut through it. The first stars were shining mistily above the crowns of the trees. I saw the thug's silhouette in the road. I saw him bent over double, clutching his middle in pain, but still pushing his way to his feet.

I got up first, the iron in my hand. I leapt at him. Swung. The heavy metal hit the side of his head. Halfway to his feet, he grunted, staggered. I roared. I hit him in the head again. He stumbled down onto one knee, trying to keep his hand up in front of him. I brought the iron down overhand, smashing it into his well-groomed hair. He dropped onto his butt. He tried to crab-walk away, keeping his hand up. I hit him again, roaring, and hit him again and kept roaring and hit him again, and that last time, I felt something give—his skull: I felt it cave in under the blow and that was it, finally, he went down, not in stages, but dead weight, *bang,* to the ground. He lay there twitching violently.

Staggering with the force of that final swing, I lost my balance and sprawled onto the road beside him.

I lay in the dirt there, gasping, cursing, sobbing while the thug next to me spasmed and shuddered—a long time, it seemed like. Then he lay still.

The owl hooted again in the gathering dusk. I climbed slowly to my feet. Took two unsteady steps to the car. Grabbed hold of its opened door, leaned on it, trying to catch my breath.

I lifted my eyes to the forest around me. The pines stood straight and tall like shadow sentries. I followed the sound of the owl and saw him, high on a dead branch, a black shape against the indigo sky. A thin mist was rising from the ground, I noticed now. It swirled in the double gleam of the car lights. It rose above me and dimmed the light of the early stars. It grew luminous at the horizon line where the edge of the moon was just rising, a bright arc visible through the trunks of the trees.

I turned this way and that and turned again, but there was no other light in the woods that I could see.

I glanced at the killer. Not shuddering anymore. Motionless.

Still breathing hard, I lowered myself into the car.

It was a Chevy, old, maybe ten years old. The radio was playing low. A man singing, his voice grainy with yearning. A GPS glowed, mounted on the dashboard, but there was no course highlighted on it: This road was off the map. With the door open, the car's top light was on. I could see my jacket lying on the passenger seat. I lifted it. My gun and holster were underneath. So was my wallet and my phone. So was the manila envelope I'd found behind the wainscoting at Samantha's place.

I worked the holster on. Checked the gun: still loaded. I worked my jacket on. I slipped my wallet and the manila envelope into my pockets. Finally, I checked the phone. There was no signal out here in the middle of nowhere. Just as well, I thought. I didn't plan on calling anyone. Who would I call? The cops? The cops weren't going to stop Stark. By the time they got here, he'd be long gone. Even if he wasn't, even if they caught him, even if they slung him behind bars for a while, that wouldn't end it. Not for me. The skeleton-man would keep coming after me. He would keep sending his people, his thugs. I had killed his brother, the only thing on earth he loved. As long as he was alive, I would live in a world of waiting. Waiting for him to find me. Waiting for him to drag me into whatever hell of vengeance he could imagine. There would be no end to his vengeance. Not as long as he was alive.

I stood up out of the car. Peering down through the deepening darkness, I found the thug's fallen Taser. I scooped it up, tossed it into the car. Then I went to the fallen thug. I squatted beside him. Pressed my fingers into his neck. No pulse. He was dead. Oh, well. I wasn't all that fond of him anyway.

I came out of my squat and grabbed the corpse by the ankles. I dragged it around to the back of the car. It was a big corpse. Thick and heavy. It wasn't easy to lift the flopping awkward weight of it and work it over the edge of the trunk. But I did it. The cadaver tumbled in. I took hold of the trunk lid. Before I closed it, I paused—just a second. I looked down at the body in the trunk—in the trunk where I had been just moments ago, tied up, helpless. I sneered at the thug lying dead in there, thinking about how he'd Tasered me and drugged me.

Fuck you, punk, I thought.

Then I closed the lid.

The trunk latch was broken now and wouldn't catch but the lid stayed down. I walked back around the car. Lowered myself behind the wheel. Pulled the door shut after me.

Through the windshield, the headlights illuminated a few feet of dirt road. I could see the road beyond the glow, rising sharply up the forested hill. I took a breath. I knew that I was sick with fear and half-crazy with rage. But I didn't care. I didn't want to think about it. I just wanted to find Stark. I just wanted to put an end to him. I wanted to silence his voice in my head.

Count the minutes till it begins . . .

I put the car in gear and started up the road.

That's right, I thought. *Count the minutes, Stark.*

9

The Cabin

I DROVE. THE DIRT road climbed. It got steeper and began to
wind and went on climbing. The moon rose, a full moon,
misty and enormous, sometimes in the windshield, sometimes at
the window as the road switchbacked. The moonlight shone on
the standing pines, on a forest that seemed to go on forever all
around me, vanishing from sight in the deep shadow that closed
over the distance. I kept driving, up the hill.

I figured there'd be a place at the end of the road. I figured Stark
would be waiting there. He'd be waiting for the car, expecting it.
He'd be expecting the thug to bring me to him. I figured when
he saw the car, he would think I was the thug and come out to
greet me. I figured that's when I would shoot him and put an end
to this. That was my plan anyway.

The road crested suddenly and I saw the cabin, just as I'd figured.
But it looked empty. There were no lights on. It was just a black
shape in the moonlit mist: a rustic one-story house stretched against
what looked like the edge of a cliff.

I had been wrong then. Stark wasn't waiting for me here after
all. At least he didn't seem to be.

I stopped the Chevy. Killed the engine. I got out, drawing my
gun as I did. I felt the mist chilly and damp against my skin. I

approached the cabin cautiously, my shoes making soft crunching noises on the dirt. I knew I was visible in the moonlight. If there was anyone inside the house, I would make a pretty easy target for him, a pretty easy shot.

But I didn't think there was anyone inside.

I moved around the side of the cabin. I moved to the edge of the cliff. That's what it was, all right: a sharp drop-off into thick brush. I looked out over the steep slope and saw a big river far below, the rising moon glittering on its running surface. I saw the scattered lights of towns winking in the distance straight ahead and to the south. I saw cars as small as Christmas lights moving over a highway.

I turned back to the cabin. Went around the rear of it. Found a door. The door rattled against a lock when I tried to open it. I stepped back and kicked it under the knob. I didn't have to kick it very hard. It flew open.

I went inside.

I turned the lights on in each room as I moved through the place. I wanted the cabin to look occupied. I had a new scenario in mind now, a new plan. I figured Stark would be here soon. I figured he'd think the thug was inside, holding me prisoner. I figured Stark would come into the cabin and that's when I'd kill him. Seemed as good a plan as the first one. I didn't care when I killed him, as long as he died.

I turned on the lights in the kitchen first. A country kitchen with copper pots and pans hung up on the rough wood walls like decorations. I went through and turned on the lights in the big front room. It was a wide, open room, done up like a hunting lodge. Braided rugs by the fireplace. A sloppy old comfortable stuffed sofa and a couple of rocking chairs. The heads of a stag and a bear mounted on the wall.

There were doors to the left and the right. I checked them out. Two bedrooms and a bathroom on one side of the main room. I turned their lights on as I checked them out. On the other side of the main room, there was a master bedroom with another bath-room. There was also a study there.

I ended up in the study. It was a large room. There was a large desk in there that looked as if it had been made from the cross sec-tion of a massive tree trunk. There was a computer on the desk. I turned the computer on and let it boot up while I looked around. There were bookshelves built into the wall; the books were about fishing and hunting mostly. There was a mounted salmon a yard long. Another braided rug. A leather easy chair.

There were two windows here, one behind the desk chair, an-other one, a longer one, on the front wall. There were drapes with prints of stags on them. The long window looked out at the drive-way. When I pressed my nose to the glass, I could see the Chevy sitting out in the moonlight, low mist curling around the tires.

I turned out the lights in the study. I figured this would be a good place to wait. I would see Stark coming up the drive from here. He would be focused on the front door. When he got close enough, I could take my shot.

As I stood in the darkness, the computer finished booting. The very next moment, it started to give off a musical tone. I hurried around the desk and looked at the monitor. Someone was calling on the computer phone system. A video call, the readout said. Whoever it was, they must've been standing by, waiting impatiently for someone to turn on the machine.

I took hold of the mouse. Clicked the program. "Video load-ing . . ." the readout said.

But the audio came on first. A voice said: "Are you there, Stark?"

I'd thought my rage had died down but I guess not. I guess it had just sunk to a low flame, ready to spring to life again at any moment. It sprang to life now, burning high, filling my heart with red murder.

Even before the video came on, I knew who was speaking. It was the Fat Woman.

I leaned into the screen, waiting to see her image.

Then there she was. Horrible. A horrible creature. Obese, ge-latinous, practically shapeless. The features of her bloated face had been destroyed—by fire, I thought; I was almost certain. Her nose and lips had been burned away. Her skin had been left a paisley pattern of pulsing pink and cancerous brown. Her lidless eyes—of some pale color—gazed merciless and viperlike out of unnaturally smooth flesh.

"Have you got him?" she said eagerly.

I almost spoke—but before I could, she must have realized some-thing was wrong. Even if there was a camera on my side—and there must have been—I don't think she could've seen me clearly in the dark. But something unnerved her. I saw her move. The connection shut down. Her image winked out and vanished.

A second later, headlights appeared at the study window. A car was coming up the drive.

I had to move fast. I hit the "off" button on the computer to kill the monitor light. The study sank into shadow, though the out-glow from the living room still came through the door, making the space visible. I moved to the side of the window. Drew back into the stag drapes to keep out of sight. I peeked around the drapes carefully, my gun held up by my face, ready.

A car—a big black Audi—pulled to the edge of the dirt driveway. It came to a stop a bit behind and to the side of the Chevy. The engine died. A second passed. The headlights went out.

I waited. Watched through the window, keeping my body back in the drapes, keeping my gun held high.

The front two doors of the Audi opened together. Two big men got out and stood guard. More of Stark's killers. Both had automatic rifles. They paused there with the stocks braced against their hips, the barrels raised, so I could make out the deadly, insectile shape of the weapons. Brand-new Colts of some kind, I guessed. Prob-ably a hundred rounds in each. They could shred me with them if I didn't get them first.

Now the back door opened too and Stark got out. God, he looked like Death. That was the way I remembered him but it was still a shock to see that face again in the flesh. If it was flesh. The white skin glowed in the moonlight like bone. The sunken, skull-like shape of it cast the cheeks into deep shadow and made the big, yellowish eyes seem even bigger, even brighter. The rest of him was harder to see. He was dressed in black and melded with the night. But his hands were as white as his face and visible enough. I could see he wasn't holding a weapon.

Stark nodded at the two gunmen and they started walking toward the house. They looked relaxed. They weren't expecting trouble. They were expecting to find their fellow thug here—and me hog-tied, ready to be butchered. Stark trailed behind a few steps, his big eyes moving, taking in the scene.

I slipped my finger off the Glock's guard and let it curl around the trigger. I had to play this just right. Two or three more steps and I'd have the gunmen within fairly easy range, but Stark himself would still have time to bolt when he heard the shots. If I took out Stark first, the riflemen would riddle me with bullets. I had to let all of them get closer—very close—so I had a chance of getting them all in three fast shots.

I waited. They took another step toward the house, and another, crossing the driveway.

My finger tightened on the Glock's trigger. Another two steps and I might take out all three of them before they had a chance to react.

Then Stark said, "Wait."

I could hear the rough rasp of his voice clearly through the window. Just the sound of it sent a chill of fear through my groin. He was a spooky son of a bitch, there was just no doubt about it. And I guess his threats of torturing me forever added to my negative impression of him.

He had stopped moving. Now, at his command, the riflemen stopped as well. I cursed under my breath. I started to lower my gun, to take aim through the window. But no, it was too late. At a gesture from Stark, the gunmen retreated, backing away as their eyes scanned the house, searching for signs of trouble.

I thought of taking my shot, but I had no chance. I couldn't get them all at this range, and in a running battle between me with my Glock and them with their automatic rifles, I'd be a dead man for sure.

Stark moved across the driveway now, moving toward the Chevrolet. He'd noticed something about the car. The trunk. He'd noticed the dent in it, I guess, or maybe the fact that it wasn't fully shut. In any case, he moved to it with his two gunmen trailing after, watching the house, scanning the dark, ready for anything. Stark opened the lid and peered into the trunk. His bright eyes gleamed in his skeleton face as he saw the dead thug in there.

I bolted just before they opened fire.

I was diving for the door as the window shattered. The night pulsed and pounded with the rattle of the Colts. The room exploded with flying lead. The wall splintered, a lightbulb burst, a lamp fell over. The stuffed salmon dropped off the wall. The leather chair danced into tatters. Glass broke everywhere.

I heard Stark shout, "Cut off the rear exit! Don't kill him! Take out his legs!"

I hit the floor and rolled and was out in the living room, in the light, exposed. But I dived again, and got to my feet and ran—just as I heard the front door come crashing in behind me.

I was in the kitchen now, at the rear, racing for the back exit, hoping to make it before one of the gunmen came running around to cut me off. I felt weirdly, wildly exhilarated. As bad as this was, it was better than waiting. It was battle, them or me. I had been in battle. It was something I knew how to do.

One of the gunmen was right behind me, marching inexorably after me, firing as he came. The kitchen tiles chipped and sang as he stepped down the little hall, as I rushed for the door. The back window dissolved into sparkling shards of glass.

I had to stop on my heels to pull the door open. Then I charged out of the cabin into the night.

And there was the second gunman. He was just coming around the side of the cabin. I leveled my Glock at him as I ran and fired blindly. He pulled back behind the wall. Set himself there. Took aim with his rifle, ready to mow me down.

I fired once more, forcing him back. Kept running all the while, barreling toward the cliff's edge.

The rifleman at the wall pulled the trigger. I caught the flashes from the corner of my eye. I looked back and saw the gunman from inside the cabin come out. He took aim.

I reached the cliff. I threw myself over.

A long, tumbling fall through empty air. I remembered the moment—it flashed through my mind—when Stark had stuck his gun barrel in my eye, ready to pull the trigger. I had known I was going to die in that second and it had felt like falling—helpless, raging. Now I went turning through space and it felt like the helpless rage of dying and it seemed like a long, long time before I came crashing down.

I crashed into branches, smashed through them, smashed into the solid earth and slid and tumbled. The underbrush was soft but I heard the drier limbs crackle as they broke. I felt them scratching and tearing at my face and hands. The impact of the earth jolted the breath out of me and all I could think was *Hold on to your gun* and I did hold on as I rolled, still helpless, down the slope.

I somersaulted over one shoulder as I picked up speed. I cracked through more branches. Dropped through nothingness for another heart-stopping moment, then hit the earth again; rolled again. I tried to get my feet under me, tried to get control of the fall. I felt something sharp whip by me and take a chunk out of my cheek. I shouted a curse. I fell.

Then the gunfire started.

The rattle of those automatic rifles sent a fresh, wild wind of fear through me. Half-blinded by darkness and speed and brush, falling and tumbling, I expected the bullets to tatter my flesh at any minute. But no, I just kept sliding and tumbling over the sheer slope.

Out of nowhere, the trunk of a sapling slugged the bicep of my gun arm. The blow made my hand spring open, knocked the weapon out of my grip. I managed to crook my elbow around the sapling and hold on. It stopped my fall.

I hung there on the plummeting cliff, breathless, wide-eyed with fear. The gunfire continued in coughing bursts above me. I lifted my eyes to the sound. Saw the muzzle flashes up there. Saw the silhouettes of the killers on the ridge above me. I could tell they were firing blindly into the night below them, but all the same I heard bullets zipping through the brush on either side of me, not far away—not far enough.

It seemed forever before the firing stopped. I hung where I was, breathless, dazed. Craning my neck, I watched the killers' silhouettes on the ridge. They were peering down the cliff. Searching for me in the dark.

I tried to think. What now? I looked around for my gun. There it was, below me, black on the brown and moonlit ground. It had slid down the slope a ways, then caught in the brush. Untwining my arm from the sapling, holding on to it with my hand, I might be able to stretch down and retrieve the gun. I moved cautiously. I didn't want the branches around me to snap. I didn't want to alert the gunmen, to draw their fire. I stretched. I reached down. My fingers brushed the butt of the Glock where it lay in the dirt. I stretched a little farther. I snagged the weapon. Pulled it toward me, grabbed hold of it. With a grunt, I brought the gun back to me and slipped it into my holster. I pulled myself back up to get a better grip on the sapling.

Just then, a beam of light shot through the darkness. It played over the slope a few yards away from me, then steadied. My breath caught. I looked up. The killers had a flashlight now. They were panning it slowly across the slope, trying to find me. I looked down quickly so the light wouldn't catch my eyes. I lay still, as still as I could with my heart pounding, my lungs heaving. My cheek stung and I felt the warm, sticky mess of blood on it. I didn't dare move to wipe it away.

The flashlight's beam had started to my left. It moved slowly across the steep slope, coming toward me. It picked out a line of branches and brush and tree trunks. Then another line, closer. I stared at it as it covered the ground, sweeping in my direction.

Now it fell across me, lighting the line of dirt and bracken on which I lay. I clung to the sapling. I kept my head down, my face buried in my shoulder. I didn't move. I breathed hot and hard. I felt the white light on me like a beam of fire. I waited for the gunmen to see me. I waited for them to open fire again. I wondered if I'd even hear the shot.

But once more the shadows folded over me. The light moved slowly on. The killers couldn't see me down here in the brush, in the dark.

Still, I waited. The beam kept moving. Another few feet. Another yard. Only when I was sure the light wouldn't gleam in my eyes did I lift my gaze to the cliff again.

There were the two gunmen. There was Stark now with them also, the three of them conferring. After a moment, Stark moved away from the edge of the cliff, out of sight. The gunmen remained. They shone the flashlight on the slope again but they were searching another section of the cliff, several yards away.

I seized the moment. I started to move, to descend. I went down foot by foot, grabbing at roots and branches to keep from falling, clawing at the earth and outcroppings of rock. I reached an open stretch of ground. With no plants to hold them, the rocks and dirt were loose there. They gave way under my shoes and fell in a pattering whisper over the slope, into the air. I froze, sending a stare at that flashlight beam as it panned across the brush above me.

But I was too far away for them to spot me now—out of reach of the light.

I continued to climb down, slowly making my way toward the river below.

Just as the ground seemed to curl out under me, just as I reached the base of the cliff and found my footing, my phone rang. A shocking noise. After the gunfire had stopped, the night had seemed still and quiet around me. The sounds of the woods had seemed like a kind of silence: The wind, the water moving down below, even the distant wash of traffic over the highway on the far shore—they'd sort of blended in with the scene so I didn't really hear them. There was nothing—nothing but the sound of my movement and grunts and breathing as I made the slow descent.

Then, suddenly, the Army song—my ringtone—was singing out in the silver night, startlingly loud and bizarrely electronic.

Then it's hi-hi-hey—the Army's on its way . . .

I glanced up quickly to see if the gunmen had heard the noise. But I was too far below them, out of earshot. Even if they did hear it, even if they saw me, they'd never be able to take me out at this distance, at this steep angle, through the branches, through the dark.

Panting, sitting against the base of the slope, I fished the phone out of my pocket. I checked the readout but the caller's number was blocked. I felt my insides turning sour as I lifted the phone to my ear. I knew what was coming.

I didn't say a word. I just listened. There was a beat of quiet, a beat of harsh breathing. Out ahead of me, a short stretch of shaggy grass ran through the moonlight to the riverbank. The lights of the town and the lights of the moving traffic gleamed peacefully on the far side. I braced myself for what I was about to hear, but it didn't help much. Stark's gravelly rasp released a nauseating vapor of fear inside me all the same.

"Champion."

"You were one step away from a bullet in the brain," I told him.

"You're only putting off the day," he rasped back.

"One step away, Stark. Next time you won't be so lucky."

For once, he didn't have an answer. I could feel his rage and frustration boiling over the wire. I hoped it twisted his guts like my rage twisted mine. I lifted my shoulder and swiped the blood off my burning cheek. Every part of me seemed bruised and scratched and hurting. I stared blankly out at the gleaming line of moonlight on the river water. Waiting.

"I'm going to kill everyone you love," Stark said finally.

My throat went dry. Maybe it was already dry—I don't know. But I tried to swallow and couldn't. "I don't love anyone, Stark," I managed to say.

"Oh, now. There's always someone, isn't there? There's that sweet little girl in Gilead, isn't there? What's her name? Bethany?"

I forced out a laugh. "I bang a bargirl and you figure it's love. You're sweet, Stark. Really."

"Then there's your cop friend. Monahan."

"Yeah, go after Monahan," I said. "I want you to go after Monahan. It'll save me the bullet it takes to kill you."

"And then, of course, there's Samantha, isn't there? Samantha Pryor."

I tried to answer again but I choked on it. I didn't even know who Samantha was—not really—but the thought that he might hurt her clutched me, wrung me.

It was Stark's turn to laugh: that sound he made like a viper slithering through the grass. "That'll be fun," he whispered.

Fury and fear pushed the words out of my throat, out of my mouth. "Yeah. Go ahead, Stark," I said into the phone, my lips hard against the phone. "Go ahead. Do it. Because I'll be waiting for you. Whoever you go after, wherever it is, that's where I'll be. And I won't miss this time. I'll kill you this time. I'll kill you like I killed your brother. I'll send you to hell like I sent him."

The silence that followed went on so long, I actually moved away from the base of the cliff and looked up toward where the cabin was, as if I'd be able to see what Stark was up to. There had been no cell phone signal up there so I figured he was in the cabin itself, using the landline on the study desk. But in fact, of course, I couldn't see the cabin at all. All I could make out was the steep slope in the moonlight, the ridge above.

The silence went on.

"You hear me, you bastard?" I said finally, nearly crushing the phone in my fist.

Still, no answer. Then, as I stood there, as I clutched the phone, peering up the cliff, I caught sight of something. A weird, red flicker. A flickering red glow. Swiftly—with awesome swiftness—the glow spread. It brightened. It took shape. Flames. Bright whickering flames rising over the top of the ridge. Rising and spreading. Spilling a red stain across the hem of the moon-gray sky. Stark had torched the cabin.

I stood and stared. And as I stared, Stark laughed again, soft in my ear. What a sound, what a sound. Like a snake slithering, like a snake coiling, a snake smiling its fanged smile, its dead eyes gleaming. It really did make me sick with dread. And where was he? Where the hell was he? Not in the cabin where the landline was; the cabin was in flames. And there was no cell signal on the ridge. Yet there it was. That laugh. There he was, with me, laughing, as if he were just a presence somehow, just present somehow in the texture of the night, in the air itself, in the silver darkness.

"Stark," I said. I didn't recognize my own voice.

He answered me—out of nowhere. "See you soon, Champion."

Then he was gone.

I stood another long moment staring up at the flames rising on the cliff. Then I turned away, breathing hard. My hand, the hand with the phone in it, fell slowly from my ear, lowered to my side. I stood staring out over the river, across the gleaming water at the lights shining peacefully on the far shore.

I could still hear him laughing.

Furious, I lifted the phone and threw it. I hurled it as far as I could into the darkness. I saw it turning in the moonlight. I saw it fall. There was a soft splash as it dropped into the river.

But I could still hear him.

10

A Joke from God

Now I was hunkered in the dead of night, rapping my knuckles on the bedroom window at the back of the house. Suddenly her face was against the pane, terrified. Bethany.

"Champ!" she said. Her voice was muffled through the glass. "Oh, my God!"

I slumped against the wall. I didn't think I could stay on my feet much longer. I tried to think of her coming through the house to help me. Pulling her bathrobe on as she hurried across the living room to the front door. I *hoped* she was hurrying, anyway.

There she was: I heard the front door open. I heard her footsteps whisper on the grass. I heard her whisper: "Champ?"

Then she had her arms around me and I felt the softness of her cheek, her hair. Smelled that fresh, natural scent of her, that somehow innocent scent.

"You're hurt. Oh, look at you. God! Your face," she said. One of her hands gripped my shoulder, the other gripped my arm. She was shepherding me back over her little lawn, back to the yellow light of the open door.

"I'm okay, I'm okay," I kept saying. "Have to get you out of here. He's coming."

But I stumbled, my legs wobbly. And she said, "Just get inside. Just let me have a look at you. You need a doctor."

"I'm okay, I'm okay."

I tried to tell her that we had to run, that Stark would come for her. But the words came out of my mouth in an inaudible mutter. Even I couldn't understand them.

"Everyone's been looking for you," she said. "Grassi's been here twice. The bastard." She moved me up the two steps to her front door. She was practically holding me upright, practically lifting me, carrying me. I don't know how she managed it. We spilled together into the lighted foyer.

"Close the door," I said—or thought; I don't know whether I said it out loud. Either way, she let me go and closed the door. I stumbled to an armchair in the living room and dropped into it. Now there was a new smell. That musty, purple smell of the house and furniture Bethany's mother had left her, the smell of Bethany's girlhood, thick and warm and comforting. It was dangerous, that smell, I thought. It could make me relax. It could make me forget we had to run—and then Stark would be there while I was still too weak to fight.

But another moment went by and I smelled the house and I couldn't remember what was dangerous about it anymore. I just sank into the softness of the chair and breathed in the homey atmosphere gratefully.

Bethany was hovering over me now. "Dan, Dan, what happened?"

My head lolled on my shoulders. I had to fight to keep my eyes open. That comfortable, musty, purple smell. The smell of Bethany as a little girl, dreaming. The sweet smell of Bethany as she hovered over me. The silken touch of her hair falling on my face. Her green and tender eyes.

"Hold on," she said. "Let me get some stuff to clean you with."

There were so many thoughts crowding my mind, so much I wanted to tell her. I thought I understood now how Samantha had come to wash up on the riverbank in Gilead. I didn't have all the answers—not even close—but I thought I had some. They had come to me during the long weary hours it had taken me to get here. The Starks' cabin had been somewhere in Jersey, it turned out, more than a hundred miles south. I had run and trudged to get to a road, then hitched a ride on an eastbound truck, and made my way north on foot until I could flag another truck—a journey of long, weary hours. Miles and miles through the dark, my thoughts racing, jumbling . . . I wanted to tell her about the racing, jumbling thoughts . . . Because now I understood . . .

The Fat Woman had hired Stark and his brother. I remembered the hideous sight of her on the computer in his cabin.

Are you there, Stark? Have you got him?

She had hired the death-headed killers. Why? I wasn't sure. To find me? Maybe. Maybe she wanted vengeance on the undercover cop whose name hadn't been revealed to the media, the man who had killed her customer Martin Emory, who had come so close to finding her. Maybe. But whatever the reason, she had set the Starks loose, and they had gone after Samantha first. Why? Who was she? I didn't know. But somehow she understood their assignment and had made her way to Gilead to try to warn me about it.

They're coming after us.

But Stark and his twin had been on her trail. They had followed her and attacked me outside my house.

It made sense, so far as it went. But who was Samantha? How had I dreamed her, hallucinated her three years ago as I kicked the drug, the Z? How had I fallen in love with an illusion only to have her come to life?

I lifted my head on the chair. Stared around me, blinking. For a long moment, the room, the night outside the windows—the world—all seemed to telescope away from me into a distant unreality.

Was it *all* an illusion? I wondered. Was it all a dream—even this?

Then Bethany was there again. A warm washcloth moved gently over my face.

"Hold still."

"Bethany . . ."

"You need a doctor."

"No."

"You need stitches for that cut, sweetheart."

"No."

The warm washcloth went over my face and blocked my view of her eyes. I wanted to look at her gentle eyes. I tried to see them around the washcloth.

"Who did this to you?" she said.

"A killer. A hired gun."

"Hold still.

"I shot his brother. He's after me."

"Okay. We'll call the police."

I caught her wrist. Held the washcloth away so I could see her eyes. They were beautiful. "No," I told her. "No police."

"Dan . . ."

"They'll just arrest him. That won't stop him."

"What are you talking about? What are you going to do?"

"No police, Beth."

"That's crazy! What . . . ? You can't just kill him."

"I can. I will. It's the only way."

She didn't answer. Gently, she pulled her hand free of my grasp. "Hold still," she said.

She went back to washing the blood off my face. Frowning, her eyes dark.

"Look," I told her. "We can't call the cops here. Grassi's got it in for me. He's just looking to tie me up. You know he is."

"Well, forget Grassi then," she said primly. She disapproved of my plan. "We'll go to the sheriff."

"The sheriff is nothing against this guy. He'll wind up doing the same thing—tying me up, holding me back—even if he doesn't mean to. Even if they believe me . . ."

"They'll believe you, Champ. Look at you."

"Even if they do, even if they arrest him, it won't stop. He'll still kill me. He'll kill you too, Beth."

"Me?" She pulled back, her eyes widening.

"I'm telling you. I shot this guy's brother. He wants to hurt me. Torture me. He said he'd kill everyone I love."

She was silent again. She knelt down beside me. She held my hand. She began to wash my hand with the warm cloth. She washed each of the fingers, one by one.

"We'll go to New York," I told her. "I have a friend there. He'll put some cops on it but he'll leave me free to do what I have to do. Okay?"

I heard her make a noise. I looked down at her. She turned her head away. I thought she had started crying but then I realized, no, she was laughing. Shaking her head, laughing.

"What?" I said.

She couldn't stop giggling, like a kid. "That *would* be the way I'd find out you love me," she said. " 'Why are you murdering me, Mr. Bad Guy?' 'Because Dan Champion loves you.' 'Oh, that's sweet! I never knew he cared!' Next time, Champ, could you send me, like, flowers or something? A greeting card . . ."

I laughed. Looking down at the top of her head as she went back to cleaning my bloody fingers. Looking at the delicate white part in her blonde hair. Why hadn't I held on to her? Married her? Built a life with her like Monahan had a life?

What was the point of asking? I knew the answer.

Samantha . . .

Later, I woke in the car beside her. Stiff, aching, but clean now. Showered. Bandaged. In fresh jeans and a sweatshirt and windbreaker—clothes I'd left at her house one time. I turned my head on the seat to watch her driving. I watched her profile framed against the swiftly running dark.

Then it occurred to me: my gun. I reached for my shoulder holster.

"It's in the backseat," Bethany said, watching the mirror, watching the road. "Don't worry. You can still shoot people." She smiled at me.

I sat up slowly. My mouth was sour with sleep. "I had papers, an envelope."

"It's all back there. I brought everything."

I blinked. "Where are we going?"

"New York City. That's what you said."

I nodded. "Right, right. I remember. Stop at a gas station with a market when you see one, would you? I need a burner. A phone they can't trace."

I waited in the car—her car: a jazzy old Mustang—while she went into the store. I watched her move under the gas station's bright lights. She was wearing an orange trench coat against the cool of the spring night. Her legs were bare. She had good legs.

When she was inside, I scanned the area through the Mustang's windows. It was after two in the morning. No other cars in the lot. No one had followed us. No one was on our trail. I didn't think they would be. Not yet. I'd scotched their plan for now, forced them to burn their safe house. They'd want to regroup before they came for me again.

Still, there was always a chance. They might act fast, hope to take me off-guard.

I stepped out of the car as Bethany came back toward me carrying the phone. I stretched. My body was aching, sore.

"I'll drive," I told her.

She tossed me her keys.

I drove—and as I drove, I talked to her. The broken white line of the highway zipped under the fender. The dark miles passed. In the rushing quiet of the car, I told her about being an uncle, an undercover, in the NYPD. I told her about my obsession with the Fat Woman. The sting on Martin Emory. About how I took the drug, Zattera—Z—to help me sleep. And the hallucinations that followed: the ghost of the little boy, Alexander, haunting me. Then I told her about the house—Emory's house in the woods—and the little girl tied to the bedstead. I told her how I pumped five bullets into Emory and killed him dead.

I glanced over at her when I told her that. To see how she took it. She gazed at me from the passenger seat, her eyes flashing in the passing lights.

"What," I said.

"Nothing," she answered.

"He was a child-murdering son of a bitch."

"I know that. And I know what that kind of thing does to you. When someone hurts a child—or a woman, for that matter . . . or anyone who can't defend themselves—I know how you take it, how angry it makes you. I happen to love that about you, Champ."

I looked away, back at the road. Made me feel funny, her saying that. Embarrassed. Exposed. "But you don't like that I killed the guy," I said. "You don't like that I'm going to kill Stark."

"I don't care about them. I'm just afraid of what it'll turn you into. All the killing."

"I've killed before. I was in a war, remember? I've killed a lot."

"I know."

"From far away and up close. I'm good at it."

"I know."

I drove silently.

Bethany said, "You know what I *do* like?"

"What."

"To hear you talking. You never talk."

"Well . . . now I am."

"I like it. I'm glad."

"Okay."

I kept driving. I started talking again. The highway wound past darkened woods, under streetlights suddenly there, suddenly gone. I told her about kicking the drug, sick and crazy, curled on the floor of my room upstairs. I told her about Samantha, about seeing Samantha, and how she was the same girl who had washed up out of the river that night I was at her house . . .

"Well, she must have been real all along then," Bethany said. "You must have really seen her."

"She wasn't real. She couldn't have been. Unless the ghost boy was real too. Alexander."

"I don't understand."

"I found a picture of him hidden in Samantha's apartment."

"You found a picture of the ghost boy? A photograph?"

"Yeah."

"How . . . ?"

"I don't know."

"He was an hallucination. He had to be," she said.

"That's what I'm telling you. He was and so was she. I imagined them both. Now they're real."

Bethany was silent. After a while, she turned to look out the window. When I glanced over, I could see her face reflected on the glass.

"What," I said.

She shook her head. "It's just . . . all this stuff . . . It's all been in your head." She turned to me. "All this time . . ."

I stared out the windshield. Stared out through my own reflection there on the glass. I understood what she was saying. All this time she and I had been together, there were all these things I hadn't told her, all these things about me she didn't know . . . I wondered if she guessed the rest of it. About Samantha, how I felt about Samantha. How I couldn't love her—Bethany—because I loved another girl, a girl who wasn't there. And now she was there . . .

I stole another glance at her reflection on the glass. I thought she probably had guessed it. It was the sort of thing she *would* guess, being Bethany.

"Well, now I'm telling you," I said.

"I know," she said.

She said it so sadly I thought she must have guessed for sure.

We didn't talk again for miles. We sat in the car together in silence. It felt to me as if Samantha was there too, sitting between us. The trees gathered darkly on the sides of the freeway. The lights of the suburbs winked and flashed behind them. Streetlights, the glaring lights of gas stations, the dim yellow lights of houses, lights left on through the night—I caught glimpses of them through the branches and the new leaves.

After a while, I felt Bethany watching me again. I felt she'd been watching me a long time and I hadn't noticed, lost in my own thoughts as I was.

"What," I said.

"Well, I kind of think I get this."

"Get what?"

"All of this. What's happening. I mean, do you really not see it?"

Something in the tone of her voice made me clutch inside. Something tender and knowledgeable in the way she spoke. I knew deep down I didn't want to hear what she was going to say next, but I had to. I had to know.

"What do you mean?" I asked her.

"This is actually kind of funny," she said. "It's like a joke from God or something. I mean, what am I? I'm no big brain. I know that. I wait tables at Sal's. But I get it. And you're the cop, you're the detective and you can't figure it out. And that's it, isn't it? You literally can't. That's the whole point."

I shook my head. "What's the point? The point of what? What are you talking about?" But I felt like I knew what she meant and like I didn't want to know.

"You dreamed Samantha," Bethany said. "You've been dreaming about her all this time, haven't you? And now she's real."

My breathing went shallow. I drove the car over the dark, winding road. I licked my dry lips. "Yeah?"

"The boy too. You saw the ghost of the boy while you were on the drug. And Samantha has his photograph. Which means he was real too."

I worked the wheel, worked the Mustang around a long curve, worked to swallow down the knot in my throat.

"Do you remember when we were talking?" Bethany said. "How we were in bed talking just before you got the call to come to the river? You remember?"

I tried to say *yeah* but the word turned to ashes.

"I asked you what your earliest memory was," said Bethany. "You said it was playing catch with one of your foster fathers."

I tried to say *so what?* but those words turned to ashes too.

"You said he coached Little League and wanted you on his team. You said he was shocked you'd never played catch before."

I turned to her. She was a shadow in the darkness. Only her eyes gleamed. Then she laughed.

"It really is a joke from God. You're the detective, but you can't see it. My nephew's in Little League. Little League is for seven-year-olds. Six at the youngest, but if your foster father was shocked you hadn't played catch, well, then I bet you were probably at least seven, maybe even eight."

I faced the windshield again, my reflection half-blacked out, half-visible. I licked my lips again. I tried to tell myself I didn't understand what she was saying.

"Come on!" said Bethany. "Your first memory is when you were seven or eight? I can remember stuff from when I was, like, three years old. I can remember a wedding I went to when I was four—what the bride was wearing, what the preacher looked like, everything . . ."

I was driving in the left lane, moving fast, close to eighty. I saw a green exit sign by the right side of the road. I swerved across the empty lanes, my hands unsteady on the wheel, my palms damp. I shot the car off the highway, down the ramp, braking hard, slowing. I reached the stop sign at the intersection. Took a right onto the two-lane and pulled over quickly under an oak tree by the side of the road. The tree bowed down out of the pale starry sky and hung over the roof of the car. I sat with Bethany in the deep shadows there, the glow from the dashboard light playing over us. Man, I was exhausted. I hurt. My eyes felt sunken and weak. My lips felt shivery and slack. The scratch on my face burned and ached under the gauze Bethany had taped over it.

Bethany spoke softly out of the darkness. "You're missing three or four years of memory," she said. "That's why you can't see it.

Not seeing it is the whole point of everything—everything you do and say. You don't know who you are, Champ. You don't want to know. That's the whole point of everything." She reached over and touched my arm and I started—I almost jumped back away from her—but her fingers curled gently around my wrist and held on. "Hallucinations don't come to life, Dan. Unless they're not hallucinations. Unless they're memories."

I leaned forward in my seat. I pressed my forehead against the steering wheel, holding the wheel in both hands. I closed my eyes.

"That's the joke," Bethany said. "You're the detective but you can't figure out the answer. Because the answer is you."

Now it was after three A.M. We were sitting in the Gemini Diner on Second Avenue in midtown Manhattan. We were in the last booth. My back was to the wall so I was facing the door but I was staring into my coffee. Bethany was sitting across from me. I could feel her watching me but I didn't look up. I was thinking about everything she had said. It was like I knew it was true but I didn't want to know. It was like I wanted to think about it but I couldn't.

I raised my eyes to her—I guess I was going to try to talk it out. But just then, Monahan pushed in through the glass door.

"Don't tell him," I said.

Then Monahan was standing immensely over us. He gave a short, sharp laugh when he saw the state of me.

"Jesus, Champion."

"They started it."

"How many'd you kill this time?"

"Just one."

"Jesus."

"One thug. Stark slipped me."

"Do I have to worry about a body turning up?"

"Not likely."

Monahan laughed again, not a happy laugh. He jerked his head at Bethany. "Shove over, sweetheart." He slid into the booth next to her. He loomed over her, made her look tiny, made her look like a tourist under the Rock of Gibraltar.

"I'm Bethany," she told him.

Monahan nodded, but he kept his eyes on me. He didn't care who she was. "So it's still you and Stark," he said to me.

I nodded. "He says he'll kill everyone I love."

Monahan's big Irish schoolboy face broke into a big Irish schoolboy grin. "That's a short list, anyway. I know *I* feel safe."

"He asked after you, in fact."

"Thoughtful guy."

"I gave him your address so he could drop you a line."

"Nice."

"A map to your place. Pictures of your kids."

"So I gotta move 'em somewhere?"

"Yeah."

"And you want me to take this one too." He barely tilted his thumb toward Bethany.

"Why not? I figure if you're all together, it'll save Stark travel expenses. I'm all about economy."

Monahan placed his giant paw over his giant forehead. He drew the hand slowly down over his face, as if he were wiping away cobwebs. He leaned in across the table. "How hard would you laugh if I told you to come in with me?"

"Only moderately but for a long time."

Monahan sighed. "Okay." He slapped the tabletop. Slid out of the booth. He said to Beth: "Come on, sister, let's go." She slid out too and stood beside him. He wrapped his paw around her elbow. Made her arm look like a toothpick stuck in a steak. He looked down at me.

"Really, Champ. Come in. Give us what you got. Let us handle it."

"Oh, yeah? So you'll run him to ground in a year or two?"

"We'll get him. It's what we do."

I looked up at him. I thought about it. I thought about what Bethany had said.

I'm afraid of what all the killing will turn you into.

"Right," I said aloud. "You and the NYPD—you'll run Stark down and arrest him."

"The FBI too. This isn't just a New York operation."

"Another couple of years, assuming he doesn't make bail—assuming he doesn't skip bail—you might even manage to put him on trial."

"We'll put him on trial. He's a hired gun. The feds could give him the death penalty."

"Sure, if he's convicted. Then, what, even if he *is* convicted. Fifteen, sixteen years down the line—if he doesn't win an appeal and if the laws don't change—he could have himself a date with the executioner."

"There you go."

"Good plan," I said. I glanced at Bethany. She frowned down at me. I turned back to Monahan.

"Only one problem," I said. "I *am* the executioner."

11

Desperate Measures

I HOLED UP IN a motel in Brooklyn just off the Gowanus Expressway. I didn't bother to get undressed. There wasn't much left of the night. I just kicked my shoes off and lay on top of the bedspread in my clothes. Curtains drawn, room dark. I watched the ceiling. I listened to the traffic, the wash and rumble and roar of the traffic, never ceasing outside the window. I heard Bethany's voice in my head.

You're missing three or four years of memory. That's why you can't see it. Not seeing it is the whole point of everything.

I tried to think about that but somehow I couldn't keep my mind on it. My mind kept drifting. After a while, I was standing outside. I was in the backyard. I was wearing a baseball glove on my left hand, holding a ball in my right. I threw the ball and the Fat Woman caught it. She stared at me—huge, shapeless, featureless, her face a swirl of cancer stains. Her mouth opened. It was a deep black hole.

Have you got him, Stark? she said.

My eyes jerked wide. I heard the traffic on the Gowanus.

That can't be right, I thought. *That was just a dream.*

I turned to look over my shoulder, to make sure I was awake now. I saw an open place surrounded by trees. The sunlight poured down through the branches in hazy beams. Men with shovels were digging holes in the dirt. Dead children slowly stood up in the holes. They stared at me. Alexander was one of them. He stood up in his hole and stared at me too. I watched the dead children, holding the baseball in my hand. I wanted to throw the ball to Alexander but I wasn't sure whether the dead played catch.

My eyes jerked open. Traffic.

That can't be right, I thought. *That had to have been a dream.*

It was a long night. Dream after dream, all bad. Finally I woke to see a glow of daylight under the hem of the heavy curtains. I checked the clock on the bedside table. I was surprised to see it was after 8 A.M.

I swung my legs over the side of the bed. I sat up, groaning. My body was sore all over. I staggered into the bathroom. I looked in the mirror. The face that stared back at me was hollow-eyed, bandaged, bruised. I tugged the gauze off my cheek. A thick black scab covered the cut beneath. The scarred man in the reflection looked at me accusingly.

You don't know who you are.

I turned my back on him. Walked out. Walked across the hotel room. I found the curtain string and pulled it.

The curtains parted and the gray city light poured in over me. I blinked out into it. I saw the motel parking lot. I saw the cars passing on the freeway just beyond, an unbroken, racing parade. There was a faint gray haze in the air, maybe from the highway fumes.

I looked out and thought about the dead children in my dream. I thought about the Fat Woman. Still out there somewhere. Stark too. Still out there. Coming after me. Coming after everyone I loved.

And the only link to them I had was Samantha. A hallucination come to life . . .

Hallucinations don't come to life. Unless they're not hallucinations. Unless they're memories.

But how could I have known her and forgotten her? It made no sense.

You're the detective but you can't see the answer, Bethany had said. *Because the answer is you.*

I have to remember, I thought.

After a while, I turned from the daylight back into the room. I went to the chair in the corner. The manila envelope was there— the envelope I had taken from Samantha Pryor's apartment, from the hiding hole behind the wainscoting. This is what Stark had been looking for. What was it? What did Samantha know?

I removed the sheaf of paper inside and dealt the pages out on top of the bedspread so I could see them all together. I put the snapshot—the faded photograph of Alexander—on the bedside table. I felt him staring at me the whole time.

I hung over the bed, studying the papers.

Most of the pages were printouts of newspaper stories. A lot of the stories were about my old case: Martin Emory and the "House of Evil." The other pages were from legal pads. They were covered in scribbles: doodles, words, numbers lost amidst sketches of faceless people, houses, jagged lines like flames. I made out the words *St. Mary.* I made out the words *New York.* I made out names: *Arnold, William, Jenny.* My eye flashed to the name *Samantha,* the name *Alexander*—but they were there unconnected, like thoughts that had come and gone.

I kept stalking around the edge of the bed, my eyes going over the pages with a hungry, predatory gaze. What did Samantha know? What was she looking for? I picked out other words: *Elm, Sawnee, Pothurst* . . . Street names? Towns? I wasn't sure.

Then I came to one page and saw my own name circled. *Dan Champion.* Scribbled next to it, almost illegible, was my address in Tyler, circled. There were two other addresses I didn't recognize, both crossed out.

She had been looking for me. And she had found me.

What else was she looking for?

Beneath my name was another name and address, also circled: *Franklin Hawthorne, Washington Falls, NY.* I lifted the page in my hand, stared at it, then lifted my eyes and stared at the wall above the bed's headboard. I tried to probe my memory but got nowhere. The name meant nothing to me. I did not know a Franklin Hawthorne from Washington Falls, New York.

It might be a lead, though. Something I could go on. Or maybe not. Whatever it was, it wasn't enough.

I laid the list back on the bedspread. I put my hand over my eyes, massaged my temples. I felt the snapshot of Alexander watching me. What did it all mean? What did any of it mean?

And who was Samantha? What did she have to do with me?

I walked to the window again. I gazed out again at the hazy day. Samantha had the answers. Everything kept circling back to her. It wasn't enough just to follow her leads. Words she'd scribbled on paper. Words that meant nothing without context. I had to know who she was, what she was after, whose side she was on.

I had to remember her . . .

But I can't, I thought. *I can't.*

I lifted my hand. I pressed it against the glass, against the dirty light and the pale sky over the expressway.

There's only one way, I thought. *Only one way.*

I knew what I had to do.

There was a diner next to the hotel. I ate a late breakfast there. It was nearly noon by the time I got in my car.

I drove out to Queens. I got some cash from an ATM. I bought some clothes and an overnight bag. I called some of my old cop friends and scored some fresh ammo for my Glock.

I went to the library. Used one of its computers. Looked up Washington Falls, New York, the name of the town Samantha had scribbled on one of her pages. There was a website; pictures: a small, prosperous-looking upstate town. I couldn't find an address or phone number for Franklin Hawthorne. But I figured in a town that size, if he was there, I'd find him. I would try, anyway.

But not yet.

First, I drove to the shore. I found an empty stretch of road by the quiet waters of Long Island Sound. No one could follow me here without being spotted. I turned off the engine. I peered through the windshield at the tall yellow-green marsh grass stirring and waving in the soft spring breeze.

I thought about what I was going to do. They weren't happy thoughts. It was a desperate idea, a desperate measure. But the Fat Woman was still out there and Stark was still out there. I couldn't just follow some treasure hunt of clues Samantha had left me, not knowing what they meant, not knowing what I was walking into, not even knowing who Samantha was. If Bethany was right, the answer to all my questions was locked inside me, locked inside my mind. It must have been there all this time. All my life, in fact. But I couldn't reach it. I had never reached it.

Or that is, I had reached it only once. By one path. One awful path.

And now I was going to have to take that path again.

Nothing had changed at the Harlem Lounge. A line of drinkers still sat shoulder to shoulder at the bar—for all I knew, it was the same line of drinkers as had sat there three years before. Some were hunched over their glasses, some lifted their faces into the glow of the basketball highlights on late night TV. Each raised his drink to his lips at intervals. They drank with unwavering purpose.

A narrow stretch of open floor ran between their backs and the empty tables. At the end of that narrow corridor, at the end of the bar, where the bar curled around parallel to the bathroom doors—there, as before, sat the dealer, Janks. An open stool, as before, stood beside him. As before, no one looked at me, not even Janks himself, as I planted myself on the seat.

I raised my chin to the bartender. Still the one-eyed man. Still wouldn't show a white junkie anything but his dead socket.

"Think you could get me a beer?" I asked Janks.

Janks raised his index finger a fraction of an inch off the surface of the bar. The one-eyed man saw that somehow. In response, he materialized in front of me. Slapped a glass down on the bar and filled it from a hose.

I watched the yellow liquid swirl into foam. "I was afraid you'd've caught a bullet by now," I said to Janks.

Janks didn't answer until the bartender was gone. "Never happen, my man," he said then. "Even the people who want to kill me need my shit."

I nodded. Probably true. I turned to him. He was the same hungry-looking brown undertaker. Solemn, self-important. The pharmacist of the inferno.

"What can I do you for?" he said.

"You sold me something years ago. To help me sleep. Z, you called it. Zattera."

Janks made a horselike noise, riffling, dismissive. "You don't want that shit. That shit'll kill ya. Government banned that shit."

"What're you, the surgeon general?"

"Just saying. I'm, like, a warning label. What do you want with that shit anyway?"

"It made me see things," I said, staring into my beer. "I need to see those things again."

"Man, I don't know how to break this to you. But that shit you saw? That shit ain't real."

"It was real enough. Just cut the crap and hit me, Janks."

While Janks was in the men's room, I sipped my beer and watched the TV. My stomach churned. I didn't want to do this. But I had to. I had to remember.

Janks plopped his scrawny ass down on the stool next to me. Slid his hand across the bar to mine. I took the Baggie of white pills and he took the money.

"Don't say I didn't warn you," he told me. "That shit'll make you crazy."

"I'm already crazy," I said.

I slipped the bag into my pocket.

★ ★ ★

I stared at that first pill a long time before I worked up the nerve to take it.

I was in another motel by then. North of the city—on the way to Washington Falls—plunked between a burger joint and a gas station off a strip of commercial two-lane. It was close to midnight. The television was on. Some old comedy playing. The laugh track in my ears.

I stared at the white pill on the bedside table.

You're missing three or four years of memory. That's why you can't see it. Not seeing it is the whole point of everything you do and say. You don't know who you are. You don't want to know. That's the whole point of everything.

Ha ha ha, went the laugh track.

I took the pill.

I had forgotten how the Z worked. How easy and natural it was. It didn't feel like taking a drug at all. It just felt like a change in your point of view. There I was, at first all worried, all balled up and twisted inside. Getting off the bed every few minutes to peek out through the curtains into the night. Watching for Stark or another one of his men. Knowing they were out there somewhere, looking for me.

Then, maybe ten minutes later, I just didn't care.

I was lying on the bed again and I wasn't afraid of Stark and I wasn't obsessed with the Fat Woman and I was very philosophical about all the dead children in my dream—very philosophical about everything.

That's just the way it goes sometimes, I was more or less thinking.

Then I was asleep. Suspended in a deep and peaceful nothingness. I only woke up once, startled out of a dream of fire.

Ha ha ha. People were still laughing on the television set, although I guess they were different people than before, laughing at something else.

I found the remote and turned the TV off and went back to sleep in the comforting silence.

In the morning, I drove north. I kept off the highways. The Z made me calmer, but I still felt Stark at my back. I didn't know how close he was or how sophisticated his tracking methods were. The first time he found me was at Samantha's apartment. He might just have guessed I would go there but maybe he could track my credit cards or ATM transactions. I didn't know what he could do.

So I stayed on the two-lane for a while. Then I stopped for gas and bought a sandwich at the minimart. I washed another Z pill down with a Coke. I figured the more I took, the faster it would do what I needed it to do.

I drove another few miles, then got off the two-lane and drove down a winding country road past rolling hills. The hills gave way to a forest, red with new spring branches, and pale green with new spring leaves. I drove through the woods for about twenty minutes. I felt good. I felt calm. But I kept watching the rearview.

Then, suddenly, I caught a glimpse of someone. I turned my head and—yes, there!—a figure was standing in the woods, staring at me as I drove past . . .

I hit the brakes. The tires squealed. The car wove unsteadily onto the road's shoulder, sending up a cloud of dust.

I jumped out into the mild weather. I was wearing jeans, a T-shirt, a windbreaker. I felt the cool of spring on my skin. I walked cautiously back down the road, my hand inside my jacket, my fingers brushing the butt of my gun. There was no sound at all except the breeze through the forest and the distant thrum of an airplane.

I stood and peered into the woods where the figure had been. Nothing there but tangled vines and lacework branches. The sun in hazy beams. No one watching. No one I could see.

The drug, I thought. *It's the drug. It's starting to work.*

I got back in my car and drove on.

Another motel room. I doubled the dose of Z. All my terrors left me and I fell fast asleep.

I was fast asleep several hours later, two hours before dawn, when I heard Stark laughing right beside me.

The sound was so like the slither of a viper that I felt the cold snake-skin coil around my throat and tighten. My eyes flashed open and I went for my gun, but too late—he was already there, standing over me, that skeleton head leaning toward me with its fixed rictus, the silver blade flashing in his white hand . . .

Then, in the next moment, he was gone. The light from the motel sign outside bled in through the thin curtains and I could see that the room was empty. I sat up, my heart hammering hard.

It's the drug. Just the drug.

I hung my head. Drew in a deep breath.

I smelled smoke.

Quickly I turned on the bedside light. I looked around me with wide eyes. There was no smoke, no fire. But I could smell it still.

I got out of bed. I was in my underwear. I padded barefoot into the bathroom. Ran the water in the sink, grabbed some in my hands and splashed it over my face to clear my head.

As the water dripped down, I looked in the mirror. I saw myself, my face unshaven. I saw the black slash on my cheek, still jagged and raw. I saw the frightened look in my eyes.

And I saw the dead child standing behind me.

It was Alexander. He was standing in the room, very still against the far wall. He was wearing a white shirt and dirt-stained corduroys. His skin was as pallid as the shirt, bloodless, lifeless. His stare was lifeless. He was holding a candle in his hand.

He stood and stared at me and I stood staring back. I didn't want to turn around because I knew if I did, he wouldn't be there, he'd be gone. I wanted to keep him there, I wanted to ask him who he was—or who he used to be. I wanted to get the truth out of him.

So I stood and stared at him as he stood there holding his candle. Then something caught my eye. I noticed a hole in the wall behind him, a hole down low against the floor. My glance flicked to it only for a moment, but when I looked up again, Alexander was gone.

I swung around. The room was empty. My eyes went down to the base of the wall, the place where I'd seen the hole. There was no hole there now. But I had seen it.

He hid the candle in there, I thought suddenly. *In the hiding hole behind the wainscoting. A candle and some matches. Because he was afraid of the dark.*

I let a long, slow breath come out of me. I stood with my mouth open, my eyes on the place in the wall.

It was true. Somehow I knew it was true. He hid the candle behind the wainscoting because he was afraid of the dark.

I remembered.

I took more Z. Careless now. I wanted to see more, to know more. I had to.

In the morning, I drove on. I drove for hours on back country roads. Every few minutes, I looked in the rearview to make sure no one was following me.

Once I looked up and the Fat Woman was sitting in the backseat, grinning at me. Her face was melting like wax.

I lost control of the car and it swerved back and forth, tires screaming, before I wrestled it back into the lane.

Now I was on an empty stretch of country road, about ten or fifteen miles from Washington Falls. I was thinking about Franklin Hawthorne. Who was he? Why was Samantha looking for him?

There was birch forest on either side of me, slender white trees with new leaves hanging from their high branches. The midday sun poured down through the open spaces, striped the white bark with gleam and shadow and made the greenery shine nearly gold. There was nothing ahead of me on the road and nothing behind.

I was feeling the drug now. I was dosed up and hazy. The road, the woods, the blue sky up ahead were all covered over with a layer of mist. I couldn't tell whether it was in my mind or outside or where the border was between the two. I remembered that feeling from the last time I'd taken Z.

Sometimes I felt as if I were about to remember other things as well—things I had forgotten for a long time. Sometimes I heard those lost things speaking to me. Whispering.

Don't let them take me . . .

They're not real . . .

I'm afraid of the dark . . .

I strained to draw out the memories, but they wouldn't come. I drove through the birch forest. Then, all at once, my heart lurched. I hit the brakes. The Mustang jolted, screeched, and stopped.

I had seen something. Something back there by the side of the road.

I put the Mustang in reverse and drove backward, weaving over the winding lane. I braked again, stopped again. Looked ahead.

There it was. An old sign. Weathered wood. An arrow pointing down a broken road into the forest. Words nearly faded away: *Old Washington Falls.*

Old Washington Falls, I thought.

I turned the car off the two-lane, and drove into the woods.

The road was broken macadam at first, then dirt. As it descended through the forest, the birch trees gave way to high pines, old oaks, and elms. The taller trees and spreading branches blocked out the sun and made the narrow passage gloomy. Somehow I knew this was the right way.

The mist grew deeper as I drove down the hill. The sun poured through it in hazy beams. Maybe it was in my mind but it seemed to spread through the forest around me. And in the depths of it—in the depths of the mist and the tangled branches and the twining vines and underbrush—I caught glimpses of dark figures, standing very still, watching me as I passed.

I turned this way and that, trying to catch them. But whenever I tried to look at them directly, no one was there.

Just the drug.

I forced myself to face front, to look out the window.

And as I did, the woods fell away and I drove into a ghost town.

There wasn't much left of it. A broad sandy avenue, some patches still paved with asphalt and others where the asphalt had been shattered to gravel. There was the ruin of a clapboard store up ahead of me, the structure slumped, the porch roof fallen aslant. And down the way, there was the ruin of a once stately house: hollow, empty, staring at me through empty windows.

In the trees around, I could see other structures: foundations and piles of stone. In the distance, the road tapered off into a forest trail, and the wild brush and bushes closed over it.

What is this place? I thought. But I felt that I somehow knew.

I pulled the car to the side of the road and killed the engine. I stepped out into the street, feeling the air cool on my damp T-shirt and my damp skin. The mist swirled around the ruined buildings, swirled around the trees, around my feet. I heard whispers in the distance.

I'm afraid ...

Don't let them take me ...

I'm afraid of the dark ...

They're not real ...

I started walking through the mist. Down the avenue toward the big house. My footsteps crunched on the broken road. The sound was loud in the surrounding emptiness. It was the only sound besides the sound of running water—a stream somewhere—and the sound of wind in the branches. There was nothing else. No birds singing. Nothing.

The dead house rose up over me as I approached. There was another road, a remnant of a smaller road, running alongside it, perpendicular to the avenue. There was a street sign planted where the two roads crossed, its pole tilted over, its metal markers rusted.

I stopped by the sign and read it: *Washington Avenue*. That was the name of the main street. Poe Street—that was the side street's name. I understood at once—and I knew I had been right to come here. I had been heading for a different Washington Falls—a new Washington Falls—but this was the one I needed to find. I needed to stand right here, right at the corner of Washington Avenue and Poe Street. I needed to see that the streets were named for American statesmen and writers.

Franklin Hawthorne wasn't a person. It was an intersection. Here in Old Washington Falls.

I turned away from the house. The back of my neck prickled as I felt the house's dark windows staring down at me. I gazed off into the forest and saw the mist coiling itself around the tangled branches. I heard the breeze out there and I heard whispers in the breeze. I saw ghosts—dark figures. I saw them from the corners of my eyes, here and there in the woods, here and there beside the ruined foundations and piles of stone. Just standing there. Just watching me. Each time I turned toward one, he vanished before I could look at him.

They're not real . . .

I'm afraid . . .

That voice. That voice kept whispering. I knew that voice, that whisper. I had heard it before. I had been here before, in this place, in this town . . .

I felt the old house looming over me as I stared into the woods.

You don't know who you are.

I caught a glimpse of another figure in the forest—another dark figure watching me from the mist, from right beside a ruined chimney. I turned toward him, knowing he would vanish when I looked at him directly.

But he didn't vanish. He just went on standing there. A tall, thin man in black jeans and a black windbreaker.

Slowly, he lifted his hand. He was holding a gun.

He wasn't a ghost. He was real. He was one of Stark's killers.

I dove to the dirt just as he opened fire.

★ ★ ★

The bullet thudded into the broken road. Gravel flew up around me. I rolled and leapt to my feet and dove again even as the pebbles showered down. I heard another report as the gunman let off a second round hard on the first—I heard the double-bang and then the cry of birds and the flutter of their wings as they rose from the trees and scattered.

Bent low, I rushed to the side of the house. Pressed close to it, out of the gunman's sight. I drew my Glock and waited for him to appear. Seconds passed. No sign of him. I started to edge away, toward the rear of the house. As I did, the killer appeared across the road. He fired again. There was a liquid *chuck* as the slug entered the house's rotten wood.

I turned and ran. There were two brick steps up ahead of me. They led to a side doorway, the door gone. I leapt up the steps and charged through the open frame into the house before the gunman could let off another round.

It was dark in the old ruin. Dark and filled with mist. It was quiet except for the faint patter of rats scrabbling in the walls. It was quiet outside too, except for the cries of the frightened, circling birds. I gripped my Glock in my sweaty hand. I tried to blink the mist away, but it just grew thicker.

I'm afraid . . .

Don't let them take me . . .

I moved deeper into the house, deeper into the dark. I kept my head low and stayed away from the broken windows.

The place, I saw, was gutted, empty. No furniture, no structures, just rubble surrounded by scarred, peeling walls. I came out of a narrow corridor into a central space, large and open. There were jagged edges here where once there had been dividers and arch-ways. The floorboards were bare, splintered, studded with nails, covered with debris. I kicked through piles of garbage. The rats scattered and vanished as I came.

There was a window up front—a window frame, all the glass long gone. And there was an exit to my right with the door still in it, closed.

I went to the window frame. Knelt by it, pressed to the wall to keep out of sight. I shook my head, still trying to clear away the haze. My lungs were heaving, the breath wheezing in and out of me. Sweat was pouring down my face, dripping off, tap-tap-tapping on the wreckage around my feet. My stomach rolled over. My throat was tight. I couldn't think straight. I couldn't clear my mind.

I curled around the edge of the window frame. Peeked out at the street and at the woods beyond. I caught a quick glimpse of motion out there—but then it was gone. I wasn't sure if it had been the gunman or a ghost. Was the gunman real? How had he found me? The ATM transaction? The credit card I used at one of the motels? Or maybe he hadn't found me at all. Maybe he was just a hallucination too . . .

I drew back out of sight; listened for movements. I thought I heard footsteps outside but I wasn't sure.

Then, suddenly, a whisper at my back.

Don't let them take me . . .

I glanced over my shoulder.

The Fat Woman was standing right there behind me.

I cried out in shock, spun around, and fired wildly at her mutilated face. Plaster flew in a white cloud as the bullet hit the ceiling.

But the Fat Woman had vanished.

The cloud of plaster drifted down to the floor. I gaped at the empty room. I quickly swiped the sweat from my eyes.

She was here, I thought. *I was here. And she was here too.*

A footstep on gravel. I froze. There was another. Just outside. Just behind the house. I held my breath. I listened. But the sound didn't come again. Had I imagined it?

My eyes scanned over the darkness of the empty room. The shadows. The piles of broken wood. Alexander standing in the corner, gazing at me.

I'm afraid of the dark ...

I stared terrified at the dead boy and he stared back at me. Then the shadows engulfed him and he was gone.

I'm going to die in here, I thought. I could feel it.

I had to do something. If there really was a killer out there, I couldn't just wait here for him to charge in and take me. If there wasn't, I couldn't just hide away, afraid of ghosts. I was crazy, drugged up. I didn't know what was real and what was hallucination. But either way, I had to do something.

I edged along the wall, trying to get a better angle on the view outside, trying to see if there was anyone there. The street was empty now as far as I could make out. Maybe I could make a run for my car.

Then—a movement in the room. On one knee, I whipped around, gun leveled. A ghostly figure dissolved into shadow. No one. My eye darted to a noise from the closed door on the wall across from me. I saw a rat scurrying for cover there. Then it was gone. No one.

I stayed where I was, staring at the emptiness. Openmouthed. Sweating. My gun trained on the darkness.

Every day they come for us. There's no way out.

I waited. I listened. I watched.

Whispers. Scrabbling. Half-seen phantoms. Nothing.

I had to get out. I came off my knee. Rose up. Moved quickly to the window.

And there was Stark, standing right outside the house, looking in on me. His skeleton face was jacked wide, his eyes were gleaming. He shrieked—shrieked—and a gout of flame shot from his mouth. Engulfed me.

I cried out, swallowed in flame. I staggered back—so paralyzed with terror I couldn't pull the trigger.

Then the door flew in to the right of me. I spun round and there was the gunman. Still screaming in fear, still surrounded by fire, I loosed a shot at him. He shouted and staggered, his arm flying wide, his pistol falling. I wheeled back in horror and confusion, thinking to see the death-headed flame-spewing Stark bearing down on me from the window . . .

But there was no one there. Just the open frame—a rectangle of daylight.

In a panic, I grabbed the edges of it. Stepped up onto the moldering sill. Pulled myself through and hurled myself into the outdoors. Flying through the air . . .

Then I hit the gravelly sand and went down and rolled and stood again and came face-to-face with the Fat Woman. She was screaming at me and all in flames. I screamed back insanely. Swiped at her with my gun barrel. She dissolved into nothingness.

I ran.

I ran for my car. I didn't know if the gunman was behind me. Had I shot him? Was he dead? Was he even real? I didn't know.

I neared the Mustang. Someone was waiting for me in there. The skull-headed Stark. He was grinning at me through the windshield from behind the wheel. I lifted my gun to shoot him dead but before I could, a bullet sizzled by my ear . . .

I looked over my shoulder and saw the gunman in the house, at the window, aiming at me through the frame. I fired at him and he tumbled back into the house's darkness. I faced forward, ready to blast Stark in the Mustang.

But the car was empty. Stark was gone.

I ran for the car. I looked around me wildly. In the misty woods, there were children everywhere, dead children standing among the trees, in the mist, staring at me.

I reached the Mustang. Yanked the door open. Dropped in behind the wheel.

Stark leapt at me out of the backseat, his flaming fingers reaching for my throat.

I screamed in terror, my arms flailing wildly, but then he was gone. "Christ!" I shouted.

I turned the engine on—hit the gearshift, hit the gas, and wrenched the wheel. The Mustang whirled around on the broken road, throwing up gravel. I straightened it. Jammed my foot down, driving the gas pedal to the floor.

There was a fire, I thought crazily. *That's why I keep smelling smoke. That's why I keep seeing flames. There was a fire in the house.*

I drove as fast as the car would go, back up the broken forest road, the dead children watching me from the mist.

There was a fire, I thought.

I was beginning to remember.

12

Flashback: The Room in the Tower

THE WASHINGTON FALLS library was nestled under a pair of maple trees on a small leafy street off the main road. It was an impressive white stone building with a square tower like something from an old English church. There was a stately white columned mansion on a rolling acre of lawn nearby. There was a sprawling glass and metal schoolhouse across the way.

This was the town I'd seen on the website. The quaint prosperous modern country village ten miles north of the ghost town I'd just left behind.

I parked the Mustang around the corner, alongside the library. I killed the engine and fell back against the seat. I raised my eyes and looked at myself in the mirror.

Jesus, I looked like the walking dead. My skin was the color of cement. My forehead and cheeks were clammy with sweat. My mouth was slack and my eyes . . . unfocused, crazy. Had I just shot another of Stark's killers? Did they know where I was? How could they? Was it all just the drugs, the hallucinations, the fractured memories . . . ?

There was a fire, I thought.

That's why I kept smelling smoke, seeing flames.

There was a fire in the house. And I was there.

And so was Samantha.

* * *

Samantha wore a purple dress. She had curling red hair. Her face was ethereal and gentle. I stole glances at her across the classroom. Sometimes she would look up from whatever project was on her desk. She would lift her face to the sunlight streaming in through the window. She would close her eyes and bask in the warmth of it. The gold light would gleam on her auburn ringlets. I would watch her, breathless.

We were seven years old.

She had an aura of stillness and calm. At recess, she sat in the sandpit. She dug holes and built castles and played with dolls and figures. Sometimes other girls would join her, but she didn't seem to need them. Often she sat alone.

I was drawn to her helplessly. I scrambled up the climbing frame, which was in the sandpit too. I monkeyed my way to the top rung, grabbed it with my two hands.

"Hey, Samantha!" I called.

When she looked up, I lifted my feet up over my head, standing on my hands upside down.

"Watch this!" I said.

I swung my legs down through my arms and sat on the bars again, then pitched off backward until I was hanging by my knees.

Samantha watched me from the sand below, shading her eyes from the sun with one hand.

"I'll bet you can't do this!" I shouted to her.

I swung myself up until I was sitting on the top bar again and then slowly stood, balancing up there with my arms stretched out on either side of me.

"You're going to break your stupid head if you're not careful," Samantha said.

I was thrilled to hear her say that. She was worried about me. She cared about me. I squatted quickly and grabbed the bar and flipped myself around—very nearly braining myself on the bar beneath—and flew out into the air. I landed whump in the sand beside her, posed in a dynamic crouch I'd seen the heroes use in comic books.

Samantha's eyes were wide. Her lips were pressed tight together.

"What's the matter?" I said. "Scared I'd hurt myself?"

"I don't care if you kill yourself," she said.

But she had to lower her face to hide the fact that she was blushing.

Given the ancient look of the stone façade, the library was surprisingly bright and clean inside. Tidy blond-wood chairs at tidy tables with a blond-wood finish, a row of carrels with computers and microfilm readers, all surrounded by stately shelves of books.

Behind the front desk just within the entrance sat a woman about my age. She was tidy and stately too. She had frosted blonde hair and wore a more or less colorless skirt suit. According to the nameplate on her desk, her name was Mrs. Bell. She looked at me the way I guessed her settler ancestors looked at the Indians who dropped over for dinner red and naked except for their tomahawks. I didn't blame her. I knew what I looked like.

"Can you tell me about the old town?" I asked her. "Old Washington Falls? The ghost town I saw a few miles south?"

I was distracted and didn't really listen to her answer. I was thinking about the little girl digging in the sand. Samantha. And me on the high bars of the climbing frame.

Watch this!

I could feel a sort of mental dam breaking inside me, the memories flooding through. I had gotten it started, yet now I wanted it to stop. But it was too late.

"... then when they built the new highway, the population shifted and the old town died," the woman said. She had a crisp, distant voice like a recorded tour in a museum. "The old property is part of the wildlife management area now. The state runs it. Not that anyone ever comes through but the occasional ghost hunter or television reporter, that sort of thing."

I nodded, thinking about the little girl lifting her face to the light, her red hair gleaming.

"Is there a local paper from back then?" I asked her. "You know, *The Washington Falls Gazette* or something like that?"

"*Recorder,*" Mrs. Bell said with only the faintest smile. "*The Washington Falls Recorder.* It goes back over a hundred and fifty years. It's not in the computers yet, but we have most of it on microfilm. Is there something you were looking for in particular?"

"A fire," I told her. "Thirty years or so ago. A fire in the old town."

In the orphanage, they kept the girls and boys separate. But in school, Samantha and I could be together. Especially at recess, out in the playground, I would find her where she was sitting alone in the sandpit, building castles, playing with dolls and figures.

I stood on my hands and walked in circles around her. She pretended not to notice. I finally tumbled down into the sand and sat beside her. She went on digging.

"You have to be really strong to do that, you know," I said.

"I know," she said as if it didn't matter to her one bit how strong I was.

"I'm really fast too. I win, like, every race."

"I know," she said again.

"You ever see me racing?"

"Maybe sometimes. I'm here, after all. You shouldn't brag, you know."

"I'm not bragging. Why are you always building sand castles?"

"I just do, that's all."

"You do it, like, all the time."

"They're part of my stories, that's why."

"What stories?"

"Just stories I tell."

"Tell to who?"

"Just to myself."

"Well, like what?" There was a silver knight figure mounted on a white horse—it lay on its side in the sand under the castle. I picked the figure up and made it charge around. "Like about knights and dragons?"

"Not dragons exactly," said Samantha. "But a terrible beast. At night, the handsome knight was climbing in the princess's window to visit her. Because he loved her. But the king, her father, caught him and put him in the dungeon and in the morning he was going to feed him to the beast."

"Well, that's stupid—wasn't the knight strong enough to break out?"

"He was in chains. No one is strong enough to break chains."

"Well, what did the king do that for?"

"Because he wanted his daughter to marry a prince from another country."

"Oh."

"But the princess loved the knight, so when everyone was asleep, she snuck down past the guards into the dungeon. She had to be very careful because if the king caught her, he would put her in the dungeon too, even though she was his own daughter. You see, the princess knew a magic spell that would help the knight fight the beast . . ."

I sat cross-legged on the sand beside her, mesmerized—by the story and by her voice and by the sight of her white, white hands working on the castle.

"In the morning, the guards brought the knight up into the castle court-yard . . ." she said.

I watched her hands. I could picture the knight and I could picture the beast waiting to devour him and I could picture the pink princess fretting in the bleachers. I was so wrapped up in it that a long moment passed before I realized Samantha had stopped talking.

Then I did realize. I looked up. Samantha had gone straight and stiff and still. She was gazing over my shoulder into the distance. Her calm, ethereal face was taut and alert.

"What's wrong?" I asked her.

"There she is again."

"Who?"

But even as I asked, I twisted around to follow Samantha's gaze. I looked to the edge of the playground, to the diamond link fence that bordered the parking lot, to the figure on the other side of it.

"That fat woman," Samantha said. "Over there."

"Oh, yeah. I see her. What about her?"

"She keeps coming back. She keeps watching us. She's been watching us for days."

I sat at a carrel with a big old relic of a reading machine hovering vulturelike above its partitions. I pressed the button, scrolling the microfilm through, watching the editions of *The Washington Falls Recorder* flash past. Now and then I had to pause to wipe the sweat off the side of my face. My stomach was queasy. I felt the mist gathering around me as the memories flooded my mind . . .

She keeps coming back. She keeps watching us . . .

My God. How had I forgotten? All this time. More than thirty years.

I scrolled through the *Recorder*. It was quick work. It was a small paper without much news in it. Anything that happened out of the ordinary made the front page. Inside, it was all pancake breakfasts and charity picnics and weddings.

The library door came bursting open. Lost in my search, I was startled by the suddenness of it. I nearly jumped out of my chair, twisting toward the door, my hand slipping inside my windbreaker to my holstered gun. But it was just kids—a bunch of kids just out of school. They came barging in, shouting. Their babysitter—a cheerful pie-faced brunette teen—followed behind them, telling them to hush. The brunette gave a wave to Mrs. Bell behind her desk. But the librarian sat frozen, staring at me, aghast. Her stern, widened eyes were trained on the bulge of my hand inside the windbreaker . . .

I let out a long breath and brought my hand out of my jacket and settled down again behind the microfilm machine. I tried to ignore Mrs. Bell's stare. I pressed the button again and scrolled through the *Recorder*.

And there, all at once, it was.

Even though I had been searching for it, the sight hit me hard. I felt the library telescope in and out around me. I felt the mist grow so thick it nearly blotted out the world. I stared dully at the paper's headline:

"One Dead in House Fire."

Thirty years ago. But I could still smell the smoke.

"Daniel, wake up now. Wake up and get dressed. You have to come with me."

What time was it? Too early to wake up. Still dark—but with some faint gray sense of dawn bleeding into the blackness. Night, just before morning.

"Wake up now, Daniel. You have to get dressed. Come on, hurry up."

What was the woman's name—the one who woke me? The Night Monitor—that's what we called her. A sullen woman with very dark brown skin and a baleful yellowish glare. Rubbing my eyes sleepily, I followed her gray slacks down the dormitory hallway.

"Where are we going?"

"You're getting a new home. Isn't that nice?"

That woke me up all right. My gut was suddenly churning with all kinds of emotions—hopes and anxieties.

"What about my stuff?"

"It's gonna be sent on to you. Don't worry. Everything will be taken care of."

"But how will you know where to send it?"

"We'll know. Don't worry. Hurry up now. There's a very nice lady waiting for you outside. She's gonna take you to your new mommy and daddy."

In the confusion of my thoughts and worries, I wondered about Samantha. Would she and I still go to the same school? Would I still be able to see her? But before I could ask, we reached a door—a side door down a side hallway—one of those doors that I knew, that all the children knew, were always locked, were never to be used.

But the Night Monitor had the key. She unlocked the door and pushed it open. The cold night air washed over me.

There was an alley outside. A car sat in the darkness, the engine running. Its headlights beamed at me, making me squint and recoil. Holding up my hand to shield my eyes, I peered through the glare.

The Fat Woman stepped out of the white glow. She was holding Samantha by the hand.

I don't know what I was about to ask, but the sight of them shut me up. The look on Samantha's face—the stark, deadpan terror there—that more than anything made me clamp my lips closed tight to keep all my questions in. I could tell right away that something was horribly wrong.

The Night Monitor put her hand on the small of my back and gently pushed me forward.

"Come on, Daniel. Hurry up. This is the lady who's going to take you to your new home."

The Fat Woman leaned down toward me. Her broad, bland face with its ballooning cheeks blocked out everything, every other sight and every thought I had.

"Hello, Daniel. You can call me Aunt Jane."

She extended her free hand to me. I stared helplessly at Samantha, who stared helplessly back. My hand lifted as if under its own power and I watched as if from a distance as the Fat Woman's hand engulfed it. Her skin felt cool, dry, taut: reptilelike.

"Now then. Off we go."

She turned and walked the two of us to her car.

She drove us a long way, a long time, hours and hours. The sun came up on fields and forests. Light and the shadows of branches intermingled on the windshield. I could see through the windshield because she made me sit up front while Samantha sat in the back. Samantha and I couldn't talk to each other without the Fat Woman hearing us, so we didn't talk at all. And the Fat Woman didn't talk. She played classical music on the radio. Other than that, we traveled in silence.

I daydreamed. It was a way to escape my feeling of helplessness and my fear. I daydreamed about meeting my new parents, about having a house with a lawn and a dog and my own baseball glove. Deep down, I did not believe that this was going to happen, but in my helplessness, what else could I do but daydream and try to believe my daydreams would come true.

On we drove.

At some point, the Fat Woman gave us sandwiches—peanut butter and jelly—and a small carton of milk. At some other point, she stopped at a gas station and let us use the restrooms, first me, then Samantha. Once, as we were driving, I turned from looking out the window and caught her studying me. She smiled. It chilled my blood.

The car finally turned into the driveway of a house and stopped. I bent forward and craned my neck to look up through the windshield. The house was a weird, looming gray Victorian with a conical-roofed turret that blocked out the sky.

The sight of it made me weak with terror . . .

★ ★ ★

One Dead In House Fire.

Five-year Washington Falls resident Sadie Trader died Wednesday when her three-story house burned to the ground, Washington Falls Police reported. The cause of the fire is still under investigation.

Oswald Packer, spokesman for the Washington Falls Fire Department, said neighbors reported the blaze shortly before 10:30 Wednesday night. When firefighters arrived at the residence on the corner of Franklin Avenue and Hawthorne Street, he said, the house was already engulfed in flames. Efforts to enter the house were impeded by thick smoke. Firefighters worked for nearly half an hour before they were able to reach the upstairs room and recover Mrs. Trader's body. She was pronounced dead on arrival at St. Mary's Hospital in nearby Sawnee.

The 34-year-old Mrs. Trader was the widow of financier Jonathan Trader. Locals described her as a quiet resident known for her charitable activities.

"She wasn't what you would call a social butterfly," said neighbor Paula Ardmore. "But she was extremely generous to all the charities and causes in town and I know she did a lot of giving on the national level too."

As of press time, the exact cause of Mrs. Trader's death had not yet been determined, according to Washington Falls medical examiner Adam Longstreet . . .

I stared down at the microfilmed story. At the photograph of the house. That looming gray Victorian with its conical-roofed turret. I remembered.

This is the lady who's going to take you to your new home.

Seeing that house again—that photograph of the house—I felt the same helpless weakness of fear I had felt all those years ago. There was fresh sweat suddenly on my neck and temples. A curling green mist of nausea spread inside me, making my skin go cold. The mist seemed to flow out of me and wind around me through the room.

I stood up quickly—unsteadily. My chair scraped, the sound shockingly loud in the quiet library. I could feel Mrs. Bell staring at me as I charged past the shelves toward the men's room in back. I didn't care. I had to get away.

I slammed through the bathroom's red door. I pushed quickly into one of the stalls. It took me three tries to get the stall door closed and latched shut. Then I dropped the lid of the toilet with a bang and sat down heavily on top of it. I leaned forward and brought my trembling hands up to cover my face.

You don't know who you are. You don't want to know.

They were Bethany's words.

It really is a joke from God. You're the detective but you can't see the answer. Because the answer is you.

All these years. All those memories. Not only had I shut them out, I'd somehow shut out even the fact that I'd shut them out. Until Bethany spoke those words to me, I had not even noticed how much of my childhood I had forgotten.

And at the same time, it was always there inside me. I knew it now. The terrible truth was all always there.

The Fat Woman labored up the winding stairs. Samantha and I followed—followed the massive and tremulous expanse of her backside in her shapeless brown dress. We heard the wheeze of her breathing as she took step after slow step—such slow steps that we children had to wait behind her until she recovered from the effort and moved again. We looked at each other. I knew that the blank terror on Samantha's face was on my face too. I wished I was a superhero who could do something, but I couldn't think of anything to do. The Fat Woman kept climbing and we just kept climbing after her. She didn't have to hold our hands or push us or threaten us. Where could we run? Who would we run to? There was no place, no one. We were powerless. We just climbed the stairs.

We reached a small landing. A wooden door. There was a heavy metal bolt above the knob. I stared up at that bolt and understood: This was the door to a prison cell.

I looked on helplessly as the Fat Woman lifted the bolt with her fat fingers and slid it back. She pulled open the door and smiled down at us.

"This will be your room until your new parents come for you."

As she stood over us, watching, Samantha and I walked into our prison as if we were asleep, as if our bodies were operating on their own power and we had no wills of our own. We stood side by side as the door shut behind us. We heard the heavy bolt slide back into its slot.

We were in a small, dark, room with curving walls, more oval than circular. The conical roof was above us, open to the high rafters. It gave the place an oppressive vastness.

A boy about our age was standing directly before us. He was small and pale in his white shirt and dirty brown corduroy pants. His eyes were as wide as ours and as frightened. He was breathing hard, as if we'd startled him. He let out an extravagant sigh of relief, his shoulders sagging.

"Whew! I thought she was coming for me *that time!"*

My eyes traveled around the place. There were six beds, three on one side, three on the other with an aisle between. There were three or four ragtag stuffed animals lying abandoned in various places on the board floor. A one-armed GI Joe lay curled around a bed leg. There was a bathroom at the far end on the right. And there were two windows high on the wall—just where the roof began. The windows were too high to reach. There were grates over the glass.

It's like a cage, I thought.

I could see tree branches and the blue sky through the wires: the free world, the lost world out there.

"I'm Alexander," said the boy in the white shirt.

"I'm Samantha."

"I'm Dan. What happens when she comes for you?"

"Isn't she going to take us to our new homes?" Samantha asked. I could tell she didn't really believe that any more than I did.

Alexander gave a slow shake of his head, full of misery and self-pity. He shivered and hugged himself as if an icy breeze had blown through the place. But there was no breeze. The air in the room was old and warm and sour.

"They pretend to be mommies and daddies. But they're not real."

I stuck my chin out at him, aggressive. "Who? What do you mean?"

"The people who come for us. They're not real. They take you away. But not to real homes."

"Where do they take you then?" I challenged him.

He shrugged miserably.

"Well, then how do you know they're not real?"

"I can tell, that's all," Alexander said sadly.

He went over to one of the beds and sat down on it, forlorn. There was a stuffed puppy atop the thin blanket. The toy's fabric was torn and the stuffing was bleeding out of it. Alexander pulled it close to his leg and fiddled with it, as if he wanted to hug it tightly but was too embarrassed to do it in front of us.

"There were five of us before," he said. "Then there were three more: Alan and Billy and Sarah. They came later. Every day the grown-ups would come for us and take one of us away. Sometimes two of us. I'm all that's left from the last group. So I guess I'm next."

I saw Samantha's lips trembling. She made a little noise and began to cry. "Danny, I'm afraid. I'm so afraid."

I'd never seen her cry before. It burned in me like acid. I stepped toward Alexander with my fists clenched.

"This is stupid. You're stupid. You don't know anything. How do you know?"

He toyed with the puppy, plucking at its stuffing. "When Jody was still here, I stood on his shoulders. Jody was tall. He could boost me up and I could see out the windows. I could see them."

"See who?"

"The grown-ups. The ones who took Linda away and the ones who took Craig and Alan. Then Billy. Sarah and Charlotte were last but I couldn't see who took them because . . . they took Jody before that . . . So I couldn't stand on his shoulders anymore. I couldn't reach the window."

Samantha sobbed, covering her mouth with her hand.

I bore down angrily on Alexander. "Yeah, but how do you know they weren't real parents? That doesn't even make any sense."

Alexander shrugged his narrow shoulders. "I just know, that's all."

"Well, that's stupid."

Crying, Samantha's voice was terrible. "It's not stupid, Danny! He's right! I know he's right!"

I turned to stare at her. My balled fists began to come undone. It went through my mind that she couldn't know either—she had less reason to know than this Alexander character did. But Samantha's word had such authority with me that my objections died before I could even speak them.

"That woman, Danny," she said now. "You just have to look at her. She's so horrible. You can see she's not really nice."

I stared at her another second, hoping to find some argument, some answer. But I knew Samantha had simply had the courage to say out loud what I didn't even want to think. I knew I just couldn't face the truth the way she had.

"You've got to do something, Danny," Samantha said.

Alexander lifted his mournful gaze from the stuffed puppy. "What can he do?"

"You've got to help us, Danny," Samantha pleaded. "You've got to."

Alexander turned his eyes from her to me. "What's he gonna do? He's just a kid like us."

"Danny?" said Samantha. "No. Danny is strong. He's so strong. He can stand on his hands on the high bar. You should see! And he's fast too, fast as anything. No one can run faster than he can."

Alexander shrugged. "What good is that? They're grown-ups. And anyway, we're locked in here."

"No, but Danny is stronger than anyone," Samantha insisted. "Really. You should see. And . . . and she has to come up here sometime. Doesn't she? She has to come and get us, right? Maybe . . . maybe you could hit her, Danny. Maybe you could knock her down and run away and get help. You can do something. Can't you, Danny? I know you can."

Alexander stood up off the bed. He stood close beside me. He touched my elbow.

"*Listen,*" he said. "*Don't let them take me, will you? She's coming for me next. I know she is. Don't let them take me.*"

I looked at him—at his eyes—and at her—at her tears—at their faces, one and then the other, both of them turned toward me.

"*Help us, Danny,*" said Samantha. She was starting to cry again. "*You've got to.*"

I was in the library bathroom. In the stall, sitting on the toilet lid. Sweating . . . my head filled with mist . . . the room filled with mist.

I slid one trembling hand under my arm and grasped my gun. I told myself not to draw the weapon, but I drew it anyway. I told myself to holster it again, but instead I rested its barrel against my forehead. I felt the edge of the bore against my skin, cold and black. I felt my finger curl itself around the trigger. I wasn't really going to fire the thing—was I? I just wanted to blow those memories away, to blow them back into the darkness they came out of.

Help us, Danny!

I couldn't bear to remember what happened next, but I couldn't make it stop.

Night fell. Alexander wept.

The darkness in the tower room was thick. There were no lights here, none at all. Only the faintest glow—maybe from a streetlamp outside, maybe from the moon—came in through the windows, making shapes and shadows dimly visible.

Still wearing my clothes, I lay on one of the beds. Samantha was on the next bed over. Alexander was on the bed opposite. His sobbing and sniveling was loud and steady.

"*Knock it off already, would you?*" I said.

"*I can't help it. I'm afraid.*"

"*I'm afraid too, Danny,*" said Samantha.

At the small sound of her voice, I had to fight back tears myself.

"*We're all afraid,*" I said. "*But what good is crying?*"

"I can't help it," Alexander said again.

I tried to ignore him. I tried to think. I tried to come up with a plan of escape. I kept telling myself there had to be a way, but there was no way I could think of. Pretty soon, I was just daydreaming about it. I fantasized that our teacher, Mrs. Burke, would deduce that something was wrong and call the police . . .

But Alexander's sobbing broke in on my thoughts.

"Would you stop it?" I said.

"I told you I can't help it. I'm sorry. It's the dark. I'm afraid of the dark. I'm always afraid of the dark."

"Well, we can't do anything about it, all right?"

"Don't be mean to him, Danny. He's just scared," said Samantha.

"Well, I know that. I'm just saying. There's nothing we can do."

I lay there with my hands behind my head. I stared up grimly into the vast dark spaces beneath the roof. I thought if only Alexander would stop his crying I might be able to think of a way to get out of here. It was easier to blame him than to admit there was nothing I could do.

After a while, Alexander spoke through his tears. "I do have something that might help me. But you have to promise not to tell."

"What do you mean?" I said.

"We won't tell, will we, Danny?" said Samantha.

"Of course not. Who would we tell? What are you talking about?"

I heard the springs squeak as Alexander got off his bed. I sat up and watched his small shadow moving cautiously through the darkness. I heard Samantha's blanket rustle and made out the shape of her—sitting up too, watching too.

"What are you doing?" I asked him.

Alexander squatted down in a corner. Curious, I got out of bed and felt my way around the other beds until I was standing over him. A moment or two later, Samantha was there too, standing beside me. We watched as Alexander fiddled with the wooden panel low on the wall.

"I brought this from my stepmother's house," he said, speaking in a whisper now. "I had to hide it there too so she wouldn't find it. I have a good way of hiding things. I thought of it myself. Sometimes the wood's stuck on too hard but sometimes . . ."

I squatted down near him so I could see him better. Samantha crouched beside me. We peered through the darkness as Alexander worked his fingers into a short section of wainscoting at the base of the floor.

"If you can get one of these short ones off and make a hole in the wall behind it, no one can see it's there. No one ever looks."

He pried the panel away, revealing the small hole he had made in the plaster behind it. Samantha and I looked on, fascinated, as he fished with his fingers inside the hole and finally brought something out of it.

"What is it?" Samantha asked.

It was a package of some kind. Tinfoil—the faint light gleamed on it. Alexander laid it on the floor and we could hear it crinkle as he unfolded it. He lifted something up to show us. I couldn't make it out.

Now I asked: "What is it?"

Even as I spoke, there was a soft scrape, a hissing flare, and then—then a blinding, startling flame. Alexander had struck a match—a small paper match from a nearly empty matchbook. Anxiously and with trembling fingers, he held the flame to all that was left of a candle, the last thin white disc of wax. The fire passed from match to wick. It faltered. We all caught our breath. But it held and steadied: a teardrop of orange-blue light.

It was wonderful. Just a little dome of pale white brightness encircling a central flame, but somehow it filled me with hope, and with something else—defiance. The dim, quavering glow brought Alexander's tearstained face and Samantha's small and frightened features out of the surrounding blackness and I could see the fire had sparked the same emotions in them.

"Cool," I said.

"We can't let it burn too long," whispered Alexander. "There's not much left. But sometimes ... sometimes it helps just to see it for a minute ..."

"Yeah," I said. "It does."

"You were really smart to hide it there, Alexander," said Samantha.

He beamed with pleasure. "I thought of it at my stepmother's. She always made me sleep in the dark."

"You don't have a lot of matches left," I said.

"I know. Only three. I have to find more somewhere. I have to. Another candle too. Maybe there'll be one wherever they take me."

"Sure," I said, feeling hopeful. "It's not like they're gonna take us to a dungeon or something. There's gotta be something there."

"That's right," said Alexander, his eyes bright. "There's gotta be, doesn't there? It won't just be a dungeon."

We all gazed at the flame in hopeful silence.

"Well . . ." said Alexander. "I guess I better blow it out now."

"Okay. Sure."

"Yes. You better save it."

But he hesitated and he and Samantha and I all stared at the flame, savoring the light.

Then Alexander blew and the fire went out and Samantha's face vanished and Alexander's face vanished and the deep, deep blackness of that tower room folded over all of us.

I sat slumped on the stall toilet. I'd lowered the gun from my head now. I cradled it against my chest with my two hands. I stared through the mist—in my mind, in the bathroom—and saw the children locked in that tower. I saw myself as a little boy and could feel everything the little boy felt: the fear and the helplessness—and the shame, more than anything, I felt ashamed that I was helpless.

Like the memories themselves, that had also been there inside me all along.

Alexander carefully wrapped the candle up in its tinfoil. He carefully hid it away again in the hole behind the wainscoting and replaced the panel. We all three went back to our beds and lay quietly in the dark, clutching our little courage to us. Alexander didn't cry anymore.

I lay atop the bedding, my hands behind my head. With new determination, I tried to think of some plan, some means of escape. But it was impossible. Soon I was fantasizing again, daydreaming I had a gun or that I had superpowers and could break free and fly to the rescue, or that I was the brave knight in one of Samantha's stories or one of her magical wizards with lightning blasting from my fingertips . . .

Oh, Danny, you saved us, thank you, thank you. I knew you could do it . . .

Then suddenly, the bolt was clanking back. The tower room door was opening. The dim gray light of dawn was spreading from the high windows through the room. My eyes jacked open and my heart hammered as I realized: In the middle of my fantasies, I had fallen asleep.

I sat up quickly, rubbing my eyes. There was the Fat Woman, a massive blackness in the faint morning. She lumbered into the room, smiling thinly. I felt a surge of fear: She might be coming for Samantha . . . She might be coming for me . . . But even as the thoughts formed in my mind, she waddled over to stand beside Alexander's bed.

"Wake up, Alexander. Rise and shine. Your new father is here to take you home."

Samantha was awake now too, sitting up. We both watched Alexander as he slowly got out of bed with the Fat Woman hovering over him. He wasn't crying now. He was past crying. His pale face was a mask of grief and despair. His wide, frightened eyes gleamed darkly. He stood in his bare feet and looked across the room at me. He didn't say anything. He didn't have to. I remembered the words he'd spoken yesterday, quiet by my side:

Don't let them take me, will you?

The Fat Woman's broad, pasty face flickered with a brief, perfunctory smile.

"Put your shoes on now. Then go to the bathroom and make pee-pee. You have a long drive ahead of you to your new home."

Samantha and I watched helplessly as Alexander did as he was told. He sat on the edge of the bed, tying his shoes reluctantly, as if he could stall off the moment of departure forever. But soon he was done and was trudging to the bathroom. The Fat Woman busied herself straightening the covers on his bed. When she was done, she stood looking down at me and Samantha. She gave us the same perfunctory flicker of a smile.

"After he's gone, I'll bring you some nice breakfast. Your new parents won't be here until tomorrow."

Alexander came out of the bathroom. He shuffled back across the room, barely lifting his feet from the floor. I got out of bed as he passed me as if there were something I might do. Our eyes met. I tried to stare some courage

into him. He turned away. As he went past his bed, he reached out for the
torn stuffed puppy he had been clutching in his sleep. But before he got a
full grip on it, the Fat Woman pulled it gently but insistently out of his
hands and set it back on the blanket.

"Let's leave that for the next children, why don't we? There'll be plenty
of toys for you at your new home."

That broke through Alexander's fog of grief and fear. His lips trembled.
He began to cry.

"I don't want to go!"

He appealed to her—he appealed to all of us—with everything in him.
But Samantha and I could do nothing. And the Fat Woman . . .

"Oh, now, don't be silly," she said. "You're going to have a wonderful new
life. Say good-bye to your friends now. Don't keep your new father waiting."

She took him by the hand as if kindly. She led him to the door. I stood
and watched. Samantha sat and watched, clutching her fists under her chin.

Just as they reached the door, Alexander turned and looked back at me
over his shoulder. He didn't say anything. He only bit his lip, the tears
running down his cheeks.

I wanted to run to his aid, to rescue him. I wanted that more than
anything. But I couldn't. I didn't. I just stood there.

And then he was gone.

That look in his eyes—that final moment before the door swung
shut—*Don't let them take me, will you:* That's what I had spent my
whole life forgetting. I had stood there and watched him go and
didn't do a thing to help him.

I bent forward on the toilet seat. My gun in one hand, I covered my face with the other. I cried, the tears running through
my fingers.

I'm sorry, I thought, *I'm sorry!*

I was so ashamed.

The moment the door closed on Alexander, I raced to the wall beneath
the window. Desperate to do something, anything, I leapt up twice, trying
to snag the grate with my fingers. It was impossible, out of reach.

"Samantha, come here, help me."

She jumped out of bed, hurried to my side.

"What can I do?"

"Make a stirrup. Boost me."

Small and fragile as she was, she bent down and linked the fingers of her little hands. I stepped into the stirrup.

"C'mon—up!"

I jumped at the same moment she tried to lift me and her rising hands gave me the extra boost I needed. I got the first joints of two fingers through the lowest wire and held on. Ignoring the cutting, excruciating pain, I hauled myself up the wall. Caught the grate in my other hand, and dragged myself up the grid of wires hand over hand. Already the strength in my arms was failing, but for a second or two, I managed to pull myself up to the window, managed to hold the position and peek through.

I looked down through the grate. I saw the man waiting for Alexander in the driveway below. Then my strength gave out. I gasped and lost my grip. I dropped to the floor, stumbling away from the wall.

Samantha followed after me.

"Did you see them?" she asked eagerly. "Did you see the people who came to take him? Did they look like parents?"

I stood openmouthed but silent. I couldn't bring myself to tell her the truth, but I couldn't hide it from her either.

Alexander had been right. The man I had seen standing in the driveway below was no father, no one's father. Standing in bright-eyed anticipation by his large, dark car. Flabby-faced, self-satisfied, rotten. Even my little boy's eyes could see his foulness and degeneracy.

My stare met Samantha's, and she understood.

"Danny!" Her voice cracked. She pressed her fists against her mouth. She looked so pitiful and frightened, I had to look away. "Poor Alexander!" she said. "He was so scared." She cried with pity for him—and with fear. Her words came out brokenly through her sobs. "Maybe it'll be all right. Maybe he was wrong. Maybe we're going to nice new homes like the woman says."

I nodded miserably. "Maybe."

"*But why wouldn't she let him take the puppy? All he wanted was to take the puppy. We didn't mind. Why couldn't she just let him take it?*"

I didn't answer. I didn't know what to say.

"*He just looked so scared, Danny.*"

"*I know,*" I said. "*And he's so afraid of the dark, you know, and he forgot to take . . .*"

I didn't finish. I turned to look at the hiding place, the wainscoting. Samantha, still crying, turned to follow my gaze.

"*The candle!*" she said. "*That's right. He forgot to take the candle. Poor Alexander. He hates the dark. He'll be so afraid, he'll . . . What? What is it, Danny? Why do you look like that? What's the matter? What . . . ?*"

She fell silent as I pressed a finger to my lips.

We could already hear the Fat Woman's footsteps laboring slowly back up the stairs.

Slowly, I stood up. My hand hung at my side, holding my Glock. I stared at the door of the bathroom stall, but I didn't really see it. I saw the mist. I saw the past through the mist.

I murmured to myself, "We'll wait until after dinner."

The Fat Woman brought us breakfast: peanut butter and jelly sandwiches and milk. Paper plates, paper cups on a tray. She put the tray on a chair.

"*Here's some delicious breakfast for you.*"

Her voice was deep, coarse, toneless. Another perfunctory smile, and she was gone.

Samantha and I sat on the floor with the plates of food between us.

"*She doesn't even pretend to be nice,*" Samantha said bitterly. "*Not really.*"

I chewed my sandwich. It tasted like ashes in my mouth, ashes with the consistency of leather. I stared into space. "*She doesn't have to,*" I said. I heard my voice coming out of me as if it were someone else speaking. It didn't even sound like me. It sounded dead—dead and somehow fervent at the same time. "*She doesn't have to pretend. She knows we can't do anything. We're just kids. She knows we can't fight her. She can say she's* taking us to our new parents and she doesn't even try to make it sound real because she knows we'll believe her. Because we have to. We'll believe her and just sit here and just go with her like he did, like Alexander."

"Stop, Danny," Samantha said with tears in her voice. "You're scaring me."

I looked at her. She froze. I could see she was afraid of me, afraid of what she saw in my face.

"No," I said. "No. That's good. That's gonna help us."

"What is?"

"She doesn't think we'll fight back. That's gonna help us now." I turned away from her, back to my sandwich. I took another bite, chewing and chewing the leathery tasteless mash. "She thinks we won't do anything. She thinks we can't. She thinks we'll just sit here. That's how we'll get her."

"We can't, Danny. What can we do? If we try to run away, she'll kill us."

"I don't care. I don't care if she does kill us. I'd rather be killed than just go with her."

"What about me? Do you want me to be killed too?"

That brought me out of my own thoughts. I looked at her again. I saw that all the lofty beauty of her face was gone. Her features were scrunched and wrinkled and old with fear.

"No," I said. "I don't want you to be killed. But do you want to just sit here? Do you want to just go with her like he did?"

She licked her lips, uncertain, her eyes moving this way and that. "Maybe—maybe it won't be so bad. Where do you think they'll take us? What do you think they'll do to us?"

I didn't answer. I didn't really know, not in any clear way. But we both knew without knowing somehow. We knew enough.

Samantha began to cry again, trying to hide it, choking it back. The tears streamed down her cheeks as she nibbled at her sandwich.

I watched her miserably. "I won't do it if you don't want me to, Samantha. I don't want to just go. I'd rather die than just go. But if you don't want me to . . . Well, I'll do whatever you say."

She swallowed hard. She was trembling—so badly she could barely speak. She wiped her dripping nose with the back of her hand.

"No," she said. "No. If you think it's right, we'll do it. I'm just scared, that's all. I'm so scared I can't make up my mind. But you're brave. You decide."

"I'm not brave."

"Yes, you are!"

"I didn't do anything for Alexander. She took him away and I just stood there."

"Because it wasn't fair! It wasn't fair, Danny! She's so big and we're just kids. She's a grown-up. But you are brave, Danny. I know you are. Do it. Really. I mean it. I want you to. I do."

"Really?" I said.

"Yes. You'll save us, Danny. I know you will. If anyone can do it, you can."

I had to swallow hard to get the words out. "All right," I said. "Then I will."

I pushed out of the stall. It took an effort. My legs, my arms, my whole body felt heavy, weary. For the last few days, the drug had covered up the damage I'd taken, but I felt it all now, every bruise, cut, and sore.

I stopped in the middle of the bathroom floor. I saw myself in the mirror over the sink. What a sight I was. My face was stone-white, my flesh was fever-damp. My eyes were sunken deep but burning with my memories, my fury, my shame. The slash on my cheek seemed to sculpt my expression into a permanent grim sneer. My gun hand hung by my side.

You don't know who you are, Bethany said.

And I thought: *I know. Now I know.*

We waited in silence as twilight came. We were too frightened to speak. Samantha sat cross-legged on her bed. I sat on the floor, my back against the wall. The suspense was awful. The fear seemed to sap the strength out of my limbs, out of my core. I wasn't sure I would be able to do what I had to do when the time came. I wasn't sure I would be able to move at all.

More than anything, I wanted to call it off. I wanted to tell Samantha, "This is stupid. We're just going to get ourselves killed. What's the point of that? We should wait. We should see what happens. Maybe the Fat Woman is telling the truth. Maybe it'll all be fine." The words were on the brink of spilling out of me. I had to will myself to hold them back. Once they were spoken, I knew it would be over. Samantha would eagerly agree with me. Relief would wash over both of us. We might even laugh at ourselves for considering such a crazy plan. We might even joke about it. What were we thinking? *we would say. We would still know in our hearts what we knew, but we would pretend not to know and we would laugh at ourselves and go back to waiting, telling ourselves it would be all right.*

And then she would come for us.

Somehow I managed to keep silent. The air turned gray, then dark blue. Samantha's figure dimmed into the dusk.

Now I heard a noise downstairs. For a moment, I went on sitting there, weak with fear. Then I forced myself to move. I pushed away from the wall. I stretched out on my side on the floor. I pressed my ear to the cool, splintery wood. I listened.

The tower room was three stories up. When the Fat Woman was on the ground floor, we couldn't hear her. We could only hear her when she was on the second floor or when she was coming up the stairs.

I heard her now, shifting around in one of the rooms just below us. I could hear the creak and groan of pipes and water running. A bath, I thought, she must be running a bath. *That was good. That was the sort of thing I wanted. I had thought it through. I wanted her still awake but distracted, busy, making noises of her own so she wouldn't hear the noises we made.*

This was what I had been waiting for. This was the time.

I sat up. I looked at Samantha. The shape of her had almost blended with the gathering indigo darkness. I swallowed hard. I took a deep breath. *If I did not move now, I would never move. No one would blame me, I thought. I was just a kid. It was probably all crazy anyway. Crazy made-up kid fears, that's all.*

I took another breath. I stood up off the bed. I moved to the wall and crouched down by the wainscoting.

The bedsprings squeaked at my back as Samantha climbed down off her bed too. She moved across the room to stand next to me. She crouched down too and watched, her eyes gleaming eagerly, as I worked my fingernails in behind the panel. I got a grip and pried the wainscoting off.

It came away easily. White bits of plaster, glowing in the dark, sprinkled to the floor.

I reached my fingers into the hole. Felt the tinfoil. Drew it out. I tried to unwrap the little package but I was so nervous it fell from my shaking fingers. I made a noise of frustration.

Samantha put her hand on my shoulder. I heard her whisper.

"Go on, Danny. You can do it."

I nodded. I took a breath. I rubbed my sweating palms dry on my thighs. I tried again to unwrap the foil, leaving it on the floor this time where I could keep it steady. I got it open. The thin disc of wax, all that was left of Alexander's candle, seemed to gleam in the twilight. I picked up the book of matches to get a better look at it. Three matches left. That was all.

I put the book of matches down—tossed it down so Samantha wouldn't see how violently my hands were trembling now. I lay down on the floor again, listened again. I could still hear the Fat Woman moving around beneath us. I could still hear the bathwater running.

I pushed to my feet and glanced at Samantha. She looked as terror-stricken as I felt. A liquid came into my throat, sharp and metallic. The taste of fear. I swallowed it.

"Okay," I said. "Be very quiet."

We had discussed my plan. We both knew what to do. I went to one of the beds. Samantha went to another. Working quickly and in silence, we began stripping off the blankets and the sheets. We gathered bunches of them in our arms and carried them over to a spot on the floor about two yards in from the door. We piled them up there and went back for more.

All the while we worked, I was telling myself: There's still time to stop, there's still time to call it off. *But we didn't stop. We went on, the two of us, back and forth from the beds to the pile of sheets. We added blankets and pillows too. And soon it was done—all the sheets were in a pile and the pillows were piled up near them—and there was no time left. This was the point of decision. We had to call it off now or do it, one way or the other.*

I stood, trying to swallow, hardly able to draw breath. I looked at Samantha, at her face, so pale now that it seemed spotlit in the dark. I barely heard her gasping whisper:

"I'm so scared!"

She reached out to me and I grabbed hold of her shaking hands and clutched them with mine. That helped to calm us both a little. I nodded to her. She nodded back.

Then I let go of her and went to fetch the candle and matches.

Samantha waited by the piled blankets and sheets. I returned to her and knelt down. She knelt down next to me. I set the candle on the floor. I pinched the matchbook between my fingers. I was careful to keep the matches away from my palms so they wouldn't be ruined by sweat.

One more time, I hesitated. One more time, I looked at Samantha in the dark. One more time, the whispers passed between us.

"Maybe . . ." I began.

"No, Danny. Go ahead."

"Right. Right," I said. "Okay."

My trembling breath was loud in the dark room as I leaned over the candle stub with the matchbook in my two hands. I tried to pull out a match. It resisted—or maybe the fear had just weakened me to the point I simply didn't have the strength to get it free. Frustrated, I tore it out forcefully, grunting with the effort.

My hand was shaking so hard, I could barely bring match and flint together. When I did, I had to press the match head hard against the flint strip in order to steady it. I pressed too hard: When I struck the match, its head sizzled and crumbled and went out. The fragments dropped to the floor without so much as a spark.

"Damn it!" I said.

I threw the useless paper stem of the match away. I shook my head. I wiped my palm on my pants and resolved to try again.

Then Samantha clutched my arm. "Danny! Listen!"

I went stiff and still. I listened. The water downstairs had stopped running. The bath was full. Samantha and I knelt there, frozen, peering at one another.

I heard a floorboard creak. A footstep. Then another. The unmistakable laboring tread of the Fat Woman. She was moving out of the room below us. Moving toward the winding tower stairs.

"She's coming up to check on us!" Samantha hissed.

I shook my head no, but I knew she was right. Samantha's grip tightened on me. In her desperation, her whisper grew dangerously loud.

"There won't be time!"

Somehow, the danger sent a new determination through me. Somehow it steadied me. I pushed Samantha's hand off my arm. I plucked the second match out of the book. I set its head against the flint more carefully. I knew if I hesitated, my hand would begin to shake again. So I struck it at once. The match sizzled and fumed. Then it died.

Then it flared. An ever-so-small, so-weak blue flame. It quivered at the end of the matchstick, threatening to go out at any second. I held the stick upside down, hoping the fire would feed on the paper stem, hoping it would burn higher.

But I knew there was no time to wait for it. Because now there was a loud, prolonged groan of wood from the bottom of the tower staircase. The Fat Woman had started coming up.

Holding the barely burning match, I let the matchbook fall to the floor. I grabbed my wrist with my free hand. Tried to hold myself steady as I lowered the small, dying flame to the wick of the candle on its tinfoil bed.

Another stair creaked loudly. Another footstep—higher, closer.

I touched the match to the wick. The flame seemed to retract into itself like a frightened animal. The darkness swarmed in around the trembling fire, about to smother it. I could see—Samantha and I staring through the darkness could both see—that we were about to lose the fire, it was about to go out.

And it did. The match-flame died in a little stream of black smoke—but before it was gone, the candle wick caught and a new flame rose, small but steady, slowly becoming yellow, bright.

"Hurry, Danny!"

Another heavy footstep on the stairs—then a pause. I remembered how we had followed the Fat Woman up here. I remembered how she'd had to stop every few steps to catch her breath. I was focused now, the way boys can be, my mind so completely trained on the task before me that nothing else seemed to exist. My hand was still shaky, but the candle flame was strong enough. I lifted the disk of wax in one hand. With the other, I pulled out a corner of a bedsheet at the bottom of the pile.

I held the flame to the fabric. A moment passed.

There was another footstep on the stairs. She must have been halfway up by now.

Then the end of the sheet browned, blackened, charred. A little crescent of material was eaten away—but there was no fire. My stomach dropped like a stone. Somehow I had thought this would be easy. I had thought the sheet would just burst into wild flames. When it didn't, I didn't know what to do. I nearly despaired . . .

Another footstep. An acid flash of panic went through me. She was going to catch us. I knew it. Our plan wasn't going to work.

Then the sheet ignited. The fire started.

I heard Samantha catch her breath. I glanced at her and saw the flame-light starting to dance in her startled, anxious eyes.

Once the cloth was burning, the fire spread fast. It raced along the edges of the sheet, then ate into the body of it, then started to flicker and rise up the other sheets and blankets piled on top of it.

Another footstep sounded on the stairs. The Fat Woman was near the tower landing, only another step or two away.

But now the pile of sheets was ablaze. The fire rose shockingly fast, shockingly hot and bright. I threw a pillow on it to keep it going, and then another, but when I went to grab a third pillow, the heat of the flames pushed me back and I had to toss it onto the pile from a distance.

A groan came from outside the door. The Fat Woman. She was very close to the top of the stairs, maybe on the landing already. It sounded like she had stopped, like she was resting again.

The fire, meanwhile, grew bigger, brighter. Samantha and I, crouching, stared up awestruck at the rising flames.

Now smoke too was pouring out of the pile of sheets and blankets and pillows. It mingled blackly with the threatening red flames. It clogged the air. It made my throat sore. It stung my lungs. I took Samantha by the arm. I pulled her away from the fire until we were pressed against the room's curving wall. I wanted to go even farther, get farther away from the heat and smoke. But I had to stay close to the door.

I cupped my hand and pressed my lips against Samantha's ear—but when I tried to whisper to her, I began to cough. I tried to pull another

breath but the smoke swirled around me, making it impossible. Coughing,
I knelt down, tugging at Samantha's arm to bring her down with me. The
air was a little better nearer the floor. I caught a breath and hissed at her.

"When I squeeze your wrist . . . go . . . don't look back no matter what."

She was coughing too but she nodded. We both turned in the glow of the
firelight and stared at the door. We waited for the Fat Woman to come in
to check on us. As soon as she opened the door, we would make our break.

The smoke thickened over and around us. The fire—eerily silent until
now—began to snicker and sough.

A long moment passed. Then we heard a riser creak again under the Fat
Woman's heavy step. And then another stair creaked right after that—and
another—quickly . . .

And I realized: She was going back down! She had come up to listen for
any trouble. Had heard nothing. Hadn't smelled the smoke. Was satisfied
we were not making trouble. Was returning downstairs to take her bath.

I had to stop her. What could I do? Shout for help. I had to start shouting for help. That would bring her back. I drew a breath—but the smoke
rushed into my lungs and the shout broke into a hacking cough that
doubled me over. Samantha caught on. She tried to shout—and she started
coughing too. The smoke grew thicker, the flames brighter. And I heard the
Fat Woman's thumping steps descending, getting farther and farther away.

"Fire! Fire! Fire! Help!"

Somehow I managed to force out the strangled cry. Samantha joined in.
We both started screaming—screaming and coughing at once.

"Fire! Help!"

But our broken voices seemed to be swept away by the growing roar of
the flames. I didn't think the Fat Woman would hear us. Even I could
hardly hear us. I could hardly hear anything but the fire. And I could not
hear the Fat Woman's movements at all anymore.

Below the burning bedding, the rotten wood of the floor was beginning
to darken and spark and send up smoke. Above, the flames were striving
toward the high rafters.

Samantha and I both managed to let out one more round of broken shouts.

"Fire!"

"Fire! Help!"

But then—like the arms of some great dark ogre—the smoke closed over us where we knelt together. Our screams dissolved into fits of deep, harsh hacking. Our bodies bent almost to the floor, racked by the force of the spasms.

The fire rose above us, its roar triumphant, its crackle like laughter. My head began to feel light and distant. I felt as if the smoke were wafting my mind away in slow undulations to some other place, some far place. I was losing consciousness.

But then, without warning, the door to the tower room came swinging open.

There stood the Fat Woman. The gross, enormous shape of her all but blotted out the light from the landing. The glow of the flames danced hellishly on her shocked, twisted, bloated features. Her mouth opened in a large, black O—and out came a string of hoarse, furious curses.

"Shit! You fucking cockroaches! What the fuck did you do?"

Bent over, coughing, clutching my throat with one hand, I was still clinging to Samantha's wrist with the other. The smoke seemed to fill my head. My mind and the smoke seemed to unify into one swirling mass of blackness and confusion. I strained to straighten my body against the spasms, to lift my eyes to see what was happening.

I saw the Fat Woman step forward. Through the smoke, through my dizziness, she seemed far away from me, unreal, almost dreamlike. I watched her as she kicked furiously at the pile of burning sheets. It seemed as if it were happening somewhere else—on TV or in some other country. I saw the pile fall over. I saw the flames and sparks spill deeper into the room.

The Fat Woman came after them—another step. She grabbed a pillow off the heap of them.

I heard her voice, thick and slow, like a recording played back at the wrong speed:

"You cockroaches!"

Slow and distant, dim and smoky, she hammered the pillow down at the flames. The movement brought her another step into the room—and with that step, she cleared the edge of the door.

And from very far away, a small voice seemed to call to me from inside my own reeling mind: Now. Now. Now or never.

I squeezed Samantha's wrist, hard—our prearranged signal. I heard her coughing somewhere in the smoke beside me. I didn't think she would have the strength to go.

But she did. She flitted from my grasp, darted through the smoke like a wraith. She flashed silently behind the Fat Woman's back and out the door onto the lighted landing. From there, she dashed for the stairs, vanishing from my sight. Just like that.

I stumbled to my feet and went after her, fighting my way through the smoke that filled the room and filled my brain, that welded the room and my brain into one great churning barrier of confusion, battling my way through that confusion toward the light of the doorway.

But I didn't go through. I didn't follow Samantha out of the room onto the landing. Instead, when I reached the door, I stopped and grabbed hold of the doorknob.

The Fat Woman was still trying to fight the fire. She was maybe half a step in from the edge of the door. When I took hold of the doorknob, she heard me—or maybe just sensed me moving so close behind her. Her giant form whipped around with stunning swiftness. She looked down from her great height and saw me below her.

Her face was caught in the firelight. Its expression of wild surprise and rage was etched in red and black. Her eyes in their folds of pasty flesh burned and danced like a demon's. When she caught sight of me, she made a noise—a wordless snarl of pure hatred that pierced me head to groin with terror.

With the speed of that terror, I started to pull the door shut. But she, with the devil's own quickness, reached for it, grabbed the edge of it with her thick fingers. Pulled back against me.

I don't know where I found the strength to fight her, but I did. I yanked the door with all my might and somehow jerked it almost shut, even with her holding on, even with her trying to hold it open. I pulled again and the door closed on her fingers. The Fat Woman gave one short cry of pain and snatched her hand away.

The next second, I slammed the door and drove the heavy bolt into its ring.

The cry of rage that reached me from the tower room seemed barely human. It was such a horrible sound that even then, hacking and coughing and half-dead from the smoke, I stood on the landing and stared at the door in a kind of dreadful wonder. I heard the Fat Woman's heavy hands smack against the wood—once and then again. I heard her shrieking—horrible curses and threats—her voice broken and hoarse.

"Open this door, you little piece of shit! Open this door or so help me you will be punished like you can't fucking imagine!"

She smacked the door again—so hard it shook on its hinges, so hard the floor seemed to shake beneath me. But now her voice became strained, and her curses were interspersed with coughing.

"You little . . . You little . . ."

But then there was only coughing.

For another long moment, I stared in horror and fascination at the door. Then my eyes were drawn down and I saw the black smoke curling out onto the landing over the sill. That seemed to bring me to my senses. I turned, still hacking and coughing myself, and stumbled away.

The prism of tears—tears streaming from my stinging eyes, coursing down my grimy cheeks—turned the light on the landing radiant and dazzling. I was half-blind as I reached the top of the winding stairs. Clutching the banister, I started down. I dropped from one riser to the next. Then my heel slid out from under me. I sat down hard, the edge of the stair jarring my butt. I grabbed the banister with both hands and hauled myself up again, coughing and weeping. I went on, descending the spiral, down and down and down.

I reached the second floor. Woozy, I looked around me. I was in a corridor. There were brass lanterns in sconces on the paisley wall, but their bulbs seemed dim to me, their glow swallowed by the flocking. I could barely see. The smoke was still in my brain. The furious, inhuman cry of the Fat Woman was still ringing in my ears.

Openmouthed and bewildered, I began to feel my way along a piece of raised paneling, working toward the next flight of stairs. I reached it. Grabbed the newel post. Clung to the newel post like a sailor clinging to a rail in a stormy sea. In fact, the floor did seem to be dipping and tilting and rising up under me. Some black-tasting bile gurgled up my throat as I curled around the post. I half-spit, half-vomited the stuff onto the stairs. Then I started thumping down.

I held fast to the banister. Descended clumsily, nearly falling stair to stair. Somewhere along the way, I caught a breath—fresh, cool air from the outdoors. I blinked and straightened as if I'd been slapped in the face. My head was suddenly clear, my vision suddenly clear. I dragged my sleeve across my eyes to wipe the tears away. I squinted and peered and saw the door. The front door to the house. It was open. Samantha. She must have gotten out. The night—freedom—lay just below me.

With elaborate caution—each step a stiff and deliberate thump—I made my way down the staircase to the foyer below. I staggered across a gold and purple rug. Gold and purple chairs lined the striped walls. They seemed to watch me as I lurched past them to the door.

Then I was out of the house, into the night. I coughed violently, fighting to suck down mouthfuls of the glorious cool air. I shuffled and stumbled down the front two steps, out onto the dark lawn, looking around me, blinking, dazed. I heard Samantha somewhere. She was coughing too. Where? Where was she?

Then I heard her gasp: "Danny!"

There she was. Kneeling on the lawn in the moonlit darkness. Bent over under a small maple tree. Convulsively grabbing handfuls of dirt and grass as she hacked and coughed and spat up black phlegm.

I took two wobbly steps toward her, then paused and turned and looked back and up, over my shoulder.

The tower was in flames. I could see the fire flickering at the high windows. I could see the smoke beginning to seep out through the walls, a coiling blackness staining the blue of night.

I turned and scanned the dark around me. Nothing but trees visible on every side of me. Trees and, down the road, the porch lamp of a house, its yellow glow obscured by leaves and branches.

I listened as I looked. Sirens—I heard sirens in the distance. Someone had seen the flames. The firemen were coming. The police—the police would be with them too.

I took the last few steps to Samantha's side. Exhausted, I dropped to my knees beside her. Still coughing, she reached out for me blindly. I took her hand in both of mine. She seemed to follow my grip up to me, rising from the grass. She flung her arms around me.

"You did it, Danny! The police are coming! They'll help us! You did it! We got away!"

The press of her body against me, her coughing whisper against my face, seemed to snap me back to full consciousness. This place, this night, the grass and dirt beneath my knees, the fire burning behind me, the smoke twining inside me—all of them suddenly became clear and real.

And Samantha herself—Samantha pressed against me, shaking, crying.

"We'll be all right now, won't we, Danny?"

I started crying too. I hated to. I wanted to be strong. I wanted to be a hero—for her. But I couldn't help it. I held Samantha against me as she wept. I held her close so she wouldn't see how hard I was sobbing.

As the sirens in the distance came closer, grew louder, we knelt together like that, hugging one another on the lawn beneath the tree, our figures lit by the moon and the flames that rose in the burning tower: two little children, crying in each other's arms.

I took a step closer to the bathroom mirror. I looked at my reflection, my scarred face, my burning eyes. I could still smell the smoke. I could still hear the Fat Woman shrieking. I could still feel Samantha's arms around me.

And I could still see Alexander's forlorn figure. I could still hear his voice—that voice I had tried so hard to forget all these years, all my life.

Don't let them take me.

I lifted my hand, the hand holding the gun.

You don't know who you are.

I turned the Glock this way and that, studying it as if I were just seeing it for the first time.

I know, I thought. *I know now.*

She was still alive. The Fat Woman. She hadn't died like the newspaper said she had. I had known that somehow. I had always known it. She was still out there, still in the wind. She and her pet murderer Stark.

I slipped the gun inside my jacket. I put it back into its holster. I was going to need it.

I know now, I thought. *I know who I am.*

I lifted my eyes to the mirror again and saw myself.

I am the executioner.

13

The Coroner's Widow

A LONG TIME PASSED in darkness. I sat in an antique armchair in the foyer. A grandfather clock tick-tocked steadily against the wall. Every fifteen minutes, the clock chimed. At the hour, it tolled.

The house settled around me, strangely alive. It had a presence, I mean a personality: dignified and self-possessed and melancholy with time.

Or maybe that was just my imagination. Maybe it was just the drug. A lot of strange thoughts came to me, sitting there so long.

I could see the scene outside through the mullioned windows that flanked the front door. The cars went back and forth on the main thoroughfare, whizzing past the stand of birches across the way. After night fell, I could see their headlights, the glare spreading over the white trunks of the trees, then falling away. Finally, one pair of lights pulled to the curb and went dark. The antique armchair let out a stuttering creak underneath me as I sat up straight, waiting.

I heard the brisk clop of a woman's heels on the front path. I heard her key in the latch and saw the door open, the movement dim and obscure in the evening shadows. She switched on the foyer light—a lamp of glass and iron hanging from the ceiling—but she still didn't see me. She had turned away and was stripping off her spring overcoat as she took the step to the closet by the front door. I sat watching her fit the coat neatly to its hanger. I thought she must have been pretty once in that haughty, demanding way some women have, like they are standing on a hill above you, looking critically down. She still had a majestic face, worn and wizened as it was, her hair an uncompromising silver, her body lean and ramrod-straight.

When she did face forward, when she did notice me in the chair against the foyer wall, her reaction was restrained. She stiffened. Her wrinkled hand went briefly to the top of her cardigan. She drew in breath through her nose—I could hear it across the room. But that was all. Pretty good, I thought, considering I must've scared the old girl half to death.

Her hand came down unsteadily and clasped her other hand in front of her skirt. She regarded me sternly, her steel-gray eyes anxious but hard. She was afraid—she didn't hide that, but she didn't make a show of it either. I don't think she considered it any of my damned business.

"Are you going to hurt me?" she asked calmly.

"No," I said.

She drew another breath and nodded once. "And I suppose if you were going to kill me, you wouldn't have made such a production of it."

I smiled wearily. "Probably not. I'm a police inspector. Or I was. I want to ask you some questions about your husband and a woman named—"

"Sadie Trader. Yes, now I understand. You must be Detective Champion. Your . . . coming was foretold to me."

Surprised, I was about to ask *by whom,* but the answer was obvious. I was working off Samantha's notes, after all, following her footsteps. Of course, she'd already been here. Of course, she'd already found what I was looking for. That's why the Fat Woman sent the Starks after her in the first place. "How did she know I'd . . . ?" I began to say. But the answer to that began to occur to me too and I didn't finish.

The elegant old woman looked around the room as if searching for a polite response to my half-muttered questions. "Would you care for a cup of tea?" she said finally.

I was exhausted from the flood of memories, my mind hazy with the drug. "Would coffee be too much trouble?"

"Not at all." The woman hesitated. "I would have to go into the kitchen, though."

"Go anywhere you like. It's your house."

She started across the foyer—then pulled up short, wary, as I rose from my chair.

"I thought I would come in with you," I told her. "So we can talk while you make coffee. You don't have to be afraid of me. Really."

"Of course not. Come this way."

She started walking again, turning on lights as she went. I followed her down a hall into the kitchen. It was a broad, bright country kitchen: white walls, wooden floors, and a big gray granite-topped island in the center. I sat at one of the tall stools by the island. I watched her as she moved with womanly briskness and efficiency from cupboard to counter to sink. She was eighty if she was a day but there was a vitality and sureness to her movements you don't see all that often, even in much younger people. I admired her. She was sort of like one of those antiques you look at and think, They don't make them like that anymore.

"So ask your questions, Detective Champion," she said—at the sink, running water into a china pitcher, her back to me.

"Inspector. You can call me Dan—although somehow I don't think you will."

She showed me just enough of her face to let me see her small answering smile.

"I'm sorry I had to break in, Mrs. Longstreet," I said. "I wanted to make sure I wasn't being followed. There are some bad people after me and I didn't want them to see me talking to you."

"Well, that was very thoughtful of you. Though really, I sup-pose, if they were going to bother me, they'd have done it a long time ago. They haven't much reason to trouble themselves. I don't really know very much—nothing that can hurt them anyway." The pitcher full, she carried it across the counter. She poured some water into a coffeemaker and some more into an electric kettle, speaking as she did. "On the other hand, they seem to have given *you* quite a working over."

I raised my bruised hand to touch the gash on my cheek. "We had some areas of disagreement."

"Yes, I imagine you did." She set the coffeemaker and the kettle working. Then she faced me, leaning her back against the counter. She fiddled with a little silver cross she wore on a plain steel chain around her neck. "In any case . . . your questions."

"Thank you," I said. "According to the archives of the local paper, your late husband, Adam Longstreet, was the coroner here thirty years ago."

Mrs. Longstreet shuddered, glancing away. "I can't bear to look at those old papers. I can't bear to see his name in them."

"He declared Sadie Trader dead. Said she died in the fire at her house."

"Yes. Yes, he did."

"But she didn't die, did she?" I said.

"No," said Mrs. Longstreet flatly. "She did not. As, of course, you know."

She gave me a bland, patrician look. I didn't think she was going to stonewall me. She had already spoken to Samantha. And anyway, I could see she had been raised in the old way, to respect the virtues, honesty among them. But she had been raised to dignity as well, and she didn't want to feel she was being interrogated.

So I said, "You know, I remember him, I think. Your husband." And when I saw her widen her eyes, properly startled, I went on, "It's possible I just imagined it after the fact, but I really think I do. I think he showed up at the house while they were still fighting the fire. Samantha and I were still there on the front lawn and I think he showed up just as they were carrying the Fat Woman—Trader—out to the ambulance."

"That would make sense," she murmured, impressed. "He did go out to the scene that night. Well, of course, he was the only doctor in town."

The kettle snapped off automatically, drawing her back to her work. She turned away from me, rooting briskly in the cupboards for coffee mugs and drawing a tea bag out of a glass jar.

"If it *was* him," I said, "I overheard him talking to . . . the police chief, I guess it was."

She set the tea bag in its mug, poured the water, poured the coffee. "Yes, Bob Finch," she said. "He died five years ago."

I watched her hands as she worked. They were swift and expert but quavery with age—or maybe with grief, I don't know. They were quavery with something.

"I remember your husband told the chief, 'I want those children taken someplace safe. I'm going to check on it. This ends tonight.'"

She paused, the coffeepot in her hand. She seemed about to glance over her shoulder at me, but she didn't. She kept her face turned away. "Did he really say that? 'This ends tonight?' You're not just telling me that?"

"That's the way I remember it."

She sniffed and set the pot back in the coffeemaker. Paused thoughtfully and looked at it there a moment. "Well. That's something, I suppose." She came to the granite island, carrying the two mugs. Set one in front of me. Her eyes were not as guarded now. "Milk and sugar, Inspector?"

"No, thanks. I take it black."

"Of course. What was I thinking? Tough-guy detectives don't use milk or sugar."

"It's bad for business if it gets around."

She smiled—kind of sweetly, I thought. Like her grandchild had said something cute. Then she perched herself on a stool across from me, warming her hands on her mug of tea, blowing on the surface of it.

"Poor Adam," she said after a moment. "He wanted so much to be a good man. He really did. I think he would have been too, except for the alcohol. I'm not making any excuses for him, mind. Or for me. But drink does take the soul out of a person. Literally. It wraps itself around him like strangling vines and chokes the image of God right out of him. I believe that. I saw it happen with my own eyes." She drank, looking over her mug at me. "You might want to remember that, by the way, the next time you take a dose of whatever it is *you're* on."

I gave a short laugh. "I took a drug to help me remember," I said. She was the sort of woman who made you feel you ought to explain yourself. "Now that I do remember, I'll get off it."

"Mm."

Properly reprimanded, I sipped my coffee. It was strong, solid, no-nonsense stuff, appropriate to the woman.

"In any case," she went on, "my powers to save Adam were limited. And *her* powers . . . her money . . ."

"The Fat Woman, you mean. Sadie Trader."

"She corrupted everybody. Absolutely everybody. I don't imagine there were ten people in that town who didn't know what was going on—or who couldn't at least have found out if they'd wanted to or allowed themselves to. That was her trick, you see. Her secret. She made it so you didn't *have* to see. You didn't have to know unless you wanted to, unless you made the effort—and who would? All you had to do was look away and take the money—or the investment or the job or the donation or whatever it was you needed from her. And that was how the town thrived—on her money. Her ill-gotten wealth. That was why, when it was over, and the new highway came, it was so easy for all of us to just leave the old places behind and go on to the new homes and stores we'd already built in the better locations. I suppose we were trying to move away from what we knew, but of course that was foolish. We took it with us. In some way, this whole town is still hers, Inspector Champion. This whole town is built on what we never admitted to ourselves. What we never saw happening right in front of us—but what we knew nevertheless, every single one of us."

I had been raising my coffee mug again but paused with my hand half-lifted. "There must've been . . . To declare her dead like that. To make it stick. It must've taken so many people."

Mrs. Longstreet lifted her slender shoulders. "Not so many really. My husband was the only doctor, as I say. For miles and miles. We were in the middle of nowhere then. Bob Finch and the rest of the police, of course, had to protect themselves . . . As I say, everyone was involved. By the time they got her to the hospital in Sawnee, they had given her a false name. She had prepared for that. She had any number of aliases ready, complete with social security numbers and so on. Not surprising, when you think about it. All those children who disappeared. All those little souls who fell into her clutches. Then my husband or Bob made up some story about her . . . There was another woman in the Trader house who had survived the fire . . . Something like that. Adam never told me the details, and I never made much of an effort to find them out. But it was all apparently much simpler than you would think." She drew a long, unsteady breath of steam. "My husband always insisted he only went along with it to insure your safety—protecting the police in return for making sure you and the little girl would be taken care of. But of course . . ."

". . . it protected him too."

"Yes. And me. All of us."

I brought the mug the rest of the way to my lips—and froze again, just holding the mug there, not drinking, feeling the heat of the coffee on my face, my mind three decades away.

"I remember her hand moving," I murmured.

Mrs. Longstreet observed me from her critical height.

"No, I do," I said. "On the stretcher. As they were taking her to the ambulance. I remember seeing her lift her finger. I didn't tell Samantha. Samantha was crying and she kept saying, 'She's dead, she's dead, she can't hurt us anymore.' I wanted her to go on believing that. So she wouldn't be afraid."

"Of course."

"But I saw her finger move. That's how I knew. All this time—I knew she was alive, I knew she was still out there somewhere, still in the wind. That's why I was hunting her. Without even knowing it. I didn't remember, but I knew."

For a long while after that, we both sat there without speaking, both of us holding our mugs on the counter, both of us gazing distractedly into space, into our own thoughts and memories.

"If it's any consolation," Mrs. Longstreet said finally, "it finished him—my husband. That night—it killed him as surely as a bullet. The drinking after that—it became outrageous. Truly, it beggared belief. It only took him a year to make an end of it." She frowned. "I felt that very deeply. If *that's* any consolation. I took his death—his suicide really—as a personal failure. I suppose it sounds horribly old-fashioned now, but I had tried to make a better man of him. I felt it was my duty as his wife. We still did that then in these backward parts." She shook her head at something I couldn't see. A strand of silver hair fell across her brow. She lifted a finger and set it back in place—an unconscious gesture, girlish and appealing. "I did always intend to make it right, you know. To tell someone. The state police. Or some newspaper somewhere. Somehow, there were always so many . . . considerations. Loyalty to my husband. Just . . . the *number* of people involved. One wondered sometimes if one even had the *right* to clear one's conscience at the expense of so many other people. Especially after they became old and were sick and suffering, so many of them. Most of them are gone now—the key players . . ." Her hand rose absently to touch the silver cross at her throat. "And so the days go by . . ."

With a sharp intake of breath, she came back from whatever distant place she'd been, and I came back, as far as I could. She sipped her tea. She smiled very faintly, a sad smile. I remembered when I'd been sitting in the house alone, waiting for her, how the house had seemed to have a personality: dignified and self-possessed and melancholy with time. It was her personality, I realized now.

"And here we are," she said.

"Here we are."

She cocked her head a little and regarded me in what I thought was an odd sort of way, inward and distant. "So then . . . what else?"

"I need her name," I said. "The alias your husband gave her. I need to know what it is."

"Oh, I don't know that," said Mrs. Longstreet. "I never did. You'll have to go to the hospital to find it. St. Mary's."

"St. Mary's," I echoed in a low murmur. I remembered the words scrawled on Samantha's notes.

"In Sawnee. It was the closest place with a burn unit, where they thought they might be able to help her. They'll have her alias there. They'll have everything you're looking for."

I shook my head. "A patient's records. They're confidential. They won't give them to me. And it was thirty-one years ago. They might not even have them anymore."

She smiled at me—a strange smile too, I thought. Gentle, but somehow . . . just strange. "They'll have them. They'll give them to you. Trust me. It isn't far. A hundred miles or so."

I found myself gazing at her. I felt she was trying to tell me something—that there was something hidden beneath her words. But she spoke again before I could think it through.

"Are you a merciful man, Inspector?" she asked me.

I thought about it. "Not really. More of a justice guy, I think."

She lifted her chin. It made her look regal—even more regal. "You're going to kill her, aren't you? Sadie Trader. That's your plan, isn't it?"

I figured it was just as well not to answer.

"And so it all just continues," Mrs. Longstreet declared. "The violence, the cruelty—it all just goes on and on."

"I guess that's one way to look at it."

"Is there another?"

"Sure," I said. "She's evil. And soon she'll be dead."

"And the world will be a better place."

"I didn't say that."

She smiled again, that same, strange smile. Then she startled me by reaching out her hand toward my face. The gesture took me aback. I recoiled from her, at first. But it was just her hand, an old lady's open hand, and I came forward again in my seat and she laid her palm against my scarred cheek. Her skin was soft with age and warm from the mug of tea.

"Go to St. Mary's," she repeated, quietly but firmly. "You'll find all the answers there."

14

St. Mary's

I SHACKED UP FOR the night in some hellhole or other. The Roadside Cottages, I think it was called. I checked into a little box of aluminum, plywood, and linoleum with a bed like a board and a bathroom the size of a sink. I went into the bathroom and coaxed the faucet into coughing some cloudy water into a cloudy glass. I washed down half a tablet of Z. I was hoping to taper off the stuff slowly this time, hoping to ease my way clean without all the craziness of going cold turkey.

Fat chance. I went to sleep, fully dressed, on the stiff bed, and almost instantly found myself walking in a nightmare world more real than reality. I was a child again. I was lost in a forest. There was a wind moving through the spring leaves, making a high, eerie singing sound. I turned to look beside me and there, suddenly, was Samantha—Samantha as a little girl—holding my hand, watching me, her eyes wide and staring.

"What's that noise?" I asked her.

"It's the dead children," she explained.

So it was. They were all around us, I noticed now, gray figures here and there among the trees, some even sitting in the branches. That high eerie singing sound was the sound of their voices. They were reciting their stories to the empty woods, each repeating a fragment of the whole, the sentences overlapping into a single, simultaneous narrative . . .

They kept me alive a long time . . .

I wanted to be dead but when they killed me, I was afraid . . .

I want to be dead now, every day, but I still have to live . . .

I cried every night for my mommy, but they said she didn't want me and she would never come back . . .

I turned my eyes from one to another of them, discovering each gray form as if it were appearing suddenly among the gray mazes of branches and vines. As the weird whispered song of their laments went on, another sound, another whisper rose beneath them, growing louder by the second.

I searched the forest for the source of that other noise until my gaze rested on Samantha again, little Samantha staring up at me.

"The fire is coming," she said.

Then the fire came, from all around us, a circle of flame eating in from the periphery of the forest, closing over the trees, devouring the trees and devouring the ghostly forms of the children standing among them. Very quickly, I could taste the ashes on my tongue. I felt the harsh, raw, rasping smoke in my throat. The circle of fire closed on itself, consuming the trees and the children and everything but me and Samantha, who were at its center . . .

And then it closed in on us, the heat raging . . .

I woke with a wordless cry. I lay gasping for breath, my eyes wide, my heart pounding. I stared up into the shadows, into the low, dark cobwebbed rafters of the Roadside Cottages. It was a long time before I calmed down. Then, sweating, I turned my head on the pillow.

Stark—the skull-faced killer—sat in a chair right beside me.

He grinned. Casually, he lifted a Glock and pulled the trigger, firing a slug into my stomach. I doubled over in agony, clutching myself . . .

But it was all just part of the dream. All just part of the process of withdrawal.

★ ★ ★

I had another flash of vision in the morning, on the road to Saw-nee. I had taken another small dose of Z just before setting out. Now I was driving on a two-lane past a patch of woods dappled by sun and shadow. I saw a figure watching me as I went by. I turned back to scan the woods. There was no one there. But I had taken my eyes off the road too long. When I faced forward, I was heading toward a ditch at the shoulder. I wrenched the wheel—too hard. The tires screamed. The car skidded and spun, the rear fishtailing away as the front went into the oncoming lane. I just had time to catch sight of a truck—coming out of nowhere—speeding toward me. I kept turning the wheel, fast as I could, into the skid. The Mustang did a one-eighty. I forced it back into the right lane, going backward—back the way I'd come—just as the truck thundered by my window, inches away, air horn blaring. The car shivered with its backwash. Then the truck was gone—speeding away. I eased my foot down on the brake, bringing the Mustang under control.

I guided the car off the road, onto the shoulder. I cracked the door open and stumbled out, nearly falling into the ditch myself.

I leaned against the side of the car, my head bowed as I fought to catch my breath. Then I lifted my head—and there was Samantha.

It was not the child Samantha. It was the woman. Walking toward me through the woods. She was wearing a flowered dress that blended with the scene. She gazed at me steadily, a slight smile playing on her lips, as she passed through beams of sunlight and into fields of shadow and out again. She looked so solid, so real, that even after I understood what she was, I could barely believe it—and I couldn't turn away.

I stood there watching in fascination as she stepped into another column of light, closer now, smiling now more fully, serene and kind and lofty and beautiful. Another step and she was once more in the blue shadows of the forest, melding with the blue shadows, becoming one of them. She did not come out of them again. She was gone.

I knew by the way I ached with disappointment that I still loved her. I had loved her ever since we were kids, I guess, and I had never stopped. More than that: We were part of each other. I understood that now. Maybe it was because we'd gone through hell together, or maybe that was just the way we were made from the beginning. Like Stark when I killed his brother, I had lost a piece of myself when I lost her, when they took her away from me after the fire, when they sent her off to her foster homes and me off to mine, so that we never saw each other again ...

How did I hallucinate her as a woman then? I thought suddenly. *If I only knew her as a child, how did I know what she would look like as a woman ... ?*

I shuddered as a chill, eerie feeling went up my spine.

I pushed off the car and got back in behind the wheel and drove on.

St. Mary's Hospital. There was a sign by the side of the road. There was a pair of stone gateposts nearby leading onto a driveway that curled out of sight up a tree-lined hill.

Right away, I knew by the look of the place that something was wrong.

The town of Sawnee lay behind me. It had probably been a nice little place once. But the farms around it had died and the town itself was ailing. The cluster of brick stores at the center of it were black with grime. Some of their windows were boarded. Most of the cars by the curb were old. The houses on the outskirts were un-cared for, many of the windows dark, many of the lawns unmown.

Beyond that, there was a winding road. A motel or two. A forest. Nothing. Then the sign: *St. Mary's*.

I turned the Mustang up the hospital drive. I passed between the gateposts. There was still a wrought-iron gate on one post—only on one—green with verdigris, chained back, half off its hinges. There was a rusted sign on the other: *No Trespassing*. Something wrong.

The road twined through the trees, a long way. Sunlight and shadow played on the Mustang's windshield, the reflections of the forest flashing on the glass. The haze of the drug was passing, but my thoughts were still jumbled and uncertain. As I felt myself getting closer to the hospital, I felt a rising anxiety. I caught glimpses of the building now through the trees: a large red-brick structure. But something wrong . . . I thought of the look on Mrs. Longstreet's face—that strange smile of hers. *Go to St. Mary's. You'll find all the answers there.* What was she trying to tell me? What did she know that she wouldn't say?

Or was I being crazy, paranoid? Withdrawing from the Z, even slowly like this, had to have an effect. The dreams. The hallucination by the side of the road. Maybe this dread I felt was just another symptom.

I came around the last bend in the drive and saw the place head-on. It was a massive brick ziggurat, the first four stories three broad wings across, the next two stories narrower, the next narrower still, and then a structure on top like a pyramid's peak, as if the place were some sort of ancient temple.

There was a cul-de-sac out front. I stopped the car at the entrance to it. I could see even from there that the hospital's broad glass doorways were chained shut. The glass was opaque with dust and overrun with climbing vines—where there *was* glass. Some of the tall panes had been replaced with plywood boards. I bent forward to look up at the building through the windshield. Window after window, rising up to the highest story, all dark. Some of the glass broken.

The place had been abandoned.

I shut off the car. Got out. The quiet of the day folded over me. A spring breeze whispering in the forest below. Traffic noises whispering somewhere in the distance. And then emptiness—that high hum of emptiness—surrounding everything.

I thought of my dream. The voices in the forest. The gray ghosts of children standing among the branches. Telling their sad stories in a song like a breeze. The thought made me shiver.

I walked up the cul-de-sac, my eyes lifted to the louring, deserted building. Its shadow fell over me and the air grew cool.

Go to St. Mary's.

Why did the old woman say that? Was it some kind of trick, some kind of trap? Was Stark behind it all, somehow using Mrs. Longstreet to lure me to this abandoned spot?

But no, I didn't believe that. I didn't believe she was speaking under duress or playing a role. She struck me as just an honest lady with an old sin on her conscience. I thought she wanted me to know the truth . . .

Then another idea came to me—an idea that made more sense: Mrs. Longstreet had known who I was. It had to be because Samantha had told her. Maybe Samantha had also told her to send me here . . .

I stopped. I stood still in the building's shadow, the old hospital looming over me. I looked up and scanned the dark windows slowly.

Finally—as happened so often since I'd started taking the drug—I caught a movement at the corner of my eye. I turned to it—to a window on the second story.

And there was Samantha. Standing behind the glass. Watching me.

The moment I saw her, she sank back into the darkness of the building and was gone. I was so crazy with the drug and the memories, the dreams and the visions and all that, I had no idea —no clue—whether she had been real or not.

My heart was beating hard as I moved over the last yards of the cul-de-sac to the front doors. I reached through the vines. Grabbed the metal handle. Pulled and pushed on it so that the chain rattled. But the doors wouldn't open. I tested the wooden boards, but they were stuck fast. I moved to a section thickly overgrown with ivy and pushed the green leaves and vines aside.

There I found what I was looking for: a jagged patch of shadow— a section of broken glass that had been hidden by the vines. An entryway.

Carefully, holding the ivy aside, I stepped into the darkness, into the hospital.

The quiet was deeper in here. No sounds of traffic, no whispering breeze. The light was pale gray just by the doors, but then slowly drained into dark shadows in the broad hall beyond the abandoned front desk.

I moved forward cautiously. Nervous. Hopeful. Was she real this time? Had I really found her? Was that really why Mrs. Longstreet had sent me? Because Samantha told her to? Because Samantha had been hiding from Stark here, waiting for me. Because she didn't know how to reach me without giving herself away. But she knew I would follow the same path she had. She knew I would find Mrs. Longstreet. Because she knew my mind. Because we were part of each other . . .

That was the hope anyway. But I remembered too that Stark's hired gun had tracked me to the ghost town outside Washington Falls. Maybe tracing my credit cards. Maybe trailing my car. I didn't know. I didn't even know how much of that had been real. But there was always the chance that it might be the skull-faced murderer or one of his goons who was waiting for me here, hiding somewhere in these dark hospital halls.

I drew in a deep breath. Moved slowly past the desk. Into the broad corridor beyond. No windows. Gray light. Empty doorways— door after open door. Shadows everywhere. Emptiness everywhere. Ghostly movements at the corners of my eyes. Stark? Samantha? No one. The dark gathered around me as I went deeper into the hospital, farther down the hall.

I heard the footsteps first. Light steps on a stairwell. I stopped in the dark. Open doors and empty rooms on either side of me. I listened. Nervous, my heart going a mile a minute, my hand slipping into my windbreaker, touching my holstered gun. I knew the death-headed Stark might emerge from the shadows at any minute.

But what if . . . ? What if it was Samantha? What would it be like to see her again? After all this time.

There was the sound of a heavy door opening. I could just barely make it out—the stairwell door—swinging open in the shadows at the end of the hall. It fell shut again, loudly: *boom*. The sound echoed in the emptiness. Only when the echo faded did I hear the footsteps again.

My fingers closed around the butt of my Glock, ready to draw.

Then, slowly, she came out of the shadows. She was wearing black jeans and a black sweatshirt. The auburn of her hair, the gold and rose of her skin, her blue eyes were all gray in the darkness.

For another moment, I still wasn't sure she was real. I still half expected her to vanish. But she didn't. She approached me steadily. Nearer and nearer, step by slow step. She came close to me. I could smell her scent. I watched every motion as her hand lifted to draw a strand of her hair from her forehead. I was afraid to move. Afraid to speak. I was afraid if I did anything at all, she would be gone.

Samantha smiled, laughed silently, as if she knew exactly what I was thinking. She did know—exactly. I smiled too.

I released my gun. My hand came out of my jacket. I reached out and touched her shoulder. She was there. She was real. On impulse, I leaned down and kissed her.

I kissed her very gently. Just pressed my lips to hers. She didn't resist. She let me. Her lips were soft, responding to mine. But when I drew back, I saw that something frightened, even frantic, had come into her eyes.

I started to lean toward her again.

She shook her head. "Don't."

I tried not to—but it was no good.

"I can't help it," I told her.

I kissed her again. Again, she let me. She kissed me back. I put my hand in her hair and drew her close. I put my arms around her and held her and caressed her as I kissed her.

She turned her face away and pressed her cheek against my chest. "Don't, Danny. Really. I mean it."

I went on holding her. I kissed her hair. I stroked her hair with my hand. I put my face in her hair and drew in the scent of her. Lost to me—lost even to my memories. All this time.

"Samantha," I said. She couldn't know, I thought, how much I'd longed for her, how deep it went, the power of it . . .

She lifted her face to me.

"This is . . ." she started to say.

At the sight of her lips, I kissed her. I couldn't stop myself. I pulled her body into mine. I lingered on her mouth as she drew it slowly away.

"This is insane," she whispered, breathless.

"I know," I said.

I drew her in to me again.

Her body was unbearably sweet, painfully sweet and fresh, like someone you remember but can't have anymore, like remembering the first time you ever touched a woman.

Because it was supposed to be her, that's why. It was never supposed to be anyone but her.

She had camped out in a room upstairs. She had spread a sleeping bag over the mattress of an old hospital bed. The afternoon light slanted in through the uncurtained windows. The room was a little bastion of light in all the hospital's mazelike halls of darkness. I still didn't know what was in that darkness—what, if anything, was waiting out there, watching, coming for us. But for a little while, I didn't care. For a little while, as I was making love to her, there was nothing for me but feeling her body, watching her face, hovering over her and watching her face and stroking her hair and studying every naked inch of her. Except sometimes . . . sometimes I had to hold her closer, bury my face in her neck to shut out the memories, the voices drifting to me from the darkness all around . . .

Don't let them take me, will you . . .

They kept me alive a long time . . .

We'll be all right now, won't we, Danny?

Outside, the afternoon deepened, the sun shifted, the shadows covered her.

Only when I touched my lips against her cheek—only then did I feel the tears there and realize that she was crying.

The smell of smoke woke me. I sat up out of a nightmare of fire, but the smoke was still there. My heart racing, I looked around in a murky panic. Where the hell was I? How could I have fallen asleep? The drug. The damned drug.

It took a long moment before everything came back to me. St. Mary's. *You'll find all the answers there.*

I tried to think, tried to clear my head. Was I alone? Was Samantha gone? Had she ever really been there in the first place . . . ?

The smell of smoke again. It was real enough this time. Someone had been smoking a cigarette in here and the smell lingered.

Could it be Stark . . . ? One of his men? Were they here? Had they found us, come for us? Taken Samantha?

Fighting the heaviness and confusion in my mind, I got up quickly. Tugged on my clothes. Strapped on my weapon. Covered it with the windbreaker. Made my way out of the little room.

I stood still a moment, out in the hall. Scanned the shadows. Then the smell of smoke reached me yet again, stronger now. I moved forward cautiously.

I came to a small common room right next door: an alcove off the corridor. A table and a sofa were the only furniture left here. There was a balcony beyond them. The glass doors were open and the thin white curtains were blowing in, billowing in with the cool afternoon wind. As the curtains moved, I caught glimpses of her. She was standing at the railing out there, looking out over the forested hills. She lifted her hand to her mouth. I saw a red glow: a cigarette. As she exhaled, the smoke blew in to me.

I felt my tense muscles relax a little.

Samantha.

★　★　★

I made my way through the curtains and stepped out onto the balcony. The day was cooler now, and the light deeper. Samantha didn't turn to me, didn't look at me. She just went on smoking her cigarette. As I got closer, I could see the tears glistening on her cheeks. She was still crying. Drawing on her cigarette fiercely; gazing out over the hills; crying.

I stepped up beside her. "We should go," I said gently. I tried to brush her tears away with the back of my hand. With a harsh, startling gesture, she knocked my hand away with her arm. She glared at me through her tears with fierce defiance.

I didn't understand at first. "We should," I said. "There are people after us."

"I know that."

"They've found me twice already. They could do it again. I have to take you someplace safe."

"You're not taking me anywhere. No one's taking me anywhere. I'm going to tell you what I need to tell you, and then I disappear, I'm gone."

"Samantha . . ."

"Why did you do it?" she said savagely.

"What?"

"Kiss me. Make love to me. I told you I didn't want to." She spat out the words. Then she turned away. She stared furiously out into the distance.

"Look," I began to say. "I couldn't . . . it just . . ."

"I told you!" she repeated.

"But you did want to."

She didn't argue. She didn't answer at all. The cigarette in one hand, she brought her other hand to her mouth and chewed angrily on the thumbnail.

"You must be out of your mind," she said after a while. "I mean it. You must be living in some kind of fantasy world."

I sighed. What could I say? She had a point: I wasn't even sure where my fantasies ended anymore. "I don't know," I said. "Maybe you're right. Maybe I am. It's just that when I saw you . . ."

I reached for her again and she pushed me away again. "Don't."
She sniffled violently. She wiped her cheeks and nose with her
sleeve. "Did you think it would be like . . . nothing had happened?
All these years. It's been almost thirty years . . ."

"I know how long it's been."

"Well, what did you think?"

"I don't know. I told you. I don't know. Look, there's no time
for this. We have to go."

"I'm not going anywhere."

The wind rose and we could hear the trees whisper and rattle
below. When the air reached us, it was cold. Samantha's whole
body shuddered. I wanted to wrap her in my arms again. But the
anger rose off her like an atmosphere. All I could do was stand
there and watch her seethe.

"I used to dream you'd come and rescue me," she said. Her voice
was low and quick. She spoke into the empty distance. "Whenever
some new bastard of a foster father put his filthy hands on me. I
used to think, *Danny will come. Danny is so strong, Danny is so fast,
he'll find me, he'll come in and save me any minute.*"

I went on standing there. I wanted to tell her: I used to dream
the same dream—that I would find her, that I would rescue her.
After a while, I couldn't stand dreaming it anymore. I couldn't
stand living with my own little-boy helplessness. So I stopped the
dreams altogether. I stopped remembering her altogether. I forgot
her. Her and everything.

"I'm sorry," I told her.

She made a sharp, dismissive noise, wiping her eyes roughly with
the back of her hand. "I don't need you to be sorry. I know it's
not your fault. We were children. I'm just saying . . ." She glanced
up at me. Quickly looked away. "I'm just saying you don't know
me. You don't know my life. You weren't there. You don't have any
right to just . . . I mean, Jesus, Danny! What was it supposed to be?
Love's sweet song?"

"Come on, Samantha . . ."

"Things change. The things they do to you . . . change you. Twist you . . . We don't become the people we're supposed to be. We become . . . something else."

I couldn't stand there anymore, couldn't watch her anymore. Biting her fingernails, smoking her cigarette. Bitter, angry. Spitting out those words. Trying to hurt me with them. Hurting me.

I turned from her to the balcony rail. The rail was painted white, the paint chipped, the red rust showing through. I gripped it, looked over it, out across the trees. The sun, out of sight, laid a wedge of gold over their green crowns.

"Oh, don't sulk," Samantha said with a hard laugh. "I'm sorry I'm not what you expected . . ."

"Stop."

"Well, I am. I am sorry. Believe me, I'd be Sleeping Beauty if I could."

I felt a surge of anger at her—anger and, I guess, disappointment too. "You're the one who brought me here," I said. "You waited for me. You told the Longstreet woman to send me . . ."

"Because people are trying to kill me. I don't know who else to trust."

"All right then. Trust me. Let me keep you safe."

"I don't trust anyone. I can't." Beside me, she dashed her cigarette to the concrete platform and crushed it brutally under her sneaker. "Damn it," she said—and she muttered again: "I told you I didn't want to . . ."

"You didn't exactly scream for help."

"Yeah, well . . . I'm a little screwed up in that regard, all right? I was hoping you'd be the sane one."

I swallowed my answer. It tasted bad.

She started crying harder now. Trembling and crying. Swiping angrily at her cheeks with her hand. Sweeping her sleeve across her nose. I stood it for a while, but it was too much, too brutal; I couldn't let it go on.

I turned to her. Reached for her. "Samantha, we have to . . ."

She cried out—"Don't touch me!"—a hoarse scream of fear and grief. And suddenly her hand moved, and a blade flashed in front of my eyes, sweeping by me, missing my face by inches.

I cursed, ducking back, out of range. She held the knife up at me, brandished it, her teeth bared, the tears pouring down her cheeks.

"I'll kill anyone who tries to hurt me again. You, them, anyone. Understand?"

"Put that down," I said. "I'd never hurt you. Are you crazy?"

She glared at me past the blade, shaking, crying. And then the glare faltered. Her lips quivered like a child's. She lowered the knife. Shook her head at me.

"Why didn't you ever come, Danny?" she said. "Why didn't you ever come?"

She turned and hurried off the balcony.

As I stepped inside, pushing the white curtains out of my way, I faltered a moment. A haze of dizziness passed over me. Now that the excitement of finding Samantha was fading, now that the excitement of making love to her was fading, the effects of my withdrawal from the Z were rising up in me again. I fought them off. Came unsteadily into the common room.

She was there. Sitting on the sofa arm. She had her belt off. She was working the blade back into it. It was clever, the way it was hidden in there. The belt was a series of canvas straps linked by buckles. The buckle in the rear was the handle of the hidden knife.

"Where the hell did you get that thing?" I asked her.

"A store . . . where I got the sleeping bag," she murmured, sniffling. "If they come after me again, I'll kill them with it, so help me. I'll slit their throats."

I shook my head. I admired the idea, but I hated to think what would happen to her, going up against Stark and his people. I lifted my eyes and peered past her into the shadows of the corridor. I wondered where the killer was—how close he was, how fast he was approaching as we stood here quarreling through our reunion.

I could feel the time closing in on us like a hard hand. I could feel Stark and his men closing in on us like the time . . .

When I looked down, I saw Samantha slide the knife back into place. She swiped at her tears again. Then she began to thread the belt through the loops of her jeans.

"Have you seen them?" she asked grimly. "There are two of them. They look, so help me God, just like skeletons. Like Death and his twin brother."

"The Starks. I've seen them. And there's only one of them now."

"What?"

"They came after me. I killed one."

She stared at me. "Did you? Seriously?"

"Under the circumstances, it seemed like a good idea."

She stared at me another second, then bowed her head so I couldn't see her face. She gave a lot of attention to buckling her belt. After a while, she made a noise—and I realized she was stifling a laugh.

"You think that's funny?" I said.

She shook her head, trying not to laugh again, laughing again anyway. "Sort of. I mean, it's just what you would have done. You know? I mean . . . you're still Danny. You're still just like you were."

I couldn't help smiling a little too at that. "Unfortunately," I said, "the other one's still alive and the whole killing-his-brother thing has sort of soured relations between us. While we're sitting around here chatting, he's doing everything he can to track us down."

Samantha gave a slow nod, let out a slow breath. For a moment, I thought she might listen to reason and let me take her away from here.

But she simply said, "Listen then. I'll tell you the whole thing quickly."

"I never wanted any of this," she said.

We were back in her room. Away from the window, out of the cold. With all the hospital darkness hunkered around outside us like a threat. Samantha was on the bed, hugging her knees, curled in a grim little ball of self-defense. I was slouched in the wooden armchair across from her, my legs splayed out in front of me.

And yes, I knew we should run. Sure I knew. Whether she wanted to or not, I knew I should grab her and put her into the car and drive her to some hidden nowhere as fast as I could. But I didn't. I didn't have the strength. A weird heaviness had settled over me and I didn't have the will to fight with her or to withstand her anger. It was the drug, of course. The hazy lethargy of withdrawal creeping through me so subtly I didn't even notice it at first.

And so I didn't run, and I didn't make her run. I just sat there in the chair. Feverish. Watching her. Listening.

She spoke quickly, quietly. Her face was ravaged: with crying, but not just with crying—with anger too and hurt and fear, and I don't know what, maybe just living with the whole damn thing all this time. It was painful to look at. My eyes kept wandering away as she spoke. I kept gazing at the scarred and broken linoleum floor or at the walls or at nothing, at anything except her.

"I mean, I just wanted to leave it alone already. I'd been over it and over it, you know. Not just Trader—what happened to us in that house. That was only the start of it for me. Then there were all the foster fathers, all the . . . It was all such a mess. I'd tried every kind of therapy there was. Remembering. Forgetting. Drugs. Alcohol. Sex."

She glanced at me on *sex* to check my reaction. I didn't react much. "Just tell me," I said.

"But I thought at least Trader was dead. I thought at least there was that, at least you'd killed her. And then . . . that man . . . the dead children . . . The 'House of Evil,' they called it."

"Martin Emory," I said.

"I couldn't stop watching the stories on TV. They had it on 24/7. The graves in the forest. The children's faces. And then that picture. That photograph: the man, Martin Emory, sitting in a car . . . And right next to him, there she was . . ."

"The Fat Woman. Our old friend Aunt Jane."

"Our old friend . . ."

I forced myself to look at her. She was gazing past her clenched fist, lost in her own ferocity. And I was lost too—lost in her story, lost in the sight of her, lost in my own hurt at what she had become. I couldn't help but think of how she was when I dreamed about her. Serene and sweet, womanly and kind—grown-up, but still the way she'd been as a little girl: like the princess in her own stories. All that time, these last three years, I'd been so swept away by that dream of her, I couldn't really care for anyone else. Not for Bethany, not for anyone. Because in my mind, it was always Samantha. Now here she was, the same face I dreamed, the same woman, but not the same, her mouth twisted and her eyes sour and her whole aspect poisoned with terror and betrayal and a whole childhood of abuse.

"I drove to New York," she said. "The second I saw that photograph. I just turned off the TV, walked out of my apartment, and got in my car . . . I drove without stopping. I went to the first police station I could find. No idea what I was doing, what I was looking for or what to tell them. I mean, it's not like I knew the woman's real name or where that horrible house had been, or where the orphanage was or anything. I asked the sergeant at the front desk if I could talk to the detectives on the case, but she said it was an undercover operation and their identities were confidential. But then I overheard two patrolmen talking about a cop who'd been wounded in the house, who was in a hospital in Westchester. So I just . . . I got back in my car . . ."

I grunted, as if I'd been struck. Suddenly I understood. She had been to the hospital in Westchester. Of course. I must have seen her there. That must have been it. I remembered how I had blacked out as I was leaving the place. I must have walked right by her and somehow recognized her and shut the recognition out of my mind. Until later. Until I was sick with withdrawal—just as I was sick again now. Then I dreamed about her coming to take care of me. The adult Samantha.

"Danny? Danny, are you all right?"

I started to answer but the words died on my lips and no—no, I was not all right. A new and denser fog had engulfed me. I grew wildly dizzy sitting there. Dazed, I stared at her through fever and confusion and I thought I was seeing her now as I must have seen her then, at the hospital in Westchester, seeing her in a strangely bright and visionary way. I felt beads of sweat breaking out on my forehead. And I thought: *Of course I recognized her.* I would always recognize her. I would know her anywhere, everywhere—forever. Right this minute, I could see her not only as she was. I could also see the face of the six-year-old child she had been, just as clearly as if no time had passed at all. Not only that—I could see what had happened to her afterward, every incident of cruelty and violation. I could see her memories—I could *remember* her memories—I could see the whole miserable life she must have lived, the life I think I knew in my heart she *would* live when they tore her, sobbing, away from me, when they dragged us out of each other's clinging arms, mouthing their grown-up lies about how we could write to each other and visit each other, because they didn't understand, they were grown-ups and they *couldn't* understand, that it was violence to separate us, because we were one thing, meant to be together.

"Danny? Are you sick?"

I lifted a trembling hand to my face. My skin was cold and slick with sweat. "Samantha, we . . ."

Our eyes met—and her eyes went wide, and I knew she understood as well. She saw what I saw: that we were one thing. She saw that she could never hide from me, that she was naked to my eyes, all her secrets and the humiliations and violations of her childhood exposed.

Her face contorted. She uncoiled herself quickly. She stepped away from the bed. "I need another smoke," she said.

I wanted to go to her, needed to go to her, but I couldn't. I sat where I was, sprawled in my chair, heavy and feverish. "Got to . . . got to . . ." I murmured, my mind drifting.

The afternoon was wearing on. The room was growing darker. By the time I managed to work myself to my feet, the air around me was hazy and gray. I moved out into the common room. Saw

her there on the balcony again behind the billowing white curtains. The curtains fluttered and danced, covering her, revealing her,
making her seem like a phantom one moment and real the next.

I pushed through them, went out onto the balcony, glad to get
a breath of the cold evening air. She was out there, bowing her
head, lowering a fresh cigarette to a fresh match, a fresh flame. I
wiped the sweat off my face. Squeezed my eyes shut, opened them,
trying to clear my head.

"Samantha . . ." I started.

"Just let me finish, Danny. For God's sake, just let me tell you
the rest of it and get out of here."

She stood with her back to me, smoking in curt, jerky, angry
motions, looking out over the railing as the gold went out of the
daylight and the evening came.

"It took me three years," she said. "Weekends. Vacations. Looking
for the places. Looking for all of it. Three years."

I nodded. Those were the three years I had spent in Tyler County,
working for the Sheriff's Department, recovering from the Emory case.

"I didn't want to do it. It was like an addiction. I kept telling
myself to stop. I kept *trying* to stop. But I couldn't. And slowly,
bit by bit, I dug it up. The missing-person reports on Alexander.
The old orphanage where we lived. And you—the detective who
turned out to be you. And finally, Washington Falls. And Sarah
Longstreet. And her."

She drew in smoke and I drew in the air, fighting off the fever
and the withdrawal haze that kept threatening to close in on me.
The curtains blew up around me and I saw her through them,
standing against the dusk, backlit by a rising moon.

"Her," I said thickly.

"Our old friend. Aunt Jane."

Right. That had to have been it. She had found the Fat Woman.
She had done what I couldn't do. Because she remembered who
she was and I didn't.

She said, "Once I found Sarah Longstreet, once I understood what happened, it didn't take me long to locate one of the doctors from here, St. Mary's. Dr. White, his name was. He was part of the team who treated . . . our old friend . . . after the fire . . . At first, he went all confidential on me, but when I told him my story, he went back to his records, found her name . . ."

Despite the cool air, despite darkness falling and even colder air starting to blow in off the trees, I felt the fever sweat break out on my forehead again. I clenched my fists. "What was it?" I said. "What was her name?"

Samantha's face was bathed in red as she pulled on the cigarette again and it glowed. And as she blew out the breath of smoke, she said: "Bobbi-Ray. Bobbi-Ray Jagger."

The wind swirled and the curtains swirled and my mind swirled as the withdrawal vertigo rose in me again.

"Bobbi-Ray Jagger," I said. It came out of my throat in a hoarse growl.

"Once I had her name, I used my library's research tools and found her address," Samantha said. "It wasn't hard. She wasn't far. Just about four hundred miles away from here." She told me the address. I was losing focus and had to work hard to lock it in my mind. "I called the police, the NYPD, to tell them what I knew . . . And that's when they came for me. The brothers. What did you call them?"

"The Starks."

"The Starks. That's why I couldn't trust the cops anymore. You see? They said they'd have a detective call me back. And then, that night, as I was coming home from work . . . I saw them." She turned and faced me, her eyes flashing with anger. The curtains were blowing all around me, all around us both, so that we only caught clear glimpses of each other off and on. In my fever, the effect was dreamlike.

Samantha tossed her cigarette away and immediately worked the pack out of her pocket to get a fresh one. She struck a match like it had struck her first. Lit up. Tugged hard. Hissed out smoke.

"They were in my apartment," she said flatly. "I saw them through the window, going through the place. I didn't know how they'd found me or why. I thought maybe it was because I called the police, maybe the Fat Woman had connections with the NYPD . . . I've never been so scared in my life." She made a miserable noise deep in her throat. "Except I have. As we know."

Weak, fading, I moved to the railing and leaned against it. I tried to keep focusing but she seemed very far away, her voice small and distant.

"I ran. I got my car. There was only one place I could think of to go. To you, Danny. I drove—and I thought I'd lost them. I kept checking my rearview. I used every back road I could. But then, in the middle of nowhere, on an empty stretch of highway—suddenly these headlights . . ." She took a breath, biting back her rage and bitterness. "They ran me off the road. I managed to get into some high grass. They came hunting for me . . . God, Danny! God! They kept moving through the grass, making these threats, telling me what they were going to do to me. These evil, evil things they were going to do . . ." She threw away this cigarette too. She shook her head angrily. "I made it to the river. It was the only way I could hide from them. But the water was so cold . . . and the current . . ."

"Why didn't you come to me before?" I said, speaking carefully to keep the words from slurring. "Once you knew who I was, why didn't you just come?"

"You know why," she said. "I didn't want to see . . . that look in your eyes. That look there now—the disappointment."

"I'm not disappointed," I lied.

She didn't answer. She only smiled bitterly—and I realized: It was all that way with her. Bitterness and tears. It was that way with her all the time.

"After they found me in the river . . . when I woke up in the hospital, I just . . . I panicked. I started running again. And I kept running. Too afraid to try to contact you again. Too afraid to do anything except run and hide. Until I came here, the only place I could think of where they might not find me, and you might.

And I just waited. I waited, thinking, *Danny will come. Danny will find me. Danny is so strong, Danny is so fast . . .*" She choked on the words and was silent.

I nodded. She'd made it happen too. Finally. After all these years. She'd left a trail for me and I'd found her.

"That's it," she said. "That's everything." And after a moment's hesitation—a moment's thought—she tapped the balcony railing twice with her two palms and said, "I've got to go, Danny. I'm gone."

She moved abruptly into the billowing curtains.

I reached for her, took her arm. "No . . ."

But the fever rose in me again, much stronger, and she and the curtains and the night spun off sickeningly into a haze. She pulled from my grip easily. She went in through the doors.

"Samantha . . ."

I stumbled in after her. I was going dark fast, my legs weak under me. I clawed my way through the swirl of curtains. Pushed out of the night into the common room.

She was already moving toward the hall and its shadows. I tried to go after her. But the fever quickly got worse the moment I was in out of the fresh air. I felt the room growing smaller, the walls pressing in. I gripped the back of the sofa and held on, the room dipping and swaying around me.

"Samantha . . ."

She turned, a dim figure in the dying light. "I'm sorry, Danny. I really am."

"Trust me. Let me keep you safe."

"I can't. I'm sorry. I'll be safer on my own."

"No . . ."

I saw her tilt her head. I saw her eyes glistening. "You're so sweet, Danny. Brave—you're still so brave. Like one of those knights in the stories I used to tell you. Really. Like one of those knights who married the princess, remember?" On the last word, her voice broke. "I wanted so much to be that girl. I was supposed to be, you know. They ruined me. They had no right, Danny. They had no right."

"Don't . . . don't," I said thickly. I tried to go to her, but I knew if I let go of the sofa, I would tumble down—down and down into unconsciousness. "Don't cry, okay? I hate it when you cry."

She laughed and sobbed at once. "Too bad. I cry a lot. As we see." She started to fade from me as the shadows folded over her. I couldn't tell if she was moving away or if I was sinking down into the deeper depths of my fever. "You go get them for me, Danny, all right?" she said. "You get them and make them pay. Get her, Danny. Stop her. Don't let there be any more Alexanders. Remember him. Remember me."

"Samantha . . ."

"Oh, Danny," she said, her voice growing fainter and fainter, almost a whisper now. "Brave Danny. You're still you. I wish so much I were still me."

Then she was gone.

I took a step after her but that was all I had in me. The strength went out of my legs and they folded. I only just made it onto the sofa. I lay down there, the darkness deepening. Deepening . . .

Did she come back for me? At one point, I thought she did. At one point, I thought I saw her sitting above me. Looking down at me with those tender eyes. Drawing her cool hand over my forehead. Just like before. Just like I dreamed her when I was in withdrawal before. Just like Samantha . . .

I flashed awake in darkness. I sat up fast. I was weak and my head felt heavy, but my thoughts were clear. I knew where I was. I knew we had to move, had to get out . . .

I peered around me until the shapes of the common room showed themselves. It was the moon that did it, the light of the moon shining through the thin white curtains still dancing around the balcony doors.

"Samantha?" I said.

No answer.

I stood. I moved—too fast. I hit the table, stumbled, nearly fell. Then I put my hand out, felt my way through the deep shadows to the hallway. Moved down the hallway a few steps, away from the moonlight coming in from the balcony, into even deeper darkness.

The huge hospital stretched empty and silent all around me.

"Samantha!" I shouted. My voice died without an echo.

I knew she was gone.

I felt . . . too much to describe. Grief. Twisting, terrible grief. Frustration. Rage.

Fear. Fear that I had lost her this time forever.

I stared down the hall into pitch blackness. Only then did I remember . . . the name . . . She had given me the name . . . the address . . . The address about four hundred miles from here . . .

Well, that's what I had come for, wasn't it? That's why she had led me here and that's why I had come. For that name. For that address.

Go get them for me, Danny. Make them pay.

My face set, hard, my lips pressed tight together. My hands balled into fists at my side. At least there was that, I thought—at least she had given me that before she left. At least, wherever she was, I could do what she wanted now. Get the Fat Woman. Make her pay. Make sure she wouldn't hurt anyone else. Make sure Samantha didn't have to be afraid of her and her hired killers anymore.

I could put an end to this—finish it for good this time.

I lifted my eyes into the emptiness and darkness.

"Bobbi-Ray Jagger," I whispered.

15

The Fat Woman

A NIGHT OF FEVERED half-sleep in a nearby motel—then I
drove all the next day. The fog of withdrawal was still thick
in my mind and the ghosts were everywhere. There were dead
children watching from the fields outside the car window. There
was Stark suddenly sitting in the passenger seat beside me, and
just as suddenly gone. There was Samantha like a mirage drifting in and out of sight on the road ahead or in the rearview
mirror—following after me or drawing me on, as I knew now
she always had.

Sometimes—when my mind really misted over—there were only
eyes and half-seen faces, gazing at me through the haze. Once or
twice, it got so bad I had to pull the car to the side of the road and
go to sleep. After an hour or so, I'd wake up smelling smoke—in
a panic until I remembered: *Oh yeah, the fire. A long time ago.* Then
I kept on driving—through the ghost-world of my withdrawal—
toward the place where I would finally meet those ghosts face-
to-face, finally find the creature I'd been hunting all these years.

But the hunt was different now than it had been. Everything
was different—and I knew that everything would be different for
me from this time on. Before, I'd been propelled into pursuit by
a darkness in the back of my mind I didn't even know was there.

Now I knew. Now I had found my past, nightmare that it was. I had uncovered . . . well, I won't say the events that had made me who I was, because now that I remembered my childhood, I could see that, in fact, I had always been pretty much who I was. But I had uncovered the events that had given me the language of my obsessions. Alexander. The burning house. Aunt Jane. Samantha. The past had given names and faces to my fears and desires. And now my fears and desires led me back into the past.

Because I had to go back. There was no getting out of it. I still had to face the Fat Woman before this would finally be done. I didn't know what I was going to do when I found her. Driving through the haunted landscape, I was still so heavy with grief—so hot with anger—at having found Samantha and lost her again, having found her and lost my dream of her, having seen what they made of her, what they turned her into . . .

They had no right, Danny. They had no right.

All I wanted was to rain unholy death on anyone who'd been responsible. Stark. His men. Bobbi-Ray Jagger. Unholy death.

But all that was up ahead and I didn't know what it would be like, what I would do, what would happen. I just kept driving.

By nightfall, all the ghosts were gone. The last effects of the drug had worn off. My mind was finally clear again.

I drove through the dark. Down another winding forest road. Past deep watchful pines. Through thick moonlit mist. I searched for the address Samantha had given me. And there it was: another dirt drive by the side of the two-lane. It was hidden among conifer branches. I almost missed it.

I drove on a little ways. I found a place to pull over. I steered the Mustang under some trees, as far off the road as I could get. I killed the lights. Killed the engine. Got out of the car. The night was moist and cool. The mist was glowing under the high and gibbous moon. The woods were loud with the sound of frogs and crickets. As I walked back along the two-lane, I heard creatures scrambling away through the underbrush. I looked up ahead and

back behind me. No lights. No houses. No cars passing on the
road. I hadn't seen one for the last half hour at least. Must've been
miles away from everything out here. I guessed that was the way
she liked it these days. Bobbi-Ray. Aunt Jane.

I reached the drive. I walked into the forest.

There's no darkness like the darkness of the woods, like its heavy,
hunkering blackness. I moved slowly, feeling my way. I had a small
flashlight on my key chain. I used it sparingly. Flicked the beam
on and quickly off to pick out the path, then edged on under
cover of the night. Now and then the moon shone through the
crowns of the trees. Even then, I couldn't see much besides the
brooding shapes all around me and the tangled meshwork of
vines and branches silhouetted against the sky.

The path went on a long time. A long time. And all the while I
was thinking: *They had no right, Danny. They had no right.*

I sensed the road turning. When I looked up—when I peered
through the trees—I caught my first glimpse of the house lights
ahead of me.

They had no right.

I walked on.

I came to the end of the path, the edge of the woods. There was
a broad grassy clearing. The house stood at the center of it.

I could see it clearly by the light of the moon. It didn't look anything like the old house, the one with the tower, the one I burned.
I realized now that I had half-expected to find that place, that old
place, waiting for me, as if I really had walked back in time. But
this was a big, broad, shingled, all-American country home, two
stories and an attic beneath one of those cross-gable roofs. There
was a balcony at one window on the second floor. A wraparound
overhang above the first floor with pillars holding it up over the
porch along the house's side. A nice, comfortable, secluded place
in the woods.

I stood still, watching it. The house was all but dark. There was only one light burning in one small second-story window. As I looked up at it, a shadow passed through the yellow glow. I felt my breath catch. Someone was in there. I felt a moment of unbridled childish dread—as if this were the old house, after all; as if I were still just a boy who might fall helplessly into Aunt Jane's clutches ...

Just then, another light went on—a pale outdoor light under the porch roof off to the right. The light cast a glow up over the house walls and gave the place a living, looming, waiting aspect. Or maybe that was my imagination.

Now there was a movement. A flashlight beam. I saw the watchman.

He was just stepping off the porch. The light there caught his face and I saw he was one of the two men who'd nearly blown my head off at the cabin up on the cliff. He was wearing a black suit and I could tell by the hang of it that there was a big pistol hiding beneath it, a real cannon of some kind tucked in a holster under his arm.

He held the powerful flashlight in his left hand, keeping his right hand free to draw the weapon. He shone the beam before him as he walked across the front of the house, moving toward where I was at the edge of the clearing. He passed the beam over the woods to my right, then moved it in my direction. His appearance had caught me off-guard and I froze right where I was. The light almost reached me before I reacted. But then, just before he saw me, I darted to the side of the path and dropped down on one knee behind a tree. The flashlight beam passed over the tree and on into the woods beyond without touching me. The watchman kept walking past the front of the house, searching the area, making his rounds.

He went by the front door and kept moving, scanning the dark with the flashlight. He reached the driveway on the far side of the house. He moved around the large black sedan that was parked under the carport there. He explored the carport with his flashlight.

Then he kept going, on to the far side of the house. He stood there with his back to me and shone the light toward the trees in the rear.

I drew my gun. I started moving toward him.

I moved in a crouch, soft-footed, trying not to make too much noise on the dirt drive. Even in his dark clothing, the watchman was plenty visible in the clearing moonlight. He was tall, broad-shouldered, strong-looking. He didn't go beyond the edge of the house, but stood where he was, his back to me. He panned the flashlight right to left slowly, making a thorough exploration of the forest that edged the backyard.

I reached the grass of the front lawn without alerting him. The watchman went on searching the woods. But I could already sense that he was about to finish—that he was going to turn around before I reached him. I moved quicker, closing the gap as he brought the flashlight back along the forest, completing his search.

I was still maybe fifteen yards away from him when he started to swing around to face me. I went faster, coming off the grass, stepping onto the dirt drive, passing behind the big black sedan. I drew my gun back, ready to hammer him into the ground with the butt of it.

Then the dirt crunched under my sneakers.

The watchman heard it. In an instant, he drew his weapon and spun around toward me.

I leveled my gun at his face. He leveled his gun at mine. The light from the swinging flashlight danced around us, making his eyes gleam and go dark, gleam and go dark again.

We stood still, pointing our guns at one another. I saw him grin in the dancing light.

"Stand off," he said.

I pulled the trigger and killed him.

As the blast echoed to the sky, he tumbled backward, his gun falling, his arms flailing, the flashlight swinging and the beam going violently—crazily—this way and that so that the bloody horror where his face had been shone in the night and then vanished as he fell. The sound of the gunshot faded just before he hit the ground.

I dropped down to one knee beside him. I put my hand on his chest. I heard him give a whistling groan out of his ruined mouth. I felt his heart stop beating.

After that, silence. Even the noises of the surrounding forest had stopped cold.

I stood up slowly. I was behind the big sedan. The smell of gun smoke was drifting up around me. I watched the house over the top of the car. Still dark. Still only the one light in the upstairs window.

The shadow passed through the glow again.

I knew whoever was up there must have heard the gunshot— knew I was coming, for sure.

I started moving. The pistol blast had blown every thought away. There was only the grief in me now—only the rage in me— pushing me forward.

I came around the car, keeping low. I went quickly to the side of the house and pressed against the wall so no one could take a shot at me from the windows. Bent forward, I raced through the house shadow, along the border of the moonlight. I made it to the front door.

No point in stealth. It was time to move fast. I leveled the pistol. Blew off the doorknob. Kicked the door in and pulled back quickly, waiting for the answering gunfire from inside.

Nothing. Only more silence, the house hunkering over me.

The door swung in on the darkness inside. I crouched low and took a look. An open living room, sofa, chairs, tables, shapes in shadow. I went in fast and rolled, once again expecting the blast. Once again, nothing. Silence. And I was in, crouched down behind a chair, the moonlight at the windows, the darkness thick around me.

I was breathing hard. I was sweating hard. My heart was pounding. I stayed where I was and listened—for a movement, a whisper, a breath, anything at all. But no—still—the silence was profound.

The house sort of ticked and settled around me—that was the only noise. And yet I felt there had to be someone, Stark or one of his men, someone somewhere in the darkness—waiting to take his shot and bring me down.

I stayed where I was till my eyes adjusted. Then I could make out the stairs, across the room. A flight with a railing rising out of sight. There was a soft glow above—that upstairs light—bleeding onto the landing from the room up there. I took a breath and moved out from behind my cover, traveling quickly toward that light, toward the foot of the stairs.

I held my gun tight, the grain of the grip digging into my wet palm. My eyes were scanning the dark but there was just too much of it, too many shapes and forms I couldn't make sense of, too many places for a killer to hide. I couldn't fight blind. My best bet was to keep moving, get upstairs, get to the light.

I reached the stairs. I started up, traveling fast, staying low. I came onto the landing. I looked for the source of the light and saw a door standing open at the end of the hall—just standing open on a lighted room. The light spilled out over the landing's shiny wooden floor, the glow of it fading as it spread from the source, dying away completely a foot or two from where I stood at the top of the stairs.

My eyes moved over the corridor. Door after open door into other rooms, dark rooms. A killer could come out of any one of them, shoot from any one of them as I went past. I could feel the adrenaline flowing through me like an electric current. I felt as if every nerve was alive and crackling.

I heard something. A sound from that final room, the lit room at the end of the hall. A piece of furniture shifting.

Someone was in there. Waiting for me.

I leveled the gun and started down the corridor. I went quickly, still bent low. I pulled up before I reached each of the dark, open rooms. Each time, I waited, listening. Each time, I heard nothing. I moved on.

The light at the end of the hall grew brighter, the doorway closer. I could feel my pulse in my neck like a bird beating its wings against a window. Somehow, even before I stepped to the threshold, I knew what I was going to see.

Then I did step to the threshold—and I saw what I was expecting. What I had been expecting, I think, since I was a kid.

I saw the Fat Woman.

What a strange, nightmare moment that was. I was so wired that every detail seemed written in my brain with electric fire.

I recognized the room. I had glimpsed it only for a second on the computer screen in Stark's cabin, but I knew it was the same place. There were dark windows on the wall across from me. There were books and ledgers piled up against the walls to either side—no shelves, just the piles of ledgers. There was a large oak desk that seemed to take up most of the floor. A laptop open on the desk, plugged into an extension cord. A phone. A cup full of pens. Every detail of it hit me . . .

And there sat the Fat Woman, behind the desk. An immense seething mass of living meat, heaving with every breath. Her hair was blonde—a wig, I think; a cheap one—stiff as straw and poorly combed. The features of her face, obliterated by the flames I'd started so long ago, were barely visible in the mottled brown and white scar tissue. But her eyes were still alive in there, alive and gleaming, and her mouth was twisted in a strange, distant smile . . .

How familiar she was. How well I knew the sight of her. The image had been inside me all these years—secretly for a long time, but always there. Not one day of my adult life, not one hour had passed without her presence. Now I saw the great wicked breathing mass of her, and she seemed almost hyperreal, the stuff of imagination sprung to life. I stared at her, fascinated.

She was wearing a shapeless brown jersey dress. It had a scooped neck. That's where my gun was trained: on the point where her pendulous breasts met in a deep cleavage. I battled an urge to pull the trigger and destroy whatever it was she used for a heart.

Staring at her—I couldn't stop staring at her—I moved into the room. I pushed the door shut behind me. I didn't want anyone creeping out of one of those rooms in the corridor and taking a shot at my back.

I moved to where I had a clear view of her burned, bloated hands. I glanced at them quickly to make sure she wasn't armed. She wasn't. One hand rested on the desktop, like a cut of some putrid beef. The other hand held what at first I thought was a mirror, its surface pointed at me, the reflection on it so dim it was barely distinguishable.

That made no sense—a mirror—but I couldn't pay attention to that now. My eyes kept going back to what was left of her face, the mottled mass of it. She went on sitting there, following my movements with those beady, soulless eyes, smiling her eerie smile. I couldn't tear my eyes away from the sheer fact of her.

"Do you know who I am?" I heard myself say. I barely recognized my own voice, it was so strangled in my throat, so furious, so sad.

The woman didn't answer. She didn't move. Her lips didn't move. And yet a noise came back to me from across the room—a noise that made something shrivel at the core of me, a harsh rattling disturbance of the atmosphere like a snake makes when it coils up suddenly out of the grass.

I knew that sound. It was Stark. It was Stark, laughing.

And in his harsh rasp of a whisper, he said, "Champion."

I blinked, stunned, confused. Then I shifted my eyes and saw him.

That thing the Fat Woman was holding in her hand—it wasn't a mirror. It was a computer tablet—an iPad or something like it. The face I had seen there dimly was not my reflection. It was clearer now and I could see it was Stark. That bizarre face so much like a death's head—the gray-white skin, the hollow cheeks, the huge, staring eyes . . . It was grinning out at me from the screen.

My glance shifted quickly, briefly, from his image to the Fat Woman at the desk. I thought I saw some light of triumph in her eyes, some satisfaction in the twist of the hole that had once been her mouth. What did she look so damned happy about? But a wisp of dread curled through me like a wisp of smoke, and I began to understand.

I looked back at the screen in her hand. At the skull on the screen.

"Stark," I said. "I expected to find you here in person."

"I'm on my way, Champion," the skull rasped.

He was too. I noticed the background of the scene as he spoke. Darkness but with a sense of motion, occasional glimpses of passing light. He was in the rear seat of a moving car, filming himself with a mounted camera.

"You're a little late," I said.

"Sorry. I had some business to take care of."

"Well, too bad. I killed your guy. And now I'm taking your client in. You and I will have to settle our little feud another time."

Stark smiled—a chilling grin. "I knew a man once in another country," he said quietly. "He had trained himself not to feel pain. Physical pain, I mean. Can you imagine that? It was an amazing act of mental discipline. I never saw anything like it."

He pressed a button on the arm of his seat. The camera shifted and I saw Samantha.

She was sitting next to him in the backseat. Duct tape over her mouth, her shoulders wrenched back so I knew her hands were bound behind her. The green camera light on the computer tablet was lit so I knew that she could see me too. She gazed at me, sadly. Her eyes were far away, as if she were hiding in the mazes of her own mind, unable to face the world outside her. I'd seen that look before. It was the look of an abused child. I had let her down again. I had not protected her from this.

"Being able to transcend pain—it gave this man a false sense of security, you know," Stark went on. "It made him fearless and he mistook that for courage. Do you understand what I'm saying?"

My throat closed as I watched his bony fingers twine around Samantha's hair, slide past her hair to stroke her cheek, to cup her chin. He traced a slow curving pattern down the front of Samantha's sweatshirt. All the while, Samantha stared at me from those faraway inner places. Dull, dead, not even reacting. I knew that, for her, it wasn't just Stark molesting her, it was all the men, a childhood full of them. All the men who'd hurt her while she'd prayed that I would come to her rescue.

"He thought he could defy me, this man," Stark went on. "He thought he was exempt because I couldn't hurt him. It was . . . a limited view of human life, don't you think?"

I swallowed my helplessness, my helpless rage. Like swallowing a rock made of fire. "It was," I said hoarsely. "It was a limited view."

"Do you know what I did?" Stark said. His hand trailed down Samantha's front. It went out of the camera shot, but I knew what he was doing by the way she jerked behind her gag. "Do you know what I did, Champion?"

"Yes, I know what you did."

"I took his children, one by one . . ."

"I know what you did, Stark."

"He broke right away, but I didn't stop." He pressed the button on the seat arm again. The camera panned away from Samantha. The skull face came back into view. "I wanted him to understand before I killed him. I wanted everyone who knew him to understand: There are all kinds of pain; there's no end to the varieties. And no one is exempt. No one. You're hard-core, Champion, I admit that. But even you, in the end, are not exempt."

I glanced at the Fat Woman. She went on sitting there, an enormous, motionless mass, her eyes gleaming with triumph.

"What do you expect me to do, Stark?" I said.

Stark leaned forward. His skull face filled the screen, grinning out at me. "You're going to hand your gun over to dear Aunt Jane. You're going to give her the gun and she's going to hold you there until I arrive."

"Right," I said. "And if I don't?"

"I'm going to spend the brief little rest of this car journey butchering your woman in amusing but not entirely fatal ways."

A long, shuddering breath came out of me. I'd been holding on to it without realizing it. If I didn't do what Stark said, he would torture Samantha. If I did, he would bring her here, and then torture her, forcing me to watch. He needed me to watch . . .

"Give her the gun," Stark said. "Do it now, Champion, or I'll get started."

I licked my dry lips. I did not know if I could do what I needed to do. I did not know if I was cold enough.

I shook my head. "You're right about one thing," I said.

"Give her the gun, Champion. Now," Stark said.

"We've all got a weakness. No one's exempt."

"Do it."

"You know what your weakness is, Stark?"

"Hand over your gun."

"Your weakness is that you need me to suffer."

"You'll suffer, Champion."

"You promised your brother. You can't just torture Samantha. You want me to watch. You need me to watch."

"You'll watch," said Stark, grinning. "You won't be able to stop watching."

I grinned back at him, feeling like Death myself. I lifted my Glock.

For once, I saw the skull's smile falter. I saw uncertainty in Stark's glowing eyes.

I pulled the trigger. In that small room, the explosion was so loud it sent a stabbing ache through my ears. It drowned out the Fat Woman's startled scream—but I saw her scream, saw her scarred mouth opening in a black O.

The computer tablet flipped out of her hand, shattering in mid-air before dropping with a crash to the floor.

I turned to the Fat Woman. Her mouth was still wide open. She was staring at me in shocked surprise.

"What . . . ? What the hell do you think you're doing?" she said. They were the first words she'd spoken since I'd walked into the room. They came out in a deep, dull croak, but I could hear the tone of outrage in them. Outrage.

"Did you think I'd bargain with him?" I asked her. "Did you think I'd plead for mercy like the children do? You taught me better than that."

I stepped toward her. She recoiled in her chair. "You stay away from me!"

I came stalking around the desk. She panicked, went for the drawer. Scrabbled the drawer open with her fat hand and reached inside.

I used the butt of the Glock to hammer the drawer shut on her fingers. She bellowed like a cow at a slaughterhouse.

"Ow! Stop it! What's wrong with you?" she said. "Who the fuck do you think you are?"

"I'm the little boy who got away."

I knocked her chair back so that her hand pulled the drawer open. I found the Colt .32 in there, a delicate lady's handgun. How would she even have gotten her fat fingers through the trigger guard? I pulled the gun out. Tossed it aside. It fell behind one of the stacks of ledgers in the far corner.

Then I yanked the power cord out of her laptop, pulled the long, narrow extension cord out of the wall. I grabbed her by the wrist, twisted her arm around.

"Let go of me!" she shouted.

"I'd like to kill you. I ought to kill you. But I'm not what you are. I'm still not what you are."

I wound the extension cord around the thick flesh of her wrist.

"Ow!" she shouted. "You're hurting me. Are you insane?"

She tried to punch me in the head with her free hand. I caught the blow on my raised arm. Wrenched her other hand back and tied that too.

"I'll think of you when you're on death row, though," I told her. "A decade of waiting, and then the needle. I'll think of you every day."

I started to tie the cord to the chair.

"Ow!" she snarled. "I mean it. You're hurting me, you asshole!"

I tied her to the chair, her arms behind her.

"You gorilla! You piece of shit!" she shouted, bouncing her fat ass up and down as she struggled. "You have no right!"

That did it. The fury exploded through the center of me. With a growl, I jammed my Glock into her eye, hard. She gasped and gagged on her own fear and shut up. I felt my finger tighten on the trigger. I wanted to put a bullet in her so badly it felt like a kind of lust.

"No right," I heard myself whisper. Pressing the gun into her eye, I leaned down to put my lips against what was left of her ear. "You think I have no right?"

"Don't . . ." she said. She was panting with fear—fear of the gun. "You can't. It's stupid. It's crazy. You kill me like this—in cold blood? You'll go to prison."

"Will I? Maybe. Maybe I don't care."

"For Christ's sake . . ."

"Maybe it would be worth it."

"What the hell is wrong with you?" she croaked.

"Why don't you bargain with me?" I said. "Why don't you plead for mercy like the children do?"

"This is crazy! It's crazy! What're you so all-fired angry about?"

I laughed wildly, still pushing the gun into her. I did sound crazy. But it was such a nutty thing for her to ask, I thought she must be babbling in terror. But no, she meant it. She didn't understand.

"You and that girl," she went on, in her deep, dead voice. "Hounding me like this. Tormenting me. Why? What for? You're both all right, aren't you? You got away. Didn't you? Obviously. You're fine. So what're you complaining about? I'm the one who should be doing all the screaming and yelling here. Look at me. Look what you did to me. You set fire to me. Look at my face! I almost died. Now you come into my house like the hound of hell or something. Shooting and threatening people . . . Why? You're fine. You're fine."

I stared at her. I drew the gun away from her a little but kept it trained on her face. "It's a limited view of human life," I said hoarsely.

She stared at me. "You're a madman, if you ask me," she said. "I had to hire a very expensive security agency just to keep myself safe from you. And you come in here, shooting and threatening like I don't even know what."

I could only go on staring, shaking my head.

"And all the while, you're fine," she blithered on. "I'm the one who got burned. Look at me. You're just fine and you nearly killed me."

"What about Alexander?" I don't know why I said it. What was the point? But the words just came out of me.

"Who?"

At once, the rage exploded in me again. "Alexander!" I shouted. And before I could stop myself, I drew my free hand back and slapped her. The blow cracked against her cheek, knocking her head to the side. A line of blood appeared at the corner of her mouth and trailed down the side of her chin.

She gaped at me, licking at the blood. "You're insane," she said. "Alexander? I don't even know who that is?"

"What about *all* the others?" I growled at her, my voice scraping in my throat, my gun hand trembling. "The ones you sold to Emory. All the others all these years."

"What the hell are you talking about?"

Shaking my head. "Good God."

"What others? What do you mean?" she said. "Oh, wait. You mean the other *kids*? Jesus. What business is that of yours?" She stared back at me, uncomprehending. "I mean, what the hell do you expect? This is what I do, for Christ's sake. People want what I sell. They have their rights, don't they? What are you, the judge over them suddenly? You're the judge over me suddenly? Jesus! Is *that* what you're here about? The *other* ones? You come in here, shooting guns, hitting a woman . . . a disabled woman . . . after you're the one who burned me . . . and it's all about *that*? The other ones? What do they even have to do with you? You got away. You're all right. You're fine. I'm the one who got burned in the whole business. God! You are a seriously disturbed person!"

I laughed again—or made a sound like laughter—backing away from her, shaking my head. I had no answer. What answer was there? It was as if we were speaking two different languages.

"Well, go ahead," she said then, turning to look at me. She was frowning with her mouth open and I could see her teeth were stained with blood. "Go ahead and shoot me if that's what you want. Go to prison. Die in prison for all I care. Your big revenge. For what? You can't bring any of those children back. No one can. What's the point? What's the point of any of it?"

I still had the gun on her. It was aimed at her heart. I still had my finger on the trigger. I still yearned to send her to hell. Maybe I would have.

But just then, the glow of headlights passed across the dark window behind her and I knew that Stark had arrived.

Still, I stood there another moment. I could hear the tires of Stark's car outside on the dirt road coming out of the forest. I knew I had to go, had to move fast. But still . . . I couldn't take my eyes away from her. *All these years,* I kept thinking. *All these years . . .*

Then, with a breath, I came to myself. I turned my back on her. Walked to the door.

"Hey! You can't just leave me here like this!" the Fat Woman shouted angrily behind me. "Take this goddamned cord off me, you maniac! Let me go!"

I pulled the door open. I saw the hallway ahead of me, lit by the light from the room, receding into shadow, then into darkness.

"Don't you dare!" the Fat Woman shouted. "Don't you dare just leave me here, you bastard! How could you?"

I stepped out and pulled the door shut behind me.

I walked down the corridor, gun in hand. The Fat Woman was still ranting behind me. I could hear her voice, her curses coming through the door. I didn't pause. I just went on down the hall. I didn't worry about the open rooms now, the dark rooms. I wasn't afraid some gunman was waiting for me. The place was empty,

I could feel it. The Fat Woman had no one left now. Only Stark and whoever was with him in his car.

I reached the stairs. I started down. The room below came into view. I saw the headlights of Stark's car glaring on one of the ground-floor windowpanes. I heard the car pulling to a stop, the tires crunching on the drive. The headlights went out.

I stepped off the last stair into the living room. There wasn't much light here, just the moon glow coming through the windows. I could make out the shapes of furniture. A sofa right in front of me, chairs here and there, a low table, and so on. I maneuvered through the gaps, crossing the room.

I reached the window where I'd seen the headlights. I pressed close to the wall, curled my head around the frame, and looked out.

Stark's car, a long, broad black machine, had stopped at the base of the lawn. It stood there another second, motionless beneath the moon. Out of range. No shot from where I was.

The doors came open. The front door opened first and a rifleman got out, a man in an overcoat. The other thug from the cabin probably. He lifted his weapon and propped it on his hip.

The back door opened. Stark got out. He was dressed in black. It made his white skull face look even whiter, especially with the moon shining on it. The moon made his eyes glint as he surveyed the house and the grounds. I saw him stop as he spotted the dead watchman by the sedan in the carport. When he turned back to face me, he was grinning as if the sight of the dead man amused him. His teeth shone in the moonlight too.

He bent down and reached into the car and dragged out Samantha. With her hands bound behind her, she stumbled as she came to her feet. Stark jerked her arm roughly to hold her upright. I could see him speaking to her but I couldn't hear his voice.

He yanked her body close to his. He wrapped his arm around her throat. He lifted a pistol and pressed it against the side of her head.

He spoke again and the rifleman started walking over the grass toward the house, toward me. Holding Samantha around the throat, holding her in front of him all the while, Stark followed after.

I moved, shifting from one window to another so I could watch them cross the lawn to the front door. I thought if they got close enough, I might get a shot at the rifleman before they came into the house. But as I was considering it, I saw Stark speak again—I heard the rasp of his voice this time, though I couldn't make out the words

Then, he lifted his head, and he shouted in his hoarse rasp—one word: "Champion!"

At first I didn't understand—but now the rifleman lowered his weapon from his hip and I realized: The shout had been a warning.

I started running. My eyes had adjusted to the dark enough for me to see my way. I reached the sofa at the base of the stairs and hurled myself down behind it, even as the rifleman opened fire.

The gun had the steady chiggering roar of a jackhammer. There wasn't a break in the noise. The windows shattered and the walls splintered as the bullets came through. The whole house felt like it was trembling, like it was about to shiver to pieces and collapse.

I lay on the floor behind the sofa. There was nowhere to go. The barrage felt like it went on for hours, but it must have been less than half a minute. Then a pause—the rifle was empty. I heard the rifleman pop the magazine. I knew it would take him only a second to reload.

I'd been waiting for that second. I sprang off the floor and leapt to the stairway.

I'd just barely started up when the blasting began again. Then the door came crashing open.

I ran for the top of the stairs. I heard the metallic clunk beneath me that could only mean one thing: a grenade. Probably an M84, a flash-bang. Because Stark didn't want to kill me. That's why he had shouted a warning. He just wanted to pin me down so I couldn't lie in ambush for him.

Sure enough, as I reached the dark landing, as I hit the floor, covering my ears with the heels of my palms, the thing went off below. Even with my eyes closed, I saw the white flash. Even with my ears covered, the explosion rocked me.

Then the gunfire started again as the rifleman entered the house. The darkness below flickered with muzzle flame. The air trembled with thunder. Glass and wood exploded everywhere. I could hear the bullets sweeping the room.

Another pause—the quick snapping sounds of a reload.

Stark's rasping whisper: "Upstairs."

I got to my feet and ran. I dashed through the first open door I saw, pushing it shut behind me just as the next grenade hit the landing. I was leaning against the door when the flash-bang blew. The sound and light of the explosion was muffled but the air wave jolted me through the wood. Then the shooting started again as the rifleman climbed the stairs.

I opened the door and curled quickly out of the room, back onto the landing, back toward the stairway. The air was flickering and shuddering again as the bullets rattled into the landing wall. The muzzle of the gun came into view, and then the gunman's head and shoulders as he climbed, firing relentlessly, sweeping the bullets back and forth.

Then another pause. The snap of the rifleman reloading.

I stepped to the top of the stairs and blew his head off.

It was one shot. The top of the rifleman's brow flew away in pieces. His head snapped back as his brains spat out behind him. Some portion of a second later, the message reached his body that there was no longer anyone home, and the meat that was left toppled backward down the stairs.

Stark laughed. Of course he laughed. The rifleman had been a sacrifice. To get him close. And now he was close. Nothing between us but Samantha.

The sound of his laughter—that god-awful sound; it really was awful—drifted up to me where I was standing, my Glock still pointed down the stairs into the shadows of the living room below.

I saw Samantha come out of those shadows first, her mouth taped, her eyes still dull and far away.

Then Stark came forward behind her. His arm still wrapped around Samantha's throat, his death's head appeared over her shoulder, grinning up at me. In his free hand, he held a gun, trained on my heart.

It was a good thing I had killed his brother. It was a good thing he hated me so uncontrollably. If it hadn't been for that hatred, he would have shot me dead on the spot and Samantha right afterward. It was only his obsession with revenge, his need to cause me the greatest pain possible: That was his weakness, and it was all that was keeping both me and her alive.

"Drop the gun, Champion," he rasped.

He climbed toward me, pointing his weapon at me, forcing Samantha ahead of him up the stairs. He kept his head moving, drawing it back behind her. I had no shot, no way to take him out without risking her life.

I drew back, down the corridor, hoping for a better angle. Samantha rose into view, but now Stark had her twisted around, a shield to protect his flank from me. He shifted his grip on her and hoisted her off her feet. I could see how strong he was by the ease of the movement. He took the last few stairs more quickly, coming onto the landing, turning toward me, Samantha in front of him again, his arm around her throat again and the pistol once again leveled at my chest.

"Drop the gun, I said." He came down the dark hall.

I backed away, my Glock on the two of them, but no shot, no way to take a shot.

"Do it now, Champion, or I'll put one in her."

He shifted his weapon. Took it off me. Stuck it into the side of Samantha's head, making her flinch with pain and fear. He kept coming toward me. I kept backing away.

"You think I won't do it?" he said. His face appeared from behind her for a second and I saw him smile. "I'd like to keep her around, it's true. I'd like to draw this out, you know I would. But I'll kill her, I surely will. Drop the gun."

He stepped toward me. I stepped back, forcing my heart to go cold as the calculations ratcheted through my mind at high speed.

"She's no use to you dead," I said. My voice still sounded alien to my own ears. "Put a bullet in her and it's just you and me trading fire. At best, she's a dead shield. At best, you kill me—kill me quick. That's no good for you, is it? You made a promise to your brother's soul, Stark. Remember? To put me through hell. You promised him you'd put me through hell for a long time . . ."

I heard the breath come stuttering out of him like a death rattle. I saw the big eyes glow with frustration and fury. He kept coming toward me. I kept stepping back—and then my heels hit the door, the door of the last room, the room where the Fat Woman was tied to the chair.

I stopped. Stark stopped. We stood facing each other. The corridor was silent. The Fat Woman wasn't screaming anymore. I guess all that gunfire had shut her up.

For one more second we faced off, Samantha between us. Then I saw the next idea—the next move—come into the skeleton's glowing eyes. I guess we thought of it at the same time, and we knew at the same time that I was finished.

He shifted the gun from Samantha's head to her elbow. He tightened his grip around her throat.

"I don't have to kill her," he rasped. "We can begin this now."

But even before he finished speaking, I threw down my gun. I spread my hands.

"You win, Stark," I said.

Stark made a noise: a long, groaning breath of satisfaction. His grin and his pleasure-glazed stare made his face look like something that might pop out at you in a funhouse. He had to lick the salt of joy off his lips before he could speak.

"Go through the door now," he said. He pressed his gun harder against Samantha's writhing body by way of emphasis.

But I didn't need to be told twice. I reached behind me for the knob. Opened the door. Stepped through.

The light in the room made me squint after the shadows of the corridor. Before I got my bearings, Stark stormed in after me, shoving me aside. He took one look around: the Fat Woman struggling in the chair, the cluttered desk, the night-hung windows, the papers and files stacked up against the wall . . .

"Good!" said the Fat Woman at once in her loud, blunt voice. "Get this cord off me—now!"

Stark ignored her. With every breath, he was still making that sound, that gratified groan. He tossed Samantha away from him—as if she were a crumpled piece of paper; as if she were garbage. She hit the wall and stumbled, struggling to keep her feet. She stood there, breathing hard behind her gag, her hands bound behind her. She watched us with her wide, distant eyes.

Stark, on the other hand—he was all focus, fully alert. He gestured at me with the gun.

"Take off that jacket."

"Get this cord off me, damn it!" said the Fat Woman. "It's cutting off my circulation. I'm going to get gangrene."

"Shut up," Stark told her. And to me again: "The jacket—take it off."

I stripped off the windbreaker. He gestured with the gun again. I tossed the jacket to a spot near his feet. Stark kicked it aside.

"Turn your pockets inside out," he said to me.

"Goddamn it, Stark!" shouted the Fat Woman.

"You'll get out," he told her. "Just hold your water."

The Fat Woman made a guttural noise of rage. She struggled against the cord for a moment, then sagged, gasping with the effort.

Another gesture my way from Stark's pistol. I started to turn my pockets inside out.

"You're a hard case, Champion. I have to give you that," Stark said as I went at it. He was beginning to come down from the high of winning our confrontation. The bitter rage was welling up in him again. "Those were good men I sent after you. And you took them out. I have to give you that. You're a hard case. We're going to see how hard."

I didn't answer. I went on turning out my pockets.

"Go ahead. Say something funny," Stark told me. "I like it when you say something funny."

I was done. I lifted my hands.

"Turn around," said Stark.

I turned. I looked down at the Fat Woman. I saw her glaring up at me from the chair, her mottled ruin of a face contorted with furious triumph. Her marble eyes glinted her hatred at me.

"Good," said Stark behind me. "You're unarmed. Turn around again."

I faced him.

"All right," said the Fat Woman. "Now let me out of here."

Stark nodded—but for another moment, he made no move to go to her. He went on standing there, went on looking at me— looking at me almost dreamily, covering me with the gun. He was really enjoying this now.

"You know what's funny about this," he rasped. He cocked his head as if the clever idea had just occurred to him. "Here you are again. You see what I mean? All this time, all this running, all this killing you've done . . . this whole journey of yours—where has it taken you? You've returned right back to where you started, haven't you? You and your girl—prisoners of my fat friend here. Locked up—oh, yes, she told me all about it. Locked up in the high room, about to be sent into a world of my pleasure, and your pain." His laughter made my skin crawl. "Isn't it amazing, Champion? How it's all come full circle? After all that trouble and time and death, here you are again, same place, same situation, you and your girl both, and what's the difference?"

I shook my head slowly, my hands still raised. "Only one," I said, "only one difference."

Stark snorted through his weird, wide, sunken nose. "What's that?"

"This time, my girl has a knife."

★ ★ ★

275

I had kept watch on Samantha during this past minute or two. I could see her working at her canvas and metal belt, getting the knife out, sawing at her zip-tied cuffs. I could see she was ready—or as ready as she was going to be. I just wasn't sure she had the will or the courage.

But if she was capable of doing anything, she had to do it now.

There was a second after I spoke—what seemed to me like an unnaturally long second—when I saw my words begin to make sense to Stark, saw his eyes begin to reflect his understanding. He had probably searched Samantha. Of course he had. But she was just a librarian. It hadn't occurred to him that she had planned for this, that she had thought of a way to fight back, to turn herself into a weapon. My weapon. He hadn't thought of that at all.

Too bad, skeleton-man.

As the understanding dawned on him, he turned—and still, the time seemed to stretch out, the movement seemed to me slow as slow could be—he turned, bringing his gun around toward Samantha.

I threw myself at him. And at the same time, Samantha launched herself off the wall, her hand lashing out from behind her with the strength and flexibility of a bullwhip. The little blade jutting from her fingers caught the light and winked. The Fat Woman had time to let out a short bark of surprise behind me.

Then Samantha slashed Stark's face. A scarlet line of his blood arced through the air, following the arc of the blade. And at the same instant, I grabbed the killer's wrist with one hand and drove the edge of my other hand into the crook of his elbow.

The blow sent his gun hand flying up. The pistol discharged—a blast that filled the room, that overwhelmed the atmosphere with noise. The bullet went into the ceiling and fragments of wood and white plaster rained down on top of us.

Chaos then. I twisted Stark's wrist and he dropped the gun. He twisted around to strike at my throat but sent only a glancing blow to the side of my neck. Samantha, making a high, gravelly noise behind her gag of tape, tried to cut him again, leaping at him, jabbing the point of the knife into his shoulder. He drove his elbow back into her—a hard shot in the center of the forehead. Her blade went flying. Samantha went reeling backward. She smacked into the wall. Her legs went rubbery underneath her. She reached for purchase but found nothing and slid down to the floor, blinking, openmouthed, dazed.

And Stark and I came crashing together, grappling with each other, our contorted faces inches apart.

My hands were on his arms and his on mine and both of us were struggling to strike a blow. Locked in combat like that, we also smacked into the wall, trying to punch or tear or knee or kick one another but only turning violently around the doorjamb as one body, stumbling as one body through the opening, out into the hall.

We moved from the light of the room to the shadows of the corridor, struggling, wrestling. Those sinewy arms of his were strong; I could feel it. I couldn't get a hand free and had to use all my own strength to hold on to him. We turned again and my back hit another wall in the corridor. The impact jarred me and Stark used the moment to spin me off the wall and lift his leg between us. In a single, swift motion, he jammed his foot into my belly and hurled himself backward to the floor, dragging me down with him.

I let out a grunt as he lifted my body on his foot and somersaulted backward, hurling me through the air.

I took a long, helpless, turning fall through the darkness. My back hit the floor hard, the jolt punching the breath out of me. Still, I managed to roll forward, managed to scramble to my feet, managed to swivel round and set myself, ready for Stark's next onslaught. But while Stark was on his feet too, he wasn't coming after me. He was turned away from me, bending forward . . .

And I realized: the gun. My Glock. I'd thrown it to the floor right there, right at the doorway. I started racing toward him, but too late. He already had the weapon in his hand. He was already straightening, already turning.

Then I reached him. Caught his arm in both my hands as it came around toward me. I tried with all my strength to wrestle the gun away from him as he tried with all his strength to strike me down and pull it free—and battling like that, we spun and banged and jostled down the corridor into the dark, the rectangle of light from the open doorway getting smaller and dimmer as we moved.

He wouldn't let go of the gun. I couldn't get it away from him. I had to hold on to his arm—which left him free to try to strike at me with his fist. He looked for a way to get at my throat or my eyes. Finally, he hit. Hard. A blow to the temple that made the shadows spark around me. I lost my grip on him. I fell back. Stark staggered, his hand thrown high—but he still had the gun. He lowered it at me.

I had one half-second before he fired—one half-second to see and understand that we had come all the way down the hall to the stairway, that Stark was standing right at the head of the stairs, right at the edge of the stairs, with me against the wall in front of him.

I ducked and charged him and he fired.

The gun must have been right by my ear because the explosion seemed to go off inside my head and for the next few moments, I could hear nothing. I didn't know if I'd been shot. I didn't know if I was wounded or bleeding out, seconds from death. All I knew was that I had barreled full force into Stark's midsection, driving him over the edge of the top step. Now he and I were falling—falling and turning and tumbling together down the stairway into the lightless living room below.

It was a weird, dreamy fall, a weird, dreamy spiral of pain and fear—fear because I couldn't stop it, couldn't control anything: all the jolts and jars and somersaulting confusion—a helpless tumble through dreamy silence that wasn't silence but the endless deafening explosion of the gun obliterating every other sound.

Then we hit the floor. We spilled into the living room, losing our grips on each other, so that for a long, long, terrible second, I had no idea where Stark was or where the gun was or what was about to happen.

Searching in the dark, I made him out, the awful figure of him, a skeleton scrabbling like a lizard across the floor, his white head lifted, luminous in the shadows, his white hands clawing their way over the edge of the rug—and toward the gun. The gun had fallen and spun a few yards away from him. He had almost reached it. I somehow got my feet under me and sprang at the crawling killer. Landed on top of him. Wrapped my arm around his throat.

I got a good grip, a good choke hold, the crook of my elbow wedged in his gullet, preventing him from tucking his chin in, from getting a breath. He knew it too—and he knew he had only seconds before he lost consciousness. So he didn't try to fight me. He just kept going. He just kept crawling, scrabbling, driving across the floor, dragging me—amazingly—along with him as he tried to reach that gun.

I tightened my stranglehold. I could hear again now—and I could hear him gagging. But he kept crawling and now his fingers were on the gun's grip. I choked him. Choked him. He had to stop. Had to go under. But he didn't. Wouldn't. He willed himself on. He wrapped his fingers around the gun. He raised it with an unsteady arm.

I tried to hold him down. Tried to stop him. Tried to cut the blood flow to his brain, closing my grip around his throat with all the force I could muster.

And still—God help me, still—he kept lifting the weapon in his hand, lifting it over his shoulder, pointing it back at me so that I had to choose whether to get out of the way or to keep my hold on him.

I kept my hold on him. I would not let him go, not again, not ever again. Even if he did it. Even if he shot me. Even if he killed me. Even if he sent me straight to hell, I would keep this grip around his throat and drag him into the fire with me.

I squeezed his throat tighter ... tighter. He lifted the gun over his shoulder. The barrel touched my head. He pressed the muzzle against my eyebrow.

I felt the cold metal on my flesh. I felt the black bore burrowing into me. I waited for Stark to pull the trigger and went on choking him, defying him, defying the bullet that was going to go through me. Waiting for the explosion I would never hear.

But he collapsed then, before he could pull the trigger. His hand—his gun—dropped heavily to the floor. His body went slack beneath me, twitching weakly, trembling weakly, finally falling still.

I would not let him go—I couldn't; I couldn't relax my arm—until long after he was dead, until long after I felt the life go out of him.

Then, at last, my own strength broke. I lost my hold. I rolled off Stark's body onto the floor. I lay on my back beside the corpse, gasping for breath.

And suddenly: a gunshot. From upstairs.

Samantha . . .

I choked on my terror. The Fat Woman . . . had she gotten free?

I had to get up there.

I turned quickly to Stark. Saw him lying dead, his face twisted to the side, his skeletal features still, his tongue lolling out between his bared teeth, those eyes, those bulging, glassy eyes, staring, empty. Quickly, I reached for his hand. Got the gun, the Glock, peeled it from his limp fingers. I climbed painfully to my feet. Staggered forward.

Samantha . . .

Weak, I moved unsteadily to the base of the stairs. A sour acid of fear was running through me. I took hold of the banister. My legs were so rubbery, I had to use the strength of my arm to haul myself up. I climbed slowly, gripping the banister, gripping the gun. Only my will kept me moving. Because I had to get to her.

I reached the landing.

The door at the end of the hall was half-open. I could see nothing but a narrowed wedge of yellow light at the end of the long corridor of shadows. I willed myself step by step through the darkness to that light. Step by slow step with no strength, the light growing larger in front of me.

Two steps before I reached the door, I smelled the gun smoke. Then I came into the doorway. Pushed the door back. Moved over the threshold.

I saw Samantha first. She was standing in front of the desk, her arms down by her side, her face in quarter profile to me. She was looking at something but her eyes were empty. Her mouth was slack. She seemed in a state of waking unconsciousness. She had Stark's pistol gripped loosely in her fingers.

I followed her gaze to the Fat Woman. The creature was still tied to the chair. Her head was thrown back. What was left of her face was tilted up toward the ceiling. In the midst of that nearly featureless swirl of burned brown and white flesh, the bullet hole seemed merely another blemish, this one right between her marbly, soulless eyes. Funny: Those eyes looked no more dead now than they had when she was living. Her body, though—the huge mass of it seemed to have sagged into itself, like a hollow thing that had been stepped on, crushed; that's where you could see that she was gone. And by the blood, of course, dripping heavily from the back of her head. In the quiet of the room, I could hear it pattering on the floor behind her.

We held our places there a moment, we three—Samantha, the Fat Woman, and I. Still and speechless. I felt dazed—dazed to find that it was all over. Or at least I thought it was all over . . .

But it wasn't. Not quite.

Because then, in one smooth, deliberate motion, Samantha lifted her hand, lifted the gun, and put the barrel into her mouth.

I had time to shout—one word: "No!"

I had time to rush to her, to drop my Glock, to grab her hand. But there was no time to stop her. If she had not hesitated, she could have pulled the trigger, could have blown the back of her head all over the walls.

But she paused. Just a second. Just long enough to shift her gaze—just long enough to look at me.

I don't know what she saw, but it seemed to wake her up some-how. That look that had been in her eyes, that look I'd seen in the eyes of so many abused children—that look of retreat into distance or fantasy or empty despair—seemed all at once to be overcome, the emptiness all at once flooded with life from within, her eyes like the eyes of someone coming out of a trance.

The gun barrel was still at her lips. My hand was still on her hand. My eyes were on her eyes and now her eyes were awake to me.

"No," I said again, more gently.

She let me pull her hand away. Turn the pistol away. Gently draw it out of her fingers. Toss it aside.

I wrapped my arms around her, pulled her to me. She pressed her face into my shoulder. She let out one loud, awful sob—one spasm that racked her entire body—but she didn't cry.

"I killed her," she said.

I kissed her hair. "She deserved to die."

"She was tied to the chair and I . . ."

"It's all right."

She shuddered against me. Placed her palm against my chest and pushed away until she could look up at me. Now that she was awake to herself, she had no defense. Her eyes were wide. She saw everything.

"Danny . . ." she breathed.

I lifted my hand to her cheek, touched her soft skin. "It's all right," I said again. "It'll be all right."

She looked around, only now beginning to think about it, really think about it, only now beginning to understand. "Will I have to go to prison?" She seemed to ask it more of herself than me, but when she heard the words, they went through her, and she turned to me in fear and repeated, "Will I have to go to prison? I couldn't do that, Danny. I couldn't go to prison, I . . . There isn't enough left of me. I don't have the strength for that . . . I'd die. I'd die."

She was drifting away again, but I brought her back. Touching her cheek, gently moving her head till she was looking up at me, into my eyes.

"You're not going to prison," I said.

"I'd die."

"You're not going to die and you're not going to prison."

"But . . . but what's going to happen? What's going to happen now?"

I drew her face to me and pressed my lips against her forehead. "Don't be afraid," I told her.

I sat Samantha down on a pile of files against the wall. She went where I took her, docile, quiet. She sat where I left her with her hands folded on her lap, like a little girl waiting for the bus to take her home from school.

I went to work on the scene. I found a letter opener in the desk drawer. I went around behind the Fat Woman's corpse. I cut the cord off her. Her big arms swung free. That was the only time Samantha flinched—when the Fat Woman moved like that. But then she saw how it was. She settled down again and sat quietly.

I got Stark's pistol off the floor. Wiped Samantha's prints off it with my jacket and tossed it down again. I found the little knife Samantha had used and pocketed that.

Finally, I took a look at the laptop. It took only a few seconds to discover what was there. The sight of it made my heart speed up. I shut it, tucked it under my arm.

Then I took Samantha by the hand and led her to the doorway.

She paused there, in spite of my tugging at her. She paused and looked back over her shoulder at where the Fat Woman sat in her chair, her big arms dangling down beside her, her head thrown back, her mouth open, her dead eyes staring at the ceiling. Samantha went on looking at her until I shifted my grip and took her by the arm.

"Come on," I told her. "There's nothing there now. She's gone."

Samantha went on looking back over her shoulder as I led her away.

I torched the place. It was wood mostly, easy to burn.

I found a plastic gas can in the carport, a length of tubing wrapped around it. I siphoned a couple of gallons out of the big sedan. I stood and let them flow into the can while the dead watchman lay at my feet, showing me what used to be his face, watching me with what used to be his eyes.

When I was done, I carried the gas can back inside. I sloshed the gas around the ground floor. Splashed it over the curtains and the walls. Went back out for two more gallons and spread those around as well.

Everywhere I went, Samantha followed me. Quiet, docile, like an obedient child. She watched everything I did but only in the most distant and uninterested fashion. Her eyes were wide and her gaze was steady, but for the most part, her face was expressionless.

When the smell of the gas first reached her, she wrinkled her nose. "What are we going to do, Danny?" she said. Just like that. As if she were still a child.

"No one needs to know what happened here," I told her, working the gas can. "Not exactly anyway. I'm going to burn the place."

She nodded thoughtfully. "Like we did before."

"That's right, baby. Like we did before."

She glanced upward at the ceiling then. "She'll burn again too."

"That's right," I told her. "Only now—now she'll go on burning."

She didn't say anything else after that. She just went on following me around, silent, staring. When I emptied the last of the gas can onto Stark's body, she turned her head away with a little pout of distaste. That was the only sign she gave that she was paying attention, that she understood.

Stark had taken Samantha's matches, but I fished them out of his pants pocket. I lit the gas and watched the blue flames splash around the floor and race up the curtains and up the walls. I watched a line of fire find Stark's body and crawl over his fallen skeletal form.

Quickly then, I led Samantha to the door. I sent her out into the front lawn. But I hesitated a moment alone in the doorway to make sure the fire took.

It took, all right.

The last time I saw Stark, his death's head was staring at me through the steadily rising flames.

★ ★ ★

Samantha and I stood on the lawn together, shoulder to shoulder. We watched the house's dark windows flicker. We watched the flickering light grow brighter as the dead building became big and alive with flame. We flinched and drew back as the ground-floor windows exploded. Through our raised hands, we saw the glass spinning down through the night, flashing with firelight. Black smoke poured out of the empty frames and billowed up into the sky, obscuring the moon, covering the stars. Inside, the fire rose swiftly to the second floor and when the second-floor windows shattered, the flames, released, breathed and roared and flared into the darkness, making the darkness shimmer and glow.

We stood and watched another little while. Samantha was right. It did feel as if we had been here before, done this before together, as if somehow we had had to come back, were fated to come back to finish the job.

Some things are like that, I guess. Some things don't die the first time.

When I was sure the house was beyond saving, I used my cell phone to call the fire department. I didn't think the flames would spread to the woods, but I didn't want to take the chance. When the call was done, I hurled the phone through a window and watched it disappear into the churning depths of smoke and fire.

I picked up the Fat Woman's laptop from where I had left it lying in the grass. Then I took Samantha by the arm. Tried to draw her away.

"Come on," I said. "We have to go before the firemen get here."

She resisted a moment. A section of the roof collapsed, flinging sparks up, making the black smoke glimmer. Samantha went on standing there, watching the house as if hypnotized by the roaring spectacle.

I put my arm around her.

"Come on, baby," I said. "This time we're gone for good."

She finally moved away with me. We crossed the lawn to the edge of the forest. I slipped my arm off her shoulder and took her hand.

Hand in hand, we walked off into the dark woods, the house in flames behind us.

EPILOGUE
Something Like Good-bye

WE DROVE THROUGH the night in silence. A long time. Samantha sat beside me, staring out through the windshield. Sometimes I would glance over at her, thinking she had fallen asleep, but no, she was awake all the while, just sitting there, just staring ahead.

I worked the car along country roads, heading for the highway. I tried to think about what had happened, everything that had happened, but I couldn't really, not yet. It was still too fresh; I was still too shaken by it. It came to me in scenes and flashes and obsessive little loops of memory that kept repeating and fading and starting up again.

I remembered Martin Emory. His round, bland, flaccid face, coy and corrupt. I remembered the ghost of Alexander haunting New York City's streets. And the night I raced through Emory's house and found him in the cellar and shot him dead—I remembered that too, at least some of it.

I tried to ask myself what I would do now, where I would go from here, but I couldn't come up with an answer—I couldn't concentrate long enough. Those scenes and flashes kept rising into my mind. Samantha washing up out of the river. Fighting the Stark brothers at my house. The feeling of lying in the trunk of the car, my hands bound behind me. The ghost town. Moments of rattling gunfire . . .

I drove on through the dark country, watching the road through my reflection on the windshield, watching the flashes of memory playing out like movies on the shadowed glass.

Shortly after we crossed the border into P.A., I heard Samantha say something, very low.

I turned to her. "What's that?"

But it hadn't been meant for me. She was murmuring to herself, the words tumbling out of her very quietly, very fast.

"I didn't mean to. You have to understand. She did such terrible things. My whole life. Who I am . . . My only life . . ."

I understood. She was talking to the police in her mind, explaining things in her mind. On and on like that, until it started to spook me. "Samantha," I said. And still she went on, so I said more loudly, "Samantha. Stop."

She turned to me, blinking, as if startled to find that I was there with her, beside her, behind the wheel.

"But what will I say to them?" she asked. "What will I say to the police when they question me?"

"The police aren't going to question you," I told her. "Why would they? All they're going to find is some ashes and a body, the remains of some professional killers and a sex slaver, probably killed by one of their own. Public service murders, we call them on the job. You think the cops'll come looking for a librarian from Pennsylvania? They're probably not going to come looking for anyone, but if they do, it won't be you. No one will even know you were there."

She faced forward again. We were on the interstate now—81, heading for Wilkes-Barre. Traveling fast, the road nearly empty except for the big rigs rumbling south.

For a while, Samantha fell silent again, as if she were thinking about what I'd said, about how it was going to be.

Then, without turning, still gazing out at the interstate and the darkness beyond it, she whispered, "I just . . . came to . . . in that room. I was dazed. That horrible man. Stark. He hit me and I was dazed and then . . . I came to and . . . and I stood up and . . . I saw her."

I wanted to stop her right there. I wanted to tell her it didn't matter anymore, none of it mattered anymore. I wanted to tell her to forget the whole thing. But I figured she couldn't stop thinking about it, same as me. She had her scenes and her memories too, just like I did. I figured she had to tell it now, to get it out of her system. So I just drove and listened and let her go on.

"I didn't really . . . *see* her there before that, you know. Not really. With that awful man—Stark—with him holding the gun against me . . . and knowing the whole time I had to use the knife . . . I had to cut my hands free with the knife, Danny, that's all I could think about and somehow . . . I didn't really take in the fact that she was there or who she was or . . . anything. And then I came to, and I did see her. And I knew who she was."

I nodded. "Of course you did."

"I was over by the wall. I was . . . I was sitting—kind of half-lying—right against the wall. And I stood up and I saw her and suddenly . . ." She let out a trembling sigh, talking more to herself than to me, explaining it more to herself than to me. "Suddenly it was like . . . it was like being inside some kind of big glass bubble or something. There was nothing else inside it . . . there was no other sound or . . . or anything . . . There was just me and her. Me and her." She turned. She looked at me. We looked at each other. "It was Aunt Jane," Samantha whispered. "It was Aunt Jane, Danny. It was really her."

"I know."

"And she was just . . . She was all there was. She was all I could see. And all I could do was stare at her . . . stare at her. And I was thinking, *You! You! There you are. After all these years. After every-thing. There you really are. Right there.* And she was . . . she was *real*, Danny. Alive and . . . she was talking . . . saying things . . . I don't know what . . . about how I should help her, untie her . . . how she would fix everything . . . give me money. All these things she was saying but . . ." Her lips began to tremble. Her eyes filled up with tears, glistening dimly in the glow from the dashboard. Her voice broke. "But she didn't say she was sorry, Danny! She didn't say she was sorry!"

"Jesus," I muttered.

The lights of the highway blurred a moment. The oncoming headlights, the red taillights of the trucks—they all blurred as my own eyes filled helplessly at the sound of Samantha's pain.

"And then I saw the gun," she said through her tears. "I saw Stark's gun . . . just lying there . . . just lying there on the floor . . . like it was waiting for me . . ." She pressed her hands over her nose and mouth. It almost looked as if she were praying. "I didn't really mean . . . I don't know what I was thinking . . . I just wanted her to see me point it at her . . ."

"I know."

"I wanted to feel like I had some . . ."

"Some power."

"Some *power,* you know? I wanted her to be . . . *afraid* . . . afraid of me . . ."

"Sure you did. Of course."

She gulped down a sob. "But she wasn't. She wasn't afraid. She didn't think I'd do it. She *laughed.* She said I was crazy. That's what she said. 'What are you, crazy?' And then . . . That's when . . . I heard the gun go off . . . I saw . . ."

That was as far as she could get. The tears came hard after that. She covered her face and sobbed without stopping.

As soon as I could, I pulled off the road. I pulled into a dusty turnout and parked. I put my arms around her and held her while she went on crying and crying.

"I'm just so sick of being unhappy!" she said.

She went quiet again after that. We got back on the highway and drove for more than an hour and she didn't say a word. She was different now, though. I could tell when I glanced over at her. Her eyes, her expression—her whole demeanor was different. She was alert now. She had returned to herself. She was working it through.

I left her to it. I drifted back to my own thoughts. Where would I go from here? What would I do? What *could* I do? My days as a lawman were over. I was sure of that. I would probably survive Grassi and the grand jury investigation into my killing of Stark One. I'd catch some flak for disappearing the way I did, but I'd probably get my badge back all the same.

Still, grand jury or no, I knew I couldn't return to being a small-town cop. Rounding up gas thieves, meth dealers, wife beaters, drunk drivers. Visiting Bethany from time to time, taking her love and secretly wishing she were someone else. It felt too much like being in exile from my own life, from the life I was supposed to live.

I guessed I'd have to go out on my own somehow. Start my own security agency maybe. Help people out when the cops couldn't or wouldn't ...

"Can I ask you something?" Samantha said suddenly, breaking into my thoughts.

"Sure."

"Do you think ... this is finished? *Really* finished, I mean. Do you really think no one will come after me or question me or anything? You're not just saying that."

"I'm not just saying it. It's finished. For you anyway."

"You mean because big strong Danny is going to take care of it all for me."

"That's right. That's what I mean."

She gave a soft laugh. "Danny!"

"What?"

"Can I ask you something else?"

"Sure."

"What do you think of me? Really."

"I don't know. What do you mean?"

"When I saw the way you looked at me, back at St. Mary's, the disappointment ..."

"No."

"Like you thought I'd be . . . the same as you remembered. Something I can't be. And now . . . I don't know. Am I just a complete pain in the ass to you at this point?"

It made me smile. At least she didn't sound like a child anymore. She sounded more like she had before, back at St. Mary's.

"You're not so bad," I said.

She gave a heavy, cynical laugh. "All this time—all this time, I've been trying to get over my childhood. Now I'll have to spend the rest of my life getting over tonight."

"Well, it'll be something to occupy your idle hours," I said.

"Idle hours nothing. For me, being damaged is a full-time job."

"Ah, right."

"Ah, right, yourself." She reached over and touched my leg—then withdrew her hand quickly, as if she hadn't meant to do it and hoped I wouldn't notice that she had. "You think I'm pretty neurotic, don't you?"

"Maybe a little."

She hesitated. I could feel her gaze on the side of my face. "So am I just supposed to get over it? Killing someone? Having killed someone. Is that something you get used to? My new normal?"

I started to answer but then I didn't, not right away. Because I realized my answer wasn't her answer. I realized, even as I was starting to speak, that what had happened in that house tonight was a shock to her. But for me . . . Well, in some ways, it was the work I was born for.

"You'll learn to deal with it," I said finally. "It's not like you got drunk and ran over a kid in a crosswalk. You snuffed out a monster. You owed it to her and she had it coming. You can live with that, Samantha."

"Right." She sighed. "Right. I guess it just goes to show, doesn't it? All this time I've been trying to . . . process my anger. Learn to forgive. Learn to let go of the past. But to just put a bullet in the monster's head—I never even thought of that."

"It's quicker. Cheaper too."

"Mental health through assassination."

"Exactly."

I glanced over to see her smiling wryly. I felt a pang of—something . . . Loss, that's it. A pang of loss. I found myself thinking about the little girl I used to know, the girl Samantha who built castles in the orphanage sand and told me stories about the knights and princesses who lived there . . . I wondered what that little girl would have turned into if there had been no Fat Woman, no foster fathers and all the rest. I wished I knew. I missed that girl. I missed—not just the child Samantha . . . but also the other Samantha, the one I saw in my hallucination, the Samantha she would have grown up to be. I liked this woman sitting beside me. She was tougher than she thought she was and righteous in anger and sort of funny too, though I could still see the gentleness and generosity she hid away under that. I liked her a lot.

But I missed Samantha, the woman I would have loved.

We came into Greensward in the hours before dawn. I drove down State Street. It was empty—silent except for the buzz of the streetlights and the clunk and hum of the changing traffic lights. But there were no cars, no shops open except one diner at the edge of town. Everything seemed in suspension, hung between the end of one day and the beginning of the next.

I drove by the public lot to see if my G8 was still there. It was, though there were several parking tickets stuck under the windshield wipers.

"I'm going to leave this car with you and send the girl who owns it to come get it," I told Samantha.

"Nice," she said. "I'd like to meet her. We can compare notes about you."

"Good luck with that."

I drove her home. She didn't have her keys anymore and I didn't want to wake up the landlord, so I picked the lock while the security camera watched me. We walked up the stairs to her apartment. I picked the lock up there too. We went inside and stood together in the litter of bedding and papers and utensils strewn around the floor.

"Look at this," she said, turning in a circle to survey the wreckage. "They really ransacked the place."

"They didn't know where to look," I said.

She smiled. "But you did."

We both glanced down at the wainscoting that covered her hiding place, the place where I'd found her papers. She didn't say anything and neither did I. But I'm pretty sure we were both thinking about Alexander.

I stayed with her for what was left of the night. We slept in each other's arms, wrapped up together like two lost children. In the morning, when I opened my eyes, I saw her face first thing—that beautiful face, close to mine. My heart tightened at the thought of leaving her, and at the thought of everything that had happened to us.

In the next moment, she opened her eyes too. She saw me watching her and smiled.

"I could stay," I whispered. "We could . . ."

"Ssh." She put her finger against my lips.

We made love to each other for the last time.

Later, we stood in the doorway. I held her against me. I kissed her hair.

"You're never alone from now on," I murmured to her. "Remember that."

"Okay," she said.

"I mean it. I'll let you know how to get in touch with me, soon as I can. You'll always be able to reach me. I'll always come."

"Danny!"

"Anything happens, anything frightens you, anyone hurts you, you call me, I'll make it stop."

She nodded, her head pressed against my chest.

"You go out with some guy and he's a son of a bitch, don't call your psychiatrist, call me."

She laughed.

It wasn't easy to let her go, but I did it. I took one final look at her face, letting my eyes linger a while on every feature. Then I turned away.

I walked down the short hall to the stairs. Just as I reached them, she said behind me, "Don't be a stranger, Danny."

I raised my hand in good-bye. I went down the stairs. Out the door. Into the morning.

I got in my car and headed for the interstate. I got on the interstate and headed for New York. I drove east at an easy pace, into the rising sun.

I had to go see Monahan. I had to tell him that his family was safe, that they could return to their lives. I had to talk to Bethany too. Tell her where her car was. Tell her that things were going to be different now. More than that. I had to tell her something like good-bye.

The miles passed. At the hour, I turned on the car radio. I listened to the news. The networks had the story about the fire in the New York woods and the bodies that had been discovered there. "Suspected criminals," the newsman said. "The murderous result of a criminal enterprise, according to the police."

Right, I thought. I turned the radio off. A criminal enterprise. Public service murders. No one would ever know the truth.

Except Monahan, that is. Because finally, when his family was resettled, when Bethany was gone, I would sit down alone with Monahan and tell him the whole story from the beginning.

And then, when I was done telling it, I would give him the Fat Woman's laptop—the laptop lying on the passenger seat beside me.

I had seen what was in it. Everything was in it. Her records. Her contacts. Her suppliers. Her customers. In New York and across the country and around the world. There had probably been more in the ledgers too, but I couldn't save those and still cover for Samantha. That was all right. The laptop would be enough. It would be more than enough.

I smiled to myself. I pressed down the gas pedal and drove a little faster, racing into the morning.

It might take a while. Some months, even some years. But they would get them, a lot of them anyway. The buyers, the suppliers, the Fat Woman's whole network. They would break down their doors in New York and Los Angeles. They would drag them off the streets of London and Paris. They would come in shooting in Moscow and Tallinn. Even in Bangkok, they would arrange for them to disappear forever.

The monsters might never know who had brought them down. But I would know. I'd be watching the whole time and I would know exactly who it was who had tracked them, hunted them, and finally destroyed them.

It was the little boy who got away, you bastards. I'm still here. Still in the wind. I'll be here as long as it takes.

I am the executioner.

And I'm coming after you.